CW00740827

NEW
BLOOD

The Wrong Man Part 2

M J ELLIOTT

Copyright© 2021 M J Elliott

Published by Compass-Publishing UK 2021
ISBN 978-1-913713-83-6

Designed by The Book Refinery Ltd
www.thebookrefinery.com

The right of M J Elliott to be identified as the author of this work
has been asserted in accordance with the Copyright, Designs and
Patents Act, 1988.

All rights reserved. No part of this publication may be reproduced
or transmitted in any form or by any means, electronically or
mechanically, including photo copying, recording or any information
storage or retrieval system, without either prior permission in
writing from the publisher or a licence permitting restricted copying.

This is a work of fiction. Names, characters, places, and incidents
either are the product of the author's imagination or are used
fictitiously. Any resemblance to actual persons, living or dead,
events, or locales is entirely coincidental.

All rights reserved. No parts of this manuscript may be reproduced
or used in any manner without the permission of the copyright
owner.

A CIP catalogue record for this book is available from the
British Library.

I would like to dedicate this book to two people who have both believed in me unconditionally.

Firstly, my wife, Debbie, who has always had faith in me and who I knew I would marry the first time I set eyes on her.

Secondly, my dad, Geoff, who was diagnosed with cancer whilst this book was being published, but who looked it in the eye and accepted the news like the man I always knew he was – a man of the old school.
A man of the like we may never see again. Love ya, Dad.

chapter one

Manchester – Early March 2019

George Burbanks was sat in his plush Manchester office – and it was plush. Very plush. The carpet was so thick you felt like you were walking on air. He and his brother, Ivan, were waiting for their 3 o'clock appointment. Ivan had nipped to the loo. It was now 2:53. George hated lateness and was surprised that the man he was waiting for had not made the effort to turn up early.

George and his younger brother ruled Manchester; well, at least half of it anyway. Along with a guy called Fletcher O'Brien, they controlled the criminal underworld in and around Manchester and many parts of Cheshire and Lancashire. George and Ivan had taken over from their father, Jim Burbanks, who had ruled Manchester alongside Fletcher's father, Arnie O'Brien. George was 59 years of age; Ivan a couple of years younger. Their father, Jim, had for many, many years controlled their half of the city with an iron rod and had always had a very mutual respect and understanding with Arnie, who had ruled the other half. The Burbankses had always kept to the northern half of the city, continuing out to Bury, Rochdale and Greater Manchester and into Lancashire; Arnie had always kept to his half of the city and out towards Cheshire, Stockport, Wilmslow and Prestbury.

This is how it had been for decades and, save the odd fallout over specific territories, they had always managed to settle their differences without major violence or bloodshed.

The Burbankses had a problem that they were keen to sort, that problem being Fletcher O'Brien. He was a loose cannon, with very few of the old-school values that his father had; the same values that George and Ivan had, and their father before them. Fletcher upset people – for no reason. He caused friction, violence, rifts, all of which, a lot of the time, were unnecessary.

The meeting they'd arranged was going to be a tricky one. The conversation they were about to have was not one they were used to. It could go tits-up big style. If handled incorrectly, it could bring trouble to their door; trouble they did not want, but trouble they would deal with if needs be. George and Ivan had discussed this issue many times and how to best deal with it. Manchester was becoming unstable. They couldn't let it continue.

Ivan came back through. 'Is he not here yet, for fuck's sake?' he said, as he stood there wiping the last bit of water off his hands on the tops of his trouser legs. Ivan was 6ft 2in, with receding dark hair that bore very little sign of greying. He stood proud, was always immaculately dressed, with particular attention paid to his shoes. They always looked mirrored, they were so highly polished. He was a broad man who carried the scars of his lifestyle. He had quite a few scars on his body, the result of a lifetime of fights.

'Nope, not yet,' George replied. 'He best not be fuckin' late, though. That would not be a good start. If he's late, then the deal's off. I fuckin' hate lateness.'

George was a little shorter than Ivan, at 6ft, and, like his brother, had dark hair, though he'd managed to keep a full head. Much to the annoyance of Ivan, George had reminded him of that a lot lately. George had very few scars, mainly because he was the more measured of the two. George would weigh things up and look at things more long-term. They were a good match and both had characteristics of their father, yet were both quite different personality-wise. The one thing they both shared was their nerves of steel. Neither of them had ever backed down from anyone. They were well respected, well thought of in their area and the ones that everyone would talk about. They were the real deal and alongside Fletcher O'Brien, Frank Pearson from Nottinghamshire and Rory Hammond from the West Midlands, they were the main players outside of the capital. They had good dealings with Frank and Rory, both of whom were of the same make-up as George and Ivan.

The three main London players were Tariq Mali, Paul Dutton and Greg West, all of whom understood the rules of the game in the same way the Burbankses, Frank and Rory did. They would cross paths, of course, but they were of the same ilk. They understood the value of peace and none of them wanted a war, so any crossovers were sorted out between themselves over a stiff drink and with a firm handshake. The only problem seemed to be Fletcher – and he was getting worse.

The phone on George's desk rang. He picked it up.

'Yeah.'

'He's here, Boss. He's clean. Shall I show him up?' came the reply from one of George's most trusted men, Shaun Bonsall.

George checked his watch. 2:57. Three minutes early. That would do. 'Yeah, bring him up. We'll see him in here.'

George replaced the receiver. A minute or so later, Shaun brought him in. George eyed him up and down, and noticed how he was trying to appear confident. George liked that. He needed to know this guy was what he thought he was. George held out his right hand. They shook a solid handshake. George gestured to the chairs near the door.

'Sit down.'

The guy took a seat. He still didn't know why he was there. He'd just received a visit from three of George and Ivan's men and was told in no uncertain terms to be there at 3 o'clock. That was only just gone midday and, of course, he'd been told, again in no uncertain terms, not to tell anyone. It was clear what would happen if he did.

'Now, I'm sure you want to know what this is all about?' George said, leaning forward.

'You could say that,' the man said. George noticed he'd not addressed him as George or, more importantly, as Mr Burbanks. That struck a nerve. He let it go, but he wouldn't let it go twice.

'We want to talk to you about Frank Pearson.'

chapter two

Nottinghamshire – 28th May 2019

Archie got back into his X6 and started the long drive out of Clumber Park. It always seemed to take ages to get out of there, it was so big. He knew he had to deal with the two guys that Paul had rung him about whilst he'd been with the family. He knew his grandad, Frank, now knew about this little issue, and he also knew Frank knew it was the second time they'd caused the family bother. They were two guys who could get a bit above themselves; two guys who could, if left alone, cause Archie bigger issues and he didn't want that. He was still on probation so to speak. He was now running the firm. At 22 years old, he was in the position that it took most men until their late thirties at least to get to. Even Frank had to wait longer to be running a criminal empire like this. Even though Archie was his grandson, there was no way Frank would ever let him fuck things up. He was doing well, was earning his own respect but Grandad Frank would often remind him that he was on probation. One major fuck-up and he'd be history. He knew his grandad wanted more than anything for him to succeed and that he'd taken a major gamble putting Archie in charge at such a young age, but then he did have his grandad's and his dad's reputations to ride on.

In the seven years since Daniel's murder, Archie had been determined to keep his dad's name alive. He was far too young then to do anything about it, but Frank had told him not long afterwards that it was his duty, his job, to step into his father's shoes and take over the family business, just like Daniel would have done had his uncle Richie not been such a dickhead. He still, to this day, could not believe everything that had happened. He'd loved his dad, loved him dearly, but he'd idolised his uncle Richie. It was his uncle who had taught him to ride a bike, to play football and all those things. His dad had been too busy stepping into Frank's shoes and, at the time, Richie hadn't been that involved, so Archie had spent a lot of his childhood with him. It was Richie who had taken him to his first match and done a lot of the things a father should do – but he could never forgive his uncle.

Today, the seven-year anniversary of his father's murder, he still hated him with a passion. He could happily kill him, but Grandad Frank had insisted that he should be left to rot in that vegetative state as that would be worse than being killed. Archie knew Frank was right, but he still wanted to kill him. But, as he told himself often enough, it is what it is. Frank was still the guv'nor in this family and what he said went. End of story. Frank would tell Archie that he was the CEO, the guy in the background overseeing everything, and that Archie was like the managing director, still very active in the day-to-day running of things. But when push came to shove, it was Frank who called the shots and Archie liked that. If he was honest, at times he felt out of his depth. He liked the fact Frank would pull rank when needed. Frank would never retire fully; he would be the CEO until the day he died. Archie just hoped that day would not be for a while yet. Archie was only 22 after all, and was different to Frank, and different to how his dad would have been. Frank was old school, as people would say. Archie just saw him as old, but he understood what people meant by old school. Frank was as straight as an arrow – well, as straight as a major criminal underworld figure could be – but in this world, Frank was respected as a man of honour, someone who you could trust and whose word meant something. He had integrity and conducted himself accordingly.

Daniel had been the same and many people, too many to count, had told Archie that his father was a chip off the old block. Daniel was every inch his father, whereas Archie was a bit more reckless and wanted everything now. He saw Frank's old-school characteristics as slow, as if things would happen at a snail's pace. Take Frank's empire for example. Frank had started to build it in his early twenties, around the same age as Archie was now, but it had taken him until his forties to expand outside of Nottinghamshire. That was a lifetime to Archie, who would often tell his grandad that if it had been him building that empire, he would be ruling the whole of the UK by now.

Frank ran the East Midlands, which included Nottingham, Derby and Leicester, and then Leeds and, more recently, Doncaster, but that was it. And even though all that, along with the old-school bollocks, made Frank a major player in the UK, respected by everyone, it was still only a small piece of the overall action. Archie wanted Manchester, Birmingham, the whole of the North and then he wanted to get into London. He was itching to. He'd already made a few contacts down there, with Frank's help, of course, through a guy called Greg West. He was a good ten years younger than Frank but still a dinosaur in Archie's eyes. Archie wanted to get in with a guy called Tariq and another called Paul Dutton, but Frank wouldn't make any introductions and had told Archie to keep out of the capital as it would bring nothing but trouble. Frank would tell Archie to just enjoy what they had and to protect it well and that alone would give him a life he could only dream of, but Archie knew that he would need to branch out sometime soon. Frank had things sewn up so well that Archie, even at 22 years of age, would get bored.

Today was a day that would not bore him, though, as he had the two fuckers that Paul had rung him about to deal with. He was going to make an example of them, go a bit overboard really, just because he could. He still felt that he needed to do things like this to prove himself. People would say that he hadn't yet done that – not to his face, of course – but he'd heard the rumours and if he was honest, it bothered him. He had never had to prove himself really. Being Daniel's son and Frank's grandson meant he didn't have to, never had done, but he still took opportunities like this to show people what he was capable of.

His mobile rang. It was Paul.

'Archie, it's me. Are you on your way back?'

'Yeah, five minutes and I'll be there. Where have you got them?'

'In the main room. My dad's here still and Michael too, so there'll be no bother, but I didn't want to touch them until you got here.'

'Good man. Four minutes and I'll be there.' Archie felt the buzz he always felt rise up inside of him.

Frank pulled into his driveway at his house in Papplewick. He closed the electric gates behind him and looked at Gloria. 'Get that kettle on, luv, I'm bloody parched.'

Gloria smiled at him like she always did. She'd been with Frank a long time now and even though they'd never married, they were, for all intents and purposes, an old married couple. Gloria got out and walked towards the front door. Frank stayed sat in the driver's seat of his Jag. Gloria looked around and mouthed 'Come on, chop chop', as she motioned with her head towards the door.

Frank mouthed back, 'In a minute. Just give me a minute.'

Gloria nodded and smiled that smile that always made Frank feel warm inside. He loved Gloria. She was the one person who had finally taken a place in his heart alongside Renee, the one he lost so young all those years ago. She'd never replaced Renee – she never would – but she never tried to and that was what had made her so attractive to Frank in the first place. Gloria was happy to be who she was despite knowing how Frank felt about Renee. Frank had thought about marriage over the past few years, but he had promised himself all those years ago that he would never marry. He'd wanted to marry Renee, but, alas, it was not to be and he said that if he couldn't marry Renee, then he was marrying no one. He watched as Gloria walked into the house and thought about today.

He thought about Richie, he thought about Daniel, he thought about everyone and how they'd got to where they were today, but he mostly thought about Richie. On one hand, he hated his son with such passion that he revelled in seeing him suffer every year; but on the other, he missed him. He would never tell anyone that, though – never. That was not Frank and no one could ever know how every time they came away from seeing him on the anniversary of Daniel's death, it hurt him like hell.

He sometimes wished that he could just be his real self and not his perceived self. As he sat in his car thinking about it all, he wished more than ever that he had the courage to say to everyone that he forgave Richie and that he regretted doing to him what he did. He had told Bonnie exactly the result he wanted and he'd got his wish: his son as a cabbage. He smiled to himself and chuckled inside at what the PC brigade would make of that – "cabbage". He'd get a longer stretch at Her Majesty's pleasure no doubt than he would do if he murdered someone in broad daylight. 'It's a mad fucking world,' he said out loud.

He did have regrets, though. He wished he could turn back time and either kill Richie and have done with it, or try and understand why Richie did what he did. After the dust had settled, Frank started to reflect on it all. He realised that Richie didn't actually kill Daniel. All he did was stand by upstairs and allow it to happen and then pretend he knew nothing about it. It was a mistake after all. The guys who came for Richie just got the wrong man.

It was them who Frank should have taken his revenge out on. Frank was scared of no one but he'd concluded that it must have had something to do with Richie in Venice because if it had been someone in the UK, who had thought themselves brave enough to kill Daniel Pearson, then someone would have talked. Of that Frank was absolutely certain. As much as he'd tried, he couldn't get anything from anyone as to who did it. All he knew was what Richie had done and for that, he had to pay. And pay he did – but that did not stop Frank mourning his actions.

Frank had to keep face, had to carry on the hate every year on 28th May because showing remorse to the outside world would show weakness. And Frank would never do that. No one could know how he really felt and no one could know of Frank's visits to see Richie once a month, every month. Frank went on his own, round the back into Richie's room, through the French doors that looked out into the garden. Frank paid the manager to keep her mouth shut, even though he knew she would do it for nothing. She knew who Frank Pearson was and wouldn't dare breathe a word. Frank believed he was indebted to her and paid her a fee. In Frank's world, that was only right and proper. He wouldn't take advantage of her just because he could. That wasn't Frank.

Richie knew how his dad felt. He was the only one who did, but, of course, he wasn't in a position to tell anyone. Frank wanted him to know. He talked to him when he visited despite seeing the hatred in his eyes. Frank convinced himself he was frustrated at his dad's refusal to be honest with everyone around him. But deep down, Frank knew Richie would never forgive him for doing what he did.

'Come on, luv, tea's ready,' Gloria shouted from the doorway. Frank nodded to say he was coming, but first, he called Archie. It rang four times before Archie answered.

'Hi Frank.' That told Frank Archie was at the club in Nottingham. He insisted on Archie referring to him as Frank when it had anything to do with work or if anyone was in earshot. He only got called "Grandad" when it was just the family.

'You sorted 'em yet?'

'Just pulled into the car park. I'm just talking to Paul now. Del's inside with them.'

'Make 'em fuckin' pay, Archie. We ain't anyone's fool. They must know there ain't gonna be a third time.'

'I know. I'll make sure they know,' Archie replied.

'Good. Don't give 'em a fuckin' inch. Let me know all about it later.'

'Will do, Frank.'

Frank hung up and got out of his car. Unfortunately, for the two men at the club, someone had to pay for the way Frank was feeling. He needed to take it out on someone. Frank was angry – angry at himself, but angry all the same. Someone had to pay. They always did.

Archie looked at Paul. No words were needed. Paul knew what Archie was telling him just by the look on his face. Frank wanted these two to pay. Paul was a big black fella, a carbon copy of his dad, Del – biceps like breeze blocks and balls just the same. He was four years older than Archie and Archie trusted him with his life. He was loyal too. Wasn't one to get above himself. In this game, Archie had already seen and heard of young blood out to try and topple the men at the top, but Archie had none of those concerns with Paul, just like Frank or Daniel never had any issues with Del. Del's brother, Michael, was just the same. Three guys you could rely on, and just the three guys you needed here today.

'Come on then, Paul, what they said?' Archie asked, as he walked towards the club front door.

'Just that you ain't got the balls to do much about it. You know the stuff, Archie. All mouth and that.' Paul stopped and turned to look at him.

Archie stopped a pace or two in front and turned around. 'What's up?' he asked.

Paul took a deep breath. 'You've got to sort 'em this time, mate. If we don't, then word will get out that cunts like these can take liberties.'

Paul didn't like to appear to be questioning Archie's credentials, but he needed to make a point. He'd already heard whispers of some of these county line gangs saying that the East Midlands was becoming easy pickings. Things had slipped somewhat since Frank gave Archie the reins. Everyone knew that but then again everyone also knew that Archie had it in him – he just needed to show it a bit more. Maybe today was the day.

Paul looked up to Archie, even though he was that few years older. He respected him totally but also knew that he could take his eye off the ball with what was happening on his own doorstep and was sometimes too busy thinking of taking over the world to keep control of his own back yard.

Archie took the two steps up to Paul. He fixed his gaze. Paul held his own. He didn't want any trouble with Archie, but was prepared to go toe to toe if needed.

'They said I ain't got the balls?'

'Yeah, that's what they said,' Paul replied, trying his best to sound confident. He didn't want any weakness in his voice.

'And what do you think?' Archie asked.

'I think they're talking bollocks. I know you have, but they need to know it, too, Archie. I don't want to hear them saying those things about you. I have your back; I always will. Wherever you go, I'll be with you. Whatever you do, I'll do it with you. You'll never get any grief from me, Archie, you know that. But if you need to hear something, I'll always tell you as it is – no frills – whether you want to hear it or not. And you needed to hear that.'

Paul felt a flutter of fear in his stomach. Archie curled one side of his lips into a bit of a smile. He then nodded his head in appreciation of what Paul had just told him.

'Don't ever stop telling me, Paul. Anyway, come on, let's deal with these two fuckers.'

Archie led the way into the club. He saw Del and Michael stood at the bar. He then glanced over and saw Rob Simpson and Carl Waites sat down on two chairs. They'd obviously had a few slaps to the face.

'I thought you said you'd not touched them?' Archie said sarcastically.

'Well, a few slaps just to keep them quiet but, you know, not really touched 'em,' Paul said with a chuckle.

'All right, Del … Michael,' Archie said, as he nodded to them both and shook their hands. 'So, what have these two been up to this time?' he asked Del.

But before Del could answer, Carl shouted out, 'Oh, here he is, the young pretender. Bunking off school, are we?'

Archie turned and looked at Carl. He said nothing. He then turned back to Del.

'Sorry, Del, let's start again. What have these two been up to this time?'

'Where's Grandad Frank? You're fuck all without him, Archie. Go and get the real man if you're gonna dish it out today, 'cos you are fuck all! Just a fuckin' kid!'

Carl turned to Rob, obviously looking for a bit of moral support. Rob was the younger of the two. Carl was in his early forties and had been a drug dealer most of his life. He did have a bit of a rep and by all accounts, ten years ago, was someone to be wary of. But he was over the hill now and was just dealing on his past reputation. Rob on the other hand was mid-thirties and still wanted to be somebody in this world. He secretly wanted a way in with Archie, but was too impressionable and would be easily led astray by the likes of the Carl Waiteses of this world.

'Yeah, go and get someone we're scared of at least. You ain't got the fuckin' balls for this!' Rob hollered, sure that that would impress Carl. 'I tell you what, Archie lad, why don't me and you have a straightener, eh? Come on, just me and you,' he continued. If nothing else, Rob wanted to let Archie know that he wasn't afraid and that he was game. He hoped that might pave a way in for him. He was wrong.

Archie looked at Paul and Michael. 'Shut them two up, please, fellas. I need to talk to Del.'

Paul and Michael strolled over to the two mouthy fuckers, who needed a lesson in respect. They hit them so hard they knocked them clean out before either of them had had time to react.

'Thank you,' Archie said, turning back to Del. He made no reference to the fact Carl Waites and Rob Simpson were lying on the club floor. 'So, Del, what have they been up to?'

'They've been buying gear off a firm in Manchester, from Alderley Edge apparently, and have been bringing it back here. Second time, Archie, and second time off this Alderley Edge set-up. I don't think the warning last time really hit home.'

Archie could feel his blood starting to boil. This was the second time in the past few minutes that one of his men had insinuated that he was too soft. It was now starting to bother him.

'So, you think I'm too fuckin' soft, is that it?' he replied with a definite air of aggression.

Del knew he'd touched a nerve, but, like his son Paul, he knew Archie had to hear it. 'I'm not saying that, Archie. I'm just saying maybe the last time they didn't get the full message, that's all.'

Archie looked him straight in the eye. 'And I suppose with Frank it would have hit home first time, is that it?'

Del bit his lip. He didn't know how Archie would take this from him. He decided to be diplomatic. He didn't want any aggro.

'Archie, all I'm saying is I think they need it with both barrels this time. The word needs to get out there. Listen, Archie, no disrespect intended, but you're young. You have a lot to learn. Frank was not the man he is today at 22 years old, nowhere near, but Frank didn't have what you have to deal with on a daily basis, did he, so he could make those mistakes with limited damage, whereas with you, you can't afford that. You understand?'

'All I understand is that you lot think I'm too soft. Well, if anyone wants to try their luck, step forward.' With that, Archie leant against the bar and folded his arms. No one spoke. No one took up the challenge. No one dared. They all knew where they stood, that was one thing for sure. Archie was Frank Pearson's grandson and that alone meant no one would take him on. But aside from that, all three of the men stood in that club with Archie all liked him and respected him. They'd all die for him. Archie just didn't really appreciate it at that moment. The silence was broken by the noise of both the men on the floor coming round.

'For fuck's sake, my jaw! I'll fuckin' kill ya, whoever did that!' Carl roared, as he tried to get up.

'Get 'em both up. Sit 'em down!' Archie barked.

No one knew who he was barking the orders at, but Paul and Michael did as he asked. Carl struggled, as if it was what he was expected to do but he and Paul, who had hold of him, both knew it was nothing more than for show.

Rob said nothing. Archie walked behind the bar through to the office at the back. He came out a minute or so later with a gun in his hand. He walked over to where Carl and Rob were sat. He pointed the gun at Carl's temple. 'Who is supplying you with the drugs? I want their names.'

'Fuck off, boy,' Carl replied, looking straight ahead.

Archie fired a bullet. The gunshot made Rob jump so high he fell off his chair. Carl screamed in agony. His thigh now had a hole in it the size of a golf ball. Archie nodded to Paul, who sat him back up straight. He was still screaming. Archie put the gun to his head again. 'Who is supplying you the drugs? I want names.'

'They'll kill me! They'll fuckin' kill me!' Carl shouted, snot and saliva streaming from his nose and mouth. Archie walked around to the front to face him square on.

'I'll fuckin' kill ya if ya don't tell me, so by the looks of it, either way, you're fucked. At least if you tell me, you have a chance of living. If you don't, you will die right here, right now. Your choice.'

Carl Waites now had a simple decision to make. To keep silent and die here, a snivelling, pathetic excuse for a hard man, or to grass on the men from Manchester and be on the run for the rest of his life, with only one good leg. He thought about it for a few seconds.

'Benny Lancashire. That's all I know. That's who I get them off. I swear, that's all I know.'

Archie looked at the pool of piss underneath Rob's chair. He then looked up at him and knew that no matter what he did to him, Rob would never get over pissing himself right in front of Archie Pearson.

'If you needed the toilet, you only had to ask,' Archie said, shaking his head.

Rob could see everyone in that room looking at him in utter disgust. Even Carl, who was still screaming like a baby, managed to look at him with disappointment written all over his face. Rob Simpson knew at that very moment that, in this life, it was all over for him and that he would never work for Archie Pearson.

'Still fancy that straightener?' Michael said to Archie. Archie laughed.

Rob wished that Archie would just shoot him dead. He would never recover from this.

Archie turned his attention back to Carl. 'So, where do I find this Benny Lancashire?'

In between screams of pain, Carl told him he only ever met him in a bar just outside the centre of Alderley Edge. Archie knocked him out with the butt of the gun. He then turned to Rob, who looked like he was about to wet himself again. He took the two steps over to him.

'Some men are cut out for this world, Rob. You are looking at four of them here today. And some aren't. You aren't, but you took your chance, so you pay the price, just like anyone else.'

With that, he nodded over to Carl, who was lying on the floor, with blood pouring out of his leg. Archie then shot Rob in the same leg, in just the same way. Rob screamed, just like Carl had, but louder. Archie ordered Del to leave them on some wasteland in St

Ann's, just outside Nottingham. He knew the message would get out.

Archie walked back into the office and left his three men to sort it all out. Archie had other fish to fry and that fish was Benny Lancashire. Who the fuck was Benny Lancashire and why would he risk the wrath of Frank and Archie Pearson? Archie rang his grandad.

'Hi Frank, all sorted. It won't happen again, but listen, are you in? I want to pop over and talk. I need to know who Benny Lancashire is.'

'Benny who?'

'That's what I thought. Listen, I'll explain when I get there. I'll come over now.'

Archie then rang Pat, his number two. Pat had been with Frank a long time. He was one of the original crew, now in his fifties, and had seen it all. Archie liked Pat and Pat liked Archie. Archie had told him he wanted him as his right-hand man because he trusted Pat implicitly, plus he wanted someone old school at his side. After everything he thought about that old-school crap, he was astute enough and wise enough to know that it counted for a lot in this world, and Archie knew that a very dependable older hand at his side was what he needed.

'All right, Archie. How did today go?'

'Fine mate, fine, thank you. Well, fine as in he's still suffering, which is always a pleasure to see, but listen – I'm on my way to Frank's. Meet me there ASAP. We need to talk about a guy called Benny Lancashire. You heard of him?'

'Have I fuck. Doesn't ring any bells, but yeah, no problem. I'll be there as soon as I can.'

'Ring Raquel. She needs to get to Frank's ASAP, too. We need to talk about what's happened on her patch. I want to know what she thinks of it all.'

'Will do, Archie. I'm on it. See you at Frank's later.'

chapter three

Michael and Paul drove into St Ann's with the two still-screaming men in the back of the van.

'For fuck's sake, shut the fuck up! It's only a flesh wound!' Michael shouted.

'Anyone would think they'd been shot or something!' Paul chuckled to himself. 'Make sure you've learnt your lessons this time, boys, won't ya ... we don't want to have to kill you next time.'

'But we fuckin' well will do if we hear either of you've been dealing anything that's not ours on our patch again!' Michael bellowed.

'Fuck you!' Carl shouted.

Michael and Paul both laughed. 'Yeah, whatever!' they replied in unison.

They pulled onto the piece of wasteland where they'd planned to dump them. Michael got out first from the passenger side and walked round to open the back door. Paul opened the driver's door and did the same. They both climbed in the back. Michael got hold of Carl's face with one hand and squeezed his lips together.

'Now listen. You guys know the score. I don't have to tell either of ya, but I'm gonna anyway. You both need to get those wounds seen to. Where and how you do that is up to you, but...' – he squeezed Carl's face even harder whilst looking at Rob – 'if either of you breathe a word, or even think about breathing a word, as to who did this to you, it will be the last thing you do. We will kill you, slowly and painfully. Do I make myself clear?'

He looked back at Carl, who nodded his head. He couldn't speak with Michael's big hands around his cheeks. Rob muttered, 'We won't say anything, I promise. Well, I won't anyway.'

Michael nodded to him. He looked back at Carl and let go of his face. Carl remained silent. 'I mean it, Carl. I'll kill ya if you breathe a word.'

He held his stare; Carl dropped his. 'Well, I'm dead anyway. Benny will see to that. He's bound to know it's me. That tosser will grass me up.'

Michael shook his head. He then looked at Paul. Paul looked at Carl.

'If by that tosser, you mean Archie, you can be rest assured he won't breathe a word. That's not his style. He's a Pearson after all and neither Frank nor his father, Daniel, would ever have stooped so low as to grass anyone up, not even the likes of you. So no, he won't. If Benny whatshisface hears it was you who told him, it won't have come from Archie.' Paul then pressed hard on Carl's leg.

'Fuck me!'

'That was for the tosser remark.'

Michael opened the van doors and he and Paul kicked them both out onto the gravel.

'Remember, boys. Mouths shut,' Paul reminded them, as he closed the doors.

He and Michael got in the van and drove off leaving Carl and Rob to make their own way to wherever it was they were going to get their wounds attended to. Michael looked in his side view mirror. He could see them both struggling to get up. He laughed loudly.

'I assume we're not gonna tell Archie that twat called him a tosser?' he said, looking back through the front windscreen.

'Well, I'm not,' Paul said. 'But hey, what Archie did today was needed. It might seem a little overboard for selling a few drugs from outside the manor but it was their second offence, plus he needed to show his strength, didn't he?'

Michael nodded in approval, but remained silent. Paul looked over to him. 'What's up – something on your mind?'

'No, nothing really. I just hope that's the end to it and that Archie has nipped it in the bud early enough. I was worried it was getting out of hand, you know, with the likes of them doing their own thing. Frank would never have had to deal with the likes of them. They'd never have tried it.'

Paul raised his eyebrows slightly and nodded slowly in recognition of what Michael had just said. 'Yeah, fair point, but neither of us knows what Frank was like at Archie's age, do we? I'm sure he had a lot of knobheads like those two to deal with back then. We just didn't see it 'cos it was before our time. I'm sure he did, though. Listen, Archie's the real deal, ya know. He's the right man, no danger. He's just gonna need the likes of us and me dad by his side. He's got a good team around him. As well as us, there's Pat, don't forget, and Pat's his right-hand man, isn't he? He's been around the block more times than I would like to recall. You know that. You've known him long enough.'

'Yeah, Pat's solid, Paul. He's the real deal all right. I remember him going up to Leeds and sorting that shit out up there. Plus, Jez is still about when needed, I s'pose, and Brian too. He'll never fuckin' retire. He's still got big bollocks ain't he, so yeah, when you put everyone together, including Raquel ... Now *she's* a top fuckin' brass is that Raquel. I remember her when she first came on the scene, down at Leicester. I never thought she had it in her but I tell ya what, she's shrewd and as game as any fella. She's got bottle, fuckin' loads of it, and no one gives her any bother down Leicester or Derby, or Notts for that matter. She's well respected, she is, and takes no shit. So, yeah, put us all together and the top table looks pretty healthy. I just wish I knew who this fuckin' Benny fuck face was. Never fuckin' heard of him.'

'Me neither. We'll find out sure enough, though, 'cos Archie will be on him like a shot. We might need that top table.'

'Pull in 'ere. I'm starving. You want owt?' Michael asked.

'Er, yeah, I'll have sausage and egg. Brown sauce too.'

Michael got out to get the sarnies and Paul sat back and looked out of the side window. 'Who the fuck's Benny Lancashire?' he said to himself quietly.

chapter four

Archie pulled into his grandad's drive and got out his car. Sarah, Archie's wife, came out to meet him with their daughter, Mary, in her arms. He kissed them both and then took Mary off her. He then kissed her again. 'Been here long, luv?'

'Five minutes or so. Your mum wanted to come – you know, with it being today. I think she thinks your grandad struggles today, after he's seen Richie.'

'Struggles? Me grandad?'

'Yeah, she reckons she can see it in him; that deep down he's sad.'

'Yeah, probably sad that he's still not killed that twat.'

'He is his son, Archie...'

'Yeah, and also the reason my dad is dead, so no, luv, I doubt he's sad, but anyway let's not give Richie any more time. He's had enough off us today.'

Sarah followed Archie in, took Mary off him as he kissed his mum, Phoebe. He then shouted 'Hiya' to Gloria.

'Hiya luv, you OK?' Gloria shouted back. She was in the kitchen as usual, making cups of tea and getting the biscuits out. That was Gloria. She'd really become the matriarch of the family, the person that any one of them could go to for a chat. Whether that was to just shoot the breeze, share a problem, get advice or just to have a shoulder to cry on, Gloria was the one they all went to. There was never an angle with Gloria, never conditional. She was happy to be out of the business and just be on the sidelines looking in. Gloria never wanted to be anyone within the family business, not that she couldn't have been. She'd been more than an outsider for so long now that she was just one of the family; the mother hen of the brood. Everyone liked her and loved her, and she liked and loved everyone back. She kept Frank grounded and, at times, that had been a godsend.

Archie got a brew and went into the lounge to say hello to his sister, Alice. He kissed her on the cheek. She kissed him back. 'Where's Johnny?' Archie asked.

Johnny was Alice's boyfriend. A decent lad, stocky, 23 years old and a physiotherapist. He'd recently qualified and worked at the local hospital, in Sutton-in-Ashfield. He wasn't a villain and, to be honest, he never would be. He didn't have it in him and as far as anyone could see, he didn't harbour any ambition to be anything he wasn't. Alice had met him at The Burnt Stump country pub one summer's day three years ago. She'd been there with a couple of friends, just chilling on the large expanse of grass at the back of the pub, when some local idiot tried it on with her. Johnny intervened and sorted the lad out. Alice was impressed and he'd been on the scene ever since. He was a good-looking young man, brought up somewhere in Leicestershire, though he never really talked about his childhood much. He was raised by his grandparents as his mum apparently fucked off when he was a toddler. He'd never known his dad, so once it was apparent Alice was keen on him and he was a keeper, he'd been accepted into the family core. He treated Alice well, had ambitions in his chosen field of therapy and got on with everyone.

'He's had to go to work. That's why he left Clumber Park early. Didn't you notice?' she asked, putting her hands on her hips.

Archie chuckled. 'No sis, sorry. You know me, always got something on my mind.'

'I'm only messing. You OK?' She could sense something was bothering him.

'Yeah, no worries, me. Just something to talk to Grandad about. You know what I mean.'

Alice did know; she knew too well. She worried about her brother. She knew her mum did too although Phoebe had become more involved in the business over the past few years than Alice felt was good for her. Her mum had always been such a placid, lovely woman – she still was – but now she could be rather cold and seemed to enjoy getting involved in any of the decisions.

Alice could see that Frank was torn with this. On one hand, he didn't want Phoebe exerting too much influence. He was still old school like that and very much believed that the women in the family should remain in the kitchen, out of the way of the man's world that Frank controlled.

He was okay with Raquel; she was somewhat different. For one, she wasn't family and two, she had proved to be a real asset to Frank in this man's world. She was respected by all of the men within it, both within Frank's extended set-up and by those she dealt with outside of Frank's influence. She set up her own deals on Frank's behalf and ruled her empire for Frank from South Leicestershire, through Nottinghamshire and Derby, with an iron rod.

But with Phoebe – his daughter-in-law and wife of his son Daniel – it was different. Frank cut her some slack; she had proved to be more than capable in her thoughts and advice on business matters and had recently been invited to the top table. That was really Archie's idea, one that Frank had reservations about, but one that he went along with, mainly for Archie but also because he could see the influence Phoebe brought. Even though he didn't like to admit it, he knew she was an asset to that table; she brought a different voice to things. Phoebe had killed before, though – something that Frank often forgot and something Archie was not aware of. Phoebe had killed an intruder who tried to rape her, back in the mid-nineties, after he had dropped off some photos of Raquel. Richie had saved her from being raped that day, which she'd never forgotten. It was why she still found it hard to feel comfortable with what had happened to Richie, even though he had, in part, been to blame for Daniel's death. She had never told Archie what she did and neither had anyone else. There had not yet been a reason to bring it into conversation.

Frank came into the room. 'All right, Son?' he asked. He always called Archie "Son" these days. Archie never knew if it was just a term of endearment like "luv" or "pet" or "duck" that people often used or whether it was because he was Daniel's son, but either way he liked it. It made him feel special.

'Yeah, not bad, but I need a word.'

'Yeah, you said. Come on, let's go through to the boardroom.'

Frank had built an extension onto his property three or four years back that included a large room that he liked to call the boardroom. Previously, any business discussions had taken place in the kitchen or at the dining room table, but Frank had wanted a room especially for business meetings, so he had this one built. It was just how you would expect a boardroom to be. It had a plush carpet, a round, solid oak table, a drinks cabinet, a coffee stand with biscuits on it and, of course, CCTV in every corner. Frank sat down. Archie sat next to him.

'So, who's this Benny guy then?' Frank asked.

'No idea, but he's been supplying drugs into Nottingham. I sorted those two out by the way. Shot 'em both in the thigh and had Del organise to drop them off in St Ann's somewhere. They'll not say owt, but they were a bit cocky. Well, Carl Waites was. You know what he's like. You know him from years back, but he soon shut up once he had a little bullet in his leg. Anyway, he told me that he'd been supplied by a guy called Benny Lancashire from over Manchester way. Alderley Edge, he said. Fuck knows who he is over there and if you've never heard of him, then I dare say he's a nobody, but we need to sort him in some way to quash whatever he's doing and to send a message to that lot over there that what they are doing is bang out of fuckin' order.'

Frank sat and listened. He liked listening to Archie and liked it when he was in this kind of mood, a mood that was not gonna take any shit. He saw himself in Archie from when he was first starting out and knew he'd picked the right man when he gave him the responsibility. Some thought he was mad, but he just knew that with his help, Archie had what it took, just like his father had. He just needed guiding as he sometimes wanted to run before he could walk, maybe like now. He sounded like he wanted to rush in feet first. Sometimes that was good, but you needed to know who you were dealing with first. That's where Frank came in.

'OK, listen, who else knows about this?' Frank asked.

'Well, Del, Michael and Paul obviously 'cos they were there when they told me his name, but that's it. I've asked Pat to come here. He'll be here soon and I told him to bring Raquel with him. She runs Nottingham, so I want to know why the fuck she's allowed it to happen. Twice.'

'OK, let's talk to her and Pat when they get here, but first thing's first, I'll make a call to Fletcher over in Manchester. Alderley Edge is Fletcher's patch, so if this Benny Lancashire is anyone at all, then Fletcher will know him.'

Fletcher O'Brien was the son of Arnie O'Brien, who had run half of Manchester up until he passed away around ten years ago. Arnie was like Frank – old school – whereas Fletcher was like Archie: more of a loose cannon. The guys who ran the criminal empires these days never seemed to be cut from the same cloth of the likes of Frank and Arnie. Frank had had some dealings with Fletcher since he'd taken over from his dad and, to be fair, thought he was OK, but was always on his guard whenever he did have to deal with him. Where Frank had trusted Arnie and knew his word was solid, with Fletcher there was always a little niggle. But saying that, he'd never done anything to wrong Frank, so until he did, Frank would take him at his word. Frank rang him.

Fletcher answered almost immediately. 'Frank, what a surprise! How the devil are you?'

'I'm OK, Fletcher, thank you. And you?'

'Always OK, me, Frank. It's the others you have to watch. How's that grandson of yours? Is he turning out to be the real deal? I hear good things about him.'

'He's here with me now and, yes, he's a true Pearson. No fear there.'

'Good. Anyway, you haven't rung me because you've got nowt better to do, so what can I do for you?' Fletcher asked, with a sudden change of tone.

Frank sat up in his chair and put the phone onto loudspeaker. 'Benny Lancashire. What can you tell me about him?'

Frank looked at Archie as he spoke. Archie remained cross-legged, his right hand stroking his chin. There was silence for a couple of seconds. Frank knew instantly this was Fletcher considering his response. He didn't like that.

'Benny Lancashire?' came the reply.

'Yes,' Frank replied, 'Benny Lancashire.' Silence again.

'Well, he's one of our soldiers, if you like, on the ground around the Alderley Edge, Wilmslow and Prestbury areas. Quite a posh lad, all told. Knows some of the money men around that area. Was brought up around there, see, and supplies them with whatever drugs they need on our behalf. He's decent enough and can look after himself for a posh lad. Why, what's he to you?'

Frank could sense the sharpness in Fletcher's voice. This was where he differed from his father. Arnie would have known instantly that if Frank was phoning about someone from Arnie's patch, then this someone must be causing Frank some grief, so Arnie would have been on the defensive without having to think about it. Arnie would never have met Frank's phone call with a threatening tone, unless it turned out Frank was being unreasonable of course. Fletcher was different. Aggressive. Frank decided to let it go. Even at his age, Frank knew the importance of remaining in control. He always had and it'd never let him down yet. Something he was still trying to teach Archie.

'He's been supplying drugs into Nottingham, Fletcher, right under our noses.' Frank waited. Silence again for a moment or two.

'Then I will deal with him, Frank. Leave it to me. I assure you it will stop immediately. There will be no repeat,' Fletcher replied, the aggression now absent from his delivery.

'Then I will do just that, Fletcher. Thank you for your assurance.'

'Always a pleasure, Frank. Say hi to Archie for me.'

Frank heard the line go dead. He disconnected the call his end and placed his phone on the table, just as Pat and Raquel walked in. He glanced up at them and nodded to two chairs at the table. They walked over to take their seats. He looked at Archie, who was still sat cross-legged stroking his chin. Archie glanced over his shoulder and acknowledged Pat and Raquel.

'What do you think?' Archie asked his grandad.

'He's lying. I don't trust him,' Frank replied.

'Why? He said he'd sort it, so why would he not do that if he's said he's going to?'

Frank sat back in his chair. 'What was missing from that call? Think about why I called him. Me, Frank Pearson, someone respected and trusted in this world, someone who had many dealings with his father, someone who was a bearer at his father's funeral. What was missing?'

Archie nodded a couple of times as the penny dropped. 'No apology.'

'That's right, Son. No apology. No "I'm sorry to hear that, Frank, I had no idea". No "Please accept my apologies, Frank". No nothing. Fuck all. And the silences ... he was thinking on his feet. He had other people in the room. He's planning something. He fuckin' knew all right. He knew full fuckin' well.'

Frank took a deep breath and sighed. He knew that this was going to be Archie's big one. He'd hoped something like this wouldn't rear its head for a while, but it was here. It was maybe coming on top, and Frank knew he had to watch and wait and see what Archie would do.

Frank picked up his phone again and dialled the number of George Burbanks, one half of the firm who ran the other half of Manchester. Frank trusted them and their word, like he had their father, Jim.

'Frank, how are you? Nice to hear from you.'

'George, listen, I know we haven't spoken in a while but I haven't rung for a chat.'

George laughed. 'I thought not! Anyway, what can I do for you?'

'I might have a problem with Fletcher. Well, I'll rephrase that. I have a problem with Fletcher. He's treading on my toes, George, and pressing down hard. Now, at this stage, it's just a feeling I've got, but I think he's pushing me. I've no idea why, but unless I'm wrong, I'm going to have to deal with it. I'm letting you know out of respect for you and your brother and, of course, your late father – God rest his soul – but if Fletcher pushes any harder, then there'll be bloodshed.'

'Frank, we've known each other a long time. I trust you, so you have mine and Ivan's blessing to do whatever you need to do. There's also a lot of criminals in this town who would probably thank you, Frank, if truth be known. But listen – I ask two things of you. One is, and I say this strongly, Frank, I want to know when you plan to exact any revenge. Please assure me you will extend me the courtesy of informing me before you do anything this side of the Pennines. Number two is if, and I say *if,* you have to deal with Fletcher, in the only way people like us sometimes have left to us, then once you've finished, you leave Manchester for good and leave it to us. I don't want any beef with you, Frank, but Manchester is not your town.'

George waited for a response.

'Understood, George, and I wouldn't have it any other way. As you say, Manchester is your town and, yes, I assure you I will let you know when we do anything. I won't tell you what we plan to do but I'll give you 24 hours' notice.'

'Agreed. Oh, and Frank—'

'Yes?'

'Don't underestimate him. If you take him on, make sure you win, 'cos if you don't, he'll spray your guts all over that nice city of yours.'

Frank ended the call and sat back in his chair. He knew Fletcher was at the top of his game, but now that he knew he'd get no beef from the Burbankses, he could go in hard – and hard was what was needed.

Fletcher placed his phone on his desk. He was in a club in the centre of Manchester, one of his many clubs around the city.

'Hook, line and sinker, Benny. I fuckin' knew they'd react. Frank's too old; Archie's still wet behind the ears. It's time. Get back over to Nottingham tomorrow and get that gear shifted. In fact, give the fuckin' stuff away. I want my gear all over that city. I want every fuckin' drug user in Nottingham snorting my gear up their noses, smoking my gear into their lungs and injecting my gear into their fuckin' veins. I don't know about the Major Oak, Benny, me old lad, major fuckin' dope more like. My dope, my fuckin' dope, all over that city.'

Fletcher raised his glass. Benny joined him. 'I knew it was a good idea of mine, Boss,' Benny said, looking for recognition. He didn't get it. It'd been Benny who'd suggested venturing into Frank's territory and taking him on. Fletcher knew that, but there was no way he was going to remind Benny. The fact it all looked to be going to plan now meant it was Fletcher's baby. If it had gone wrong, then it would have stood squarely at Benny's door. Tomorrow, Benny was going back to Nottingham.

Archie stood up and looked out of the window into Frank's beautiful garden. He then turned round to Raquel. 'How the fuck has this been allowed to happen, Raquel? What did you know about any of this?'

Raquel looked surprised; surprised at Archie's tone and his apparent assumption that she'd messed up and let something go unnoticed.

'Archie, come on, no one knew anything about this until today – not you, not Del, not anyone,' she replied, mindful not to appear too aggressive.

'It's the second fuckin' time it's happened, don't forget. The second time that Rob Simpson and Carl Waites have been dealing other people's gear. The second time in six weeks that they've bought gear elsewhere and had the audacity to deal it on your fuckin' patch,' Archie shouted. He looked pissed off.

For the first time since coming on the scene in the mid-nineties, Raquel felt the pressure from within. She'd had it from outside, lots of it over the years, but she wasn't used to feeling pressure like this from within the business, certainly not from Archie. Since she'd proved herself from around the time Frank and Daniel had taken over Leicester, she'd had no bother.

She'd had the Midas touch and any issues that she'd had controlling her patch had always been met with support from within. This was the first time she'd felt accused of not being up to the job – and she didn't like it – but Archie was right. It *was* the second time and it *was* on her patch. She was annoyed at Del too, though, as well as at herself. He was her ears on the ground. Then again, she quickly thought to herself, he had dealt with it as soon as he'd been made aware. He had rung her that morning and she was the one who had told him to go and get both men and let Archie know straight away. She'd been at one of the clubs in Leicester sorting out a problem, but maybe she should have rung Archie and made sure she was there herself earlier. She decided to be firm.

'Two things here, Archie. Firstly, with respect, I can't be expected to keep tabs on every lowlife dealer in three counties and, secondly, again with respect, Del did, on my orders, round them up as soon as he knew what was happening and alert you. We can only react to these situations, and react we did – swiftly. Del called me at 10:30 this morning. By lunchtime, he had them both and had Paul, I think, ring you. I'm sorry but I don't think we could have done any more any quicker.'

The room was silent. Archie didn't take his face off her. She could feel Frank's gaze too but Archie knew she was right. He could tell in her body language that she was under pressure but, like she always did, she stood her ground, and that was one quality he liked about her. He sighed as he looked out of the window.

He knew she was right, but she wouldn't hear that from him. He would let her stew. Archie then turned to face them all again.

'Tomorrow morning 10am, a full top table meeting. Raquel, you let everyone know. 10am sharp. We need to sort this. Or rather, *you* need to sort this,' he said, staring her down.

Raquel left the meeting feeling very pissed off. She had served the family well over the years, but since Daniel had been murdered, she'd often felt cast aside. She knew that she had the respect of the family and beyond – respect that she had earned – but she was feeling more like an outsider than ever before. Raquel thought that when Daniel had been taken out and Richie had been dealt with, she should have taken over at the top with Frank. Raquel was ambitious and knew she had the grit and presence to be Frank's wingman. Jez had never courted leadership. He was always happy to be at Frank's side, to be his personal bodyguard so to speak, but Raquel had wanted the top job. She knew she could do it. Everyone knew she could do it, but she wasn't family and that meant she would always be answering to one of them. And by the looks of it, that person would be Archie for the foreseeable future. Raquel would do what she always did. She'd swallow it and keep her counsel. She liked what she did, but at times she wondered how long she could keep watching Archie do the job she'd wanted for so long. She'd just tell herself that's how it was and unless she was prepared to launch a takeover bid, she'd have to just keep on swallowing.

chapter five

Archie walked into the house at Southwell that he, Sarah and Mary all shared with his mum, Phoebe, and sister, Alice. The house was so big that they could all comfortably live there. It was the house that his father, Daniel, had bought, so Phoebe would never leave it, plus he felt a duty to stay and look after her. Sarah enjoyed it there too. She got on with Phoebe and Alice wonderfully well, and she liked the girlie chats and things they did when Archie was off running the business with Frank. It suited them all well. Johnny, Alice's boyfriend, would stay over some nights but he also had his own place in Blidworth, a village about three miles outside of Mansfield. He was a bit of a home bird and, like Archie, he felt a duty to return to Leicestershire, to look after his grandparents as they were the ones who had brought him up. Archie liked that in him – that Johnny was family-orientated and had those values and morals that ran strong through the Pearson family.

Archie sat on the huge sofa in the lounge. He flung his head back, put both hands over his face and took a deep breath. He felt someone sit beside him. He knew it would not be Sarah as she had gone straight upstairs to put Mary down. He guessed it would be Alice as he could hear someone in the kitchen and assumed his mum had gone straight in to put the kettle on. He opened his eyes. He was wrong. It was his mum. She smiled. He smiled back.

'Alice making a cuppa, is she?'

'Yeah. Do you want something stronger?' his mum asked.

'No, it's OK, Mum. Tea will be fine.'

Archie was not a big drinker. He liked a beer or two now and again but he wasn't someone who needed a drink at the end of each day to unwind. He had seen and heard how keeping a clear head had given his grandad the edge down the years, and without really making a conscious decision to follow suit, he was just the same.

'It's been a tough day, Mum,' he said, throwing his head back over the sofa once more. Phoebe stroked his hair. She still saw the young boy in the man that sat before her. Part of her wished he was not in the position he was, but the other part was proud to see him emulating his father; proud that he was taking over the role that Daniel would have done. She knew that most mums would want their son to stay well clear of this world, given what had happened to her husband, and part of her did. But the stronger part wanted him to keep his father's name going.

When Daniel was murdered, she initially wanted to kill the murderers herself, she was so angry. That anger had remained, although it had subsided somewhat over the years. Once she found out what had happened and that Richie had seen it all and kept quiet, trying to fill Daniel's shoes, she felt nothing but hatred. Then she felt broken, as if she just wanted to give up. But she came to realise that Archie was in Frank's sights and no matter what she did to try and prevent the natural course of things, Frank would make sure Archie was the man to take over the reins of his empire. At that moment she decided that if you can't beat 'em, then you may as well join 'em and she made it her business to get more involved, mainly to keep her eye on Archie. This way, she told herself, she could at least protect him as much as she could.

Her involvement did not sit well with Frank, she knew that, but she also knew that he was aware of her motives and so he gave her a place at the top table after a request from Archie. Phoebe was now privy to all the decisions that were made in the family business, so she knew as much as she could about what Archie was getting into at any one time. That was as much as she could do for him. In their world, she was never going to be top dog, but whilst she was a Pearson, she commanded respect, and that respect made sure she was taken seriously and influenced any decisions that were made. Any influence she had was always with Archie in mind.

'Every day's a tough day, Son, in this game. You can tell me about it, you know. I'll hear it tomorrow but if you want to talk, you know I'm here,' she told him, hoping it would make him feel just that little bit better.

'Do you think Richie regrets what he did?' he asked.

Phoebe turned to the fireplace. She thought for a second. 'No, I don't think he does to be honest. I still see the hatred in his eyes when we go. Why, do you?' she asked, intrigued as to what Archie's response would be.

'No, I'm with you. I don't think he does. Anyway, what's this I hear about you thinking Grandad's got regrets?'

Phoebe smiled. 'I think he's sad when we go and see him, Archie. I see it in his eyes, you know – sadness. Just like I see hatred in Richie's eyes, I see sadness in your grandad's. It's the way he looks at Richie. He won't realise he's doing it, I'm sure, but your eyes don't lie. Your mouth lies but your eyes, never. They always give you away.'

'So, do you think he regrets what he did to Richie?' Archie asked, quite surprised at what he was hearing.

'Maybe. I think maybe he does.'

'What – sad that he didn't just kill him and be done with it or sad that he did anything at all? Archie asked, his tone a little strong.

'Hey, don't snap at me. You asked me, so I'm telling you what I think, and I think he's sad. Why, I'm not sure, but I see sadness in his eyes, that's all I'm saying. You'll have to ask him if you want to know if

I'm right or not.' Phoebe made sure Archie knew he was out of order.

'Sorry, Mum. Hey, here she is, tea lady,' he said, as Alice walked in with a tray.

'Well, you weren't gonna make it, were you? It's about time you started to pull your bloody weight around here. We don't work for you, remember?' she said, half joking, but at the same time making her point.

'Shut up and just put the tea down. Any biscuits?'

'How many?' Alice asked with a sigh.

'Two.'

'Yes, sir, three bags full, sir. Yes, your honour!' Alice shouted, heading back to the kitchen.

'So, have I to wait until tomorrow then to find out what the meeting's about?' Phoebe asked.

'Yep, I've had enough of work today, Mum. Let's wait until tomorrow.' He then caught the biscuits that Alice threw at him and popped one in his mouth whole.

'You're a pig!' Sarah shouted as she came in the room. Archie smiled at her and patted the seat next to him. She sat down and he gave her a big hug that nearly squeezed the life out of her.

Alice's phone rang. 'Hey, have you finished work?' she asked. 'OK, no problem. Don't work too hard. See you tomorrow. Love you.'

'He's a grafter that lad,' Phoebe said, as Alice placed her handset on the coffee table. 'Is he still working?'

Alice nodded. 'Yeah, don't know what a physiotherapist can be doing at this time of night, but yeah, he's still working.'

'Hospitals don't shut, you know, sis,' Archie said. 'They have to work long hours, so you'll have to get used to it.'

'Yeah, I know. I shouldn't let it bother me. It's just anti-social sometimes, that's all.'

She brought her legs up onto the chair and put the cushion on her lap. She then cuddled it like a little girl, obviously disappointed that she wouldn't see her Johnny. It could be worse, she thought. At least he's out of our world.

chapter six

Archie was up early, ready and out of the house at 8:30. He was on his way to Frank's for the 10 o'clock meeting. He was dressed in a navy-blue suit, black highly polished shoes, a crisp white open-neck shirt and a navy-spotted handkerchief in his left breast pocket. One thing that Frank had always taught him was the importance of dress. Frank insisted on him looking smart and business-like whenever he was on official family business. Frank always dressed very smartly himself, as had Daniel. Frank had drummed it into Archie, partly because Frank had seen the young blood of other firms being too casual, something he did not approve of, and partly because looking the part was something that, in this world, made more of a difference than anyone outside of it ever realised. Archie wholeheartedly went along with it as he always felt a sense of power whenever he was dressed appropriately, like he was today. If he turned up for this meeting in jeans and a jumper, he would unconsciously feel underdressed and therefore not able to deliver anything with the same level of authority.

He could never explain why clothes made such a difference, other than likening it to when his Uncle Richie was a football hooligan. He would dress in all the terrace football gear and say that looking the part made all the difference to who you were in that world. Archie remembered his uncle telling him that back in the day a firm could be half-beaten before any ruck started if the opposing firm were better dressed. He'd heard the saying often enough from Frank that "the clothes maketh the man" and he'd learnt to understand what that meant.

He was going in early so that he could talk to his grandad first about the purpose of the meeting. Archie knew that he needed to make a statement today as this was really his first big problem, or potential problem, and he knew that those around that top table this morning would be looking to him for leadership, decisiveness and direction. He was not going to fall short but he still needed a bit of reassurance from Frank. He needed a sounding board, and he knew Frank would be happy to oblige.

As he pulled into Frank's drive, he noticed the white car parked near the front door that told him Gloria was having her feet done. He looked at the clock on his dashboard. 9:05. Who has their bloody feet done at this time? he thought to himself as he came to a stop. The lady who did Gloria's feet was called Emma Black and was as mad as a box of frogs. She lived in Skegby, a village outside of Mansfield, and did pedicures and something called Reiki. Archie never really understood what Reiki was but Gloria said it was some sort of healing thing; universal energy, or something like that, she'd told him. Anyway, Gloria swore by it and had this Emma lady come twice a month to do her feet and give her a blast of Reiki. The only trouble was Archie always tried to avoid Emma as once she got talking she never stopped. She never came up for air. Archie hoped that by now Gloria would be in her studio out the back either having her feet massaged or having her blast of energy.

This Emma also visited the home where Richie was, giving some of the older residents pedicures. Gloria got her into that and now she did the same thing at a few of the nursing homes around the area. Archie walked into the hallway. It was quiet. Gloria must already have her out the back. He walked into the kitchen. No one was around. He put the kettle on and started to make a brew. He'd just sat down at the kitchen table when Frank came through.

'I was hoping you were gonna be here, Son,' he said, as he got a mug from the cupboard. 'I told that Emma I had to come through as I was expecting you at 9 o'clock. I'd have never gotten away. Boy can she talk, that one. Thing is, I never have a clue what she's on about. She's trying to persuade me to have some of that Reiki shit. Gloria swears by it, reckons it will do me the world of good. I told her I might have it next time.'

Archie smiled. 'I'll let everyone know that at this morning's meeting, shall I?'

'Yeah, righto, Son, very funny. Anyway, let's get down to business, shall we? What's your plan this morning?' Frank asked, making his cuppa.

'I want them all to know that we may have a problem – to keep their eyes and ears to the ground and to let them all know that we're taking no shit. One more sign, no matter how small, of Fletcher and his blokes peddling their fuckin' gear on our patch and we take the fight straight to 'em. I want them to know that this is a real proposition, taking into account your gut feeling on this and to make sure everyone is up for it. Fletcher's no mug and if it comes on top, we need to be ready for them.'

Archie stood up as he spoke. He then leant onto the table top with both hands.

'If you're right, Grandad, and let me tell you I think you might be, then this will be my first real test. As I say, Fletcher O'Brien is mainstream. He's the real deal and I need them all fuckin' wound up this morning, ready for a fuckin' war if needs be.'

He then sat back down. Frank could sense his nervousness, which given the potential problem was understandable. He was right: Fletcher O'Brien was a major player. His dad had been before him and Fletcher had carried on that tradition. Frank knew that if Archie took the fight to Fletcher, then it could and probably would be a bloodbath. Frank wanted to avoid that – who would want a bloodbath if it could be avoided? – but he was also more than prepared to take the fight to Fletcher if he had to. He knew Archie needed him and even at 69 years old, Frank could feel that adrenaline rush pump through his body. It was the same rush he'd always got whenever he could feel a fight coming on. It was game on. Frank was going to show Archie, his grandson and heir, what to do, how to handle this and how to grow into the real deal. But first, he needed Archie to remain in control and show leadership.

'First of all, Archie, you need to be calm. I can sense an air of apprehension.'

'What do you mean "apprehension"? I'm not scared, you know,' Archie replied angrily.

'Oh yes you are, Son. I can see it. And you bloody well should be,' Frank said, waiting to see his reply.

Stone-faced, Archie kept quiet. He knew Frank was right.

Frank continued. 'Being afraid is good, Son. It's a mechanism that can work for you if you understand it. I'd be scared if I was you, any fucker would, but you need to channel that fear into something positive – and that positivity is control. Learn to control your fear. Keep calm. Aggression is often a mask for fear; a mask that serves a lot of people well, but the real players are the ones who can remain calm whilst at the same time being scared shitless. That's who you need to be, Son: the one person in the room who always remains calm.

'I learnt that very early on in my career. And then on the doors in Mansfield in my late teens, I realised that when the dickheads were kicking off outside, threatening to do this and that to me and my family, I had to remain calm. I just had to stand there in silence, looking as though I was in control of the situation and as though none of that aggression had any effect on me at all. Ninety-nine times out of a hundred, they just blew themselves out and ended up walking away, still shouting what they were going to do to me. I, on the other hand, even if I was stood there feeling scared inside, looked as cool as fuck, and everyone around me became scared of me. I had to do nothing, nothing at all, other than remain in control. I learnt to control that fear and then, as time went on, there was no fear, only control. I soon became fearless and very quickly became feared, all because I knew how to control my fear early on.

'Soon, I only had to be present to see that same fear in other people's eyes, in their reactions, in their responses. And that's when I knew I was something different. I was the cool one in the room. I always kept my head, hardly raised my voice, although, as you know, I still do shout from time to time – but that's not to mask fear, that's just to get my frustrations out into the open and to remind people that I can be a nasty fucker when I want to be. You need to be the one who keeps their head, Archie. The one who's different, the one who appears unnerved, even when you're bricking it. The advantage you have is that you have me with you. I'd die for you, Son. You have nothing or no one to fear, only yourself. Understand?'

Archie listened intently, so proud to have his grandad talk to him like this. He took in every word. It all made sense. He now knew what he needed to do. He took a large gulp of his tea.

'Fuck me, that's still hot!' he gasped, taking far too much in one go. 'I understand, Grandad.'

They gave each other a hug, a proper bear hug, and patted each other on the back at the same time. Frank pulled him closer.

'But on top of all that, Son, the one thing you also have to have is bottle – the bottle to do what's necessary. Never back down, never back out of doing something that you know needs doing. Always stay in control. Be feared and fear no one.'

Frank then stepped back. Archie nodded. Frank did the same.

'Come on, they'll be arriving,' Frank said, walking towards the door to go into the boardroom.

chapter seven

Benny Lancashire was in his car. He was on the phone to Harry and Stuart, his two men who were on their way across country to Nottingham.

'How many runners you got, Harry?' Benny asked, wanting to know how many men were going to be getting the drugs onto the Nottingham streets.

'Twenty, Boss,' Harry replied. 'They're in the van behind us, crammed in like sardines, but don't worry, it's all in hand. I can't get hold of Rob and Carl, though. They're not answering their phones. I tried 'em last night and again this morning. No answer, nothing.'

Benny thought for a moment. 'They'll have been done, both of them, I bet ya. That's why Frank rang Fletcher last night. They'll have fuckin' grassed us. I knew it would be them two, the tossers. Do you know where they both live?' Benny asked.

'Yeah, both of them,' Harry replied.

'Right then, go to their places first and if they are still alive, beat them to within an inch, and I mean a fuckin' inch, of their lives. Make sure you don't kill 'em – Fletcher wouldn't want that at this stage – but close enough. Then get onto the large estates and get that gear on the streets. Word will soon get back to Archie and Frank, and then we'll see what they're fuckin' made of. Once your guys are distributing it, ring me so I can let Fletcher know.'

'Will do, Boss.'

Benny shook his head and hit the steering wheel. He fuckin' knew they'd grass. He rang Fletcher to tell him.

'Harry can't get hold of those two we've been using over there to supply, so I've told him to get his men on the streets and just sell the gear round the estates. You OK with that?'

'Yeah. Get the gear on their streets any way you can, but listen, when word gets back to Frank, he will have his men on those estates pronto, so our men will be vulnerable. Harry and Stuart included. So, listen. Get Phil and his little mob together and get over to Frank's main club. You know where it is. Park close to it and when I get the call from Frank, I'll ring you to go in and smash it – and whoever is in there – to fuckin' pieces. Frank and Archie included if they're there. Fuck 'em, it's game on, Benny lad.'

Benny smiled. He loved it when it was game on. 'No problem, Fletcher, I'll get onto Phil now. I'll take him, me and five others, in two cars. We'll smash 'em to fucking pieces.'

Benny ended the call. He was excited. He couldn't wait to fuck up Frank and Archie Pearson. Benny was 32, from a well-to-do neighbourhood in Cheshire and had had a very privileged upbringing, but it had bored him silly. His parents disowned him when he was caught shagging a young brunette a few years back on his father's golf course. Benny had her from behind, near to the fairway of the 9th tee, just as his father and his ten-bob millionaires walked past with their trolleys. Benny nearly killed the golf club owner when he tried to eject him from the course.

Luckily for Benny, Fletcher O'Brien was also on the course that day and he'd found it hilarious. He took an instant liking to Benny, offered him a job as a doorman at one of his clubs and, very soon, after being so impressed with him, gave Benny the opportunity to control the drugs being sold both on the doors and inside the club. Within two years, Benny was selling in and around some of the sleepy villages in Cheshire; higher end drugs to some of the more wealthy individuals who needed something to fill their dreary lives once the missus had stopped opening her legs as often.

Benny fit in. He talked posh, he looked posh but he was as hard as nails. He visited the gym five times a week, took every steroid there was going and had muscles on top of muscles. He was very handy for Fletcher. Benny was going places. The golf course incident was just under five years ago and now he was fast becoming one of Fletcher's most trusted inside men. Benny wanted to get to the top and saw opportunities like the one here today as a way of getting there quickly. His Achilles heel was that he was driven by money. Benny knew that if someone came along with a big enough stash, he'd be off following that pot of gold.

The man he was taking with him today was a guy called Phil, who Benny knew from the gym. He was a fucking psycho. He had his own little crew who dealt and was well respected in and around Manchester. Phil didn't harbour any ambitions to rise to the top like Benny did. He was just happy to make a few quid and be hired muscle when needed.

Harry went to the homes of Carl Waites and Rob Simpson. Neither were in. He said he'd go back. He never did and no one remembered to ask him about them. They'd both got lucky and had recovered in hospital. Coppers on Frank's payroll made sure no one made anything of it. Rob Simpson ended up working in a factory on an assembly line. Carl Waites left Nottinghamshire and was never heard of again.

chapter eight

Alice took the tea and coffee orders. That was what she always did. She wanted to be involved but no more than that. She was happy to be what some people would call an old-fashioned tea lady, but she liked it and it meant she was involved.

Phoebe took her place at the table in her usual spot. They all had their own place and own chair. It was never planned like that, but over time everyone just seemed to sit in the same chair, so it had become a bit of a standing joke. She looked over at Archie and smiled. He smiled back. She then looked around the room, first at Frank. He smiled. She smiled back. Frank was at the top of the table, as he always was. Phoebe studied him and saw the same smouldering good looks that he'd always possessed. She saw what Renee and Gloria had both seen in him. Yes, he was old now, but he looked younger than his 69 years and still had that barrel chest and sturdy, solid frame that gave him presence.

She returned to Archie, who was deep in thought as he waited for everyone to get settled. Phoebe then glanced around the room at the top table that she hoped would help keep her son safe in the years ahead. She took in Jez, Frank's trusted right-hand man for so many years. Jez had been loyal. He had given Frank his life and, like Frank, he had worn well. He looked good for his age, despite his big nose, and was still as feared as ever, although he only ever came out for the big days. People would say things like, "Fuck me, it must be serious shit today. Jez is here." No one had said that yet, but there was time.

Then she moved to Brian, another original member of Frank's empire. Frank had known Brian since his doorman days in Mansfield all those years ago and, like Jez, Frank trusted him with his life. Brian had been forever single, never marrying, never having anyone to share his life with. People would say he was married to the job, and in a way he was. Unlike Jez, he was still very active and even at his age, could still mix it with the best of them.

She then turned to Pat, Archie's right-hand man. Pat was only in his fifties, so still very much part of daily life within the family business, and had proven himself to be cut from the same cloth as Jez and Brian. He was good for Archie. He could be trusted and had an old head on his shoulders.

Then Phoebe scanned the room, seeing Raquel, a woman in a man's world who, had she been born a man, would have ruled the UK. She was a diamond was Raquel and, again, someone who would die for her employers.

And then there was Del, a man who still had arms the size of breeze blocks; his brother, Michael, who was just the same; and then John Hughes from Leeds, who had taken over from Pat when Pat came back home to Nottingham. John ran Leeds and Doncaster. He was a broad Yorkshireman who ate chips with everything. Even with chips, he'd have some more chips on the side. He was a very quiet, unassuming man of few words, who, if you didn't know better, was someone you would never think was in this kind of work. He was the quiet assassin, though; someone who never raised his voice but was ruthless just the same.

Phoebe looked around at them all again and knew that these people, a mix of old and younger blood and loyalty unrivalled, would not let her son down. There was just one more person, who she'd not yet seen. In fact, she'd forgotten about him until he walked into the room.

'Sorry, just been to the toilet,' he said, wiping his hands on his trousers.

Phoebe noticed his missing fingers, which made her smile. Steven Wallace had only recently been invited onto the top table; in fact, it was only his second meeting. Steven had been, quite a few years back, rival to Frank and Daniel, when he and his brother, Gary, controlled Leicester. Frank and Daniel had taken them out when they'd tried to muscle in on Frank's territory, along with a guy from Leeds called Gerry Clarke. Daniel had killed Gary Wallace stone dead. Steven had survived but had lost an eye and two fingers in the process. He now had one glass eye and would sometimes wear sunglasses as he was quite self-conscious. Today was one of those days.

Frank had taken some persuading, but Archie, like his mum, felt that the top table needed more members. He felt that Steven had proved himself many times over, which in all fairness he had. He had proved his loyalty but Frank still saw him as a bit of a threat, even though it had been nearly thirty years since they'd taken them out.

Frank had made him work for him after they'd killed Gary so as to shame him in some way. Steven had been a major player, along with his brother, but Frank thought that making him skivvy for him was more shameful than being killed along with Gary. Steven had taken it on the chin and had shown to be a good asset. He was a good villain after all and was very handy, but Frank held a grudge, and could never agree that Steven could forgive what happened to his brother, even though Steven had told Frank it was ancient history many times.

Archie liked Steven. He worked as Raquel's number two and served her well. She spoke very highly of him too. Phoebe, like Frank, was still a little unconvinced even all these years later. It had been her husband, after all, who had killed his brother.

Steven took his seat. Archie cleared his throat.

'Right, ladies and gentleman. We may have a problem.'

Frank immediately scanned the room for any reaction. It was just something he instinctively did these days. Since Archie had taken over more of the reins, he was able to watch from behind and see what people were thinking, purely down to their body language. He'd become interested in it after watching a TV documentary on it and now, whenever he could, he watched for signs of what people were thinking.

Two people adjusted their seating. One was Archie, so that said he was nervous, which in essence Frank thought was a good thing (although he hoped no one else noticed it), and the other was Steven. That interested Frank. He made a mental note. He then continued to listen to Archie.

Steven asked who the problem was with.

'It's a guy called Benny Lancashire, Steven – a guy from over Manchester way, that's who,' Archie replied. 'But he's not the biggest potential issue. The biggest issue is Fletcher O'Brien. Now, you all know Fletcher and you all know he's Arnie's son, God rest his soul. So, if he turns out to be a problem, then it's major, hence this morning's meeting.'

Del piped up. 'So, what did you find out then, Archie, about this Benny Lancashire guy that Carl and Rob told us about?'

'That he works for Fletcher, as a foot soldier, he said, but Frank reckons Fletcher was lying. Now listen, and listen good. We can't afford any mistakes if we are dealing with Fletcher O'Brien. Fletcher reckoned he would take care of this Benny case, but we're not so sure. Something just didn't ring true about the conversation, so we need to be on our top game. We reckon Fletcher knew all about Benny Lancashire dealing his gear over here and if he did, then that's a major fuckin' liberty, one that we cannot overlook, no matter who Fletcher O'Brien is. And if it is true, then we cannot see Fletcher stopping whatever it is he's planning. So, expect more of that gear to hit our streets. That may be today, may be tomorrow, may be next month, but it will hit our streets. So, when it does, we have to take this fight to Fletcher. There's no alternative.'

'Bring it on,' Brian said.

'Yeah, we will take it to him, Brian, but we need to be in control. This is a major UK player, one that won't be easy. He obviously sees the fact that Frank has taken a bit of a back seat as an opportunity to either test us, or muscle in, but either way we'll be ready.'

'So, what's the strategy, Archie?' Phoebe asked. She always wanted to know what the strategy was. That was where Phoebe came into her own. She was the thinker around that table, the one who couldn't offer any muscle, but the one who would always make sure there was a plan and a rationale behind things.

'The plan, Mum, is to wait. We may have this wrong. We may be doing Fletcher a major injustice, so we wait. We do nothing except wait. If Fletcher is planning something, he may hold out to see if we make a move after yesterday's phone call. So, we wait. We do nothing, but we watch and we listen and we react. Or rather, we respond swiftly depending on what his next move is. If we find out any more gear has been dealt on our streets, then we move quickly and Benny Lancashire will be the first target. In fact, yes, John take Paul, Del's son, with you and get over to Alderley Edge and see what you can find out about this Benny Lancashire. We don't even know what he looks like, do we, so be discreet for fuck's sake. I'll give you the details of the bar when we're done here.'

He looked at Del. 'Make sure your Paul is suited up, Del. They need to look like businessmen of the area. It's a posh place apparently.'

He then looked at John Hughes, who was already in a suit. Archie smiled and nodded. 'Be discreet, though, John. Blend in. We don't want anyone knowing who you are.'

'No worries, Archie. We'll be fine. I'll come back to Nottingham with you then Del, eh, and get your lad?' John said, looking across the table at Del.

'Yeah, no worries.'

Archie then looked at Raquel. She knew what was coming. She knew she'd get brought up this morning and to be honest, she was OK with that. She was still annoyed at what Archie had said yesterday but she had to suck it up and accept some of the responsibility.

'And you,' he said, 'get yourself back over to Nottingham as soon as we've finished the meeting and keep your ears so close to the ground, I want you to be able to feel the coolness of the concrete. Anything happens, and I mean anything, no matter how small, even if it's just a feeling, I want to know about it and I want to know about it from you, no one else, just you.'

Raquel nodded. She didn't speak; she was too annoyed. She felt like she'd just been spoken to like a child, but she took it and just told herself for the umpteenth time that she would never allow herself to be in this situation again.

Archie then leant forward with his elbows on the table. 'So, that's all we know at the moment – that we may, and I say may, have a problem. But if it turns out to be a problem, then we will sort it, no matter who he is. Everyone on board?'

He looked around the room as they all nodded and said yes. Only one person said anything different and that was Jez. Jez didn't say much but when he did, you listened. He always spoke well and with sense, and Archie would never forget that it was him – along with Raquel and Marie, Richie's ex-girlfriend – who pieced it all together when Daniel was murdered. Well, pieced it all together about Richie's involvement at least.

'You do realise, Archie, that if you take on Fletcher, it will be a bloodbath. He's a loose cannon, you know. You do know that, don't you? And what about the Burbankses. Has anyone been in touch with them?'

Frank instantly looked at Archie. He turned to Jez and then back to Archie again. For fuck's sake, Jez! he thought, as he readied himself for Archie to react.

Archie resented any suggestion that he couldn't handle things and that remark from Jez certainly implied that. Frank watched as Archie took a deep breath in. He could hear it and he saw his chest move up and down.

'Yes, Jez, thank you. I am fully aware of Fletcher's standing in this world and what he is likely to do, but take it from me, if he does anything else to inflame this already delicate situation, I will go after him and take him down. No one, and I mean no one, takes a liberty with me or anyone else around this table and gets away with it.'

Archie and Jez stared at each other. Archie continued. 'And as for George and Ivan Burbanks, yes we have been in touch. Frank has made the call and that side of things is sweet. We all know where we stand. They support whatever we feel we need to do.'

Jez nodded in approval. 'Excellent, Archie,' he said. 'That'll do for me.'

Archie nodded. He said nothing else to Jez. He felt he'd said enough. Frank smiled inside. He'd just seen a different side to Archie. One that could hold the room; one that, in that one statement, had just told everyone around that table that he was ready. He had finally taken over from Frank. Frank was proud of him. He saw Daniel in him; he saw himself in him. He saw Archie, the main man, the right man.

Archie kept counsel for the next hour or so, talking further about the potential issue with Fletcher alongside other business matters. He had kept the regular meetings as a main part of the business so as to keep on top of everything that was happening out on the streets. Frank had instilled in him, early on, that he had to treat it as a business, with regular board meetings, just like any regular firm. There were, of course, many legitimate businesses within the family set-up. Frank had made sure down the years that they had many legitimate companies to both launder cash and to explain their wealth. Frank had seen many men in the underworld get taken down because they'd lived solely off illegal or immoral earnings.

Frank had been smarter than that quite early on in his rise to the top. He'd had the tax man sniffing around but he had always been able to explain where his wealth had materialised from, and to show a paper trail for any major expense or extravagance. Archie had seen the importance of this, especially after listening to far too many tales of men who were enjoying a stretch at her majesty's pleasure, purely for not keeping the taxman at bay. These meetings allowed him and Frank to keep on top of the legitimate, as well as the illegitimate, side of their empire. They would usually last most of the day, but today was a short one as it was both unexpected and unplanned, finishing around 12 o'clock.

Everyone dispersed to carry on with their daily activities. John Hughes went off with Del to pick up Paul. Jez and Brian still effectively worked for Frank. They were still his own men, although they did, when required, answer to Archie too. Pat was Archie's right-hand man, so he stayed with him. Jez went up to Archie.

'No offence meant earlier, Archie, about the

bloodbath with Fletcher. I just wanted to see what your reaction would be, that's all.'

'And why was that?' Archie replied, still wound up about his comments.

'To see if you'd explode like you normally do, or to see if you'd answer me in a calm, controlled manner. Frank said you'd learnt a lot recently about control and all that kind of stuff, so I wanted to see for myself.'

Archie gave Jez a hard stare. He'd been annoyed that Jez had spoken to him like that in the meeting and was even more annoyed now that Jez was telling him he'd been testing him.

'So, what if I'd exploded? You know, like you say I normally do?'

Jez paused a moment. He could tell this could turn nasty. He thought about where he was, he thought about who Archie was and the fact Archie was 22 years old with all of this shit to deal with: shit that Jez had never courted, shit that Jez had always left to Frank to carry. Jez had always just been the muscle to sort the shit out, never the one to carry the responsibility on his shoulders. He recognised that and respected what Archie potentially had on his plate.

'I'd have still been with you, Archie, you know that – but not without Frank. Frank would have to go wherever we went to sort this, but now, now that I can see how you are changing, I'd go with you alone. That's the difference.'

He looked him in the eye. Archie did the same; his brain working overtime, processing what Jez meant.

Without averting his gaze, he said, 'You're a fucking diamond, Jez. You've been at my grandad's side longer than I bet you even care to remember. You were there when my family needed you. When my father was killed, you helped piece it together. I love you, but don't ever question my credibility again in front of that table; in fact, don't ever question my credibility in front of anyone. If you have doubts and need questions answered, see me in private.'

Jez liked what he was hearing. Archie had every right to say that and he said it well, with authority, with calmness and with meaning. Jez knew he'd been put in his place and that was exactly where he'd wanted Archie to put him. He held out his hand. Archie shook it.

'Fair point, Archie. Understood,' he said, meaning every word. No more words were exchanged but, in that moment, Archie had grown so much in Jez's eyes. Jez, like others, had been sceptical of Frank's decision with Archie, but seeing him recently, and especially today, told Jez that Frank had made the right move. Jez knew the next few years would be tough. Archie would have it hard out there. People were watching, hovering like vultures, but one thing Jez Carrington knew more than anything else was he would be there when needed for both Frank and Archie. Jez always knew that one day his time would come; that one day he would get too old, get caught out and he'd die doing what he loved – being a criminal. He just hoped it would be whilst protecting either Frank or Archie, and that when that day came, that he'd go out at the top.

As he turned away from Archie to join Frank in the garden, he prayed that day would not involve sparring with Fletcher O'Brien, because if it did, then that day would be here far too soon.

Archie's phone rang. It was Hazlehurst, the most senior copper the family had in their pocket. Frank had groomed him for a good few years. Hazlehurst had told Frank years ago that he'd never stoop so low as to be answerable to the likes of Frank Pearson. That was like a red rag to a bull for Frank and for a number of years, early after the turn of the century, Frank made it his business to get Hazlehurst on his payroll. To do that, he needed an angle on him. He got that angle when he obtained evidence that Hazlehurst had covered up a serious crime involving people in the public eye. Frank still had that evidence to this day; evidence that would ruin Hazlehurst, and would put him in prison for a decent stretch.

Hazlehurst now did everything he could to cover Frank and Archie's tracks whenever they needed covering. He was well paid for it and Frank reminded him often of how low he'd stooped. Archie answered the call.

'All right, Hazlehurst,' he said, his tone sharp as it always was with coppers. Archie didn't like them and Hazlehurst was no exception. The fact he paid him made no difference to how he spoke to him.

'Two men with shotgun wounds to their legs. They're not talking, but was it anything to do with you guys?'

Hazlehurst replied, equally as sharp. He hated the likes of Archie and Frank Pearson but he also knew he could never afford for that evidence to be made public. Archie was always careful with what he said, even to Old Bill on the payroll.

'Just make sure they don't talk. And make sure nothing lands at our door,' Archie replied.

That told Hazlehurst that it *was* something to do with the Pearsons. He sighed. 'Thought so. OK, leave it with me. I'll sort anything that needs sorting.'

Archie couldn't help but smile. 'Good man. Your pound notes will be with you as usual. Spend them wisely.'

Archie always got something like that into the conversation. It was just something he did. He didn't trust coppers, Hazlehurst included, and always made sure he said something incriminating like that just in case anyone was listening. Frank told him he was paranoid – Hazlehurst could never afford to take them on, but Archie was always cautious. He just couldn't help it.

'Hazlehurst, right?' Frank asked.

'Yeah, just about Carl Waites and Rob Simpson somehow getting a bullet hole in their legs, that's all. He's sorting it, though. No need to worry.'

'Good. Listen, you did well in there, Son. Had real authority and presence.'

Archie appreciated that from his grandad. Frank didn't do praise well. It came infrequently, so when it did, it had real meaning. Frank looked around him and saw Jez, Brian and Pat talking amongst themselves. He put his arm on Archie's shoulder.

'If this turns into something, I'm telling ya, you'll need – well, we'll need – to go in mob-handed. We need to be strong. If we hesitate, we'll be on the back foot. We need to act fast, Son. The whole criminal underworld will be watching. Give 'em something to watch.'

Frank studied Archie's face as he spoke. It was unnerved. Archie was up for it; Frank could see it.

'Don't worry, Frank. I will be.'

chapter nine

Thirty-eight-year-old Faye Johnson was the manager of the Romsey Care Home in Walesby, about a twenty-minute drive from Mansfield. It was a quiet village with a pub, a post office and a shop. Romsey wasn't an overly big home, but its reputation was one of the best in the area, hence why Frank had chosen it for Richie, who needed 24-hour care.

Faye enjoyed her job. She had been there for the past twelve years, as manager for more than seven of them; just before Richie became a resident in fact. It was Faye who Frank paid to keep quiet about his monthly visits. At first, she had welcomed it all. She enjoyed the brown envelope that Frank gave her every month with a wad of crisp notes in it and, for the first few years, had been happy with the whole arrangement. She wasn't doing anyone any harm. She knew all about Frank Pearson and the rest of the family – she was a local girl and everyone knew of the Pearsons – although she'd only recently learnt just how big a figure Frank was. She would never tell anyone about their arrangement or that Richie Pearson was a resident, but things had changed a little.

Someone else came two or three times a month to see Richie; someone who also paid her a healthy chunk for doing so. They'd been coming for the past two years or so; at first, she'd just taken the extra cash, happy to keep two secrets. All she had to do was to make sure that they never came on the same day.

Frank always texted her to let her know so that she could make sure she was on duty. Frank had insisted she do that. He always wanted her there. Frank came once a month, so it had been easy to keep them apart, but lately she'd become worried about it all. She just knew that one day it would come out. Faye wished she could turn back the clock, yet felt she was stuck with it all. She couldn't tell Frank about this other visitor as it would surface that she'd been keeping it from him for two years and she couldn't do anything about the other visitor, who was on their way right now. Each time, they'd spend an hour or so with Richie in his room, insistent that they were not disturbed. Faye sat in her office, biting her nails.

'Ey up, Faye,' came a voice from the doorway. 'Can I go to Mrs Robinson's room? She's my first today.'

Faye looked up. It was Emma. She came once a week to do pedicures for some of the ladies. It had been Frank's better half, Gloria, who had introduced her to Faye.

'Er, yeah. No problem. Just go straight down. She's in her room,' she said, wiping her mouth.

'You OK, luv?' Emma said, concerned. 'You look like

you've got the weight of the world on your shoulders. A problem shared and all that...'

Faye sighed and stood up. 'Yeah, I'm fine. Just stuff, you know.'

'A fella, is it?'

Faye smiled. 'It's fine, honestly. Nowt for you to worry about anyway.'

'OK, but if you want to talk, I'm here and if you're stressed, I can do you a Reiki session. It's really good for stress, you know. You'll feel great afterwards,' Emma said, as she turned to go.

'Er, actually, I might take you up on that,' Faye replied. 'The last time you gave me Reiki I did feel really chilled. I finish at 3. What time you here till?'

'3:30ish probably. Come to mine for about half four if you like.'

'I will. I'll see you there. I'll look forward to it.'

Emma smiled and told Faye that she'd see her later and walked down the corridor to see Mrs Robinson. It was then that she realised she'd left her diary in her car. She always liked to pencil in the next appointment before she left her ladies, so she turned on her heels and walked back towards the front door.

As she walked out into the car park, she saw someone she recognised. She waved and shouted 'Hiya!' They waved back and walked towards her.

'How ya doin?' they asked.

'Fine, thanks. Just forgot my diary. I'm doing a couple of pedicures. Didn't expect to see you here,' Emma replied.

'Yeah, well, I need to speak to you about that. Look, no one knows I come here. I just come now and again, just every so often, to see Richie. As I say, no one, and I mean no one, knows I do this, but I just feel sorry for him, you know, all on his own and that. So, please keep it quiet. I just give him a bit of physio whilst I'm here. I just can't stand back and do nothing. That's just not me. I have a natural urge to help people. Promise me you'll not say anything to anyone, and I mean to no one, Emma. You have to promise me. I only do it 'cos I know he doesn't see anyone else.'

Emma smiled. 'Of course, I won't. Your secret's safe with me, I promise. But you do know Frank would go apeshit if he knew, so believe me I'll not tell anyone 'cos there's no way I want Frank Pearson to know that I knew. So, even if you grassed me up, I'd deny it,' she said laughing but thinking why do I have to know this? I don't want to know this!

'Thanks, Emma. I know I can trust you. Have a good day and take care.'

'It's OK, Johnny. Our secret,' she said with a smile and turned away, clutching her diary.

Johnny then followed her. She stopped and half turned.

'Have you just arrived then? Sorry, I thought you were going.'

'No, just got here. I'll spend an hour or so with him. I think he likes my visits. I know he can't really show his emotions, but you know what I mean. I can just tell.'

Emma thought how nice it was that Johnny would do this for Richie and how Johnny was probably the only person Richie saw who was nice to him. In fact, she thought he was probably the only person, except for the carers, that Richie did see. Emma knew that none of the family visited – that was common knowledge.

'I'm doing Mrs Robinson's feet today. She's in the next room. They're lovely aren't they, the luxury rooms. I think she's got a few quid, has Mrs Robinson,' Emma said, winking.

'They certainly are. It'll not be cheap to stay here. Even the basic rooms are like a 4-star hotel room. Anyway, see ya, Emma, and remember, not a word please to anyone.'

Emma touched her nose with the forefinger of her right hand and nodded. She then went through the gate into Mrs Robinson's garden and Johnny went through the gate into Richie's. A small hedge separated each garden that was just high enough to stop the average person peering over. She made the usual fuss over her client, who was so excited to see her, and then they sat in the garden while Emma gave Mrs Robinson her normal pedicure. Emma could just about hear Johnny talking to Richie. If she listened carefully enough, she could make out what he was saying – and Emma being Emma just could not help herself.

Mrs Robinson had dozed off, as she always did. She would be halfway through a tale before she'd suddenly stop talking. More often than not, she'd snore until she woke herself up. She'd done the same today, but as yet, hadn't started snoring.

Emma could hear Johnny telling Richie well done and that they were making great progress, which made Emma like Johnny even more. One thing did surprise her, though, and that was when she heard Johnny say, 'Your movement in your right hand is coming along great. I could definitely feel some power when you gripped my hand.'

Emma stopped what she was doing. 'Wow,' she said to herself under her breath. That sounded amazing. Richie couldn't move any part of his body, or that's what Gloria had led her to believe anyway. Maybe they were wrong she thought, as she started working on Mrs Robinson again, who, with that, gave a loud snore and woke herself up.

'Did I drop off again?' she asked, adjusting herself in her seat.

'Yes, you did, Mrs Robinson. You always do.'

'I know, dear, but you just make me so relaxed. Anyway, what was I telling you before I nodded off?'

Emma listened to Mrs Robinson continue to tell her of the fracas the night before with Eric, one of the residents, who had thrown his tea all over Susan, one of the carers. She listened, but her mind was elsewhere.

Johnny got in his car. He sat in silence and thought for a moment. He was slightly worried, but told himself not to be silly. He just hoped he could trust Emma – he'd be really in the shit if anyone knew he was seeing Richie behind the family's back. He'd been working hard with Richie on his physio. It seemed to be working, and he'd be mortified if he had to stop now.

His phone rang. It was Alice. 'Hiya, luv. You OK?' he said, trying hard not to sound stressed.

'Yeah, fine. What time will you be home? The meeting's finished, so I'm on my way home now. I thought we could have something to eat somewhere,' Alice replied in her usual jolly voice.

'I'll be a while yet. We're running behind, you see. You know what it's like at the hospital – never on time with anything. I'll be as quick as I can, though, I promise, but it might have to be late lunch or early tea,' he said, knowing that Alice would be disappointed.

'Aw, bloody hell, Johnny, you never get any time off! Just a spot of lunch, that's all I wanted.'

'I know, sweetheart, but I can't just up and leave. I'll be as quick as I can, honest, but listen, I have to go.'

'OK. Hurry up, though.'

Johnny rang off and started his car. He had to rush back to work to get through his workload. He knew Alice was upset but going to the home had put him behind. He drove out of the car park and headed towards Ollerton, thinking about Emma and how no one could know he'd been there. If she mentioned this to anyone, it could spoil everything. He replayed their conversation in his head over and over, focusing on her face and her body language. He convinced himself she would keep quiet.

chapter ten

John Hughes was waiting for Paul to get changed into his suit. He hated waiting, hated hanging around. John was a doer. He was a quiet man – wasn't a shouter – but he fucking hated hanging about. Paul came in through the door in a charcoal-grey suit, a white shirt and a light-grey patterned tie. He looked smart.

'Bout fuckin' time. Come on, let's go. Work to do,' John said. 'It'll take a while to get to Alderley Edge. It's all across country – Chesterfield, Sparrowpit, that way. You know where I mean?'

'No fuckin' idea, mate. I never venture far outside Notting-ham. This'll all be new to me. I've only been to Chesterfield once and vowed I'd never go again. Never been to Manchester at all,' Paul replied.

'There's a big world out there, mate. You ought to try and see a bit of it.'

They got in John's Mercedes and started their journey, first to Chesterfield off the M1, then through Baslow, Sparrowpit, Chapel-en-le-Frith, Hazel Grove, Wilmslow and, finally, into Alderley Edge.

'It's took some bloody time, John, ain't it? No wonder I stay in Nottingham. I could have flown to Spain in this time,' Paul said, looking around the very leafy place they were driving through.

'Nice drive, though, mate. I love it when I'm driving through places like that. The Peak District – fuckin' lovely, don't you reckon?' John replied.

'Yeah, s'pose so. Can't beat the city, though. Too quiet for me, all those green, hilly places. I mean what do you do all day? No action or nothing. I'd not know what to do with myself. I mean even this place, Ald Edge or whatever it's called—'

'Alderley Edge,' John interrupted.

'Yeah, that's it,' Paul continued. 'I mean, what can ever go off here? Full of posh knobs, innit. You can just tell.'

John smiled and shook his head. He remembered being young like Paul, but nowadays he did enjoy the peace and quiet a lot more. He told himself he'd retire to the sticks somewhere, once he'd had enough of drugs and violence.

'It's just down here. Four hundred yards it says,' he said, looking to the right; Paul looking out left. 'Here it is.' John pulled up a few yards past it. 'Just need to find a car park.'

He saw a blue P sign about fifty yards away saying there was a car park a hundred yards on the left. He pulled out and made his way to it. Paul paid for two hours, them both agreeing that was long enough. They then walked back towards the bar.

Paul rubbed his hands. 'Don't look like anything, does it? I mean, it looks like a real swanky bar, not the kind you'd deal from,' he said as they crossed the road.

John tended to agree with him but said, 'Looks can be deceiving, mate. Look, when we get in there, let's just sit down, get a drink, I'll get some papers out of this briefcase and we can look like we are just part of the surroundings – just two men in a suit, having a meeting of some sort over a beer. After a half hour or so, I'll ask the barman if there's anywhere we can get some powder. That should start the conversation off nicely and, hopefully, it will lead, very casually, on to Benny Lancashire. It's amazing what people will tell you once they think they've befriended you, and especially if you want to buy drugs.'

'Fine with me, John. This is your gig; I'll just do whatever you ask.'

They walked in and were immediately struck by how plush it was, to the point that they both wondered if they'd been sold down the river by Carl Waites and Rob Simpson.

'Are you sure this is the right place?' Paul said quietly, as they waited at the bar.

'That's what Archie said,' John replied, without moving his lips or his head.

Neither of them had noticed the man sat in the corner behind the front door, who had just texted *They're here.*

chapter eleven

Benny sat with Phil a hundred yards from Frank's main club. Behind them was a transit van with five men just itching to get out and start smashing something or someone up. Benny knew they'd be getting impatient but also knew that when the doors opened and they were let off the leash, they would cause mayhem. He had to hold them back until Fletcher gave the word. This was all about timing.

Benny had his two men, Harry and Stuart, distributing the gear with the others on various estates in Nottingham. He'd been instructed to "give the fucking stuff away", so he was doing just that. He needed Frank or Archie to get wind of what was happening and to put a call into Fletcher. Benny would then get the nod to unleash the psychos in the transit van behind him and trash Frank's club. They were pumped and ready to go. Benny was dying to get the nod. He sighed again as he looked at his phone.

'I've told ya, Benny – looking at it ain't gonna make it ring or make it ping. Just relax, man. Chill,' Phil told him, with his arms folded and eyes closed.

'I don't know how you can be so relaxed. It ain't

fuckin' normal. You ain't normal.'

Phil smiled as he listened to Benny rant on. He continued to rest his eyes while Benny continued to look at his phone.

Paul and John sat down with their drinks. They clocked the guy in the corner and nodded a customary single nod of the head and a smile. The guy did the same.

'Fuckin' quiet in here, John. I'm telling ya, this ain't the right place. It can't be,' Paul said, looking around.

It was dimly lit, but in a classy kind of way. The fittings were expensive, the chairs very comfortable and the beer was long and cold. Behind the bar were an array of gin bottles and a very good selection of craft beers. The prices told them it was an exclusive place. There was no hint of any special offers and no sign of any food being served.

Paul was hungry. He looked up at the barman, who was cleaning some glasses. 'Do you do food, mate?' he asked.

'Only nibbles and snacks,' the barman said, as he brought over a one-page menu. Paul thanked him and looked at the choice. There wasn't anything that was going to satisfy his hunger. He put it down. He didn't fancy olives in oil or bread and humous.

John opened his briefcase and took out some papers. He placed them on the table, as if he was going to discuss them with Paul.

'Would you like anything to eat, sir?' the barman asked.

'Er, no, it's OK, mate. Cheers. Nothing I fancy on there,' he replied. The barman went back to cleaning his glasses.

'Fuckin' weird in here, John,' Paul whispered. 'Something's not right. It's too quiet. A place like this should have some customers. Women who lunch. Men who lunch. Anyone. I've just got a feeling.'

'Shut up, ya pussy. Just look like you're interested in these papers. Once we've downed these, we'll have another and then I'll ask about that something else. Keep calm. Everything's fine,' John reassured him.

Neither of them noticed that the guy in the corner had locked the doors.

chapter twelve

Archie felt a whole mix of emotions standing in the club in Mapperley. He'd come here after the morning meeting to see Pēteris, a Latvian guy who had been working for the family a long time now. He had started by supplying migrant workers from Eastern Europe for Frank and Daniel, but was now running this club in Mapperley too. The migrant labour side of things was a side of the business that now ran itself really, and one that had diminished with all the talk of Brexit and leaving the EU. It was still lucrative but nowhere near as much as it used to be.

Pēteris was very loyal and a hard worker. Raquel spoke very highly of him. Archie liked Pēteris and had come to have a coffee with him on his way to the main club.

'They're fuckin' what?!' he shouted down the phone to Raquel, who was at the main club with Del and Michael.

Looking at Del, Raquel repeated what she'd just said. 'There's a load of Manchester gear hitting our streets today. It's all over Nottingham.'

Del looked as anxious as she was. She waited for Archie's response.

'When you say all over, where the fuck's that?' he raged.

'All over, Archie. We know it's in St Ann's, The Meadows, Hyson Green, Bulwell – it's everywhere. And that's not all,' she continued. 'They're giving it away.'

Archie paced up and down. He had felt anger in his time, but nothing like this. He was ready to explode. He was being taken for a mug.

'Stay there. I'm on my way.' He rang Frank right away. 'It's happening.'

'What is, Son?'

'Fletcher. His gear is all over the city. The wanker's taking us for a mug. I'll kill him, Frank. I'll fuckin' kill him.'

'I bet I get there before ya, Son. I fuckin' knew it. He's nowt like his father. I'll have his fuckin' balls on my fuckin' dinner plate. Meet me at the club.'

'I'm already on my way,' Archie replied. He looked at Pēteris. 'Get ya coat.'

Pēteris did as he was asked and followed Archie to his car. Archie was marching like a madman. Pēteris could only imagine what Frank was like.

Frank was seething. Gloria was worried. She much preferred it when Frank was controlled and measured. That kind of anger she could cope with – she knew that came with the life she was part of – but this was different. She'd not seen him this angry since he found out about Richie's involvement in Daniel's death. She knew it did not bode well.

'Frank, calm down. You need to calm down. Look, sit down and talk it through with me. Here, sit down and I'll make you a drink. You can't go out like this. Someone will get killed,' she said, desperate to make Frank see sense. Gloria very rarely got involved in Frank's affairs. She knew it was not her business and much preferred to keep out of it, but she couldn't just stand by and watch Frank storm out of the house in that state. It would lead to murder.

Frank looked at her. 'Sit down? Have a cup of tea? Do me a favour, Gloria, luv. How the bloody hell can I sit down and have a nice cup of tea when I have that wanker from Manchester dumping gear all over Nottingham? What do you expect me to do, eh? What am I supposed to do? I'll tell you what I'm gonna do. I'm gonna kill him. I'm gonna kill him very slowly and show him, very slowly, that no one takes Frank Pearson for a mug. Who the hell does he think he is, Gloria? Who does he bloody well think he's dealing with here?!' Frank shouted.

He very rarely took his frustration out on Gloria and when he did, it was always because of someone else. He didn't mean to.

'I'm just saying, Frank, luv, that you're not thinking clearly. Remember what you always say, what you always preach to Archie: stay in control, you always say. I hear you time and again: stay calm, be the one in control, be the one who responds and doesn't react. You say it time and again, Frank Pearson, so I'm telling you. I'm telling you because I love you. Please, take a minute, sit down, take a breath. Take a moment to think – five minutes, ten minutes. It'll make no difference to how many drugs are on your streets, but it might just give you the edge – that edge you always say the men at the top have; the edge that you always say makes you who you are, Frank.'

Gloria could see he was listening. 'Please, Frank, sit down. Let me put the kettle on, or have a whisky if you like, but just sit there and take a breath,' she said, holding both his hands.

Frank did as she said. He looked at Gloria and realised why he loved her so much. She was the voice of reason. Today, like she had so many times in the past, she spoke sense. She didn't get involved often, but when she did she was priceless.

He nodded slowly. 'Five minutes. A cup of tea,' he said, plonking himself on the sofa and stroking his chin. Frank only drank on special occasions. 'I'll have that whisky once I've taken care of Fletcher O'Brien!' he shouted. 'I'll savour every drop.'

John and Paul supped the dregs of their first pint. 'I'll get another round,' John said. 'Same again please, mate,' he told the barman, as he placed their two empty pint glasses down.

'Nice place, this. I bet you get some good clientele in here.'

The barman nodded. 'Yeah, normally busier than this. Really quiet today, it is.'

John swallowed and then ventured, 'Anywhere round here we can buy any gear? You know, any coke or such like? A bit of a pick-me-up?'

The barman smirked. 'I wondered how long it would be.'

'What d'ya mean by that?' John asked, a little taken aback by his tone. He then heard a voice that he didn't recognise and the sound of someone gagging. He turned round to see Paul clutching his throat, blood spurting everywhere. He looked at the man stood beside him, holding a knife with a blade that must have been ten inches long. Paul slumped to the floor. He was dead.

'Some coke, was it?' the barman asked.

Archie sped along Mapperley Top towards Sherwood. 'The fuckin' wanker!' he kept saying. Pēteris was unsure how to behave. He didn't know what was happening, only that it must be something big as he'd never seen Archie this fired up.

'What's happened, Archie?' he asked, unsure if Archie would even tell him.

Archie looked at him and suddenly realised that Pēteris knew nothing of what had happened or of what was likely to happen. He shook his head in bewilderment. 'Sorry mate, you don't know, do you? Well, look, the short story is that a guy from

Manchester called Fletcher O'Brien has decided to flood our streets with his drugs and now we need to sort him out. The good news is I'm gonna sort him. The bad news is there'll be a lot of blood shed. Some may be mine, some may be yours, who knows, but blood will be shed,' he said, looking over at Pēteris.

He wanted to see his reaction and it was just as he had expected. Pēteris was a hard Latvian, with one of the best poker faces around. His face didn't alter.

'Manchester, you say?'

'Yes, Manchester.'

'You remember Jānis, a guy who I used as muscle sometimes at the club? The tall guy with a squint. Remember him?' Pēteris continued.

Jānis was a friend of Pēteris's, and also from Latvia. They only got to know each other in the UK. Jānis was an electrician and a bit of an electronics whizz kid who'd installed some electrical devices for Pēteris many years ago. Pēteris had got him in with Frank at the time as he was a handy fella, and he'd never looked back. He hadn't made his living from electrics for a good few years now, but did the odd cash job now and again for the right people.

'Yeah, I do remember him. He was about 6ft 5in. Never knew who he was looking at,' Archie said, as he vividly recalled an occasion involving four football hooligans from Burnley who had stopped off at the club with their mates after a match with Forest. 'He drop-kicked those Burnley lads that time, didn't he?

They were singing "Suicide Squad", weren't they, as they goaded him and then he laid them all out?'

'Yes, that's him. Well, he now does quite a bit of business in Manchester, bringing in foreign labour for a lot of the food factories around there. That's why he moved over there – to work with his cousin, who had started to bring some workers in. He's doing well. He will know this Fletcher guy, I'm sure. Shall I ring him?'

Archie thought for a moment. He then thought some more. Pēteris wondered if he'd heard him.

'Shall I ring him? Jānis, I mean. Shall I find out if he knows the Fletcher guy?'

Archie took a deep breath. 'Yeah, OK, ring him. Connect your phone to my car, though. I want to hear what he says. I'll keep quiet and listen but he cannot know why we are ringing. If he asks, just say I've asked you to find out for me, that's all, nothing else. I know he used to work for you, but he's in Manchester now, so, no offence, but I trust no one from over that way. OK?'

Pēteris nodded. 'I understand.' He then dialled the number just as Archie reached the ring road.

chapter thirteen

John stood there and looked at Paul on the floor. He then looked back at the guy with the knife. He noticed the six-inch scar the guy had on his left cheek and then he glanced over to the barman, who was now stood at the end of the bar. He looked over his other shoulder to see the guy in the corner, behind the door, still sat there. Only now he was smirking whilst holding his phone to his chin. John thought how he was one, they were three, plus they had the advantage of a ten-inch knife. The odds were poor. He knew at that moment that he would either have to take the fight to them or wait and see how painful his own death was likely to be. He was fifteen feet from the barman at least and he was the closest person to him, so if he was going to take it to them, he'd have to wait. By the time he got to the barman, the knife would probably be in his back. He decided to wait.

'You know who we are then?' he asked, not aiming it at anyone in particular but looking at the man with the knife as he said it.

The man in the corner laughed. 'Of course we know who you are. We were expecting you. So predictable, you Midland lads. Got no class. We do our homework, see, before we do anything. We have photographs of you and anyone who's associated with Frank Pearson all over our office at the back. Benny insisted on it, on Fletcher's order of course. We have all of your ugly fuckin' mugs so ingrained in our minds, we could spot any of you a mile off. We knew someone would be here today. We had hoped it would have been Phoebe. She's a looker, she is. We'd have all shagged her, one after the other, and we'd have videoed it for Archie, but never mind eh. Ya can't have everything.'

He then got up and slowly walked over to John. He remained a couple of feet away. 'Now then, you must realise that you ain't getting out of here. The thing is, how are you gonna die? Now, I would like a fairly slow, painful death for you, ya know, to show we mean business, but I'm not sure I have time for that. Got a date with a lovely bird in an hour or so, so you'll be pleased to hear we'll make it quick for ya.'

John knew he was going to die, but he also knew that there was no way he was going down without a fight. He remembered what he'd thought about on the way there, about retiring to somewhere nice and quiet, somewhere in the Lake District maybe; walking in the hills, then stopping off for a pint at the local pub in front of a roaring fire.

He could see out of the corner of his eye the two pint pots he'd placed on the bar. The man from the corner had now walked over to him so that all three of these guys were now stood in front of him. There was no one, as far as he knew, behind him. He had a chance. The pint glasses were within reach. He grabbed them and smashed the tops off down on the bar. He now had two very nasty weapons in his hands, one in each. He lunged at the man from the corner, and the man a couple of feet away from him, driving his right hand into his throat. The glass ripped through his jugular. He screamed, putting his hands to his neck as he fell backwards.

John spun round to see the guy with the knife come towards him. He steadied himself. He noticed the barman had not moved. He was not a fighter. He was obviously someone who thought he was something he wasn't. John only had one man now to fight. The guy lunged at John and swiped the blade, cutting his left arm. He could feel his warm blood pouring from the wound. He brought his right arm round instinctively and plunged the pint pot into the man's cheek. The man brought his arm that was holding the blade back round. It crossed over John's right arm but he managed to bring his face back to miss the blade as it swung round.

John kicked his right leg out and brought it sweeping back across the guy's left calf. His leg buckled and he lurched into the bar, which propped him up, albeit at forty-five degrees. John kicked him again, at the same time pulling him towards him. The man dropped to the floor. John thrust the pint pot into his face and twisted it left to right. The man screamed.

John then felt a huge blow to his head as the

barman smashed a bottle of wine over him. He fell to his knees, as he struggled to remain conscious. Then he felt the knife from the guy on the ground thrust into his stomach. Blood rose up his throat, spurting from his mouth. He collapsed, coughing, and clutching the knife embedded in his stomach. He died thinking of Coniston Water.

chapter fourteen

Alice was sat with Johnny in a very nice tea room in Southwell. They had just had lunch, a late lunch at that, but a very nice lunch just the same. Alice had an egg salad with a little sprinkling of organic apple cider vinegar washed down with an organic smoothie of kale and lime juice, whilst Johnny went for a quiche salad with a mug of tea. Alice liked the tea room. It had very pleasant shabby chic décor, with very individual pieces. There were no high street items in there, more second-hand pieces that had been lovingly restored and no doubt sold at very inflated prices to satisfy the modern appetite for vintage when dining out.

Johnny had managed to catch up on his work and had arranged to meet Alice just before 3 o'clock for their lunch. Alice could sense something was on his mind. She always knew when he had something running through his head because he'd look straight through her, oblivious to whatever topic of conversation Alice was trying to talk to him about. This particular conversation was about Alice's favourite topic: shopping.

Alice loved shopping; it was her main hobby really. She always liked to look her best and would never tire of pounding those streets carrying bags of clothes she would probably only wear once or twice, before dropping them off at the various charity shops she loved around the area. She would alternate which ones she used as she felt it was only right to support the many different charities, and if she was honest, that was one of the reasons she bought so many clothes. Alice knew she was privileged. She appreciated the wealth that her family had, though she'd always tried to ignore where it all came from.

Alice was the spitting image of her mum; remarkably like a younger Phoebe, who she also resembled in character and personality. Alice was a giver. She'd do anything for anyone and was always happy to please, which is why she enjoyed giving to charity.

Alice was well versed on her grandad's activities and, of course, her brother's. She missed nothing when she made the tea; in fact, she would often correct her brother on discussions at the board meetings when he conveniently forgot things that had been said. Archie knew he'd never get away with anything whilst his sister was involved. Alice had a superb memory, which came in handy quite often.

'You're not listening to me, are you?' she said quite sharply.

Johnny adjusted his eyes, bringing her into focus. 'What, of course I am. Heard every word,' he replied.

Johnny was thinking about Emma and was still worried that she might let it slip one day. Everyone knew she was a real chatterbox and even though he was convinced she'd never do so intentionally, he also knew only too well how her tongue ran away with her. He really did wish she'd not seen him.

'So, what was I saying then?'

'Erm, something about shopping at the weekend … me and you going up to Meadowhall.'

Alice was shocked and impressed in equal measure. She smiled at him. 'Well done,' she said. 'You somehow managed to get out of that one.'

Johnny smiled back and held his hand out over the table. Alice placed her hand in his and he cupped it in return.

'I love you,' he said quietly.

Alice brought their hands up to her cheek and she rubbed it on the back of his right hand. She then kissed it softly.

'I love you too. I can't imagine being without you. Don't ever do anything to spoil what we have, will you? Don't ever get involved,' she said, looking deep into his eyes.

Johnny knew what she meant. She had told him from day one to make sure he kept out of it. She had been sure her brother would have enticed him in by now, but to be fair to Archie, he'd had a couple of conversations with Johnny about it, but Johnny had always been clear that he wanted to remain his own man and just wanted to be a physiotherapist. Archie respected that and had not said anything to him for a good twelve months now.

'I won't. You know I want none of that life. I couldn't handle the aggro. You know me, I'm no aggressor,' he said, self-mockingly.

Alice smiled again and kissed his hand once more.

'And that's just how I like you. I couldn't cope with you putting your life on the line every day, like the other people in my life do. I just about cope with Archie and my grandad as it is. Even my mum is getting a bit too involved for my liking. I can see she actually enjoys it. I thought she'd see what it was all about and decide against it, when she first started to show interest after my dad died, but to be honest, she's become one of the top table – and a key one at that.'

Johnny could see the anxiety that gave Alice. Phoebe was her mum after all, and Alice could not cope with ever losing her mum to a violent death like she had her dad. He then thought about Emma and again about what she knew. He had to prepare himself for what Alice would say to him if she ever discovered the truth, but what he was doing gave him so much pleasure. He really wanted Richie to improve his movement in his hands. It was coming, slowly, but Johnny was making progress and that delighted him immensely.

chapter fifteen

Archie was five minutes from the club. His mobile pinged. It was a message. He wanted to pick it up and read it but was deep in conversation with Jānis, Pēteris's friend. Archie had initially intended to just listen to their conversation but once Jānis started talking, Archie couldn't help but interject. Jānis had had dealings with Fletcher O'Brien. He'd been taxed by him along with his cousin, once Fletcher had found out about them bringing in foreign labour to the factories in and around the area.

This was Fletcher's territory. They'd got away with it for a while, but then the knock at the door came and they received a heavy beating. They now supplied the exact same foreign labour to the factories in and around Manchester, but just for less money as Fletcher always had to receive his cut. They'd also had to give a percentage to the Burbankses for doing business on their patch, but their dealings with them were far more professional. George and Ivan had visited Jānis and his cousin, telling Jānis that if they didn't pay, they would not be able to operate in their area. Jānis knew by the way they handled themselves that they were a cut above. He never argued and paid every week. Fletcher, though, just dished out the beating, leaving the talking till after.

Jānis had told Archie three interesting pieces of information. One was that Fletcher was a flash git, who lauded it over everyone and was despised by a lot of the criminals who operated around Manchester. Another was that he knew where Fletcher lived. The third was that a friend of Jānis's girlfriend cleaned for Fletcher at his house, so had access to his property through his keysafe. That was of particular interest to Archie.

'So, how many times a week does this Andrea woman clean for him?' Archie asked.

'Twice a week or maybe three times, I think, but I can find out for sure if you want,' Jānis replied.

'Yes, that would be good. Fuckin' brilliant in fact, but listen, Jānis, I can't stress this enough – for fuck's sake, do not breathe a word of our conversation. It has to be just between the three of us. That's for your sake as much as anyone's. Understand?'

'I do, Archie, don't worry. Listen, I have no idea what your beef is with Fletcher, but if you take him on, for fuck's sake succeed. You'd be doing all of Manchester a big favour if you took him out of the picture. Oh, and one more thing. If you are planning on taking him out, would you allow me to get involved? I owe him for the beating I took on his orders, so I'll be happy to oblige in some way.'

'Listen, you don't need to know any more at this stage, Jānis, but rest assured I'll be in touch if I need you. But once again, keep your mouth shut.'

Pēteris rang off. Archie picked up his phone to read the message. He screeched the brakes. The car came to a stop almost immediately. Cars behind him pipped their horns as they manoeuvred around him. Archie stared at his phone; at two photos from an unknown number. One was of Paul with his throat cut. The other was of John with a knife sticking out of his stomach. The message simply read *Surprise*.

Frank was walking towards his car. He'd had his cuppa and was slightly less enraged, but only slightly. He'd lectured his whole life about control and knew this was a time to practise what he preached.

His mobile beeped. *Surprise*. He stared at the two photos.

Archie pulled into a side street. He needed to get away from the people who were honking their horns at him. If he didn't, he'd end up committing murder. Pēteris was looking at the photos after Archie had passed him his phone. He parked on the pavement outside a very ordinary-looking detached house, with a Vauxhall Astra in the drive. It was a leafy street, but ordinary just the same.

'I'll kill him, Pēteris. I'll fuckin' kill him myself. I can't let him breathe for another day after this. What the fuck am I going to tell Del? That's his fuckin' son there with his throat cut. His youngest son. What will I tell his two brothers?'

Before Pēteris could answer, Archie got out of the car and paced up and down. He ran his hands through his hair and then banged the bonnet. He was seething so much Pēteris thought he was frothing at the mouth. Archie then stood up and took two or three deep breaths, as he looked at Pēteris through the windscreen. He then marched round to the driver's side and got in. He started the car and screeched off. He said nothing, got to the end of the road and turned left. The road to the club was right. Pēteris looked at him quizzingly. Archie stared straight ahead. Pēteris decided to break the silence.

'Where are we going? The club is that way,' he said, as he turned to point his left hand over his right shoulder.

'Manchester. We're going to Manchester. I'm going to kill that bastard today. I need retribution, Pēteris – today. Not tomorrow, not the next day, but today. That bastard has no fuckin' idea who he's dealing with.'

'Archie, that's a bad idea. Going to Manchester is not the right thing to do. It will end badly if you do that.'

Archie stopped the car. People honked again. He looked at Pēteris. 'Feel free to leave. Just open the door and fuck off if you want. I'll go alone.'

There was a moment's silence. Archie's phone rang. He glanced at the number on the screen in the car. It was Frank. He'd never even considered ringing Frank.

It then dawned on him he needed to let him know. This was not going to be a conversation he was going to enjoy. He took his foot off the brake and carried on along the road, back towards the ring road.

'Frank,' he said.

'Get over to mine now.'

'Listen, there's something I need to tell you.'

'Well, that makes two of us. So, I don't care what the fuck you are doing, but get to mine now!'

Archie took a breath. 'Frank, listen, you ain't gonna like this but—'

'Archie, save it. I take it you've had two photos sent to you?'

'Yeah, have you?'

'I certainly have. Get yaself here as quick as you can.'

chapter sixteen

Benny looked at his phone for the hundredth time. Then it rang. He jumped up in his seat and looked over at Phil, who still had his eyes shut. It was Fletcher.

'Get yourselves in that club and cause fuckin' mayhem, Benny. Smash it up and smash up whoever's in there too. No murders – I'm not that callous – but beat the fuckers up good and leave that club in a right mess.'

Benny was fully pumped, like a coiled spring. 'Will do, Boss.'

'But, listen, before you go, I'm sending you photos of two of Frank's men who went to Alderley Edge earlier looking for you. I presume it's fair to say they came off worse. You'll like what I'm going to send you as I believe one of them, the black guy, was the son of one of the men you might just find in that club you're going into. His father's called Del, I think, so if there's a Del in that club, make sure you show him these photos. He's sure to recognise one of them, even though his throat's cut.'

'Nice one, fuckin' nice one. I'll show that fucker if

he's there. Might just show him what will happen to him if he thinks he can mess with the big boys. I love my job. I fuckin' love it.'

Benny smiled a big smile. 'Start the motor, Phil. And drive thataway!' he said, pointing straight ahead.

They were at the club within thirty seconds. Benny thought how good it looked from the outside. He had heard that Frank's main club was the dog's bollocks and from what he could see, it could well be.

He liked a decent club and appreciated the sophisticated establishments. He was brought up in a very leafy part of Cheshire and had become used to drinking and dining in the finer areas of what Cheshire and Manchester had to offer. He'd remained close to his roots through his life of crime and, on rising through the ranks, had chosen to stay in the smart suburbs.

He rang Tiny, the bloke driving the van behind.

'You ready, Tiny?'

'Born ready, Benny, mate,' Tiny replied. 'What's the plan?'

'Me and Phil have a shooter apiece. Don't want to use 'em, but you know, we will if we need to. We have a bat each and I think you have two machetes *and* bats, right?'

'Yeah, that's right. Two machetes and a baseball bat each.'

'Right, well – we go in, mob-handed, steam straight in and smash up anything and anyone in there. There's eight of us, so can't see any problems, especially with the element of surprise being on our side. So, enjoy yourselves, lads, and let's do some fuckin' damage!'

Benny could hear the cheers as he ended the call. He was just about to get out the car when his phone pinged. He opened the message and grinned, on seeing the two photos.

'I hope his dad's in there,' he said, as he got out.

Del, Raquel, Michael and Steven were in the club, sat in the main office. Raquel was in the chair behind the main desk. Del was stood two feet away to her left, with his arms folded. He'd just placed his mobile back in his pocket after leaving a voicemail for his son, Paul. He'd wanted to hear how things were at Alderley Edge. He was not concerned that there was no answer, thinking he must be busy or maybe a bad signal. Michael, his brother, was stood near the door; Steven sat on the opposite side of the desk to Raquel.

There was a slight tension in the air as they were waiting for orders from Frank. It had been a while since they'd alerted Frank and Archie to drugs being distributed on their streets by the Mancunians. Raquel was a little nervous as she'd expected Archie to be there by then and for some sort of instruction to have been relayed.

Michael sighed. 'Fuckin' nightmare this. Like waiting to be hung. We need to get out there and tell our own men on the ground what to do. All we've told them is to hang fire. They'll be wondering what's happening. I know I would, for fuck's sake.'

Raquel fixed her eyes on him. 'Listen, as I've said tons of times already, Frank and Archie will have a plan, no fear. We've just got to wait. Calm down and make another brew.'

Michael shook his head as he said, 'Same again then? I've never drunk as much tea.'

Everyone nodded. 'Yeah, same again.'

Michael opened the door and headed to the kitchen. He heard voices. He turned and walked back past the main office and out into the main room. He saw what looked like seven or eight guys walking in through the entrance, all tooled up. They looked menacing and, immediately, he knew they'd not walked in by accident. They'd not seen him. He retraced his steps to the office.

'We have a problem. Or should I say, about seven or eight problems.'

Steven and Del instinctively followed Michael to the main room; Raquel, a couple of steps behind. By the time she'd entered, the intruders were already running towards the four of them, baseball bats in hand. Raquel spotted one of them had a machete.

Del, Michael and Steven stood firm. Without thinking or without word, they shielded Raquel. They all stood rooted to the spot, one foot in front of the other, slightly to the side mirroring a traditional boxing stance. They traded blows as best they could; their only weapons their fists and feet. They held firm for what seemed like an age but was, in reality, only about fifteen seconds, before they were forced back. They retreated into the corridor, desperately trying to defend themselves.

Three of the men including Benny stayed in the main room and started to smash it up and anything in it – tables, light fittings, lamps, chairs, optics, the lot. Benny could hear from the corridor that his men were having a good time. He knew Phil would be leading the way on the front line, like a man possessed. Benny, for a moment, wished he could witness it, but he wanted to be the one leading the way in wrecking Frank's club. He'd promised Fletcher he would see to it personally, and seeing to it he was. This is what Benny was made for. The adrenaline was pumping so hard around his body, he felt invincible. He stopped for a moment to catch his breath. The two men with him did the same, out of instinct really. Some men were leaders and some were foot soldiers, who just naturally followed lead. These two guys were foot soldiers. Without realising it, they were waiting for Benny to start all over again.

Benny raised both his hands above his head and did a 360-degree survey of the room. He shouted as loud as he could.

'Where are you, Frank?! Come on, Archie lad, where are you?! Look what we are doing – and you two are nowhere, fuckin' nowhere! My name is Benny, Benny Lancashire. I'm here. Come on, where are you?' he laughed, bringing his baseball bat down hard over the bar and making a crack the full width of it.

Benny continued, enjoying every moment. The two

men with him joined him and together they made a mess of the bar, the club's centrepiece. It was a full 360-degree bar that could be accessed from all areas of the main floor. It had cost Frank a fortune, but it was ruined within seconds. Benny stopped after a minute or so and walked towards the corridor to join the others, shouting Phil's name. Phil bumped into him as he came out to greet him. He was puffing hard, but smiling too. He put his arm around Benny's shoulder.

'They're done for, mate. We've just stopped. Here, take a look,' he said, as he led Benny through. Benny laughed seeing the three men on the floor all covered in blood. He then looked over at the lady, who was in a lot better condition than the three men. Raquel was hurt, but they'd gone light on her. Benny looked at Phil.

'What's up – you living in the fifties or something?'

'What d'ya mean?'

'What do I mean? I mean look at her. She's hardly been touched. Fuckin' do her, and do her like the others. She ain't nowt fuckin' special.'

Benny then stood and watched Phil punch Raquel four or five times in the face. She never squealed, and took it like anyone else. She was not going to give these bastards the satisfaction. Phil stood back. Raquel held her nose. She knew it was broken, but Del, Michael and Steven – they'd been done good and proper. She knew that these men would pay. She knew for sure that war had just been declared and she also knew, broken nose or not, she was going to be part of the retribution.

'Who's Del?' Benny demanded. He looked at Del and Michael. 'It has to be one of you two,' he said.

Del managed to speak. 'Me, it's me. Why?'

'What's your phone number?' Benny asked.

'What? Why?'

'I won't ask again. Tell me your phone number,' he said, giving the nod to Phil.

Phil stood over Del, baseball bat raised. Del struggled to open his eyes, they were so bruised. He saw the bat. He managed to lift his head slightly and tried to bring Benny into focus. He then slowly gave out his number. Benny typed it into his phone.

'Come on! Time to go!' he ordered, turning to leave. He then stopped and turned back round, as the text message came through. 'Think you have a message there, Del. Is it in your pocket?'

Del tried to shuffle, to allow him to get his phone out.

Benny looked at Tiny. 'Get his phone out for him, Tiny, mate.'

Tiny stepped forward, felt in Del's pocket and pulled out his phone.

'What's the passcode?' he asked him.

Del ignored him. Tiny kicked Del in the side of his stomach. Del winced.

'What the fuck is your passcode?' he asked again.

Del told him. Tiny opened the message and passed the phone to Benny. Benny smiled, seeing the photo of Paul with his throat cut.

'Think you might know this fella,' Benny said, putting the picture in front of Del.

Del screwed up his face and looked away. He tried to get up. Phil knocked him back down with ease.

'Come on, lads, let's do one. Welcome to the big league, gents!' he hollered.

Raquel could hear Phil laughing all the way to the door. She fell back and lay looking at the ceiling.

Del cried out. It hurt as he did so, but he lay there and wept. For the first time since primary school, Del cried. It wouldn't be the last time, though. He'd not yet seen the one of John.

Archie pulled into Frank's drive, just as Jez was getting out of his car. Brian was a few steps in front walking towards the door. Archie looked at Pēteris. He was unsure whether to leave him in the car or take him in. This was above Pēteris's pay grade. He was a good man, but he was not at the top table. He decided to take him in as he thought it would do no harm. If Frank didn't want him there, Archie would know about it.

'Come on. Come with me,' Archie said, as he opened his door.

'Is that OK?' Pēteris asked.

Archie closed the driver's side and put both his hands on the roof. He looked over at Pēteris and gave a wry smile.

'Fuck knows, mate, but we'll know soon enough. Just keep quiet and we'll see what transpires. If it's an issue, you can sit back in the car.'

Archie threw the keys at him over the car roof. He then walked in with Jez, who had waited for him. They shook hands but neither of them spoke. Jez nodded to Pēteris. Pēteris quietly said, 'All right, Jez.'

Frank was in the boardroom. Archie walked in and looked straight at his grandad. He was expressionless. Archie could gauge nothing of what Frank was thinking. It either meant he was about to explode and if so, Archie wondered in whose direction, or that he was calm and focused. Archie hoped it was the latter. Brian was already seated.

'Sit down, gents,' Frank said. Gloria then came through. 'Coffees all round, is it fellas?' she asked. They all nodded and confirmed what they wanted, though Gloria didn't need reminding, she'd made that many of them. She only had to take note of what Pēteris wanted.

'Where's Pat?' Frank asked, looking at Archie.

'Should be here any minute,' he replied, just as Pat walked in.

'Talk of the devil,' Frank quipped. 'Nip and tell Gloria what you want to drink, Pat, and then we'll make a start.'

The room was tense. No one really spoke for the few seconds Pat was out of the room. Pēteris was both surprised and pleased that no one, mainly Frank, had commented on why he was there. He glanced around the room and realised for the first time that some of the main men in Frank's operation were looking old. Frank had worn well. His dark hair was mixed in with grey, but that suited him. His skin was surprisingly smooth, with not too many wrinkles, for a man in his late sixties. Pēteris wondered if he moisturised. He suspected he did, but of course would never ask. Jez, he thought, was a similar age, and Brian too was of that same era.

He wondered at that moment whether there was a place for him to move up the ranks a little. He knew these three men were legends in the criminal underworld, especially in the East Midlands, and that they could still mix it and were certainly still up for the fight. Yet, age would at some point play a factor and he just hoped, as he looked over at Archie, that it would not be at the expense of the future Archie was hoping to build. He then thought about how two of the younger generation had been taken out over in Manchester. Paul had only been in his twenties and would have been a star of the future. And then John Hughes, the man from Leeds, was only in his forties as far as he knew, not too dissimilar an age to Pēteris, who was 39 – in this world, still a young man really. He decided to sit tight at this meeting as long as he was allowed to, and if he had the opportunity to be involved at a higher level, he would grasp it with both hands.

Pat re-entered the room and sat down.

Frank spoke. 'Right, gents, we have a serious issue here, one that will be as big as anything we've ever had to deal with. For the sake of clarity, I will spell it out for you all. Fletcher O'Brien has made his intentions clear. I sensed he was not a man of his word and he's now proved me right. He's started something we need to finish.'

Archie interjected. 'So, we need to sort this fucker out pronto.'

Frank did not reply. He just paused for a moment, before carrying on. Archie felt the message loud and clear to shut the fuck up and let him finish.

'I'm not sure if you all know, but again, for the sake of clarity, I need to tell you all that both Paul and John have been murdered. The trip they made to Alderley Edge this afternoon did not go to plan, or end well. Paul had his throat cut and John was stabbed in the stomach. Fletcher sent me a photo of them both. Well, maybe not Fletcher himself, but I'm sure on his orders. I've not yet spoken to Del, but given the time' – Frank looked at his watch: it was 5:45 – 'I need to soon because he's sure to be wondering where Paul is, or at least what's happening.'

Frank's phone rang. He looked at the number. It was Raquel. He decided to take it.

'Is this important, Raquel, as I'm in a meeting?' Frank sat back in his chair, void of any emotion as

Raquel told him what had happened, including Del knowing about Paul. She then told Frank she'd seen the photo of John too.

'We're on our way,' Frank said. He then hit the table with his fist.

'What's happened?' Archie asked.

Frank took two very deep breaths. He was trying his very best to remain calm and in control. He knew this was what was needed. The fuse had well and truly been lit now, if it hadn't already, and could spark all-out war if he wasn't careful. Frank, more than ever, needed to exercise what he'd preached down the years. He stood up just as Gloria came in with a pot of coffee and six cups. He was going to tell her the coffee was not needed, but decided to let her place the tray on the table and serve it.

'What's happened, Frank? For fuck's sake!' Archie said, this time with some frustration in his voice.

Frank sat back down. 'Benny Lancashire and seven or eight of his men have smashed up the main club and, by the sounds of it, Del, Michael, Steven and Raquel too. They left about ten minutes ago. They're in a pretty bad way apparently.'

'We need to sort him, Frank, and we need to sort him now. Right this minute, right this night. Fuckin' now. He's gone too far. He murdered Paul and John for fuck's sake. How do you think Del, and John's missus, Tina, will feel? Have you any fuckin' idea?' Archie growled. He was ready to blow his top. That chat that Frank had had with him this morning about keeping in control was long gone. Archie was pacing up and down. What he had just said had hit a raw nerve with Frank.

'Have I any fuckin' idea? Is that what you just said to me – have I any idea? Have you forgotten that I lost my son a few years ago? A son who was murdered by people unknown, people I have not been able to get to, to avenge his death. My own son, and your father for that matter. Have you forgot what happened to your dad?'

Archie stopped dead in his tracks. He had forgotten. In the moment, just then, he had forgotten. He regretted his words immediately. He hung his head in shame. He looked up at Frank and said, 'I'm sorry, Grandad.' He knew he should call him Frank in this moment, but for now, just for now, he was his grandad again.

Frank gestured for him to sit down and as Archie walked back to his seat next to him, he said, 'I know, Son, I know' and patted him on the back of the shoulders.

Jez knew this was his cue; this was the moment for him to calm the situation and take the opportunity to give Frank back the floor.

'So, what's the plan, Frank?' he asked, knowing that his long-time boss and friend would have a plan. And if he knew Frank like he did, it would be well thought out, methodical and calculated. Frank would remain in control, of that he was sure, but even he wasn't prepared for Frank's reply.

'Nothing, gents. We do nothing.'

Brian sat forward. 'You what, Frank – nothing?'

'Yep, that's right. For now, we do nothing.' He looked at five faces all a mixture of surprise and confusion. Even Pēteris, who didn't know Frank as well as the others, looked perplexed.

Brian shook his head. 'Del will want to kill him. He'll be expecting murder, Frank.'

'Yeah, well, Del works for me and if he wants murder, he may well get it, but only when I give the order. Let me make myself crystal clear, gents. For now, we do nothing. We do not retaliate, we do not make contact. We do nothing.'

Archie was struggling. Had he not said what he had a moment or two ago, he would have exploded right there and then. He could not make sense nor reason of what Frank was saying. A huge fucking liberty had been taken. Murder had occurred and Frank was saying to do nothing. He looked at Jez. Jez stared back.

Archie decided to speak. 'You're gonna have to explain this one to me, Frank, 'cos I'm strugglin' with it,' he said, trying very hard to remain respectful.

Frank sat back in his seat, turned his head to him, then looked back across the table and spoke to them all collectively.

'We do nothing, for now, and the reason we do nothing is because that is exactly what Fletcher O'Brien will not expect us to do. No response is the last thing he will expect. It will unnerve him. It will make him react, it will make him do something he wasn't thinking or planning to do. He will have tried to second-guess our move. He will be expecting us to drive over to Manchester right now, and he will be ready for us. He will have men in place tonight, tomorrow and the next day, so silence from us will make him nervous. And when people are nervous, especially people in Fletcher's position, it makes them vulnerable. And it'll leave gaps, because he'll be going off his plan. He'll start to wing it.'

Frank paused. He thought he could hear a few pennies dropping. 'And in the meantime, we will be planning our response. When I said do nothing, I didn't mean to literally do nothing, but this is the big league, gents. We can all fight, we all know that, but so can Fletcher O'Brien. This ain't about meeting in a field and having a ruck. This is about us taking out one of the main faces and that, my friends, needs planning.'

Frank tapped his temple. 'THIS is a man's best weapon. If a man can outthink another, he has the edge. It's about the long term. We'll swallow what's happened, but rest assured,' – Frank paused again, looking them all in the eye one by one – 'rest assured, Del will get his murder. But it ain't gonna be tonight. We need a plan and that's what I need us all to come up with. But right now, we need to get over to the club and see the damage, and to console Del. How well do you know Tina, Pat?'

Tina was John Hughes's wife. She was a very nice lady, one that you could always take home to your mum.

'I know her well, Frank. I spent a lot of time with her and John when I was teaching him the ropes up there. Am I paying her a visit?'

'Cheers, Pat, it needs doing, but listen, as nice as she is, she needs to keep her mouth shut. I have no idea what Fletcher will do with the two bodies. He could dump them and the coppers could find them – which I hope doesn't happen – he could get rid of 'em – I have no idea. He could even get them dropped off over here on our doorstep, who knows, but she needs to know the score and she needs to keep that shut.' Frank pointed to his mouth. 'I don't want to have to hurt her, Pat, but she needs to play the game.'

Pat nodded. He hoped she understood. He was sure she would. She'd been involved with John long enough to know this could happen.

As they all got up to leave, Archie asked them all to sit back down. He then told them all about Pēteris's friend Jānis over in Manchester, and about him knowing someone who cleans for Fletcher.

'Fuck me, Archie, that's just the piece of the jigsaw we've been looking for!' Frank said, looking up to the ceiling. 'Thank you.' He then looked at Pēteris.

'I wondered what the fuck you were doing here, Pēteris, my old pal; in fact, I meant to ask you what you thought you were doing here earlier when Archie went off on one, but it then slipped my mind, but now I know. I tell ya something, lads, the universe doesn't 'alf work in some strange ways. Pēteris, I want a meeting with Jānis tomorrow. Over here. We are not setting foot in Manchester just yet. As I said, I want Fletcher to wonder why we are not retaliating. Make sure he's here tomorrow morning. Here at my house.'

Pēteris nodded. 'No problem, Frank. I'll sort it.' Pēteris tried very hard not to smile too widely. This might just be the opening he'd been looking for.

Frank stood back up. 'Come on. We need to go to the club.'

All five of them, as they walked out, now knew where Frank was coming from. Jez smiled inside. He knew Frank would have a plan and from what he said, it all made sense. There was no way Fletcher would expect silence and that, as Frank had said, would make him nervous and want to react.

Frank shouted to Archie, 'With me, Son, come with me. Let Pēteris drive your motor.' Frank wanted to speak to Archie alone. He needed to have a word with him about his reaction in the boardroom.

Pat went to see Tina. She cried buckets and was hard to console, but she swore she would not breathe a word'.

chapter seventeen

Fletcher O'Brien was sat in his very large office in his six-bedroom house in Altrincham, a leafy market town in the Trafford area of Manchester, about eight miles from the city centre. He'd bought the house cash around eight years ago and had extended it extensively since, much to the annoyance of his neighbours. It had a swimming pool, sauna, gym and cinema room as well as three reception rooms and an orangery. It was a statement house, with large gates that led to a driveway that swept to the left as it brought you up to the house. The landscaped gardens were bordered with trees, and an electric fence ran the length of the perimeter. This was the main cause of concern for his neighbours, but Fletcher always got what he wanted and the fence was no exception, with a few crisp pound notes taking care of the problem for him.

The sauna and swimming pool were really for his wife, Katrina, or Kat, as she liked to be called. She took great pride in her appearance, exercised daily and fretted like hell if she put a pound on in weight. Kat was your typical trophy wife. She'd never worked a day in her life, had false tits, false eyelashes and a year-round tan that always looked surprisingly real, maybe in part due to loving her holidays in Marbella, at their four-bedroom villa. Kat went as much as she could. She insisted on installing a gym and a sauna there, too, to complement the outside swimming pool. Kat swore by a sauna, saying it cleansed your pores, but to get the full benefit, you had to stand under a bucket of ice water as soon as you came out. She squealed every time she pulled the chain to tip the bucket over her and irritated Fletcher immensely every single time she came back through into the main house and told him about it.

To everyone, she had it all; to herself, she was as miserable as sin. She was controlled by Fletcher in every way. She'd never wanted a pair of fake tits, but he'd insisted. She never wanted to exercise every day for fear of putting on an ounce, but he'd insisted. She never wanted to go to the villa accompanied by two of Fletcher's men each time, but he'd insisted. She'd never wanted children, but he'd insisted. They had a boy and a girl: Alfie, nine, and Courtney, seven. Kat had wanted a career, but Fletcher had first seen her when she was in the sixth form and she'd been with him ever since. She was eight years younger than him – and had forgotten what it was like to make her own decisions. Fletcher told her who she was friends with, where she went and with whom, and watched her like a hawk, convinced she was going to cheat on him. The irony was always lost on Fletcher that he had shagged more women than even he could remember, whereas Kat had never laid a finger on another man, mainly because she knew it would most probably be the last thing she did.

Fletcher savoured his scotch. He felt the burn as it slid down his throat. He'd just come off the phone to Benny and was feeling fucking good. He licked his lips, taking in the taste of the scotch. He thought about how his plan was working fine. Benny had done good, as had Phil and his boys by the sounds of it. It was now just a case of waiting to see what Frank and Archie would do. Fletcher was certain they'd react straight away. He knew how Archie's mind worked and he'd heard how he went off at times. He just hoped Frank was there too.

Fletcher was ready. He'd increased his manpower at all of his clubs, and his security at home. He now had two of his men living full time in the house, much to Kat's frustration. His troops on the ground who ran his operations had all been well versed. Whenever Archie or Frank came knocking – and he was sure it would be soon – Fletcher would be ready. He clenched his fist as he pictured Archie coming to sort this out, giving it the big 'un. He wanted to take Archie out personally. He knew that without him, Frank would be too old to keep things intact. Archie, on the other hand, could cope well without his grandad. Remove Archie and one by one they would crumble. He thought about how, as a youngster, he'd seen rows and rows of dominoes lined up on some Saturday night TV variety show, and smiled as he recalled them falling, once the first had been knocked over. That was how he saw things happening. It was all in place. Fletcher was confident he'd taken care of everything. The only thing he hadn't made changes to was Kat. He thought she was well taken care of and could see no reason to change that.

chapter eighteen

Frank pulled out onto the A60, off Blidworth Waye, towards Nottingham. He'd wanted Archie in the car with him to speak to him alone. Archie knew what was coming; in fact, he could have had the conversation with himself he was that sure what his grandad was going to say.

'What did I explain to you this morning, Son?'

'I know, Grandad, I know,' Archie replied, looking out the side; his left elbow on the top of the panel ridge where it met the bottom of the window.

'So, what the fuck happened then? There you were this morning holding court, coming across all measured, the one in control, the one in the room who everyone looks up to for leadership – and then, fuck me, with one stroke, old Archie is back again, wanting to take on the world without a care or thought for how he's gonna do it. So, come on, what the fuck happened?'

Frank was mad – disappointed as he was mad – but mad all the same.

'I just lost it, didn't I? You must have lost it in the past. In fact, I know you have. I've heard the stories,'

Archie replied, meeting Frank's attack head on.

'Yes, but you have the benefit of my experience. I didn't. And believe me, Son, I wish I had. I'd have had a much easier ride if I'd had me to teach me how to do things.'

Archie shook his head a little. He was becoming frustrated, but he recognised the signs and took a breath in. 'I know, Grandad, I know...'

'Call me, Frank, Son – we're not sat having Sunday lunch.'

'Frank, I know you're right and believe me, I'm trying my best to rein my anger in, I really am, but sometimes it just takes over. Just look at what he's done! Don't tell me that you didn't feel the same. You must have wanted to go over there and take him out just like I did.'

Archie paused, waiting for Frank to reply. He didn't. That told Archie what he already thought.

'Well, that speaks volumes. Look, I know I have a lot to learn and, fuck me, Frank, I'm having to learn fast. I want to be your heir, I want to carry on your name, but don't expect me to be the finished article now, 'cos I ain't gonna be.'

Frank listened intently. In his heart, he knew Archie was right, but this was no time for sentiment. And this world they operated in, and ruled, was no place for snowflakes.

'You are my heir, Archie, let's make that clear. Your father would have been, but he's not here, and we all know the reasons why, so that mantle is yours. So, there's no place for any of that modern fuckin' shit where we all need a bit of time, a helpin' hand. No, fuck that. This is the big league, where real men operate, so I want no more Archie-big-fuckin-bollocks. I want measured and controlled Archie. The Archie that I saw this morning. There's no room for imposters here, Son – so like it or fuckin' lump it. You've jumped in the deep end, so keep swimming. I'll throw you a rubber ring now and again, but don't you dare fuckin' drown. That should've been you chairing that meeting at my house just now, not me, but I couldn't hand over the baton to you in there. If I had, we'd have been driving over to Manchester now, and no doubt come unstuck.'

Without taking his eyes off the road, he continued. 'This is your time, Son. Time to stand up. Yes, you're young, and you are more than capable, but our world is watching, and I'm not gonna let them see you stood behind me. You need to stand front and centre. Fletcher O'Brien wants YOU, Archie, not me. He may well take me as dessert, but you are the main course.' He then looked at him and said, 'Don't get eaten, Son.'

Archie had taken it all in. It wasn't what he had expected Frank to say, but he knew it had been what he needed to hear. His grandad was right. Fletcher had brought the fight to him, not Frank. It was personal. Fletcher saw him as a weak link. He could see that now. Fletcher could have brought this on top at any time in the ten years since his dad died, but he hadn't. He'd waited until Archie was in situ.

He then remembered Frank pointing to his temple this morning and saying, 'THIS is a man's best weapon. If a man can outthink another, he has the edge. It's about the long term.' It was all about outthinking. As Frank had said, 'We can all fight.'

'It's all about THIS, Frank, isn't it?'

Frank turned to see Archie pointing to his head. 'It is, Son, it sure is. Now, are we done?'

Archie nodded, adding, 'I've only just begun, Frank. I'm a long time done.'

Frank smiled inside, but then remembered where they were going and instantly felt a pang of sadness. They'd be at the club soon.

chapter nineteen

Phoebe was sat having a glass of wine. Gloria had told her what had happened. She was a little perplexed at not being invited to Frank's house for the meeting, especially when she heard that even Pēteris was there. But she believed Gloria when she said she was convinced he had been with Archie when Frank had called. That made her feel a little better but she still felt excluded. Frank, in particular, had a habit of forgetting her, but she knew deep down it was because he didn't think; it was never intentional. He still struggled to accept her at the top table. She knew that it was not because she was a woman – although she was well aware that never went in her favour – but because of who she was: Daniel's wife. That was more important to Frank than her being his daughter-in-law. Even though that amounted to the same thing, in Frank's eyes, she was Daniel's wife and he felt a duty to protect her. Archie always made sure she was included as she should be, but it was Frank who had called this meeting. She just had to accept it.

She was deep in thought about Paul and John, and Del and Tina too. She knew how they felt. She was a broken woman when Daniel was murdered, although she'd hidden it well, so she had first-hand experience of what being in this dangerous world could do to a loved one. She would ring Tina tomorrow. She'd appreciate it. Del, on the other hand, she would go and see face to face. She'd met Tina a few times, of course, down the years and had always got on well with her; but Del, she saw weekly at least, if not most days when things were happening at pace, which in this world they often were, so she wanted to wrap her arms around him and tell him that time would heal. It never goes away, but it gets easier; she wanted to tell him that. What could she do to help? Phoebe was no fighter. She was too slender and had always been a peacemaker, though she'd proven herself to be a killer when it came to protecting her own.

Daniel's death had changed her permanently and once she'd become more involved, she'd actually grown to like the buzz this life gave her. She could quite happily offer advice and strategic influence to Archie and Frank's world, even though she knew it would lead to pain and misery for someone. Anyone she'd ever been responsible for receiving a beating, or even for meeting their maker, was always someone who had chosen this life. Anyone who gets drawn in, at any level, knows the potential consequences, and that had always sat comfortably with Phoebe.

Alice and Johnny walked in and plonked themselves down on the sofa. Alice looked at her mum. She could see she looked troubled and deep in thought.

'What's up, Mum? You look like you've got the weight of the world on your shoulders. Not more trouble with him from Manchester, is it?'

'You know Paul, Del's son, and John from Leeds?' she said.

'Yeah, what's up?' Alice replied, looking serious. She leant forward and put her elbows on her knees. Alice did this when she felt she needed to protect herself. It was instinctive. She never even realised she did it. She listened as her mum told her what had happened; that Paul and John were dead and how the main club had been trashed and how Del, Michael and Steven had been badly beaten. Phoebe forgot about Raquel and her broken nose; in fact, she'd not given her a thought. Alice put her head in her hands and exhaled loudly. Johnny put his arm around her.

'Bloody hell, Mum. What's going to happen now?' Alice was scared. She didn't do this life awfully well; another resemblance of her mum in her younger years. Phoebe had taken some adjusting when she first met Daniel, and Alice was still doing hers. She made the tea at the meetings and secretly liked the fact she was treated very well by everyone in and around Mansfield and Nottingham, but she liked to pretend the world, their world in particular, was all peaches and cream.

'No idea, sweetheart. That, I suppose, is down to your brother and grandad, but history tells me Paul's and John's blood will not be the last shed in this saga. That guy from Manchester has taken a real liberty and has ignited a very large fuse. I just hope that the ones to put it out live this side of the Peak District, 'cos if they don't, our lives will change forever.'

Phoebe looked more serious than Alice could ever remember her mum looking. She bit her lip and nestled into Johnny's chest. He cuddled her and squeezed her hard, and kissed the top of her head. He heard her say, 'Don't ever get involved, Johnny. Promise me you'll never get involved.' He kissed her again as he replied, 'I promise, I promise.'

chapter twenty

Raquel greeted them as they all pulled into the club car park. She looked a mess. She'd managed to stop the blood from her nose and Michael had somehow clicked it back into place. It hurt like fuck, but when she'd looked in the mirror, she'd realised it didn't look too bad. She was unsure of the reception she and the others would get. To her knowledge, Frank had never had his clubs trashed like this before. He'd had trouble, of course – people thinking they could take liberties on a weekend night, although these were mainly blokes who thought they were someone to be reckoned with, showing off to their mates – but it had always been dealt with very swiftly and without any major drama. He'd had his share of real players trying to muscle in, but again, men who weren't in Frank's league. Players like Frank and Fletcher's father, Arnie, never really took hassle to the doors of their opposite numbers. Respect was the order of the day and whether it was old hat now or not, the old-school players had too much self-respect to do that.

So, this was a new one for Frank. Such a show of disrespect had not been made on Frank's doorstep since Gerry Clarke from Leeds had tried his luck many moons ago. Frank had shot him in the leg, before putting three bullets in his chest. No one had really attempted to that degree since.

Raquel just hoped that Archie, and Frank for that matter, would understand that they were outnumbered and that they'd defended the club as best they could. She noticed Pat was absent, which she found strange given the severity of the situation, but she soon found out that he'd been sent to console John's wife. She was surprised to see Pēteris driving Archie's car. Pēteris worked for her. She wondered why he was with the top table. He should be at their club in Mapperley.

Jez and Brian nodded at her as they waited for Archie and Frank to get out of Frank's car. She nodded back in acknowledgement. Archie walked straight up to her and put his arm around her as he guided her back inside the club.

'You OK?' he asked, softly.

'Yeah, as well as we can be. Listen, Archie, they came from nowhere. Totally unexpected. We tried our best,' she said, feeling she had to justify the scene Archie was about to witness.

He stopped and looked her in the eye. She noticed Frank and the others had held back a step or so.

'Raquel, there's one thing I know about you and them in there,' Archie said, pointing with his right hand towards the door, without averting his gaze, 'and that is, that you will always defend what we have with everything you have. So, listen, if you or any of the others are concerned about what me or Frank are gonna think once we enter that room, don't be. I'm prepared for the worst, and I'm sure it's just as bad as I'm expecting, but if it's worse, then so be it. It can all be fixed. The main thing is that you and those three in there are all OK. How's Del?'

Raquel grimaced. She winced as she did and put her hand to her nose.

'He's hurting, Archie, he's hurting bad. He rang Ryan and Des. They're in there with him. They all want revenge. You know what I'm sayin'.'

Ryan and Des were Del's other two sons. They were both older than Paul; Ryan by 18 months at 28 and Des by 3 years, approaching 30. Even though Paul was the youngest, he was the one out of the three who was most like his dad. Ryan and Des were respected villains in their own right, and well placed within Archie's younger element of the firm. Archie knew all too well he needed some younger blood, and now that Paul had been murdered, these two would be chomping at the bit to avenge their brother's death.

'We understand that, Raquel, but they're gonna have to understand, we run this firm not them, so any revenge they want will be on our terms.' Frank pointed his right forefinger back and forth between him and Archie.

'I know, Frank, and to be fair, so will they, but I'm sure we can all imagine how they're feeling,' she replied.

'Some of us know, Raquel; some of us know only too well,' Frank said, gesturing for Raquel and Archie to move on.

Archie put his left hand up towards Frank with his palm facing outwards as if to say to hold on a minute.

'Broken nose?'

She nodded. 'Bloody hurts too,' she said, forcing a smile.

Archie entered the main room first. He put his hands on his hips and surveyed the damage. It was as bad as he'd thought. He had hoped it wouldn't be, but it was a wreck. He felt his anger rise. He looked at Frank, Jez and Brian, and slowly shook his head. He took a deep breath recalling what Frank had told him twice that day. This was going to be a hard and steep learning curve, but as Frank had told him in no uncertain terms, this was his time to be a leader, a proper leader who led from the front in all situations. This was bigger than he'd had to face thus far. Fletcher O'Brien and whoever had done this was going to pay, and pay dearly.

He led the walk over towards the main office, where he knew Del and the others would be. Without turning his head, he said, 'I'll bring them all out here. We'll be like sardines, all of us in there.'

Frank and the others congregated, leaving Archie to walk on. He could see them all in conversation through the window as he approached the office door.

Michael noticed him first and nodded. He looked like he'd been in a fight and a half.

Archie opened the door. 'All right, gents. Let's go out onto the main floor. More room there.'

Del looked at Michael. Michael could see he was a little done that Archie had not consoled him. As they came out of the corridor, Archie stepped aside to allow them to pass, but kept Del back by putting his hand on his shoulder.

'Let's go back in the office for a minute, Del,' Archie said, gesturing with his head. Del nodded. Archie turned his head towards the circle that had formed in the middle of the room and said loudly so that they could all hear, 'Frank, you got a minute?'

Without replying, Frank made his way towards the office. By the time he got there, Archie and Del were in an embrace. Archie was slapping the back of Del's shoulder blades, as men do when they want to show emotion that they are unsure how to deal with. Del broke away from Archie and turned to Frank, who did the exact same. Del appreciated the show of affection and their solidarity. He knew only too well they both knew how he felt, not that it made it any easier. Del's heart was aching like it had never ached before. He now knew what people meant when they said "You never think it'll happen to you." Del never thought it would, but it had, and it hurt like hell. And like most people who lose a loved one, no matter in what circumstances, he could never imagine a time when he would feel any different.

Archie spoke first. 'I have no words, Del. I know how you are feeling, mate, believe me I do. You will have your revenge, that I can guarantee you. But you need to trust us – me and Frank. You need to trust us. Understand?'

Del had mixed feelings. He did trust Archie and he trusted Frank like no other man alive. Del knew deep down the morals Frank had built his empire on were there within Archie too. Del just didn't want to wait.

'When?' he asked. 'When will I get my revenge? 'Cos I ain't gonna wait long, Archie. It was that Benny Lancashire fella. He was the leader of that crew today. He made that crystal clear. So, I want him and a fella called Phil. He seemed to be his number two. And a bloke called Tiny too. Big fella he was, as you'd imagine with a name like that.'

Del managed a smile and forced a chuckle. It made the three of them laugh. It was all the three men standing in that room knew to do in a situation like this – laugh. None of them was overly touchy-feely; laughing was their way of coping with it together.

Del looked at Archie and then at Frank. 'I only ask two things, gents. One is that I personally get to murder Benny Lancashire, this Phil guy and that Tiny bloke, along with Fletcher O'Brien. I wanna pull the trigger on every one of them. I need to do that for my Paul. Secondly, if we somehow get Paul's body back, that we have a proper funeral. I know we probably won't see Paul again, but if Fletcher does for whatever reason decide it would be funny to dump the bodies over here on our patch, then I am allowed a funeral. I know you may not want that, 'cos you won't want the Old Bill to know, but I need that, gents. That's all I ask.'

Archie was unsure what to say. He glanced at Frank. Frank nodded.

Archie spoke. 'Of course, Del. You have my word. If we get Paul's body, you can have a funeral, but, for now, that is kept between us. I do not want Tina to be demanding the same for John. I'm agreein' to this as a favour, Del. As you know, it will take a few favours and a few words in a few ears to organise that under the radar, 'cos that's how it'd have to be. It's a big ask, but you have my word. You look like shit by the way.'

They laughed again.

'They came fully prepared, Archie. I wish you lot had been here. I've taken some hits in my time, but today takes some beating,' Del said, unaware of the irony. Archie got it; Frank didn't.

They all walked out into the main room. Archie took £40 out of his back pocket and gave it to Pēteris. 'Go and get some sandwiches and some chocolate or something. I bet we're all starving. I know I am. And something to drink too.'

Pēteris got a decent selection of sandwiches from the local shop around the corner and came back in through the main door. He could hear raised voices and sensed tensions were high. Everyone was still in the centre of the room. They heard him coming, even over the loud chatter, as he crunched over shattered glass and smashed chandeliers. Archie broke off mid-sentence.

'Bring 'em over here, Pēteris. I'm bloody famished.'

Pēteris handed the sandwiches out and some of them swapped. Pēteris was left with tuna mayo, which he was OK with. Archie opened his Coronation chicken and carried on talking.

'As I said, Des, I ain't budgin' on this. We do nothin' until I say so. I know you're hurtin' – fuck me, I know – but you're just gonna have to swallow it. Is that clear?'

Des, the eldest of Del's sons, was not a happy man. He'd fully expected to storm them. He could not get his head around this strategy. It made no sense to him whatsoever. His brother, Ryan, felt the same, as did Del. But Del, being older and having the experience of seeing Frank always get it right in the end, knew that this was another time when he – and his two sons – would have to hang tight and see what panned out.

Des shook his head in disbelief as he said, 'You're the boss, Archie, but like my dad says, we all want to be involved in things when we get our revenge. Just promise me that.'

'I already have, but just so we're straight, I'll say it again. We WILL sort this and you WILL get your revenge, and you WILL be involved. If I can sort it, all three of you will be there when the time comes, OK?' Archie looked at them individually as he finished. They all nodded in acceptance.

'Good. Now then, one other thing I want to make

clear – and this involves you three, and you Raquel – Fletcher may just wait for us to respond, but on the other hand, he may send his lackeys over here again tomorrow, or sometime soon, to sell his gear. If he does, we take his men out. Whilst we're doing nothin' about Fletcher and this Benny guy for now, we are not gonna stand by and watch his drugs flood our streets again. I do not want his men here. Is that understood?' Archie checked their reactions.

Raquel spoke. 'So, if they come over again, we deal with his men hard and fast – is that what you're saying, Archie?'

'Too fuckin' right, Raquel. I want our men on the ground fully versed that if they see any of Fletcher's men, or anyone else's, dealing on our patch, then they have my permission to do whatever they need to take them out. Obviously, I do not want men shot dead in Nottingham or Leicester, or anywhere else, but they either take them out or get help to do so, but we hit them hard. Anyone captured is to be taken to the lock-up in Arnold and dealt with there by Del, Des or Ryan – no one else. Clear?'

They all nodded.

'OK, well, there's not much we can do here tonight. I'll arrange for this lot to be cleaned up tomorrow and for new furniture and fittings to be sorted. We'll have it back up and running in no time.'

'Double the presence on all of our doors, Raquel. All of them, including Derby, Donny and Leeds. I'll leave it with you to sort.'

Archie directed a nod at Del. It was his way of saying he hoped that was all OK for him. Del appreciated it and returned the gesture. That was enough for Archie, but he would make sure Ryan and Des accepted it too. As he motioned to walk with Frank, Raquel asked for a word.

'What's up?' he asked.

'Why is Pēteris here?'

'Oh, sorry, I meant to tell you about that when we got here, but you know, just slipped my mind. I was with him in the car when I got the call from Frank to go to his house, so he obviously went with me and then we came straight here. That's all.'

'OK, cheers. Just wanted to know what was what,' she said.

Archie grabbed her left upper arm as she went to leave. 'You OK?'

'Yeah, I'll live. I've been in this game long enough. You know that.'

Archie smiled at her as he went to join Frank. He and Frank had not discussed what to do if any of Fletcher's men came dealing again, so he knew he needed to address it with him. Yet, he was also aware that it was down to him to show the team that they were going to meet that little problem head on, even if they were holding back on how to respond to Fletcher directly. He hoped it would appease them a little, and it had.

Frank put his arm around Archie's shoulder. 'You did well, Son. Proud of ya. And I liked the plan on how to handle any dealers that he sends over. Good touch and well made. Good timing too.'

Archie sensed adulation in his voice. He was pleased. The last thing he needed now was another argument with Frank. It had been a long day, a fucking very long day. He couldn't quite believe all that had happened since they'd seen Richie two days ago. He'd not had time to sit down, scratch his arse – fuck all. He was ready for bed. He needed a good night's sleep. He thought about Sarah and hoped she'd still be up when he got home. He was just thinking about her lying there naked next to him, when Frank said, 'So, Son, what's the next thing we need to sort?'

It was a leading question. Archie knew the answer; he'd just hoped it would wait for another day.

'Leeds. We need to discuss who's gonna take over from John.'

'That's right, Son. We can't leave Leeds and Doncaster too long. For me, we need to promote Trainer. He's a fuckin' good lad, and John spoke very highly of him. Need to move quick, Son, but for me there's no one else.'

'Trainer it is then. I'm in full agreement,' Archie replied, knowing that in that moment Frank could've said anyone and he'd have agreed. He was happy with Trainer, though. He was a good bloke – solid – who knew the score, and he was itching to climb the ladder. Archie decided he'd speak to him the following day. For now, he just wanted to get home. He didn't know what was waiting for him, but he would find out soon enough.

chapter twenty-one

Del walked into his house, put the kettle on and then made himself a stiff drink. He needed it. Today had been the day he had always hoped and prayed would never come. He wished it had been him. He asked himself again as he savoured the rum why it had not been him. Why did the Almighty decide to take his son? He looked up to the ceiling and shouted, 'Why? Why, God? Why did you do this to me? Why did you take Paul?!'

Del had always told his three sons that this life could well mean an early death; probably a violent death; maybe a torturous one. They had all known the score early on in their careers but all three of them had wanted it, Paul especially. He'd always dreamt of being a face, and making it to the top table, emulating his gangster dad. Del put down his rum and dropped a teabag in his mug. He wished he could turn back the clock to before he'd ever become a bouncer at Frank's club. He recalled being told that being a doorman was a good life, one where you got to shag the women looking for a quick jump before they went back to their dreary husbands. The same life that gave you street cred, but also sucked you in. Del poured in the hot water, squeezed the teabag and got the milk out of the fridge. A tear slid from his chin and splashed into his tea. He wiped his eyes. They were sore from the punches that had rained down on him earlier. This was the second time Del had wept today and he knew he wasn't finished yet.

'I loved ya, Paul!' he choked.

He took a sip of his tea and winced as it touched his swollen lips. He then finished his rum and slumped back into the sofa and stared at the ceiling again. He thought back to how he'd gone from being a doorman to one of Frank's most trusted. He remembered that guy from Leeds coming down and Frank shooting him dead. That night his life changed; from then on, his sons were destined to live his world of crime with him. He blamed himself. If he had never become a bouncer, Paul would still be alive. If he'd walked away when Simone, his wife, had told him to, Paul would still be alive. *Simone.* He smiled. He'd loved that gal, but she couldn't take any more and had given him an ultimatum almost ten years ago.

'It's me or the life, Del. You choose,' she'd said to him in this very house. Del had called her bluff. He never thought she'd go, but she did. She took the boys with her but they all wanted to stay with their father, so within a month he was a single dad of three. He had no idea where Simone was now. He wished she was here with him. He thought about their days out as a family: days to Clumber Park, days to Holme Pierrepont, walks in Sherwood Forest and, of course, the annual nights at Goose Fair. They were good times. Del cried more silent tears as he remembered how Paul would spend hours watching the cricket at Sherwood Forest at Edwinstowe as the others walked through the woods; how he would run to tell Del the score once they'd returned. Long, sunny days they'd been. Now all Del could see in front of him was rain. Wintry days, howling gales and dark clouds above. How he longed for those sunny days.

He then thought of who had done this and renewed his vow to exact revenge. That was the one thing he could do for Paul and he knew that Paul would be looking down, telling him, "Go get 'em, Dad. Fuckin' do 'em!"

'I will, Son,' Del swore, raising his empty glass. 'I will. Promise.'

There was a knock at the door. He sat upright. Who the fuck was knockin' at his door at this time of night? He was in no fit state to fend off anyone tonight. He'd taken his fair share of blows today. The last thing he wanted or needed was another ruck. 'Fuck,' he said to himself, running upstairs to get the baseball bat from under his bed. He took a breath, as he slowly, and as discreetly as he could, pulled back the curtain. He carefully poked his head through and sighed a huge sigh of relief when he saw it was his Ryan and Des. They both lived together about two miles away. They'd bought the house between them and were as thick as thieves. Del opened the door.

'We didn't want you to be on your own, Dad,' Des said, as Del put the bat down at the side of the door.

'Come in, both of ya,' he said, as he widened it further. 'I thought it was trouble. I've never been so glad to see you both. I don't think I had another fight in me tonight.'

Del closed the door, turned round and instinctively opened his arms for a group hug. 'I'm OK, ya know,' he grimaced. Ryan and Des squeezed him tight. It hurt, but he never said anything. He cherished the feeling a parent gets when they hug their offspring. It saddened him knowing how he'd never get that feeling again from Paul.

The three of them broke off.

'Listen, if you two are planning on sleepin' over, there's only Paul's double bed. I'm just sayin',' Del laughed.

'I'll be fine down here, thanks. I ain't sleepin' in a bed with him,' Des said, gesturing at Ryan with his head.

'I'll sleep down here too. I ain't sleepin' in Paul's bed. Not tonight. I just couldn't,' Ryan replied.

Del nodded. 'OK. I'll put the kettle on,' he said and made for the kitchen. He then stopped in the doorway and looked back. 'I appreciate this, boys.'

'We'll be OK, Dad,' Ryan said.

'I know, Son. I know.'

Archie had taken the long way round from Frank's house. He'd had to drop Pēteris off to the club at Mapperley. Pēteris had insisted on going there before he went home, just to make sure all was well. Archie had stepped in for a few minutes with him. Pēteris rang Jānis and arranged for him to meet him at the club in Mapperley at 9:30 the next morning. He would then meet Archie at Frank's house in Papplewick. Archie was still playing out the events of the past two days. Paul and John were dead. He was in shock. Since being catapulted into the limelight he'd not experienced this level of violence towards him or his men. This was the first time, at his tender age of 22, that he'd felt under real attack. If he was honest, he felt vulnerable for the first time in his life.

He pondered what he would now be feeling, or doing, if Frank was no longer on the scene. What if Frank had passed away last year for example? Would he cope? Would he have the power, and the balls for that matter, to take Fletcher on? He knew one thing, and that was that he would have certainly gone for him, heavy. He would either be dead right now or World War Three would have broken out. He'd always respected his grandad, like no other man alive. His father had already been murdered by the time Archie had learnt about respect in this game, so for him, there was only one man to look up to, and that was Frank. He now knew how much he needed his grandad.

As he drove past the sign saying "Welcome to Southwell", he vowed to never flare up and question his grandad again. Well, he knew he might question him, but not to the degree he'd done previously. He smiled and shook his head in disbelief as he thought about how he'd wanted to get into London, be introduced to at least one of the three top fellas down there and to take over the world. What a prick he'd been to think that Frank was a dinosaur, that he moved at a snail's pace. He'd thought that Frank's empire of the East Midlands and parts of Yorkshire was only a small piece of the pie.

'This has been a big fuckin' lesson,' he said aloud, as he drove past Southwell Co-op.

Sarah was in bed. It was 11:50 and she'd not yet dropped off. Phoebe and Alice were still downstairs but she'd felt tired and even though she was fully aware of the day's events, she was sure she'd be able to sleep. But, of course, once her head had hit the pillow, her mind began racing. She thought about what she'd been told. She thought about Mary and how she could never imagine what she would feel like if Mary was murdered. She hated it when she had these thoughts, but also knew she'd been under no illusion when she became involved with Archie.

They'd met at Southwell Races. Archie was with some of the men who worked for him in Mansfield, a guy called Kevin and a man called Darren. Both had worked for the family for a good few years and had grown from running their own housing estates in Forest Town and Oak Tree to being Archie's men in Mansfield. They both reported to Raquel really but

Archie had known them all his life and liked to treat them now and again to a good day out at the races. Doncaster was their local favourite, but on that day, they'd chosen Southwell. Archie always told Sarah he knew he was going to marry her the first moment he set eyes on her, and if she was honest, she'd been flattered by his attention. All of her mates had told her that she'd live a life of luxury if she got in with Archie Pearson. Only her best friend Karen told her to be wary.

'You'll end up burying him before you're thirty,' she'd say.

Sarah didn't listen. Karen stopped being a friend and it had been three years since she'd seen her. She did miss her but it was Karen who had cut ties. Sarah only stopped ringing her after Karen stopped answering her calls. What Karen used to tell her had always stuck in her head, though, and after what she'd heard about today, she realised Karen may yet have her told-ya-so moment.

She looked at the clock. 11:55. Archie should be back any moment. She put on her silk dressing gown and her slippers, and walked out onto the landing. She could hear Phoebe and Alice talking. She was unsure if Johnny was still up. She headed downstairs and into the living room.

'Couldn't sleep?' Phoebe asked.

'No, too much going round my head. I'm expecting Archie to be home soon.'

'Fancy a brew?' Alice asked.

'Yeah, go on then. Thanks.'

Johnny smiled, but said nothing. He was still thinking about Emma and how she knew he visited Richie. After today, Frank was likely to be even more angry if he found out. Johnny's stomach was churning.

'You get used to it, Sarah. It just comes with the job. Waiting around at night wondering where they are. It's hard, but it becomes a way of life,' Phoebe said, trying to reassure her.

Sarah gave a faint smile and nodded but didn't really feel any better.

'You two want a cup too?' Alice shouted through.

Phoebe declined but Johnny said he'd have a coffee.

All Sarah wanted was a hug. She willed Archie to hurry up. She just wanted him with her, safe and sound.

Archie pulled around the final bend before the approach to the gates to the house. He slowed and indicated. He could see all the lights on downstairs and was happy that at least one person was still up. He drew to a stop when the sight before him came into view. There, sat slumped in front of the gates, were the bodies of Paul and John; their torsos covered in blood. They each had a message pinned to their body. Paul's said *Give Del our best*; John's, *Manchester 1 Leeds 0.*

chapter twenty-two

Fletcher O'Brien had a real spring in his step. He'd slept like a baby, very content in the thought that Frank and Archie Pearson would be over to see him today. He was going to make sure he was in his main club in the heart of Manchester all day. That's where anyone who was anyone knew where to find Fletcher O'Brien. If he wasn't in when anyone called, he would be notified of their presence immediately. Fletcher had a very strong team around him. Men who had pedigree and men who had been in the game for years. He had a mixture of old blood from his father's days and new blood from the current era, men he'd trained himself and who he knew he could rely on. His wife, Kat, was already downstairs making breakfast. Fletcher slapped her arse like a teenager. He saw their cleaner Andrea come through from the downstairs toilet.

'Bloody hell, you're eager this morning, aren't you?' he said, as she bent down to pick up the mop and bucket.

'You know me, Mr O'Brien, always keen to be here. I love it here. You're my best customer,' she said, knowing that with the wink she just gave him, he'd be shagging her as soon as Kat had gone to her spa.

Kat knew it too, but she'd given up a long time ago trying to curtail his womanising. Ever since they'd first got together when she was still in the sixth form, he'd been shagging about. At first, she pretended it didn't bother her, then she knew it did and tried to put a stop to it. Now she just accepted it and ignored it. She longed to be free of all this shit, this life and that wanker of a husband of hers, but knew whilst ever there was breath left in his body, Fletcher would never let her go. She'd lost count the number of times she'd dreamt of killing him, but she was no murderer. She just had to hope someone else would do it for her, or that he'd peg it of natural causes. This life would give anyone a heart attack. Either way she hoped it came quickly.

Andrea could never understand why Kat went to the day spa down the road. She had a swimming pool and sauna and all the bits here at home but even though she used the facilities at home most days, she also loved to go to that spa at least three times a week. She always went on the days Andrea cleaned at the house. Andrea did Mondays, Wednesdays and Fridays every week and the occasional Saturday to give the cupboards a good clean or some other job she liked to do that she could never fit in on her normal cleans. Fletcher liked to give her a good seeing to at least once a week, which she suspected would be today given the frisky mood he seemed to be in.

Fletcher ate his breakfast of scrambled egg on toasted muffin, put on his brown Oxford shoes, flung his jacket over his shoulder and kissed Kat goodbye on the cheek. He never even said cheerio to Andrea, never mind bounce her up and down on him. She knew full well she was used, but she could play Fletcher like a good'un when she wanted to. The fact she'd given him the wink and he'd fucked off without even a goodbye annoyed her like hell. She watched him get into his 4x4 from one of the upstairs bedrooms. *Twat.*

She was now even more comfortable with what Jānis had spoken to her about the previous night. She didn't yet know all the full details, but he had said to go to his that afternoon 'cos he needed to talk to her about something to do with Fletcher. She told Jānis how many times a week she cleaned there, and she confirmed that she knew the key safe and that there was CCTV. Jānis asked what she did when she couldn't make it, so she knew that whatever he was talking about was not having afternoon tea in Fletcher's garden. He assured her that if he needed her to do something, she'd be well looked after, and she was happy with that. Andrea was saving like mad for enough money to open a little beauty boutique. She trusted Jānis, so whatever this was about would not get back to Fletcher.

While she was irritated at being ignored, Fletcher, however, had forgotten Andrea was even there. His only thought today was making sure he had a welcoming committee for Mr Pearson and Mr Pearson. He rang Benny.

'You up, Benny, lad?'

'Been up most of the night, Boss. Couldn't sleep. I was buzzin' yesterday and couldn't come down. Mind you, that gear I snorted when I got back wouldn't've helped.'

'Good, well get yaself to the club sharpish. I'll be half hour or so. The traffic this mornin' is doing my fuckin' head in. Ring Phil and get his little crew down. Smiler will be there, as will Doddsy with his lot, so we'll have enough bodies. They've gotta come. I'll be fuckin' amazed if they don't show today.'

'No problem, Boss. Are we sending any more bodies over to deal some more drugs or what?' Benny asked.

'Not today, pal, no. I don't think there'll be any need. Frank's a main player, Benny, so with all the drugs we've shifted, plus those two fellas he sent over here and you lot wrecking his club up, he's got no choice but to come over. He'll never be able to hold his head up again if he swallows that lot. Should have done this before now, shouldn't we? I can't believe I left it so long. Anyway, chop chop, you might miss the action, lad.'

Fletcher felt on top of the world. 'You'd be proud of me, Dad!' he shouted, as he honked his horn at some guy in a silver Merc who'd failed to indicate.

chapter twenty-three

Frank looked at the bodies of Paul and John, which Archie and Johnny had dragged into the garage the night before. Archie hadn't told Frank until that morning, but Frank came round as soon as he knew.

'We promised Del a funeral,' Frank said, staring at them.

'I know, but they're as stiff as a board. I'm not sure we'll even get them in a coffin,' Archie replied.

'Me neither, Son, me neither.' Frank dialled a number.

'Who you callin'?' Archie asked.

'Ted. He's been a funeral director longer than I've been breathin'. He'll do owt for a brown envelope. He's done me a few favours over the years. I'm hopin' he can—"Ted, it's Frank ... Yes, I'm OK. You? Listen, bit of a problem ... Yes, I know I only call you when I have a problem, but shut up a minute and listen. I have two bodies, stiff as. I need one of them to have some sort of funeral."'

Frank listened. 'Look, don't give me that shite. How does two grand sound?' He rolled his eyes. 'OK, five grand, you robbin' fucker. You know where Daniel and Phoebe's house is, don't you? Right, I'll see you here at 12:30 ... No, I can't do it now. I need to be back at mine for a meeting at 10. 12:30, Ted. If you get here before me, just wait ... No, Phoebe won't make you a brew if you have to wait, 'cos she'll be with me. Now I'll see you later.' He hung up.

'Fuckin' slippery one is old Ted. Good as gold, though. He'll sort it. Anyway, let's get over to mine to see this Jānis guy. But listen, not a word to Del yet. Not until we've seen Ted.'

Archie stared at Paul and John a moment longer while Frank walked out of the garage to his car. He promised them once again that he'd get the men who did this to them. He then joined Frank and waved to Sarah, who was at the kitchen window with Mary in her arms. He blew them a kiss, as he stood at the car, with the passenger side door open.

'Archie, today. We need to go,' Frank said quite sharply. Archie sat in and closed the door. He looked at Sarah and Mary for as long as he could until Frank turned the car round. He then felt his mum's hand on his shoulder. Phoebe knew what he was thinking. Archie put his left hand on top of hers and patted it twice. Phoebe then leant into the back seat and instinctively looked right as Frank pulled out.

Pēteris made Jānis a brew and placed his mug on the worktop. They were in Frank and Archie's club in Mapperley. Jānis had been there about ten minutes.

He looked tense, which for Jānis was unusual. He was 6ft 5in and could more than handle himself. He wasn't a gangster as such, but he was a formidable man, one you could trust and, as hired muscle, he was as good as anyone. For him to be uneasy didn't sit too well with Pēteris.

'What's up, Jānis? You seem nervous?' Pēteris said, as he sat down and took a mouthful of his coffee.

'I am, mate, I am. This Fletcher guy is heavy duty, you know. I hope Archie knows what he's doin'.'

'He will do,' Pēteris assured him. 'He and Frank are heavy duty too, you know. Anyway, have you spoken to that lass – Amanda, was it?'

'Andrea. She's called Andrea,' Jānis replied, 'and, yes, I have. She's trustworthy, good as gold she is, so I have enough info I think for Frank and Archie this morning. Well, I hope I have, but you know, I didn't wanna give too much away with her at this stage, no matter how much I trust her.'

'So, what are you so nervous about?'

Jānis laughed. 'You seriously have to ask?!'

'You didn't sound nervous yesterday when Archie spoke to you on the phone. In fact, you said something like you wanted him to make sure he involved you when it all happened. You sounded like you were itching to be involved,' Pēteris said, a little annoyed that he was taking Jānis with him this morning and that he'd vouched for him when he was acting like this.

'I know and I still am. My mind was doing overtime last night, though. I can be like that sometimes. Irrational thinking they call it, or something. By the time I dropped off, it had all gone tits up and I was lying dead at the bottom of the Manchester canal. Anyway, hadn't we better be goin'?' he said, taking another swig of his drink.

Pēteris nodded, gulped his coffee, picked up both cups and put them in the sink. They then set off in Pēteris's car for the fairly short drive to Papplewick. All the way there, Pēteris just hoped Jānis would compose himself.

Raquel had woken up with a sore head, not from drink but from the beating she'd taken. She hadn't looked her best when she looked in the bathroom mirror earlier, so she'd slapped on a bit of lippy and a bit of blusher. She decided she looked OK. She'd been told to be at Frank's for just before ten and was five minutes away. She'd been told to come alone, which she took to mean not to bother Del or Michael. She also knew it meant Archie was either letting them sleep in to nurse their bruises or that what she was about to be witness to was not for their ears. Even though they were top table members, sometimes it was only Raquel, Phoebe, Pat and Jez that were invited alongside Archie and Frank. Not often, but on occasion. She assumed this was one of those times.

She came off the A60 down Blidworth Waye to Papplewick, taking it steady to soak up the scenery. She'd learnt, with age, to appreciate the greenery that the rural areas offered. One day, when this life was no more for her, she'd retire to the country somewhere. She used to always like the city life, the bright lights and faster pace, but like a lot of people, she had changed somewhat as the years had rolled on.

She remembered the first time she set eyes on Daniel and being introduced to the Pearson family. It seemed like yesterday, but had been close to twenty-five years. *Twenty-five years.*

She approached Frank's driveway. The gates were open. She drove in and saw the usual motors parked up. She went inside and could instantly hear Gloria shouting, 'Do you want brown sauce on that?' She loved Gloria. She'd not changed a bit in all the years she'd known her. Always the Mother Hen looking after her chicks, never interfering one bit.

'Hiya, Raquel, luv,' she said, passing her a plate with a bacon cob on it. 'Give this to Pat, will you please? Do you want one?' Gloria continued, having not yet looked at Raquel. She loved being busy, fussing over everyone, did Gloria.

'Yeah, go on then. Red sauce, though, for me,' Raquel replied, as she passed Alice on the way through to the dining room.

'Bloody hell, Raquel, that looks sore!' Alice gasped.

'Should see the other guy,' Raquel replied. 'Not a mark on him!' It still hurt to laugh, but she kept forgetting.

Raquel had just given Pat his cob when Gloria came running through.

'Ooh, Raquel! I'm sorry, luv, I never even looked at your face! Here, let me see.' She licked her finger to get the brown sauce off before taking Raquel's face in her hands. She touched Raquel's nose. Raquel winced. 'Sore, is it?'

'A bit.'

'Bastards. Sit down, luv, and I'll get you a brew and that bacon cob.'

Archie shook his head. 'Stop fussing, Gloria. She's had worse – many times.'

Gloria ignored him and went back into the kitchen. She was angry; angry that a man would do that to a woman.

'Times haven't 'alf well bloody changed, Alice,' she said, as Alice poured boiling water into the teapot. 'Beating up a woman. Just not bloody on.'

Alice made the tea. She didn't know what to say.

The doorbell rang. 'Shall I get it, Frank?' Gloria shouted.

'No, I'll get it,' came the sound of Archie. He strolled into the hallway to open the door. It was Pēteris and Jānis. 'Come in, lads. Two more sarnies, Gloria, please,' he said, as he went back through to the dining room.

'Any sauce, boys?' Gloria asked. Pēteris asked for red; Jānis said he didn't want any sauce. They then followed Archie, said their hellos and shook the hands of the men before taking their seats.

Raquel, for the second time in two days, wondered what Pēteris was doing here. Archie noticed and, for the second time in two days, he too realised he'd not let Raquel know in advance. Raquel fixed her eyes on him. He held her gaze, knowing full well what her look was all about. His hard stare told her that he knew what she was thinking, but forgetting to extend her that courtesy again was just tough shit. She knew she'd have to let it go AGAIN. He had a lot on his plate.

Archie then spoke. 'Right, ladies and gentlemen, I know we normally have meetings like this in the boardroom but—' He then stopped and looked at Jānis. 'No disrespect, Jānis, but you are not on our payroll, so the boardroom is out of bounds.' Jānis nodded in acknowledgement.

Archie continued. 'Hence why we are here munchin' these lovely bacon cobs. Now, I know Jānis has introduced himself but I'll re-cap as to why he's here. He's had dealings with Fletcher. Not all of them good ones and, like a lot of people in the Manchester fraternity, he's not a big fan. But the really interesting part is that, as I said briefly yesterday, a friend of Jānis's girlfriend, a lady called Andrea, cleans at Fletcher's house, so she has access.'

Archie paused and looked around the room. Jez, Pat, Phoebe, Raquel, Pēteris and Jānis were all listening closely, as was Frank. Archie had their full attention. 'So,' he continued, 'we might just have a way into his house. So, Jānis, tell us what you know.'

Jānis cleared his throat just as Gloria came in with two cobs and two mugs of tea.

'Here you are, lads. One with sauce is yours, Pēteris,' she said, handing Pēteris his plate and mug, 'and this one is yours, sweetheart,' she said, passing Jānis his. Jānis placed his plate and mug on the table and drew a gulp.

'Well, Andrea cleans there three times a week – Monday, Wednesday, Friday. Usually gets there mid-morning and does three hours each time. Fletcher normally makes sure he's there on a Friday. I asked her why and, well, let's just say he enjoys her company on a Friday. Not every week, but most weeks. I didn't know that previously,' he said, feeling like he had to justify it to the room.

Jez, Pat and Archie smiled. Pēteris was unsure what to do. Phoebe and Raquel looked at each other and rolled their eyes.

'No need to justify it to us, Jānis. Mind you, today is Friday and it is mid-morning,' Frank laughed childishly. Archie, Jez and Pat did the same; Pēteris joined them. 'Carry on,' Frank instructed.

'Kat, Fletcher's wife, is either in the swimming pool or her sauna, or at some day spa she goes to, so apart from most Fridays, Andrea is left alone to do her job. She has the code to the key safe to let herself in. She's been cleaning for them a few years now, so is well trusted,' Jānis continued. 'She always works alone apart from if she is going to be away, like on holiday, or if she goes to see her mother in Cornwall.' He took a bite of his cob and a sip of his tea. He much preferred coffee, didn't really like tea, but drank it anyway.

'So, how often is she at her mother's and what does she do when she's away?' Archie asked.

'She likes to go at least once every two months. When she does, she leaves on the Friday after her clean and travels back on the Monday, so it's the Monday she misses. Other times she'll go for a week, which she classes as a holiday, and then she might go abroad a couple of times too.'

'He must fuckin' pay well, old Fletcher, if she can afford that many holidays,' Jez interjected.

'No idea, but I think she goes last minute on a cheap holiday, and she's on her own, so it'll not be a fortune,' Jānis replied.

'So, who does the cleaning when she's away?' Phoebe asked, taking the words right out of Frank's mouth.

'Well, normally her friend Suzie, but sometimes she can't do it as she has a few cleaning clients of her own, so in the past she's taken quite a few different mates to do it. I asked her if Fletcher and Kat were OK with that and she assured me they were. At first, she would ask them if it was OK and that, but now she just says, *"Oh, this is so-and-so. They'll be covering for me next Monday"* for example, and they just accept it. They trust her, as do I,' Jānis replied, before munching away.

'They must do,' Phoebe responded.

The room fell silent. Everyone was thinking. You could almost hear the cogs turning.

'Oh, and it's a smart house too,' Jānis said, as he finished the last of his sandwich.

'A what?' asked Frank. It was the same question

they all wanted to ask, except Archie. He was the only one who knew what one was.

'A smart house – you know, where everything is done through your iPad or iPhone,' Jānis said carefully, not wanting to imply he couldn't believe they didn't know what one was. The thing was, he couldn't.

'You're gonna have to explain this one to me, son, in layman's terms, very slowly. What the fuck's a smart house?' Frank said, sitting forward clasping his hands, his elbows on the table.

Archie smiled to himself. *This will be fun.*

'Well, everything in the house is controlled and operated by a voice command. So, if they want to open the curtains, they just say *"Curtains open"* and if they want the heating to come on, they just say *"Heating on"* or something like that. Same with the light switches and the door locks. Everything really. It's all controlled wirelessly and through electronic devices. It's quite good,' Jānis said, sensing this was all too technical for everyone there.

'Fuck me,' Frank said. 'I've never heard of it. So, what does this mean for us then?'

Raquel spoke up. 'Before we explore this further, can I just ask about CCTV?'

'They have it outside only apparently. No CCTV inside the house, no cameras or anything. Just around the house outside. Quite surprising really for a man in his position, but then again, he reckons he's untouchable, doesn't he?'

Jez then spoke. 'So, this smart house thing – can it be rigged up to control it remotely?'

'What, you mean make it so it can be controlled by someone else other than Fletcher and Kat?' Phoebe asked.

'Definitely,' Jānis replied.

Frank was intrigued. He frowned as he tried to work out what Jez and Phoebe were getting at. Before he could ask, Archie interjected.

'Where are you two going with this?'

Jez spoke first. 'Well, if it can be rigged up to be controlled remotely and we can get Fletcher in it somehow on his own, then we would have control over whether he could get out of that house. Surely the door locks and window locks could be controlled by one of our voices and then, well, he'd be a sitting duck under our control.'

Frank was already dialling a number on his mobile. He sat back in his chair while it rang. It was answered on the fourth ring. 'Kenny, me old pal. How are ya?'

Kenny Walters was a Scotsman, who was now living in Lincolnshire. He'd moved down to England to be with his now-deceased wife, who had wanted to be nearer her mother. The mother had died nearly twenty years ago, two years after the move, and his wife, Carol, had passed away around eighteen months ago from breast cancer. Kenny knew everything there was to know about electronic devices and components.

'I'm OK, Frank, thank you. Living the dream, you know me.'

'Great. Listen, ain't got time for chit-chat,' Frank said as he laughed, 'I just want to ask you about smart houses. You heard of 'em?'

'Yeah, course. More and more people are having them. Why, you thinking of having one?'

'No! Am I fuck. I can switch my own lights off, thank you. What I want to know is, can the system be rigged so that it can be controlled remotely by a third party?'

'Can a duck swim, Frank? You do know who you've rung, don't you? I could do that with my eyes closed whilst having my cock sucked by a very tidy twenty-something.'

Frank laughed. 'I can just about see that in my mind's eye, Kenny. Listen, that's all I wanted to know for now, but if I have a job for ya, are ya interested?'

'Sure am, Frank. Who for?'

'I'll tell you that when we meet. You still in that same house in Leadenham?'

'Still here, Frank. Bonny Scotland keeps calling, though. I've got my house on the market, so be quick, 'cos as soon as it's sold, I'm off to Shetland.'

'Shetland?' Frank remarked, quite surprised.

'Yep, Shetland, bonny lad. Off to live with my brother for a while. Not for ever, but a year or two maybe. He has a croft up there. I'll be working the land for a bit, but don't worry, it's only a flight away or a ferry trip to Aberdeen, so if the price is right, I'll still do a job here and there.'

'Well, I didn't see that comin', Kenny, but each to

their own. Me and Archie will be over early Sunday mornin'.'

Frank finished his call. 'Well, it can be done,' he said.

Everyone sat back in their chairs almost in sequence, like some sort of synchronised swimming team. They all pondered for a second.

Pēteris then chipped in. 'Can I just ask, Frank, who is this Kenny guy? Some sort of techno guru?'

'More of an electronics wizard, I'd say, Pēteris. Why?'

'Well, if he's all things electronics and if he can do what you've just asked, then surely he could rig up some sort of electrical fire – you know, if Fletcher was in the house home alone so to speak.'

Archie sat up straight and pointed his finger at Pēteris. 'And if we've got control of the locks, then old Fletcher would, well, just die in an electrical fire. Some sort of accident. I like it, Pēteris. I like it very much.'

'Not our usual MO, is it, though?' Pat said, looking rather disappointed with that suggestion.

'Exactly, Pat. And that, my friend, is why it would be so fuckin' brilliant. We could take out Fletcher like that, and at the same time have men at that bar to take out whoever frequents it,' Archie said, trying to curtail his excitement. He then turned to Jānis. 'Has Andrea ever taken a fella to cover for her?'

'Don't know, Archie. Let me ring her.' Jānis dialled her number. Andrea told him that she'd only ever taken a woman with her to cover for her. She was at

Fletcher's when she answered the phone, but as usual was on her own. Kat was in her sauna and Fletcher was still out.

'What's the chances of Kenny dressing as a woman?' Phoebe asked.

'For the right money, he'd go there stark bollock naked,' Frank replied.

'Right, gents,' Archie announced, 'and ladies', he continued as he looked at Phoebe and Raquel, 'me and Frank will go and see Kenny on Sunday. Raquel, I want Del, Michael and two others, maybe Kevin and Darren, parked up outside that bar in Alderley Edge all day tomorrow. I want to know who comes and goes. I don't want Ryan and Des there, but certainly Del and Michael as they will recognise any faces from the crew who smashed up the club. I want Marie over at that day spa that Fletcher's missus goes to.'

'Jānis, get this Andrea to text you a photo of her so Marie knows what she looks like.' Jānis nodded.

'Mum, speak to Marie. I want her to befriend her. See what she's like. Don't know why, but I just want to know what makes her tick. What she likes. It might be nothing, but somethin's just tellin' me to get close to her.' He paused. 'If things go to plan on Sunday at Kenny's, then we could have Kenny in there Monday with Andrea, and have it all set up to control that fuckin' house of his by Monday afternoon.'

'Are you sure it's a good idea getting Marie involved? She's not a criminal, Archie,' Phoebe asked.

'No, but she knows enough about us to mean that at some point she needs to get her hands dirty. And she owes us. We let her keep Richie's house, you know. In fact, we transferred it to her. It's hers. All free that was.'

'I know, Son, but she did help us piece everything together with Richie and your dad.'

'Yeah, but she owes us. I want her involved, and befriending Kat is just up her street. No one knows her, so she'll be fine. No arguments,' Archie replied quite abruptly.

Phoebe knew it was time to back away. 'OK,' she nodded.

'What about their main club in Manchester?' Pat asked. 'We need to target that too, surely?'

'Not really, Pat, no. That would leave too many bodies, too much carnage. We need to remove the main man – Fletcher. We have agreed to then leave Manchester to the Burbankses. They will deal with any fallout in their own way. Fletcher's men will then have a choice, to either work for George and Ivan or fuck off. It'll be plain and simple. We do Fletcher at his house, but this bar is where Paul and John were murdered, so whoever frequents this place is of serious interest to us too. And they will get it as well.'

Archie sounded assured and controlled. Pat agreed, as did some of the others. Frank, though, was a little unsure about sending Del and Michael with Kevin and Darren. He was not a hundred per cent convinced either of them could handle that so soon after what had happened to Paul. Del was his father and Michael his uncle, and seeing the place where it all happened and possibly the people who did it could be a recipe for disaster. He decided to leave it. He didn't want to question Archie in front of everyone, especially after Phoebe quizzing him about Marie, but it was not sitting comfortably with him. He felt this was inexperience on Archie's part; maybe Archie just wanting to show he was the boss. He just hoped the decision would not come back to haunt him.

'So, does everyone know the initial plan?' Archie checked, scanning the room. Everyone nodded.

He looked at Jānis. 'Enjoying that cob, pal?' Jānis tried to speak but couldn't without showing everything in his mouth. Archie could see he was trying to hurry his food. 'Thank you for coming today, Jānis, and tell Andrea to expect to be taking someone with her on Monday,' Archie said smiling, knowing Jānis felt uneasy eating so quickly.

'Shall I tell her it may be a bloke dressed as a woman?' he asked, when he'd finally finished.

'No. I really can't see Kenny pullin' that off. I've only met him the once, but he's an old-school Scotsman. He's not dainty enough.'

'His beard would give it away,' Frank said. 'We'll just have to hope Andrea can sneak him in somehow. We'll tell you more on Sunday, so keep ya phone on.'

Archie continued. 'We meet here 6 o'clock Monday night for a briefing. By then, Marie will hopefully have made contact with Kat, the system will be rigged, and

Del and the others should have some info on who comes and goes at that bar in Alderley Edge.'

Everyone seemed OK with the plan. They all knew their jobs. As the meeting came to a close, they chatted amongst themselves. Pat, in particular, got to know Jānis a little better. He remembered him from before and wanted to know what he'd been doing, plus he enjoyed Jānis telling him how a smart house could be hacked. He was surprised at how much Jānis knew on the subject for a thug. He liked him and had always found him a reliable bloke, and thought how good it'd be to have him on the team permanently.

The only thing bothering anyone was the issue with Del going. It bothered Frank.

No one seemed bothered about the fact Fletcher had two of his men living at the house 24/7. No one seemed bothered, because no one knew.

Frank and Archie met Ted at Phoebe's house at Southwell. The three of them looked over the bodies.

Phoebe shouted, 'Tea's up!'

None of them moved. 'So, what do you reckon, Ted?' Archie asked.

Ted was in his late sixties and had been in the funeral game his whole life. He'd been legit for most of it but, like most industries, it was changing and he'd been left behind. Around ten years ago he disposed of his first body for Frank, and he'd done a few since. He still did legitimate funerals but not to the degree he had done previously. It was now just something that kept him out of mischief and topped up his pension. The five grand he could earn off Frank for this would be a lovely little bonus for him.

'It can be done, Frank, as you know, but to get these bodies lying flat will take some force. It can be done, but there'll be a fair bit of cracking and pulling to get them flat.'

'Are we cremating them both?' Archie asked as he'd thought it was just Paul that was having a funeral.

'Well, I'd assumed so,' Ted said.

Frank didn't correct him as getting two done for five grand was a nice bit of business. 'Yeah, of course. Both of them,' he confirmed.

'When do you want them cremating?' Ted asked.

'Next week sometime probably, Ted, or maybe the week after. The father has enough on at the minute. In fact, he doesn't even know the bodies have been found,' Frank solemnly replied.

'I'll keep 'em cold until then, but listen, it will have to be the same as last time. An early-morning slot straight after one of the direct cremations and we'll only have twenty minutes at most for any kind of service,' Ted instructed them.

Frank knew the score. Archie didn't.

'What do you mean?' Archie asked.

Ted explained. 'Well, some families have a direct cremation, which means no service, so the coffin gets brought in and sent down to the cremation bay underground almost immediately – so only about five minutes of the slot is taken up. The direct cremations are normally the first ones of the day. We'll pay the chapel attendant and the cremation staff off. They will let us in the chapel so we can have a bit of a service, put the two coffins on the catafalque and then send them downstairs. Plenty of time before the mourners turn up for the next one.'

Archie sighed. 'Not much of a send-off, is it? Which crem will you use?'

'No idea yet, but leave that with me. I use quite a few, so I'll sort it with one of them, don't worry,' Ted replied.

'It's as much as we can offer, Son,' Frank said, placing his arm on Archie's shoulder. 'Come on, let's get that brew, then Ted can take them with him.'

'When are we telling, Del?'

'Not until this thing with Fletcher is over. We need Del focused. He can have his cremation afterwards. So, not a word. If he asks, we ain't had no bodies, OK?' Frank insisted. Was it right to send Del to Alderley Edge the following day? It didn't feel right.

He told Ted to head on to the house and then put his arm across Archie's chest as a sign to stop. Ted carried on. As he did so, he surveyed the grounds and thought how he'd have to bury a lot of bodies to ever get anywhere near to affording a pile like this. Ted could see Phoebe through the kitchen window. He liked Phoebe. If he was twenty years younger, he'd be up it like a rat up a drain pipe.

'You must want to say something,' Archie said, knowing full well Frank needed a word.

'I do, Son. Listen, sending Del to Manchester is not a good idea. Apart from that it's not the right thing to do, he's just lost his son to murder and you want to send him to stake out the very place and maybe the very people who done it? Think about it. No need to send Del, Son. Send Steven instead. He was there at the club – he'll recognise them if they are there. I could maybe agree to sending Michael, but not Del. It's too personal.'

Archie listened intently. Frank was right. Earlier at the meeting Archie had suggested Del, thinking that someone, maybe Frank, would object. That's what he'd expected, so he was surprised no one had. He had planned to listen and reason and go with the general consensus, to show that he was a leader who could listen to people's concerns, and who was able to change his mind. He had hoped to use it as a way to seize an opportunity to be seen as less bullish and more measured. The fact no one did had backfired on him. Deep down, he didn't want to send Del. He was now grateful Frank had brought it up. He pretended to be locked in thought as he gazed across towards the paddock area. He returned to Frank.

'You're right, Grandad. It is too soon. I'll sort it with Raquel now.' He then rang Raquel after Frank had gone in for his brew. Raquel was pleased too. Thankfully, she'd not yet told Del, but that was only because Frank had quietly told her to hold fire earlier.

chapter twenty-four

Fletcher was in his office at his main club, smoking a big cigar whilst sipping on a large scotch. The club was now one of tension, not the calm jovial atmosphere it had been when he first got there. He was starting to wonder why he'd had no response from the Pearsons. It was now getting towards 2 o'clock. The main room was quite busy with Friday lunchtime punters, something Fletcher had been pleased about earlier. He was fine if the Pearsons came in wanting a war in full view of his customers. He saw it as an arena in which to show his power and authority. He was confident that if Frank and Archie came in here today wanting to sort this thing out, that they'd be leaving with their tails between their legs. That's if they could leave at all, he told himself.

The lack of contact was unnerving. It just didn't feel right. This was not what he'd expected at all. A phone call at least. Anything to show their hand. He knew if the tables were turned, he'd have been over to Nottingham in a flash and wouldn't have left until he had Frank's and Archie's balls in a vice. What the fuck was stopping them? This was not Frank and this was certainly not Archie – if anyone was to come charging over the hill, it was Archie. Fletcher sipped his scotch again. He knew, to the men he had with him today, that he must have had a look of concern on his face. Other than Benny, Tiny, Harry and Stuart, plus Phil and his crew, he also had his usual club staff, all who could mix it. Then there were his two most trusted: Newbie, a name that had stuck for over ten years from when he first joined the firm, and a time-served villain called Will, who had worked for his father. These two would die for Fletcher and he always felt invincible when they were around.

Fletcher had always tried his best to emulate his father but he could never really master the art of remaining calm when he felt the heat on him. He just did not have that skill in him. He'd always been a fighter. Even as a youngster, he would always hit first and ask questions later. His father had never had to teach him that. He never bought the argument that all behaviour was learnt. He didn't learn how to be aggressive; it was just who he was. He was convinced that he was born that way.

'You look miles away, Fletch,' Newbie said, as he stretched his arms out above his head and yawned.

'Keepin' you up, am I?' Fletcher sneered.

'Just saying, Boss, that's all. Calm down.'

'Yeah, well, I don't need no comments like that from you,' he snapped, on hearing commotion from outside his office door. He stood up. 'What the fuck's going on out there?' he asked, striding towards the door. He opened it and saw a guy in a suit arguing with one of the barmaids, pointing his finger in her face.

'I gave you a fuckin' fifty. I ain't a liar!'

Fletcher could see one of his security staff going over towards the bar area to intervene. He looked at Fletcher. Fletcher shook his head and faced his palm to him. The doorman stopped in his tracks. The man in the suit was still arguing. Fletcher walked up to him. The man looked round totally unaware of who Fletcher was and, judging by his body language and aggression towards the barmaid, he was totally unaware whose club this was. Fletcher grabbed the man by his tie and dragged him towards his office. The man struggled to stay upright as Fletcher pulled him hard. He instinctively put his hands to his neck trying desperately to loosen the knot. By now he was being dragged into the office by Newbie and Tiny. They threw him towards the back wall. He hit the wall with force and put his hands up as he struggled to breathe. He undid his top button.

'A fifty you say?' Fletcher asked.

'Look, it's no problem. Forget it. Maybe I was wrong. It's nothing. I'll apologise to your barmaid and, look, I'll buy you all a drink,' he said in desperation.

Fletcher turned to Will. 'I fancy a sandwich, Will. A toasted one.'

Will grinned and left the room. The guy looked petrified. 'Look, am I OK to go?'

'Are you fuck, my friend. You are going nowhere yet.'

Fletcher gave a small nod to Tiny, who punched him and knocked him into the wall. Blood poured from his nose. He hit him again. The man bounced off the wall and then crouched down putting his hands above his head in surrender. Will then came back in the room with a family-sized sandwich toaster. He plugged it in.

'What's your name?' Fletcher asked him.

'Richard. Richard Blake.'

'Stand up, Richard.'

Fletcher then told Newbie to sort the music. He left the room and within a few seconds the music was thumping, so much so that even in the office, you could hardly hear yourself think.

'Give me your hand,' Fletcher ordered Richard. Richard put his hands in his pockets. Fletcher held out his right hand. Newbie put a blade in it. Fletcher walked up to Richard, put the blade to his face and said loudly, 'This will cut into your face and then I'll put both your hands in that sandwich toaster, or you can give me your hands and save this pretty face of yours. You have five seconds to decide.'

Richard began to cry. 'Look, I'm sorry! I didn't mean any of it. I really am. I just want to go!' he sniffled.

'Five!' Fletcher shouted, as he cut Richard from his cheekbone to his jaw. Richard screamed, but above the music no one outside could hear him. Newbie and Will then grabbed him and pulled his hands out from his pockets. Tiny opened the lid of the sandwich toaster. Will placed Richard's right hand on the bottom grill and Tiny closed the lid. Richard wailed as it burnt. Five seconds later, Tiny lifted the lid. They did the same to his left hand. He then fell to the floor, in agony. Fletcher took a roll of notes out of his pocket and stuffed a fifty into Richard's lapel pocket.

He then turned to Benny, who had seen the whole thing.

'Take him and dump him somewhere. And make sure he knows that if he breathes a word, I'll hunt him down.'

Benny nodded. He and Tiny picked him up like a child, leg and a wing, and took him out of the back door. They dumped him three miles away.

Fletcher rang Frank. 'What's up, Frank? Lost yer fuckin' bottle? Where the fuck are ya? You're fuck all!'

Frank took a deep breath. 'There's two kinds of men in this world, Fletcher. Those who react and those who respond. Which one am I?'

The line went dead.

chapter twenty-five

Trainer was singing along to the radio as he drove down the A1. The sun was shining, he'd shagged a beautiful brunette all night and was now on his way to meet Archie. This was what he'd been waiting for all of his life – a place at the top table of Frank Pearson's empire. 'Come on!' he shouted once more at the top of his voice, punching the air with his right fist.

Trainer Williams had always been well known around Leeds as a man who loved a ruck. He'd been the kop of his school all the way through and had served his time on the doors. He'd first come to know Pat Steadman when Pat was running Leeds and had primed John Hughes to replace him when the time was right. Pat had always told John that as soon as he got the chance to go back to Nottingham, he would. The time came just after Daniel's murder. Pat became Richie's second, and then Archie's, once Archie had established himself as the successor. This meant John Hughes moving up a notch to replace Pat, and Trainer moving up to replace John.

Now that John had been murdered, Trainer was the main man in Leeds. He was in the inner circle of the

Pearson empire. He'd always loved John and so it hurt him to think it was because of John's demise that he now had his opportunity, but it had always been his ambition. In truth, he'd always known his chance would come quickly. He just wished it was because John had retired to the country, like he always said he would.

Trainer was a shrewd cookie. He was tough, would take on any man and would do whatever it took, but what set him apart and what meant he'd grown through the ranks was how smart he was. Trainer was no thug. He was a career criminal who always edged his bets and always did his homework before he acted. He'd seen too many good men never realise their true potential because they were just thugs; thugs who were too concerned about their reputation and who would just steam in, fists flying, if they ever felt threatened. Trainer was different. He'd more than once walked away from a confrontation in full view of his peers and enemies, only to return very quickly one step ahead to sort the matter out. He was clever enough to do that and comfortable enough with who he was to do that. In their small world, any retribution to set a record straight spread like wildfire. Those who ever thought he'd lost his bottle when he'd walked away got to hear pretty soon that Trainer had come out on top. When he did, his actions were brutal. His targets paid a heavy price for him walking away and risking looking weak. Now, no one wanted Trainer to walk away from them, because they knew what would be coming.

He was called Trainer because he always wore trainers. He never wore shoes; hated them. It had all stemmed from his family being so poor, he'd once been sent to school in his sister's shoes. He'd been teased brutally about it and had worn trainers ever since. Since leaving school all those years ago, he'd never sported a pair of shoes.

Trainer pulled off the A1 at the Worksop roundabout and headed down the A614 towards Ollerton. He'd been summoned to meet Archie and Frank to officially welcome him to the top table and to talk about their little problem. He knew that it was to do with one of the main faces in Manchester, but because of what happened to John over there, he was dying to be involved. If he knew Archie and Frank like he thought he did, he was sure they'd have him involved quite heavily. This was Trainer's time to step up. This was his time to make his mark. He wasn't going to fuck it up.

chapter twenty-six

Marie was nervous. She was expecting Phoebe any moment. All Phoebe had told her was that she needed to speak to her as she had a job she wanted her to do. Marie had been expecting this for a long time now. It had been over six years since Frank had gifted her the house in Blackscotch Lane. At the time, she'd had very mixed emotions. On one hand, she was truly grateful to be given such a beautiful house in an affluent area of Mansfield, even though it was where Daniel was murdered. She knew what the house meant to Frank. It had been the family home for so long; it was where he had brought up his boys and where everyone had gravitated to both in Frank's private life and in business. Frank told her he wanted her to have it because had it not been for her, Daniel's murder would have forever remained a total mystery. It still got to Frank that he never knew who did it, but, as big as Frank was in the gangster world, he knew to leave things alone when it involved men from Italy.

Yet, when he gave her the house, underneath all the hugs and thank yous, Marie knew that one day she would be expected to "do something". It had never been said or even insinuated, but she knew that favours and actions like this, as honourable as Frank was, would still carry some sort of caveat. Today could well be that day.

The doorbell rang. Marie opened it and smiled as Phoebe walked in. Marie looked at her nervously but before she could say anything, Phoebe said, 'Don't ask, Marie. It'll all come clear in a mo. Come on, put that kettle on. Let's have a brew.'

As Marie filled the kettle, she knew her instinct had been right.

'How is everyone?' she asked. Marie had kept in touch with everyone since Richie had been put into the care home. She'd been welcomed into the inner circle for her actions and had initially welcomed it, thinking she could maybe be part of it. Yet, as she'd discovered all those years ago when she'd crossed that line with Richie, she just wasn't cut out for that world.

'Well, things have been better. We've got a problem and that's why I'm here. I need you to do a job for me as part of Archie's plan to put things right,' Phoebe replied, making sure she studied Marie's reaction. It was as she'd thought. Marie was scared. Like Marie, Phoebe had known that one day she'd be asked to do something, and that it would be either her or Raquel to do the asking.

'I thought so. Didn't think when you said you had a job for me that it was painting your nails.' Marie smiled as she said it; a nervous smile, but one that told Phoebe she'd expected it and was resigned to doing whatever she'd be asked to do.

Phoebe told her about the last few days' events, which, given they'd only been together seeing Richie a few days previously, took her by surprise. She was particularly saddened to hear about Paul and John, but it only served to make her more scared than she had originally been. She listened carefully as Phoebe explained to her what her role would be.

'So, that's all I have to do – befriend her? Just get to know her a little?'

'Yep, that's it. Look, I know this is not something you're gonna relish doing, but just try to put why you are there to the back of your mind. Just treat it as a spa day; just do what you would normally do. Relax while you're there and just chat to her. This is her, look.' Phoebe showed Marie a photo.

'Archie wasn't specific, so there's no probing questions or anything. You might get very little, but you know what us women are like when we get chatting at a spa, we just let things run away with us, don't we? We all do it, even me. Just talk to her and see what she says.'

'When does he want me to go?' Marie asked.

'Today and tomorrow. She's bound to be there at some point. She's always there according to that Andrea.'

'What, now?'

'Yep. Now, girl. Come on, get your stuff.'

'I'm not a member or anything. I won't get in.'

'Already sorted. I rang them to ask about being a member and all you need is two forms of ID.'

'Not my real ID, surely?' Marie questioned, sounding quite agitated.

Phoebe tutted. 'Of course not, silly. Here, take these,' she said, getting a passport and a utility bill out of her bag. 'Your name is Joanne Bingley and you live in Glossop. If they say anything about Glossop being quite a way away, just tell them your sister lives in Altrincham. That's the best I could do in the short time I had.'

Marie looked at the passport. It had her photo on it. 'How did you get this photo of me?'

'Don't ask. Come on, we need to go.' Phoebe finished the last of her tea, placed the mug in the sink and turned to look at Marie. 'Marie, you need to go and get whatever stuff you would normally take to a spa. Quickly. If we don't get a move on, the day will be over.'

Marie lay the utility bill and passport on the worktop and in some sort of trance walked slowly upstairs to get her things. Her stomach was churning. She reached the top and took in the landing, with its plush carpet. She then glanced downstairs at the expensive flooring in the hallway and wondered if she'd have been better telling Frank six years ago that she'd have been OK finding her own place to live. She then heard Phoebe shout, 'Hurry up! Come on, we need to be going!'

Del was pacing around the office at the main club in Nottingham. He was still angry that he wasn't allowed to go with Michael, Steven and the others. Even Trainer had been told to go and he was the new kid on this block. Del wanted to be there, to be part of whatever the plan was at all stages. He'd told Raquel that he was just going to go regardless and that no one was going to stop him. The only thing that had changed his mind was when Raquel told him that either he was going to ring Frank and tell him, or she was, but either way, if Del went of his own accord, Frank and Archie would know about it. At that point, Del accepted that that would be a foolish thing to do. As hard and as game as he was, there was no way he could take on Frank and Archie. He'd lose and that would do nothing to right the wrong of his son's murder. Del knew he had to just bide his time. He'd been promised involvement – Frank and Archie had both given their word, and the one thing he was sure of more than anything else was their word meant just that.

'Sit down, Del, or go home. It's doing you no good pacing around,' Raquel said, as she watched him back and forth.

She knew he was hurting bad and wanted to mother him, but he was virtually as old as she was, and that told her to keep her distance. Saying that, Raquel wasn't really the mothering kind. It didn't come naturally to her. She'd never wanted kids, had never had that maternal instinct that a lot of women have. She liked kids, was always happy to swoon over them for five minutes, but she couldn't ever remember harbouring thoughts to have children of her own.

'I can't rest, Raquel. I know why I've been ordered to remain here, but I'm like a volcano waiting to erupt! Those bastards murdered my son, remember, so I'm not just gonna sit here quietly and read my paper, am I?'

'Why didn't you go with Ryan and Des to have a word with that fella who lives in Heanor? At least you'd have been able to take your anger out on him. You know he's going to get a kicking of some sort. He's taking a cut that he shouldn't, so a decent beating is well justified. They've only been gone ten minutes. Ring them and get them to come back. It'll do you good and, listen – any news from Alderley Edge and you'll be one of the first to know.'

Del stroked his chin. He had pondered whether to go with his sons and very nearly had. He did think that he should be with them today. They had lost their brother after all. But if he was honest, he thought he might not be able to control himself if he started to administer a beating. He didn't want a murder charge to have to deal with.

'Fuck it,' he said and rang Des. 'Turn round, Son. I need to be with you guys today.'

Des and Ryan picked Del up a quarter of an hour later. The guy who lived in Heanor was not at home when they called. They looked for him until they found him, then left him close to death by the side of the road. He spent five days in hospital and never took a cut again. Del felt so much better once he returned to the club. Much better indeed.

chapter twenty-seven

Marie parked in a car park about a two-minute walk from the spa she was to go to. She'd decided not to park in the spa car park so that her car wouldn't be seen. She then walked briskly towards the side street where the entrance door was. She'd never been to Altrincham before. Phoebe had told her that it was upmarket and, by the looks of the area, she was right. She entered the spa and waited while the receptionist dealt with another client. After around thirty seconds, she sat down on one of the leather sofas and flicked through a brochure, which mirrored the ambience of the place.

'Hello Madam, can I help you?'

Marie looked up to see the receptionist beaming at her. She had long blonde hair, lily-white teeth, a perfect smile and full lips. Marie stood up and straightened her skirt.

'Yes, er, thank you. Yes, er, I'd like to become a member, please. I did ring up earlier and you said I needed two forms of ID,' she replied, passing the documents over.

'Thank you ... Joanne.'

Marie smiled.

'I'll just ring through to Cara in our sales team and she will come through to register you and to show you round. I'll just need to take details of your credit card for the joining fee and for the first month's membership and then once Cara has your bank details, it will be taken by direct debit.'

Marie felt a rush of adrenaline run through her entire body. Phoebe had not said anything about using a credit card. *Shit!* She sat back down on the sofa as the receptionist took details from her passport and utility bill. Marie checked her purse for money. She had just over seventy quid. She took back her ID and then asked, 'Sorry, I forgot how much you said the joining fee was and all that. I'm a right scatterbrain, you know.'

The lady smiled. 'It's an £85 joining fee and then £120 per month, paid by direct debit.'

'Right. Lovely,' Marie said, as she tried to think on her feet.

Cara then came through. 'Hi Joanne, I'm Cara. How are you?'

Marie tried her best to look relaxed but inside she was shaking. She couldn't believe that Phoebe hadn't thought of payment. She couldn't use her own card and she didn't have enough money on her. As she followed Cara through, she spotted a notice on the wall that said *"Special offer – two-day guest passes available for £50"*. Marie immediately felt her fear disappear. That was it: she would just get a two-day pass. There *was* a god, and he'd just shown himself in Altrincham.

Marie let Cara go through the motions before doing a very good job of someone desperately looking for her credit card. She even emptied her bag, knowing full well she'd put her cards in the inside zip of her bag when she'd nipped to the toilet on the way through. Marie then explained that she'd had a really stressful morning and had left it at home, so, for today, could she be a guest for two days for fifty quid. Cara's face told Marie she didn't really buy her story and that she was disappointed at a missed opportunity for commission, but she played the game and told Marie that it wouldn't be a problem and that she could continue with her membership next time, reminding her that she could, in fact, do it tomorrow, if she came back for her second day then. Marie smiled, knowing there was no chance she would be doing that.

chapter twenty-eight

George Burbanks put down his mobile. He'd just had a conversation that told him all he needed to know about what was happening with Frank and Fletcher. Any serious business in Manchester was George's business. Whatever happened would have repercussions either way. Ivan sat opposite him with his hands behind his head.

'So, what's the crack?'

George smiled a little and nodded. 'Well, it all seems to be goin' as we'd expected. Frank's gone quiet, which we hoped he would, 'cos knowin' Frank as we do, he'll have a plan that will catch Fletcher off guard – the mother of all plans. And Fletcher's like a hot potato 'cos of it. He can't understand why Frank hasn't reacted yet, and is likely to do something really stupid as a result. Frank, on the other hand, because of his silence, must be plannin' something tasty. 'Cos that's Frank.'

'Why not put a call in to him? He did ring us after all to give us the nod that he had problems with Fletcher, so a phone call wouldn't seem amiss, would it?'

George sat back mirroring Ivan, with his hands behind his head. He looked at the ceiling. 'Nah, no phone call. Why would we? Nah, that would appear odd. We can get all the info we like. Our man's doin' good. Frank will be plannin' something and he'll not wait long. But we know Frank well and he's at his most dangerous when he's silent. If I had beef with Frank, I'd much rather have him shoutin' the odds. When he's silent, he's one fuckin' deadly fella. Just sit back and watch, Brother. Just sit back and enjoy the fireworks.'

chapter twenty-nine

Marie had been given the grand tour by Cara. She'd paid her fifty quid and was now eligible to enjoy the facilities for two days at least. She'd actually momentarily forgotten why she was there. Everything was top-notch, just as she'd hoped, and as she changed into her robe and slippers, she decided that she was going to try and enjoy it. She checked the photo of Kat again so that she had her image ingrained in her memory. She just hoped that she'd show up today. Marie knew she'd feel a lot better if she at least struck up a conversation with her. That way, she could convince herself that Kat knew nothing of why she was befriending her.

She didn't have to wait long. As she got herself comfy on one of the loungers around the indoor pool, she was just about to open her book when she caught sight of a lady who looked just like the one in the photo. Even though she had the image clear in her mind, she went to check her phone. It was her. She looked even more beautiful in the flesh. Her boobs were obviously false but that was no surprise to Marie. She'd come across more and more girls and young women who'd gone under the knife. It had always amazed and intrigued Marie why young women wanted to or needed to do that, but it was the way of the world now, especially in these circles, and it no longer raised an eyebrow. Marie noticed how tanned and toned Kat was. She knew she'd had two children and was impressed by how her body defied any sign of childbirth.

She watched Kat put her things down on a lounger and immediately make her way towards the sauna and plunge pool. Marie watched as she went straight in without speaking to anyone. She decided to give it a couple of minutes before joining her. She had butterflies in her tummy, so she reminded herself of the real reason she was there and took a few deep breaths. She thought of things to say, how to start off the conversation, and told herself that her name was Joanne. She repeated it a few times before she wandered over to the sauna area. She tried to look natural and smiled to the few ladies who were chilling out around the pool. She took one last deep breath before opening the door to the sauna. It was hot, extremely hot. So hot that it took her breath as she inhaled. The air was dry. As she sat down, she felt the air cool very slightly. Kat looked up and smiled. Marie did the same. She decided to just sit down and see what happened. She tried to think what she would normally do here. She had to put why she was here to the back of her mind. *Just act naturally.*

The sauna was smaller than she'd expected, probably only big enough to comfortably fit five or six people. It was circular in shape with the stove in the centre. Next to the stove was a little bucket and ladle for pouring water on the stones. Marie decided she would use that as her opener.

'Are you OK if I put a little water on the stones?' she asked.

Kat opened her eyes and looked at her. They really were the most beautiful she'd ever seen. She just hoped that her personality reflected those eyes. She smiled. 'I was just going to ask you the same question. That's fine with me. I like it hot. The hotter the better.'

'I'm glad you know what you are doin'. I can't remember the last time I was in a sauna,' Marie said, hoping that would help kick-start a conversation. Plus, it was true and Marie wanted to try and be herself as much as possible.

'I love them,' Kat said, as she sat up a little straighter, appearing as though she wanted to talk. 'I have one at home. I use it most days, but I love to come here too. It gets me out of the house. I always come here on the days our cleaner comes. I'd rather be out of the way when she's there. I sometimes come at weekends too whenever she does a Saturday clean, like today, but it's not easy, not with my fella. I haven't seen you here before, though.'

'My first time actually. I'm just a visitor though, today and tomorrow.'

'Are you local then?' Kat asked, appearing interested to hear Marie's story.

'No, Glossop. I live in Glossop.'

'Wow, that's a fair way away! What are you doing here?'

'Visiting my sister. She lives this way,' Marie replied, trying to sound assured.

'Ooh, what's her name? Where does she live? I might know her.'

'Polly. I doubt you'll know her. She's older than me and I'm quite a bit older than you, so I doubt she'd be your cup of tea. She's a bit of a recluse, hence why I'm here alone. She never comes out of the house really. My name's Joanne by the way,' Marie rushed, wanting to move on from where Polly lived. She did have a road in mind, but would much prefer to move change the subject.

'I'm Kat. My name's Katrina, but everyone calls me Kat, and anyway, you don't look much older than me!' she said laughing.

'Ooh, I am! Trust me. Anyway, I bet you have a great time in here. I bet you have loads of friends and do all the things 'ladies who lunch' do. It seems a lovely place.'

Kat dropped her gaze and went quiet for a minute. 'Come on, let's do the ice-cold water bucket outside. You'll love it. It really cleanses your pores. It's great for your skin. Then we can go into the steam room. Come on.' She held out her hand and led Marie out. The bucket of cold water *was* ice cold. It took Marie's breath away but they both stood there giggling. Marie was enjoying Kat's company and was being herself.

They spent the next two hours chatting like two old

schoolfriends, talking about all sorts. Marie had to keep reminding herself of who she was supposed to be. She did drop her guard on more than one occasion when she talked about her childhood and school life and where she'd worked, but she was sure Kat had not noticed. Kat was a real chatterbox. She always had been, and she liked the new friend she'd found. She didn't have friends of her own. She only had Fletcher's friends or Fletcher's men and acquaintances in her life. Kat was like a young lady again.

Marie could talk with the best of them but Kat took some beating. Marie had not expected this. She'd prepared herself for it being hardgoing and for there to be other women around. She imagined Kat would be with a group of friends, but it became clear that she was quite a loner; in fact, Marie had noticed that no one else had really spoken to Kat. A few had said a customary hello or hiya, but no one of any real connection. It did appear that Kat, for all her wealth, was quite a lonely figure and by the end of their two hours together, Marie had come to feel quite sorry for her. As they sat having a green tea together, Kat told her about her relationship with Fletcher. Marie listened. Kat's tone had become quite sombre. It was clear how controlled she was and how unhappy she was in their relationship. She told Marie that her husband shagged the cleaner on occasion, which he didn't know she knew. This was interesting news to Marie, given that Andrea was someone who she believed was going to assist Frank and Archie. She made a mental note.

Kat continued to pour her heart out. She told Marie how she didn't have her own life really and that Fletcher controlled everything she did, even to the point where two of his men had dropped her off today and would be picking her up in twenty minutes' time. They did that every time she came. Wherever she went, someone accompanied her. That was her life. Kat could see how Marie felt sorry for her. She could see how she pitied her. Kat knew their friendship was not real. She'd realised that a while ago. Marie's accent was not local, certainly not from Glossop. She'd decided it was probably from Nottingham as that's where Marie had seemed to spend most of her life. A lot of what Marie had said had not added up. This made Kat sad. She looked up at Marie and took her hand.

'You're not from Glossop, are you?' she said looking her straight in the eye. Marie took her hand away. She didn't even realise she'd done it.

'What? Yes, of course, I am. Like I said, I live in Glossop, but my sister lives over here.'

Kat gave a wry smile and shook her head. 'It's OK. I know you're not. No one ever really engages with me in here. They all know who I am and more importantly who my husband is. They all either despise him or are afraid of him. Probably both to be honest. As you'll have seen, I get no more than the odd hello. I like it here, though. It allows me to escape, if only for a few hours each time.' Kat again took Marie's hand. 'Look, I'm no fool. I may look dumb but I'm far from it. I know my husband has some beef, some major beef, with some guys over in Nottingham. I hear things.

I see things. I always excelled at maths and can put two and two together and I know that something big, or heavy, or whatever you call it, is coming, and I also know that you have more than likely been sent here to befriend me. Remember, I can put two and two together and you, Joanne – if that is your name – are making five.'

Marie tried to speak. 'Look, Kat, I have no idea what—'

'Shush. Just listen to me. I'm sure you are not who you say you are. I thought you were real at first, but the more we talked, the more it became clear you are not from round here. I reckon you have been sent here from over Nottingham way to suss me out. I may be wrong, but if I am right, I want you to help me and, in return, if what I think is right, I can help you.' Kat looked at her phone. She had ten minutes.

'I need to go in a minute to get changed, but if I am talking sense, be here again tomorrow and we can talk further, but if you want my husband, or should I say, if the blokes from Nottingham want him, I'll give him to you on a plate, served up with two roast spuds and a Yorkshire pudding. But, in return, I must get away. I don't want money. I don't want *these,*' she said, holding her tits. 'I just want my freedom. And unless Fletcher O'Brien is dead, I'll never have it. If I'm talking nonsense, don't be here tomorrow. I only want to see you tomorrow if I'm right.'

Kat kissed Marie's hand. Marie sat there speechless and watched as Kat walked off to get changed. Marie lay on her lounger and put her hands over her face. 'Oh my God,' she whispered. That, she definitely hadn't expected.

Steven Wallace was watching the bar across the road. Only six people had been in or out in the hour and a quarter they had been waiting: four young women on a girlie day out and a middle-aged couple. That was it. The rest of the bars and bistros on the street were busy, with a steady flow of people coming and going and customers eating and drinking outside, but this one was as dead as a fucking dodo. Steven, Michael, Trainer, Darren and Kevin were sat there like lemons watching a door that hardly opened. They'd played I Spy, Twenty Questions and even Rock Paper Scissors, but now they were bored shitless.

'Fuckin' weird this, Michael. Not one fucker's been in or out. It is the right place, isn't it?'

Michael took a deep breath and sighed. 'Deffo. One hundred per cent it's the right place. It has to be. And there HAVE been people going in.'

'Six. Fuckin' six I've counted!' Steven was pissed off.

Trainer slid along the wooden seat in the back. They had gone in a plain blue van. They'd opted against white as a plain white van looks odd. A blue one looks far more inconspicuous, or so they reckoned anyway. The two main men, Steven and Michael, were in the front, with Trainer, Kevin and Darren in the back. Even in a van, hierarchy prevailed. However, Trainer told himself that because he was now officially a top table member, he was the top dog in the back. It made this tedious operation seem just that little bit more bearable.

'Look, shall I go in? They won't know me. They'll have never heard of me,' Trainer said to Steven.

'Archie said not to, mate. He was very clear that no one goes in.'

'I know that, Steven, but fuck me, what are we actually lookin' for?'

'Anyone. We were just told to make a note of who goes in and out. You know that,' Steven replied, irritated by Trainer's remark.

'Well, no one's been anywhere near it, have they, apart from those four bits of totty and that old couple. We can't sit here all afternoon and all night, for fuck's sake. Look, I'm starvin'. I'm gonna get a sarnie. Anyone want owt?' Trainer asked.

They all put an order in for a sandwich and a drink. Trainer asked Darren to go with him and give him a hand. As they got out of the van and walked along the road looking for a baker's, Trainer said, 'Come on, let's cross over and go down that side street. It must lead to the back of that row of shops. Let's see what's happenin' at the back 'cos there's fuck all happenin' here.'

'I knew you were gonna say that. Come on, I can't sit in that van for much longer. Fuckin' stinks,' Darren replied, pleased that he'd guessed right.

They crossed the road at the crossing and jogged down a side street. Trainer was right. It *did* lead to the back of the shops. They crouched down and watched. Within two minutes, two blokes walked into the one they were sure was the back of the bar. They looked at each other. They waited. Within three minutes, the same two men came out. They waited some more. Trainer's phone rang. It was Michael. He ignored it, knowing he would be asking where they were. It rang again. This time it was Steven. Again, he ignored it. He turned it onto silent and slipped it back in his jeans pocket. Darren prodded him. He looked up. Two different men were walking in. They looked quite young, maybe late teens. Two minutes later they came out, and between them, looked at what they had just purchased. Trainer knew a bag of powder when he saw one, no matter how far away he was.

'It's just a front for a drugs operation. I bet they don't sell any fuckin' beer. I'm goin' in. Wait here,' he said.

'Fuck that, I'm coming with ya,' Darren replied, following a yard behind. Trainer stopped. 'Darren, listen. They won't know me, but you are a face in and around Nottingham. They must have known who Paul and John were.'

'Yeah, and where was John from – Leeds, just like you. If you're goin' in, then so am I.'

Trainer raised his eyebrows and nodded at the same time as if to say fair point.

'Come on then, but we need to be ready 'cos if it comes on top, we've gotta get outta there. What have you got on ya?'

Darren shook his head. 'Nowt, just these,' he said, holding up both fists. 'I didn't think to bring owt from the van.'

Trainer laughed. 'Ah, well, good job I brought this fella then,' he grinned, pulling out a gun. 'What's your Manchester accent like?'

'Dunno,' Darren replied.

Trainer told him he needed to sound like he was from Manchester if he was going in with him, which he stressed in a very good Mancunian accent.

'Fuck me, Trainer! Where did you learn to speak like that?'

'It's just somethin' I can do. Always been able to,' he said in a Scouse accent. 'I can do any accent,' he continued in a very good Geordie twang.

Darren had a go. It didn't sound bad, but nowhere near as good as Trainer's.

'Come on. Keep those fists clenched, but don't speak unless you're spoken to,' he reminded Darren, as he strode towards the back door. 'And if you do, for fuck's sake, make sure you speak in that accent. As bad as it is, it might just save your life.'

Trainer knew that if he got a wiff of them being rumbled, he'd shoot the fuckers on the spot. They'd killed his mate and mentor, John. He was up for revenge and if that came today, then so be it. This was the world he lived in. This was the world in which he revelled. Darren knew it too. He just wished he'd brought his own piece.

chapter thirty

Trainer walked in. He made sure he looked confident. He was surprised to find the back door only led into a dingy room. He knew it was the right building. He spotted a door that had to lead through into the main bar. Sat on a leather sofa that had seen better days was a guy whose face was a mess. He looked as though someone had thrust a glass into it. Trainer had seen that injury many times before. This guy had definitely had a glass thrust into his face. The scars were new – Trainer was sure this guy must have been there the other day. Paul and John would not have gone down without a fight. Trainer wondered if he was looking at his friend's murderer.

'What you after?' the man asked.

Trainer composed himself. He knew he couldn't just kill this bloke. As much as he wanted to and as much as he'd told himself outside that he'd shoot the fuckers dead, he was on Frank Pearson's payroll and that meant doing his job. In his best Manchester accent, he said, 'Just some Charlie. A coupla grams.'

The guy replied with a nod towards the door. Trainer then realised the window next to it was one-way glass. He waited. The man with the scars didn't take his eyes off Trainer. He never even looked at Darren. Trainer decided he wouldn't hold the man's stare. That was not what Joe public would do. Joe public would look nervous and intimidated. Trainer decided to be Joe public. The door then opened and a bag came through and landed on the floor.

'Sixty quid,' the guy said.

Trainer took a wad of notes out of his pocket and paid with three twenties. The guy nodded towards the bag on the floor. Trainer picked it up. 'Cheers,' he said and walked out behind Darren. They walked quickly back the way they came. Trainer looked round. There was no one behind them.

'Fuck me, my heart was goin' then, Trainer, me old pal. Did you see his scars? He's been in one hell of a fuckin' fight.'

'Yeah, and I reckon the man who did that to him was either Paul or John. We need to get this information back to Archie and Frank. The bastards who did Paul and John are in there, mate. They are there, just fuckin' sat there, and we have to walk away. Come on, let's get those sarnies and get back to that van.'

Five minutes later, they opened the van doors, climbed in and chucked a load of sandwiches onto the seat.

'You've been round the fuckin' back, haven't ya?' Steven growled.

'Yeah, we have, but listen – that place will never sell a fuckin' pint of beer all day long. It's just a front for selling the drugs round the back. And I reckon the guy who killed Paul and John is in there right now. He had new scars from what looks sure to have been a glassing, probably from Paul or John. We could go in now and sort the fucker out good and proper. He's sat on a sofa on his own, right now. Your call, Steven, but he's there.'

Steven looked at Michael, Paul's uncle. He could see the anger boiling. He knew he had to make a decision, and fast. He took his sunglasses off. He wanted to look Michael in the eye but, more importantly, he wanted to let Michael see his. Steven still, after all these years, wore sunglasses most of the time to hide his false eye, a reminder of his first-ever dealings with Frank and Daniel nearly thirty years ago.

'I'll ring Archie,' he said.

As he dialled his number, Michael didn't take his eyes off him. A small part of him was pleased he was ringing Archie and not Frank. Archie was more likely to say, "Fuck it, take the fuckers out" than Frank was. Frank would be measured and take a longer-term view of whether that's what was needed.

'Archie, it's me. Listen, this bar is no bar at all really. Hardly any fuckers been in and out all day, but, interestingly, the back door is where it all happens – where they sell their drugs. There's a guy at the back who has fresh wounds to his face, probably from a glassing. He could be the guy who murdered Paul and

John. We could take him out now. Your call.' Steven continued to look at Michael the whole time.

'Put me on loudspeaker,' Archie said. 'Nothing happens, gents, without Del being there. Today was about finding things out, nothing more, but I think it's safe to say that the guys who got Paul and John are there all the time. We'll get them, but it's time to come home, fellas.'

Michael shook his head. Out of disappointment more than anything. He knew the score, though. As much as he'd have loved to have gone in there and blown the bastard's brains out, he also knew it had to wait and that Del had to be there more than anyone.

'That's it then, lads. Home sweet home,' Steven said calmly, as he started the engine.

Frank looked at Archie. 'Good decision, Son. We have to make sure that when we strike, we strike hard and we take them all out at the same time. We now know that those fellas that Del wants are at that bar; we are pretty sure we can get access to Fletcher's house; and we know where his main club is, where his main men congregate. We hit them all at the same time. It'll take some planning, but we'll come out on top.'

'I know, Frank, I know, but I could have very easily told Steven to go in there and take them all out in that bar. He was there, just there waiting to be sorted out,' Archie replied.

Frank got up and walked towards the main window that looked out onto the garden. 'That would have been the easy thing to do, Son. The thing that, in fairness, most people in our game would have done. It would have showed strength and it would have made them feel better about themselves and the whole situation.' He then turned to face Archie. 'But only for a short while, then they'd have had the fallout to deal with. Shit they'd have brought on themselves. And that's why, Son, people like me rise to the top. People like George and Ivan Burbanks. People like Greg West in London. People like Rory Hammond. They all play the long game. I'm right, aren't I, Jez?'

'As always, Frank, as always. I remember all those years ago when I first met you, when we were doin' the doors, you were always the one who remained calm when it all kicked off, and that made people wary of you.'

'Exactly. And that's why you need to be the same, Archie. You know you're different when people are scared of you, when you do nothing. Jez here was the same. That's why he's been at my side all these years. The only difference was Jez never wanted to lead, so me and him work. You have the same with Pat here. You're the same, Pat – calm and careful. When was the last time you heard Pat raise his voice to scare anyone?'

'Anyone can shout, Archie, but the one who's shouting will be in fear of the one who's not, in any confrontation. It's just how we are and that will never change,' Pat said, feeling a touch uncomfortable that his boss was getting some kind of lesson on how to be a leader in this world, and that he was contributing to it.

Frank then heard some voices coming from the hall. Female voices. Phoebe came into the room. 'You're not gonna believe this,' she said, appearing to be quite excited.

'What, Mum?'

Phoebe sat down and straightened her skirt. 'Well, Marie has certainly had a productive day. Kat twigged who she was.'

Before Phoebe could continue, Archie flung himself back in his chair. 'Ya fuckin' jokin' me. Is she OK? What happened? Fuckin' hell! How the fuck did she twig?'

'Archie, calm down. Listen to me. I think it's turned out well.'

'Has it? Why, is she selling her husband down the river?'

'It would seem so, yes. After she'd nattered to Marie like a long-lost schoolfriend, Kat then told her she knew who she was. Well, more of why she was there really. She told her that if *"the blokes from Nottingham"* really wanted her husband, then, if we look after her, she'd serve him up on a plate for us. She HATES him. He controls every aspect of her life. She wants out. She ain't bothered about money or anything. She just wants her freedom. She's our ticket in. We don't really need the cleaner any more. Kat will serve him up.'

Phoebe stopped talking and looked around the room. They were all speechless.

'Well, Marie has certainly repaid us. And some,' Frank said. 'Good call that, lad. Even I didn't see that one.'

Archie paced up and down. Frank watched him. Jez and Pat watched him. Phoebe watched her son, waiting for an answer. He gazed out of the window and thought. Frank looked at Phoebe. She looked back. They both waited for Archie to speak.

'So, how did Marie leave it?' he asked his mum.

'Kat told her that if she was talking nonsense about who she was and why she was sent to befriend her, then Marie was not to turn up tomorrow, but if she was right, then she told Marie to be there. That way, she'd know for sure.'

'You go with her then, Mum. Go with her tomorrow. Suss her out for yourself. This sounds great, just what we needed – but also just a little bit convenient for me. Marie's OK, but she's no criminal mastermind. You on the other hand, Mum, will know if she's genuine.'

'OK. I thought you might say that. I can go as a guest, Marie said, so it'll be no issue.'

'Be careful though, Mum.'

'Frank, we'll still go and see Kenny tomorrow as planned. If Kat is kosher, then we can still rig the place up with her help, and then, if needs be, once we're sure Kat is for real, I'll let Jānis know to tell Andrea that she's not needed.'

Fletcher climbed off Kat. He'd just shot his load and was lying there thinking about the only thing other than sex to excite him these days. As he watched Kat go into the en suite, leaving the door ajar, he rang Benny. Benny answered more or less straight away.

'This is doin' my fuckin' head in, Benny. I can't sit around and wait for them to do somethin'. Get the lads over to Leeds tomorrow and get some drugs out on those streets. That John Hughes fella is no longer there, so it should be easy pickings and it's far enough away from Frank and his young pretender. Let's see what they do then, eh!'

'No problem, Boss. Who shall I take?'

'Just take Harry and Stuart as normal – they're your lads – and three or four of some of the estate lads. They'll be up for havin' the chance to shine. Any will do.'

'I'm on it. It'll make a change from a lazy Sunday afternoon.'

Fletcher put down his phone and grinned.

'Leeds, Leeds, Leeds!' he shouted, as Kat flushed the toilet. 'Come on, Kat, get yaself back in here! Round two!'

chapter thirty-one

Frank and Archie drove along the A17 to see Kenny in Leadenham, a small village in between Newark and Sleaford. They knew what they wanted out of today's meeting, and that was for Kenny to go to Fletcher's the next day. All they needed was for Fletcher's missus, Kat, to be on the level. They were sure Phoebe would know whether she was being straight up or not once she'd met her. One thing that Phoebe was good at was sussing people out. She always knew when something just didn't smell or feel right. She had a sixth sense. Maybe it was women's intuition but whatever it was, it had served the business well over the years.

Stabbing that intruder back in 1996 had changed Phoebe. At first, it was a subtle change, but it was there. And then, after Daniel's murder, she really came into her own, transforming from a timid woman who strived to please everyone into this formidable figure who wanted to be at the heart of the family business. She was no cold-blooded killer, though. She'd still do you a good turn at every opportunity. But in recent years, she'd gone from not wanting any part of what went on to being a decision-maker. Phoebe was a voice of reason; a voice that never had mindless violence behind it, but one that was methodical and measured. She was an asset, an asset that both Frank and Archie valued.

'Nice out this way, innit?' Frank remarked, taking in the open fields from his side window.

Archie looked over to him but made no comment.

'What's up – don't you like it round here?'

'Yeah, it's lovely, Grandad, but it's not much different from where you or I live. What's with the small talk? You got nowt else to say?' Archie replied, well aware his grandad was just filling time.

'What's up with you? Didn't get your leg over this morning or something?'

'No, I didn't as a matter of fact, not that it's any of your business, but we surely have more pressing matters to discuss than what it's like on the A17,' Archie retorted, wanting to get back to the business in hand.

'Fuckin' hell, lad, we've been over it so many times already. Kenny will agree to go tomorrow. I know him. He'll do anything for the right money. Phoebe will no doubt ring us to say it's all in hand and then we'll have that bastard taking his last breath before we know it. We can't discuss anything else until we know about Kat, but she'll be on the level. She's desperate to get away from him. Everyone in the game knows Fletcher shags owt that moves, and that he treats her poorly, so why would she not be kosher?'

'Yeah, I suppose, but I just can't see how we can go ahead with the original plan with the cleaner Andrea, if Kat is fuckin' us about.'

'Look, as I've said, if Phoebe smells something fishy, she'll tell us and then we'll have no choice but to take the bull by the horns and revert to plan C – and that is to go in all guns blazing when he least expects it and take him out. That's not my preferred option – far from it – as the fallout would be huge, and that's not what you need, Son. But if it comes to it, then we'll have to sort out the shit as it comes. That's life in this game. But look, I'm sure it won't come to that. Here, take this next left. It's up to the top of the hill on the right.'

Archie turned left and prayed that Kat was playing with a straight bat.

Phoebe stood with Marie, behind two men who were signing in. She smiled to herself as she thought how men had changed over the years. When she first met Daniel, he or any other man she knew would not have been seen dead in a spa. In fact, she tried to remember how many spas there were in Mansfield back then. She could only think of one. Nowadays, no one raised an eyebrow.

They moved forward towards the desk and Marie spoke to the same receptionist as the day before. After explaining that Phoebe also wanted a two-day pass, Phoebe filled in the forms and paid her money, and they went through into the main area. Phoebe used her real name as she'd not had time to sort out any fake ID and besides, she had already decided she was going to be herself with Kat. The "Kat" was out of the bag so to speak, so there was no real need to hide who she was.

Phoebe was impressed with the décor. No expense had been spared and it was certainly a place she would frequent if she lived this way.

'She's over there,' Marie said quietly, as she saw Kat over the other side of the pool. Kat got up and discreetly looked towards the sauna, clearly saying to Marie that she would see her in there. They put their things on their loungers before slowly wandering over. Phoebe noticed a few faces checking them out.

This was the kind of place where a flawless complexion was expected. Phoebe got the impression that standards were high and competition fierce as to who looked the best. Phoebe was a natural beauty, who, like Marie, had only ever used face cream to make her skin look as good as it did. They opened the sauna door and walked in. Kat was alone, as Marie guessed she would be.

'I knew I was right. I knew you'd be here today,' Kat said, genuinely pleased and somewhat relieved. 'What's your real name?'

Marie sat down, with Phoebe next to her. 'Marie. My name's Marie and, yes, you were right, but I need to introduce you to Phoebe. She is one of the main people. Nothing will proceed without Phoebe's agreement.'

Phoebe held out her hand. Kat shook it. Phoebe noticed how soft and dainty her hands were, which reminded her how much older she was than Kat. Kat had evidently had work done to her face, as well as her breasts, and was, to Phoebe, yet another example of how natural beauty was the only way to go. Whilst Kat was beautiful in her own way, Phoebe could see behind the false lips, the eyebrows and the Botox. She thought Kat looked older than her hands said she was. She looked like a doll and, to Phoebe, dolls did not look real.

'How are you?' Phoebe asked, starting off in a nice relaxed fashion. She wanted to gain her trust and to get her on side, she needed to be empathic.

'Fine, except I haven't got long. I never come here on Sundays, ever, so Fletcher was as suspicious as hell today; in fact, at one point, I thought I might not make it, but luckily, well I say luckily, he has other things on his mind today. I heard him on the phone and it kind of took the focus off me. In fact, he ended up just shouting to me to fuck off and do what I like. But I daren't be too long as his focus will come back to me soon enough. But listen, this might mean something to you, I'm not sure, but given what I do know about his beef with your guys, I suspect it will. He's sending some of his men, a guy called Benny Lancashire and others, to Leeds to offload gear in the area today. They are on their way now. I assume that will cause your guys problems. Is Leeds an area you operate in?'

Before Kat had taken a breath, Phoebe was up and out of the sauna. Kat looked at Marie.

'Thanks for that. She's just off to make a phone call. She won't be long,' Marie said. Two days ago, her life was normal. Now it seemed anything but.

Kenny was making a brew. He had not expected his services to be required so soon, but as he knew too well, in this game, he had to react when needed – he'd try and get a few more quid than normal. 'It'll cost, Frank,' he stated, as he passed Frank his tea.

'It'll cost no more than normal. Don't think you're taking me for a mug, Kenny. I know your rates – I've used them enough in the past – so any ideas you have of making me pay any more, forget them. Before we fall out proper.'

'It's just supply and demand, Frank.'

'Get fucked about supply and demand! I demand and you supply. That's how it works, Kenny. Don't try it on.'

Kenny knew he'd not win this one. He'd dealt with Frank a few times in the past and Frank had always paid him on time, in full. He charged a heavy price as it was, so he decided he'd better back down. 'OK, Frank. As always, you win. So, come on, what's the SP?'

'Fletcher O'Brien.'

Kenny nearly choked on his tea. 'O'Brien? Fuckin' hell, Frank, what beef have you with Fletcher?'

'None of your business, you know that. It's irrelevant who it is. All you need to do when we get you in there is do your stuff and rig that house up so that we can control all of the voice commands ... everything. I do not want Fletcher O'Brien to have any control over anything in that house. That's right, Archie, isn't it?'

'That's it, Frank. Look, Kenny, this is your area of expertise. We are in your hands here, but all we want you to do is rig it up and then show us how to control it remotely. It can't be that hard for fuck's sake.'

'It's not if you know what you're doin'. Look, I can do what you ask, no drama, but keep my name out of it. I don't want Fletcher after me if it goes belly up your end.'

Frank put down his tea and walked over to Kenny. 'It won't, Kenny. And you know me from way back. There is no way I would breathe your name to anyone outside of my operation and there's no way anyone in my employ who knows about this would either. So, you've got nothing to worry about.'

Kenny felt a pang of fear rise up. He'd overstepped the mark and he knew it. And, more significantly, so did Frank.

'Please accept my apologies, Frank. No disrespect intended.'

Frank moved away without saying a word and bent down to stroke Kenny's dog. Kenny felt the fear fade from his body.

Archie's phone rang. It was his mum.

'Hi Phoebe. How's things?'

Frank watched as Archie's face changed. Archie

looked at him. Frank knew whatever Phoebe was saying was serious.

'OK, thanks for that. Just carry on as you were. No change.' He put his phone in his pocket. 'So, are we done here, then?'

Frank knew that was a message that they needed to go. 'So, Kenny, wait by your phone, keep it switched on, and wait for our call. Forget whose house it is and just do your thing. We will take care of everything and you'll get your fat wedge as soon as the job is done. But expect our call either later today or tomorrow.'

Kenny nodded. He looked scared. Both Frank and Archie noticed.

As soon as they got outside, Frank asked what was up.

'That was my mum. Fletcher has sent that Benny guy to Leeds with a few others. They're planning to do the same to Leeds as they did to Nottingham – flood it with gear. We can't stand by, not this time.'

'Get in the car,' Frank said. He sat in the passenger side in silence. Archie let him think. Frank knew what he would do. He wanted to know if Archie would do similar.

'What you gonna do then, Son?' he asked.

Archie hated it when he did this. He knew Frank had thought it through in those few seconds. Archie had been too busy waiting for his grandad to think it over. He stared straight ahead. He pondered. He weighed things up. 'We can't stand back again, Frank.

We can't allow Fletcher to take the piss twice.'

'I agree, Son, one hundred per cent, but to keep him guessing, don't do what he wants you to do. What would he want you to do?'

'Go over there, all guns blazing.'

'Exactly. So, we deal with the problem in Leeds and leave it there. We tell Trainer, we get some more men up to Leeds and we take out the men he's sent – but we make no contact with Fletcher. Don't let him reel you in, but send him the message that any men he sends over will be dealt with. We are so close to taking him out he has no idea. Don't ruin it now by reacting. Remember: respond.'

Archie's phone rang. It was Trainer. 'We've a problem, Archie.'

'Let me guess ... some guys from Manchester are selling drugs in Leeds?'

'Yep. They're in Roundhay, just off Roundhay Road and into Roundhay itself. Normally I'd be there now, but given the current circs, what do you want me to do?'

'Sort them out, Trainer. Good and proper. But listen – if you can, take them to the club. I want to see them. Me and Frank will be there in about an hour and a half, give or take a few minutes. Take no prisoners, Trainer. This is your time to shine. We'll see you at the club.'

Archie sped out of the driveway and down to the A17, towards Newark and the A1. It was then a straight road to Leeds.

chapter thirty-two

Richie was staring out of his bedroom window. It was all he did. It was all he could do really. The only difference was when he received his monthly visits from Frank and the weekly visits from the one other person who came to see him. Frank would sit with him for an hour. He would tell Richie what was happening in the family and with the business, things Richie couldn't care less about. Frank just wanted to spend time with the son he'd put in a wheelchair. He'd reminisce, often talking about the period when Richie had been back in the family fold. It had been Frank's favourite time of his life. No one knew, of course, but Frank would on occasion tell Richie that and he'd say how sorry he was and how he regretted what happened.

Richie would just stare in his direction. His eyes were the only thing he could control. Richie felt nothing for his father. He had hated him all of his life. Frank had made it clear from a very young age that Richie was to blame for the death of his and Daniel's mother, Renee, and Richie had grown to despise his dad more and more because of it. He had played the game to a degree a few years back, to court favour for a short while – the same period that Frank looked back on so fondly – but save for that, he'd felt nothing but loathing for his dad. Of course, Richie knew full well that in the early part of his life that hate was only a mask for the love and adulation he'd craved as a youngster. But, as he'd grown up, it was indeed pure hatred. He'd like nothing better than to see Frank Pearson dead. The only thing that kept Richie going was the thought of maybe seeing that happen one day and finally being able to be free of him. He blamed his father for putting him in there and for him being nothing more than a dribbling, hateful man.

Frank had had a choice when he'd found out about Daniel's murder. He could have tried to understand, to try and accept some of the responsibility for how Richie had turned out, but Frank being Frank meant there was no room in his life for sentiment. Frank only knew one way to deal with what he'd seen as betrayal and that was to maim and torture. He was the one responsible for Richie behaving like he had all those years. He was responsible for Richie being the man he was then and for the wreck he was today.

Richie was hell-bent on revenge. He detested just about everyone and just about everything, and despised what his life had become. That was Frank's plan, of course – to make sure he lived out the rest of his life as a bitter man. Richie cared not that Frank felt remorse.

He was looking forward to this afternoon, though. He was expecting his weekly visitor. He loved it when they came. Today they were a little late, but Richie didn't mind. He heard footsteps and knew whose they were. It was amazing how your senses improved when you relied on them so much. Richie heard the door open.

'Hiya Dad, sorry I'm late. Work stuff and all that, even on a Sunday. How are you?' Johnny said. He could see a smile forming; a little one but a definite curl of the lip. 'I can stay a little longer as I've told Alice I'll be late getting to hers.' He held Richie's hands and started to massage them.

Richie now only cared about one thing and that was his son. He'd known nothing of Johnny until just over two years ago, when this young man came into his life. He'd never had plans to have children. He'd never thought himself worthy. Marie was the only woman who he might've considered trying with, but she'd put paid to that when she betrayed him seven years ago. He no longer wished to see Marie dead. He knew she was a good'un deep down and that she'd just found herself in a position she couldn't deal with. Marie crossed the line in Venice and was really someone who should never have taken that step. But she had, and it was Richie who ultimately paid the price. He didn't regret going to Venice – he was after a guy who owed him fifteen grand at the time – but he regretted his actions over there. Events in Venice had ultimately led to him being how he was now. He should have walked away when that Italian guy challenged him in the hotel corridor. He didn't and things were never the same from that day on. Marie had ended up with the family home, his home, and he'd ended up in a wheelchair being fed by his carers.

Johnny had been Alice's boyfriend for a few months when he first came to see Richie on his own and told him who he was. He'd admittedly used Alice as a way to get close to the family, something that was a huge risk – still was – and which Richie couldn't talk to him about. He'd been sceptical at first when Johnny claimed to be his son. He'd not believed it, but little things that Johnny knew, things that only him and his mother could know, convinced Richie that he was his father. This, along with wanting to see Frank take his last breath, was what kept Richie breathing.

It turned out that a one-night stand with a brunette in Loughborough over twenty years ago, over the bonnet of her Ford Capri, had produced the one thing that was good in Richie's life. And now he came every week, sometimes more than once a week, and the best thing about it was that no one knew. No one knew he came and no one knew Richie had a son. That was the little bit of power Richie had left. It was their secret. It would come out soon, but only when the time was right.

Johnny was a physiotherapist who believed that there was always hope. He'd not known about Richie's condition, of course, when he'd first decided to become one, but the fact that he had, meant he could work on his dad. He'd had many arguments during his training with very senior people in the field about how hope was never lost. He would get told that sometimes there was no hope, but he refused to believe it, and here was proof. Johnny would work with Richie every time he came to get some movement in his muscles. He just knew it was possible. If there was a desire, he was sure something could be achieved.

'Move your fingers, Dad,' he said, and watched and smiled as Richie wiggled them. He again saw that little smile. 'Make a fist.' He marvelled on seeing his father, who was told he would never move anything again other than his eyes, clench his hands. Johnny opened them and placed his right forefinger in Richie's right hand. Richie then closed it and squeezed.

'You're getting stronger there, Dad. Definitely stronger than last time. Without a doubt. We're getting there, Dad. Slowly, but we're getting there.'

Richie wished he could hug Johnny. He'd had that pleasure taken from him. He might never hug his son, ever, and it hurt Richie like nothing else. He looked at Johnny and as best he could, he tried to relay his feelings to him. He never wanted days like today to end. The only reason he was ever happy to see Johnny go was so that tomorrow would come, and then the next day, and with every new dawn, he was a day closer to him coming back to see him.

A couple of hours later, Johnny left and made a phone call to his uncle. He often rang him when he left his dad's room. Not every time, but more often than not.

'A slight improvement today, Unc. Only slight, but it's going in the right direction.'

chapter thirty-three

Phoebe calmly walked back into the sauna. She took her seat next to Marie. The fact Kat had given her that information suggested she was on the level. Phoebe decided to give her the benefit of the doubt and treat her as though she was fully on side.

'So, Kat, let's cut to the chase. Cards on the table, face up. You want free of that husband of yours, yes?'

'At any cost, Phoebe. As I said to Marie yesterday, I just want out. I just want to be free. I have all the money I could dream of, yet I bet I haven't got more than a tenner in my purse. I have two men waiting for me in the car park who drop me off here. I have no life, just whatever life Fletcher decides I can have. So, yes, I want free of the bastard.'

'Then we can help each other. Your husband has taken a real liberty with my father-in-law, Frank Pearson, and my son, Archie Pearson. A liberty that cannot go unpunished. He has to be dealt with. Of that, there is no doubt. How that happens largely depends on you, but we want to move quickly. We need access to your house at a time when your husband is not there. We need to get a guy in there. Your house is a smart house, isn't it?'

'Yes.'

'We need to get access to your house so we can control the system remotely, so any controls you have need to be available. That's all you need to know. Once we have access, we need to know when your husband will be alone. You and your children cannot be there,' Phoebe said, trying to make sure Kat was taking all of this in. 'Do you understand, Kat? You will not see your husband again. Do you realise what you are doing here?'

Kat nodded. 'I do. Tomorrow morning would be the best time as Fletcher has a meeting at his main club in Manchester every Monday morning without fail. He always leaves the house early, normally around 8:30. The only person who will be there other than me will be the cleaner. She comes three times a week.'

'Right, so we could sort out what we need to sort tomorrow morning then. That's good. What about after then? When is Fletcher likely to be in the house on his own?' Phoebe asked.

'The only time he's in the house on his own really is when he's shagging the cleaner. He thinks I don't know, but I've known for ages. But do you really need to wait for that. All you have to do is let me know when your guys are doing whatever you have planned and I will be ready to leave. Unless you are planning to blow the house up, I could just leave when you arrive, couldn't I?'

Phoebe nodded in acknowledgement. Kat was right. With her on board, there was no real need to wait for Fletcher to be in on his own.

'OK, so tomorrow morning we will be at your house. There will be two men. One of ours and a guy who will rig up your smart house system.'

Kat sat back. 'Shit!' she said out loud. 'I forgot about the security. Fletcher has two men at the house 24/7. He says he doesn't like CCTV. Reckons it's 'cos it can be hacked, but I know it's so no one can see the women he brings back. He has a couple of cameras outside showing some of the grounds but not on the gates or anything. It's never made sense to me but whatever. Anyway, two of his men are on rotas all day every day patrolling the grounds and the house. Shit, I never gave them a thought.'

Phoebe sat back too and tried to think. 'Could they not be distracted somehow?' she asked, looking for anything to hang on to.

Kat sighed. 'There's only really Andrea.'

'Who?' Phoebe asked, knowing full well who Andrea was.

'The cleaner. She could maybe ask them to help her with something. I know it's a long shot, but she's our only hope. Only thing is I hardly speak to her, you know – 'cos she's shagging Fletcher behind my back.'

'Leave her to me,' Phoebe said.

'Eh? How?'

'Just trust me. Can she park her car around the back of the house?'

'It's where she always parks.'

'Excellent. Just leave it to me. I will arrange for Andrea to park her car around the back as normal. I'll make sure there's something wrong with her car, flat tyre or something, that she can easily get those two helping her with. They'll both think with their cocks, won't they?'

'Oh yes, all Fletcher's men think with their cocks,' Kat said. 'Well, most of them anyway. The only decent one seems to be Duffy.'

They spoke for a while longer, ironing out the details. Phoebe gave Kat a burner phone.

'That's untraceable, Kat,' she said. 'Keep it with you and only communicate with us with that. And only if you really have to. There are three numbers in it: mine, Marie's and Archie's. Archie is under the letter A, I'm under P and Marie is M.'

Kat took the phone and nodded. They were all clear on what was to happen. They left separately, making sure there was at least five minutes between them. Kat left first, with Phoebe and Marie following. They didn't want to be seen together.

chapter thirty-four

Del was on his way to Leeds. Frank had rung him to
tell him of the situation up there as he and Archie
knew he'd want to be a part of it. They were right. He
was an angry man, but he was also a man who knew
he had to be as calm as he could. If he let his feelings
run away with him, he'd be like a man possessed and
would bring unnecessary heat down onto the firm. As
much as he wanted revenge, he didn't want to do that.
Frank and Archie trusted him to act accordingly, and
in return to trust them that he would get the revenge
he craved. He was sat in the passenger seat of an
untraceable car. His brother, Michael, was driving
and his two sons, Des and Ryan, were in the back.
Steven and Pat were in the car behind. Archie and
Frank were around ten minutes in front of them
according to the last conversation they'd had. Del was
to meet Trainer and a couple of others somewhere
near Roundhay. The sat nav said seventeen minutes
to the rendezvous. Del's phone rang. It was Trainer.

'Del, it's me. Listen, I've got three of them in my
sight now. They're chattin' on a street corner – they're

sitting ducks. I can't wait for you, mate. I can't let them go as this is a golden chance. Archie told me to explain it to you, 'cos I know how important this all is to you.'

'Look, Trainer, no problem, mate. I get it, but I assume you're gonna take them to the club to meet Frank and Archie?'

'Yes, pal, I am. How far away are you?'

'Quarter of an hour or so. Just passed Wakey.'

'OK. Go straight to the club, pal, and we'll see you there.'

Trainer put his phone back in his pocket. He was parked about seventy yards from the three guys. They looked decent blokes who could handle themselves, but he was in good company. He had three of his most trusted with him: a guy called Kempsy, from Wakefield; a bloke from Kirkstall called Garry Porthouse; and a shaven-headed psycho called Downsey, who had only recently been released for doing five years for robbery. He'd been called Downsey since he was a lad 'cos he was always getting sent down. He was now mid-forties and had never really learnt his lesson. All three were frontliners, and men to be relied upon.

'Right, fellas. Time to go to work. Nice and easy, Kempsy, but when we get close, brakes on and then straight out, all of you. No matter what resistance we get, I want them fuckers in here sharpish. There's three of them and four of us, plus we have the element of surprise on our side, so no fuckin' messin', OK?'

Kempsy drove quite slowly as he approached. They were still huddled together talking. One of them had a rucksack on his shoulder. As Kempsy reached around twenty yards away, he accelerated hard and drove straight into them, knocking them over. Garry and Downsey jumped straight out and punched two of them hard as they tried to get up. Kempsy was out before the van had stopped and headbutted the third as he rose to his feet. By the time Trainer had realised what was happening, they were in the back of the van, with Garry and Downsey somehow knelt on all three of them. They had both drawn their guns. The three guys from Manchester had two guns pointed at them by the time they knew what had happened.

They were all swearing and spouting the usual shit about how Downsey and Garry were dead meat and that they'd come back and kill them, plus they were screaming from the effects of a transit van knocking into them.

'For fuck's sake, lads, whose idea was that to run the fuckers over?' Trainer asked. Kempsy was climbing back into the driver's seat when he said, 'Mine, Boss. I said to these two earlier, if I got the chance, I would run the fuckers over. Can't run then, can they? Just thought it would be easier!' he said, laughing his head off. 'The fuckin' bellends!' he shouted as he checked his wing mirror and drove off.

Trainer shook his head. 'Well, fair play. It *was* easy. Far easier than I thought it would be!' he yelled into the back, to make sure they heard him.

One of the men on the van floor shook his head. 'Do you know who you are dealin' with? I hope you said goodbye to your missus this morning, fella, 'cos you won't see her again,' he said, as he eyed Downsey.

Downsey put the gun into his left hand and chinned the guy on the floor with his right. He said nothing. The guy just spat out some blood from his mouth and laughed.

Garry then threw the rucksack to Trainer. 'Here, Trainer.' Trainer opened it and saw it was half full with little polybags; some with pills in them, some with white powder. The usual stuff. He zipped it back up and placed it in the footwell. Kempsy then made them all empty their pockets and took the phones and cash they had on them.

Frank and Archie were at the club. They heard the sound of a van pulling into the yard. Archie glanced at the TV monitor. It was Trainer.

'They're here, Frank,' he confirmed. They both headed towards the back door that led to the rear car park. They opened it to see Downsey and Garry dragging the three of them out at gun point. Kempsy then came from round the far side. Trainer walked to stand at the side of Archie.

'These are the three fellas I rang you about.' He then heard the sound of vehicles and watched as Del and the others, followed by Steven and Pat, came into view. As Del got out, Trainer threw him a baseball bat. Downsey then passed Archie the rucksack and showed him the mobiles and cash. Archie told him to keep them.

'These are the three I told you about, Del,' Trainer hollered. Del caught the bat in his right hand and swung it through the air. It made a loud swish that everyone knew would inflict proper pain. Del looked at Archie, who gave him the green light. He then casually strolled around to stand square on. He took a step forward and looked at them all individually. None of them were any of the men who were at the club when it had been smashed up the other day. He turned to Frank and Archie.

'Well, none of these smashed your club up, Frank, but they're still gonna pay.' He then swung the baseball bat back and smashed it into the right knee of the man stood to his left, bringing him to the ground. He screamed in agony as he held what was left of his kneecap. Del could tell the one in the middle, who was next, wanted to launch himself and take the fight to them. The gun that Downsey had pointed at him made him remain rooted to the spot. Del then smashed that guy's right kneecap, and that of the one beside him. They both, as their friend had, dropped to the ground, holding their smashed knees. Archie and Frank noticed the one in the middle had hardly made a sound. He was certainly the top guy of this little threesome. He was the one Archie would focus on.

Ryan and Des, along with their uncle, Michael, dragged the three of them inside the club. Kempsy and Trainer put three chairs in the centre of the room.

They then sat each of them down. The one who was evidently the leader was placed in the middle. The other two were still moaning about the state of their knees. He, however, kept Archie's gaze, as Archie pulled up a chair of his own and sat down in front of him about ten feet away. 'You won't get away with this,' he stated to Archie.

'Oh, I think I might. Well, put it this way, I don't think the bookies would take my bet. Too short odds, you see. Now, what's your name?'

'Get fucked.'

Archie smiled. 'Nice. Now, I'll ask you once more. What's your name?'

'Fuck off,' he replied.

Archie looked at Del and nodded. Del walked round to face him. He then looked at Downsey. 'If he flinches, Downsey, before I make contact, shoot him,' he told him. Both Del and Downsey knew full well only Archie or Frank could give an order to kill, but the guy sat down didn't, and that's all that mattered.

Del swung the bat back slowly to make sure Archie was out of his range and then, as hard as he could, he smashed it right into the guy's left kneecap. He fell clean off the chair and shouted loudly and slowly as the pain ripped through his leg. 'For fuck's sake!'

Archie allowed him the dignity of quietening down before he asked him again, 'So what's your name?'

'Go fuck yaself!' he roared, using it as a way to mask the pain.

'Pass me your lighter, Ryan,' Archie shouted, so as to be heard above the noise. As he waited a second or two for Ryan to pass him his lighter, he looked at the other two guys sat either side. They did not hold his gaze, but looked away. That confirmed to Archie he was dealing with the right man. He took the lighter and flicked up the top, then lit it. It was quite a tall flame.

'Hold his left arm out straight, Michael!' he ordered. He then passed Del the lighter. Del held it under the guy's arm. about an inch or so from his skin.

'What's your name?' Archie asked again.

'Fuck you,' he answered, although this time he sounded noticeably less aggressive.

Archie nodded to Del. Michael held the guy's arm firm. He was strong, but Michael made sure it was as steady as he could make it. Del then lit the lighter and watched as it burned into the guy's skin. He screamed in agony as it blistered and bled. Del could smell the burning flesh as the aroma filled the air around the group of men who were watching. Archie was impressed how long the guy held out.

'It's Harry. My name's Harry.'

'Harry what?'

'Harry Davies.'

Archie gave a nod and Del pulled the lighter away. Michael let Harry's arm drop.

'So, how many more are there of you, Harry?' Archie asked.

'No idea. I just came with these two. I don't know.' He was now sounding quite pitiful.

'Michael, get his arm again, please.'

'OK, OK, there's four more. That's all, just four more.'

'And where are these four?'

'No idea. It's the first time I've ever been to Leeds. I couldn't tell you.'

Archie was just about to order Michael to hold his arm again when one of the others piped up. 'Honestly, mate, we have no idea. We were just dropped off here with Harry. Honestly. That's the truth.'

Archie looked at him, for a good few seconds. He believed him. 'Is Benny Lancashire with them?'

The guy looked to the floor. That told Archie he was.

'Michael, get his arm.'

'Yeah, he is,' the guy said.

'And the names of the others?' Archie asked.

'I don't know. Honestly, I don't know.'

'Harry, who does Benny have with him?'

'I ain't tellin' you any names. You can kill me if you like, but I ain't grassin' names. You can fuck off.'

Michael received the nod and got hold of Harry's arm again. Del burnt his lighter into his arm in the same spot as before. Harry cried in agony. 'Stuart Fox,' he blurted. 'Stuart Fox, Damien Morton and a fella called Dickie. Don't know his real name. Only met him this morning.'

Downsey scrolled through one of the phones. 'All of their names and numbers are in here, Archie.' He then passed it to Archie, who thought for a second. He looked at Frank. He wasn't sure why, but he often did that when he needed reassurance or guidance. Frank gave him nothing, but then there was nothing to give.

He then decided to text Dickie. He was the last name to be said, so Archie guessed he was of the least importance and would be the least likely to suspect anything. *How's things going? Where are ya?* He then waited.

As he did so, Harry said, 'You better finish me off, Archie, 'cos I'm a fuckin' dead man if you send me back there.' Archie nodded. It was the least he could do to a fellow criminal. He knew the score and so did Harry. Archie was going to have them killed anyway. These three would not see the light of day again, but he felt it was only right to let Harry know. The phone pinged. *We're on some estate in Harehills. Big council estate. Benny's fucked off somewhere. Come over, the estate's fuckin' huge.*

Frank's club was in Harehills. It was the same club that he'd taken over nearly thirty years ago from Gerry Clarke. They only used it as a meeting place now, but that meant the rest of the guys were close.

'How far is the big council estate from here, Trainer?'

'Two minutes in my van. Is that where they are?'

'Yep. Is there a row of shops or a chippy or something there?'

'Yeah, right on the big roundabout. A row of shops. Tell 'em to meet you there in ten minutes. We'll have 'em back here in no time.'

Archie texted back. *There's a row of shops near the big roundabout. See you there in 10.* It pinged straight back with a thumbs-up.

'Bring 'em back, Trainer. In one piece. All four of 'em, if you can, but that Benny Lancashire has gone AWOL apparently, so just the other three if needs be. Though I'd prefer all four.'

Trainer left with Kempsy, Garry, Downsey, Ryan and Des. The rest stayed put. Michael and Del took over holding them at gunpoint. Archie gave the order to put Harry out of his misery. Del took the gun from his inside jacket pocket. He knew this was not the man who killed his son, but he was still going to hand out some retribution.

Harry saw the gun. He knew what was coming but he didn't make a sound and he didn't flinch. Del stood poised for a few seconds, as he looked Harry in the eye. Harry thought for a moment he may have had a reprieve. But Del was just savouring it. Harry met his hard stare and Del then shot him twice. Harry slumped back and died a quiet death. Everyone there watched with respect, as Harry Davies took what was coming to him like a man.

Trainer and the rest pulled up a few minutes later in the same white transit van they'd used to bring in Harry and the two others. They were parked a hundred yards or so from the row of shops. They couldn't see anyone. They waited and watched. Trainer and Kempsy were in the front again with Kempsy driving. He wasn't planning to run them over this time. There were too many people about. More than they'd bargained for. Trainer remarked how his parents would always tell him that Sundays used to be a family day. Nowadays, everyone was out and about like any other day. Sundays were no longer a day of rest.

Trainer told Ryan to get out and hang about, and to approach the three blokes for a score once they'd appeared. That would distract them and allow the van to sneak up. The plan was to jump out and bundle them in the back. Ryan got out and walked towards the shops. He hung about outside of the chippy. It was closed at this time on a Sunday. He'd been there for around two minutes when three men came around the corner. He waited. He knew Trainer was going to text Dickie. Ryan could just hear the sound of a text coming through. A man, who looked in his early thirties, was texting a reply. Ryan then looked at his own phone. It was on silent. He stared at the screen and watched as a text came through. *It's them.*

Ryan put his phone in his pocket and approached them. 'All right, lads,' he said. They all looked up at him. 'You got any gear goin'? Some white powder would be good. Had a shit day, just need a little something for later. Know what I mean.'

One of the others nodded. He looked older than Dickie, the guy with the phone. He had presence. He was broad across the chest, with tattoos down both forearms.

'Why would you think we had any gear?' he asked.

Ryan noticed his broad Manchester accent. He wondered whether he was involved in his brother's murder. He remained calm. 'Hey mate, no drama. Just wondered, that's all. My mistake.' Ryan began to walk away, knowing they were likely to call him back, which they did.

'Hey!' the guy with the tattoos shouted. 'I didn't say we never did, did I? Here, how much you after?'

Ryan stopped and turned around. That was Trainer's cue. Kempsy started the van. He drove slowly towards the roundabout and the row of shops. Trainer had his eyes fixed on the group. The guy with the tattoos was opening a rucksack. Kempsy parked the van, just as he was showing Ryan some clear polybags. Trainer got out, as though he was going to the shops, but he wanted to be the right side of the van from the off. The three guys with Ryan were totally oblivious to him. Kempsy got out too. He stretched his arms above his head and yawned. It appeared perfectly normal, just as if he'd been driving for a while. Trainer banged on the side of the van. The three guys, along with Ryan, instinctively looked up. Des, Downsey and Garry flew out of the back. By this time, Trainer had smacked Dickie straight in the face. Ryan had headbutted the guy with the tattoos. Des, Downsey and Garry all had baseball bats, which they hit the three men mercilessly with. They had no time to retaliate; their faces now bloodied. Within fifty seconds of Trainer banging the van, all three were in the back. By the time a minute had passed, the van was driving off back towards the club.

Not one bystander said a word. Most never even looked up from tapping away on their mobiles. They knew better than to get involved. Only one person who had seen what had happened was shocked. Benny Lancashire had just parked his car fifty yards away. He'd just seen the back end of what had happened. He turned his engine off. *Fuck.*

Benny had gone AWOL around an hour before. He'd been to Leeds a few times over the years for nights out and every time he came, he had a guaranteed shag from a nice blonde who lived in Chapel Allerton. She was early forties but a real looker and an even better shag. Benny had been known to travel over to Leeds, purely for an hour or so with her, so he was not going to miss getting his dick sucked today. He now wished he had. Fletcher had told him specifically to keep the lads together and to stay with them. Benny had ignored that. He'd decided to split them into two groups in order to spread the problem for whoever was now running Leeds for Frank and Archie. And he'd also decided to fuck off for a shag. He now had a serious problem. He rang Harry. There was no answer. He left a message: *"Harry, it's me. Slight problem, pal. Looks like Stu and his lads have been bundled off in a van. Ring me mate. ASAP. We need to talk."*

Benny sat and thought. It was very unlike Harry not to answer. He always had his phone on him. He wondered if they'd also been rumbled. Benny didn't like the situation he was in. If Fletcher found out that he'd not been around when his men were attacked, he knew he'd make him pay. And if his men had been murdered, Benny knew the same fate awaited him. Benny hit the steering wheel. 'Fuck, fuck, fuck!' He always said his dick would be the death of him, but he thought it would be by some sexual disease. Certainly not like this. He knew it was time to make the call. He dialled the number. George Burbanks answered.

'Benny, lad, what's happening? Anything new I need to know about?'

'Hi George, yes, there is. Look, I've fucked up and I need out. It's time for me to collect my wedge and fuck off.'

'Steady on, boy. I tell you when it's time to fuck off. Let's get that straight for a start. Don't think you can ring me up and tell ME what's happening. Now start again. What's happened?'

'We're in Leeds today, as you know, but, well, let's just say I fucked off for a shag and when I came back, I saw Stuart and two others get bundled into the back of a white van, so I reckon Frank and Archie's men have them. I've tried Harry but no answer, so I suspect they've got them too. Thing is, I was under strict instructions to keep the group as one and well, stay with 'em, so you can see my predicament. If Fletcher gets wind of any of that, I'm a fucking dead man, so with the greatest of respect, I'd like to cash in my chips and fuck off as planned, if that's OK, Mr Burbanks.'

That was the first time Benny had called George Mr Burbanks and George knew it was because he was now in the shit, but George was a man of his word and he'd told Benny when he'd first summoned him to his offices that if he could orchestrate a war with Fletcher and Frank, where Frank took Fletcher out, he'd pay him handsomely and, to be fair, it was looking like he would succeed on that. George and Ivan had told Benny what they wanted from him and how to go about it and Benny, up until fucking off for that shag, had followed it to the letter. They'd chosen Benny because they knew he wanted to be rich and that, for easy money, he'd do almost anything. They'd also told him, whilst one of their men had a gun in his bollocks, that if he didn't agree, they'd shoot his dick off right there and then. If he ever breathed a word, they'd hunt him down and kill him where he stood. In return, if he succeeded, they'd pay him a quarter of a million pounds and give him a villa in Spain. That's how much they wanted Manchester to themselves – and Fletcher O'Brien out of the picture. Manchester would run so much better without Fletcher around. Benny had jumped at it and had come up trumps. The only slight issue was that the job was not quite finished and Benny had gone off script by popping off to see that blonde.

'Come straight to the office, Benny. Don't answer your phone to anyone. Just come straight here.'

Benny started his car and drove to meet George and Ivan. If he was honest, he was unsure what to expect.

Archie listened to the message. He laughed. 'Looks like Benny is now aware what's happened. Shall I send him a photo of his mate Harry?' he said, addressing everyone.

Frank immediately spoke. 'No, Son, definitely not. Remember our best weapon is our silence. Tell them nothing. They'll be going mad with not knowing what we are doing. Let Benny deal with it his end. Keep the element of surprise, Son.'

Archie nodded. He knew Frank was right. This was no local spat between local hard men. This was with Fletcher O'Brien.

'Well, he'll certainly be expecting a call back, so when he doesn't get one, I'd love to know what he'll tell Fletcher,' Archie said, just as they heard the sound of a van pulling into the car park.

A minute or so later, Trainer and the rest came in with the three guys they'd just lifted. Three more chairs had been placed in the centre of the room for them. The guy with the tattoos was shouting all sorts, as he was marched over to a chair, full of bravado, telling Archie he'd kill him personally. Archie said nothing. He just stared at him and let him vent his anger. After around thirty seconds of being placed into his seat, he realised there was an empty chair next to Harry's two men. He quietened down. 'Where's Harry?' he asked.

'Michael!' Archie shouted.

The guy with the tattoos looked on in horror, as he saw Michael drag in the lifeless body that was his friend Harry Davies. He dropped the bravado, recognising the mess he was in. He tried to remain strong. He knew he'd end up like this one day and had always told himself that, faced with the situation he was now in, that he wouldn't give a fuck. He always told himself that he'd never weaken. He now realised that was a lot harder than he'd always imagined.

'Eye for an eye, is it?' he said, trying to sound calm. 'Well, I heard that fella of yours Shaney did over never even fought back. A fuckin' pussy he was! Shaney slit his throat like he was spreading butter. He was fuck all!'

Pat held Del back. Steven held Michael back. Archie knew it was time to do this fucker.

'All yours, Del,' he said.

Del stepped forward. He picked a knife up off the table and slowly walked over. The guy tried to muster a laugh, but Del could see he was scared. He tried to wrestle free of Trainer, but Trainer held him firm. Downsey pointed his gun. The guy's breathing quickened. He was virtually panting. Del looked him up and down.

'My son was no pussy. He was worth ten of you. I wish I could torture the life out of you, but I promised myself you would die the same way. You piece of shit!'

The guy's eyes widened. Del pushed his forehead

back to open up his neck. He watched him the whole time, never averting his gaze. The bloke tried to move his head, but it was futile. Del slit his throat. He let go of his forehead and he slumped forward. Del then watched in silence as he died where he was sat.

'So, Del, we now know who killed Paul. You'll have your moment, Del,' Frank said.

Del told Archie that the others were just foot soldiers. He felt no need to do the same to them. He'd had enough of killing today, but he thanked him for giving him the opportunity. Downsey then shot two of them; Trainer, the other two.

Frank took his phone from his pocket. He needed six bodies disposed of. This was going to cost. By 5:30 that Sunday afternoon, Frank and Archie were back at Frank's house. The man Frank had called, a man he'd used many times before, had been in to collect the bodies and dispose of them without a trace. Trainer had paid him his share. The clean-up had been done. No one other than those who were there had any knowledge of what had happened that day.

Benny had an inkling, but that was all. He had ten missed calls from Fletcher – he'd ignored them all. Benny knew, as he drove to meet the Burbankses, he needed to move quickly.

Frank and Archie had rung Phoebe on the way down. She would be waiting for them at Frank's along with Marie, Jez and Brian. They needed to hear a full account of her chat with Kat and the plan moving forward. Both Frank and Archie knew that time was short. Once Fletcher had wind of his men seemingly disappearing, they could expect serious shit.

chapter thirty-five

Kenny Walters had a scotch in hand, while he waited for the call. He was nervous about this one, very nervous. So much so, the voice in his head was telling him to walk away. He had no desire to work for Frank against Fletcher O'Brien, but he felt he had no choice. If he backed out, Frank would make him pay – and pay dearly. You didn't say no to Frank Pearson.

He'd also done jobs for Fletcher in the past and knew him well – well enough to know that if he got so much as a sniff about this, he'd kill him. Kenny was in a predicament and he didn't like it one bit. He'd never done a job for a main player against another main player before. This was new territory, and one he was not looking forward to. He'd worked for all of the main faces – the likes of Frank, Fletcher, the Burbanks brothers, Greg West, and Tariq Mali in London, all of them – at one time or another. His line of work was one that not too many dealt in. He'd earned good money over the years, hence why he'd been able to buy the beautiful house he now had up for sale in Leadenham, in the Lincolnshire countryside.

He paced up and down. He sipped his scotch and looked at the suitcase at the foot of the stairs. He downed the last of his whisky and felt the burn on his throat. He wiped his mouth with the back of his hand, ran upstairs, picking up the empty suitcase on the way. He then quickly packed a few clothes, stuffing them in without really thinking too much about what he was taking. At this point, anything would do. Kenny decided he was going to fuck off right there and then. He grabbed his phone and his car keys, and had a quick drink of water. He took out of the sideboard in the living room, his file that had all of his personal stuff in – things like utility bills, passport, bank statements. He kept them all in one place. His whole identity was in that file; he could not afford to leave it behind. He looked around as he realised exactly what he was doing. He had to get away, though. He would ring the estate agents the next day and tell them to sell it with all the furniture included. Kenny was never coming back.

'Come on, lad,' he said softly to his British bulldog, who was snoring away in his bed. 'We've got a long drive, pal.'

Bertie yawned and stretched out as Kenny put on his lead. He got Bertie in the boot, went back in to collect his bed and food and then finally carried the suitcase to his car. He was going to Shetland. Frank Pearson could fuck off.

'This one's not for me, Frank,' he said to himself, as he locked his door.

chapter thirty-six

Benny walked up the stairs flanked by Shaun Bonsall, the same guy in the Burbanks firm who'd taken him up the last time he was there. That was just over two months ago. He could hardly believe everything that had happened in the past nine or ten weeks. That was the day that changed his life ... again. The previous time was when he'd first met Fletcher after shagging that bird on the golf course that his father used to be a member of. The shame had been too much for his dad. In fact, he'd all but given up golf. He played a few rounds on a local municipal course now and again but that was it.

Benny had agreed, in return for a very large sum of cash, to orchestrate some kind of war between Fletcher O'Brien and Frank Pearson. It had been quite easy really. He'd just planted an idea inside Fletcher's head that Frank and his grandson, Archie, were sitting ducks. Frank was in his late sixties and Archie was still very much heir apparent. Benny had merely sown the seed. He'd just dropped it in conversation a couple of times and, as expected, Fletcher had taken the bait.

George had told Benny as much. He'd assured him that was all he needed to do, and he'd been right. Benny had had to keep the thing going, though. He'd had to make sure that Frank and Archie responded, though he and the Burbanks knew they would; in what way, Benny had not been sure. He'd half expected all-out war with bodies lying everywhere. George, however, knew Frank would respond how he did, which is what he'd wanted all along. George was yet to hear the finer details of when and where, but the silence from Frank was deafening. George knew Frank was planning something and Benny had told him that Fletcher was in the dark, as he'd hoped he would be. It had all gone to plan, except for today's little escapade in Leeds. George had not banked on the Pearsons carrying that out today, but it mattered not. George and his brother, Ivan, were well off radar. They were just waiting to pick up the pieces.

Benny walked into the plush office and firmly shook George's hand for the second time in two months. Ivan never got up, like last time. Benny sat in the same chair as before, feeling slightly nervous. He was unsure what to expect from this meeting.

'So, Benny, have you heard anything further?' George asked.

'Nothing, Mr Burbanks. I've had so many missed calls from Fletcher I've lost count. I haven't even listened to the messages. I'm just hoping that he's not made contact with any of the others and, well, I'm hoping he thinks I've come a cropper, you know. Been done in like.'

'Pass me your phone,' Ivan said, as he leant forward. He took it off Benny and pressed for the voicemails. He then placed it on the desk. There were three messages.

The first one was Fletcher. *"Benny, it's me. What the fuck's happenin'? You were supposed to keep me updated. Now fuckin' ring me as soon as."*

Message two was very similar. Message three was different. *"I don't know what the fuck is going on, Benny, but you better have a very good explanation. I can't get in touch with any of you. This ain't right. If he's done you all, I'll have the fuckin' lot of 'em. It'll be all-out fuckin' war ... AAAAARRRRGGGHHHH!"*

George smiled. He sat back in his chair. 'Well, it would appear Fletcher is a tad upset, Benny. Now you obviously need to disappear. You've done your job – well, most of it – but you are leaving a few loose ends.'

He looked at Benny and Benny could see he was thinking. Benny knew he was not going to come out of this with his full wedge, but he couldn't give a shit. He could see Ivan staring at the two blokes who were stood at the door. Benny felt a twinge of terror. He was expecting a shot to the head. George then sat forward, placing his elbows on the desk in the same way he had when Benny first sat down.

'I'm a man of my word, Benny, as is my dear brother, Ivan. We carry the same morals and values as our father did, but we cannot ignore the fact you have left it somewhat messy. You fucked off for a shag and, well, let's just say that was a big mistake. A mistake that may have repercussions. A mistake that we did not want.' George paused. He took a deep breath and sighed. 'So, we will pay you half of your money.'

George stopped and looked Benny straight in the eye. He was waiting for a response. Benny was relieved. He'd expected to be done over, not walking away with £125,000. He'd be on the run for as long as Fletcher O'Brien was alive, though he hoped that would not be for much longer.

George continued before Benny could answer. 'But in return, you never set foot in Manchester again. In fact, if I was you, I would leave the country. The villa is off the table as you've only completed part of the deal, but take the money, Benny, and fuck off. And don't ever breathe a word of our arrangement to anyone. If you do, we will find you.'

Benny Lancashire accepted the briefcase full of used notes and fucked off. He booked a flight to Spain and left that night.

chapter thirty-seven

Fletcher was striding up and down his living room, like a man possessed. Will and Newbie were with him. He'd summoned them to come over. It was now 6 o'clock.

Newbie was trying to reason with him. 'Look, Fletch, you must have known they wouldn't sit back and do nothing forever. You must have known sending the boys across today was throwing fuel on the fire.'

Fletcher grabbed Newbie by the chin with his right hand and pushed him into the wall. 'Do you think I didn't know that? You talk to me like that again and I'll make sure you never walk again.'

'Fletch, come on, for fuck's sake!' Will shouted.

'Oh yeah? You think you're Billy-big-bollocks too, do ya? What is it with you two – think you've got what it takes, do ya?!' Fletcher stood with his arms out in front of him with his palms facing upwards. 'Come on, both of ya!' he raged, as he looked from one to the other. His face was red and he was spitting phlegm as he spoke. He was out of control and Will knew better than to tackle him. Fletcher was the boss. No one had ever dared take him on. Will was not about to be the first. He sat back down. Newbie straightened his jumper and waited for the silence to break.

Fletcher changed his stance. He dropped his arms and took a swig of his whisky.

'They must've known we were comin'. They fuckin' must have. There's no way they would've been able to take on Benny and his lads. I mean, Harry for one. Fuck me. He's as hard as fucking nails. They must have been tipped off. Leeds was the patch that whatshisfuckin' name was runnin' for them. Him that Shaney did. John something or other. Leeds was vulnerable. They must have fuckin' known.'

Will looked at Newbie, who returned the same look. Fletcher could never just accept that something had gone wrong. Whenever things went pear-shaped, he always suspected a grass. They'd lost more decent men over the years than they cared to remember all because Fletcher didn't trust them. Neither of them was going to say so, though. Not tonight. Fletcher could never reason that his compatriots at the top table were a match for him. He thought he was the main man and that he could take anyone on and take anyone out whenever he felt like it. Both Newbie and Will knew, of course, that he'd never before taken any of the main men on, because in reality he was no more a stronger force than they were. Taking on a main player, like Fletcher had with Frank, was suicide. Everyone knew that. Trouble was, no one had been brave enough to tell him when he'd decided to take the fight to Frank. They'd all thought it, but no one had dared speak up.

'Who fuckin' knew we were going today, eh?! Who fuckin' knew?!' he roared.

'Fuck knows, Fletch. We didn't even know until you told us this morning. You said you rang Benny last night. Who were you with?' Newbie asked.

Fletcher thought for a moment. He then looked towards the door into the kitchen. He remembered he'd just finished shagging Kat when he made the call. She was in the en-suite.

'No one,' he said. 'No one. Anyway, I have things to do here. You two get off. There's nowt we can do tonight. Whatever Frank and Archie's done is done. Meeting as usual tomorrow morning, 9am. Make sure everyone's there. And I mean everyone. We need to take this fuckin' war over to Nottingham. I need to think, but what I can tell ya is that blood will be shed, and fuckin' lots of it.'

Newbie and Will looked at each other, perplexed. Fletcher's whole demeanour had changed. He seemed transfixed on something, as though his mind was elsewhere.

'You OK, Fletch?' Will asked.

'Yeah, I'm fine. Just got things to do, that's all. Things seem a little clearer, but look, just fuck off, both of ya. Just be at the club tomorrow morning with everyone else. Make the calls. I don't want any no-shows. If anyone asks about Benny or Harry or anyone, just play dumb. Say nothin'. I'll tell everyone at the club in the morning.'

'OK, Boss. See you tomorrow.'

They both shouted bye to Kat as they left. She shouted back. Fletcher locked the door manually behind them. He didn't want Kat to know.

chapter thirty-eight

Frank tried Kenny's phone again. There was still no answer. He'd tried it repeatedly for the past hour.

'How long until Roy gets there?' he asked Archie, who looked at his watch.

'He should be there now. I'll ring him.'

Archie had sent one of their men from Newark to Kenny's house around half an hour before. At first, there was no suspicion, but after three or four attempts of getting hold of him, Frank had become concerned; concerned that Kenny may have done a moonlight flight.

'Roy, you there yet?'

'Yeah, just got here. There's no lights on and no answer when I ring the doorbell.'

Archie looked at Frank. 'There's no lights on, Frank, and no one's in.'

'Is the dog barking?' Frank asked.

Archie shook his head after asking Roy the same.

'The bastard's fucked off,' Frank said, shaking his head. 'Is there no one left in this fucking world who can be relied upon? What the fuck's up with everyone these days?' he said to Jez. Jez too shook his head in bewilderment.

'You'd never get this in our day, Jez. Fuck me.'

'He must've got cold feet, Frank. Like you said earlier, he looked nervous as soon as you mentioned Fletcher's name,' Jez said, still not taking it all in.

Archie had by now ended the call.

'I'll track the bastard down if it's the last thing I do. When this is over, I want him found, and I want him sorted. No one does that to me.'

Frank was angry. No one had ever done a disappearing act when he'd requested their services. Ever. This was new to Frank and he wouldn't handle it well.

'Well, if he's fucked off, we can't use him, can we?' he continued. 'This has well and truly fucked things up, fellas. After today's activity up in Leeds, Fletcher will be wanting revenge. We can get ready, lads, 'cos believe me, we'll have it coming.'

The room fell silent. Frank watched Archie, Jez, Brian, Pat, Phoebe and Marie gather their thoughts. Marie, in particular, was scared shitless. She just wanted to get up and run as fast as she could. She knew nothing of what Fletcher O'Brien was capable of; the rest of them knew too well. They'd all seen the photos of Paul and John. They were all mulling over what plan B could be.

Phoebe had told them of her and Marie's earlier chat with Kat, about how she was fully on board, and how, with Kat's help, they could carry out their plan with relative ease. The only issue was the two permanent guards, but Phoebe had told them about her plan with Andrea. It had all seemed to have fallen into place. Kenny Walters had fucked that up and fucked it up big style.

'Well, fuck me, don't all come up with a new plan all at once, will ya!' Frank barked. The silence had triggered him.

'Time is the problem,' Archie replied. 'If we had more time, it wouldn't be so much of an issue.'

'I'm aware of that, but we need something pronto.'

Pat sat up straight. If he'd had a light bulb above his head, it would have just gone off. 'Jānis,' he said. 'He could do it, I'm sure.'

'Jānis?' Archie repeated.

'Yeah, he was telling me all about it after the meeting last week. I had a good chat with him. He certainly seemed to know his stuff. He used to be an electrician, he said, and you know, into all things electronics and that. Gotta be worth a call into him.'

Archie was already dialling his number. Frank was feeling excited again.

'Jānis, it's me, Archie. Listen, you know that guy we rang last week to sort out the smart house hack?'

'Er, yeah. Kenny, wasn't it?'

'That's him. Well, he's gone AWOL. But a little bird tells me that you could do what he was gonna do. Is that right?'

'Yeah, I could do that, Archie. Right up my street, that.'

'Why didn't you mention this last week then?'

'Archie, come on. With respect, I was there to just tell you about Andrea. I didn't feel it was my place to question this Kenny guy or to put myself forward in his place. Frank was speaking to him before I'd even realised what he was doing. And it can be quite an intimidating place sat with you lot...'

'Yeah, fair enough, but listen – you told me when we first spoke early last week that if we took on Fletcher, you wanted to be part of it. You said you owed him for that beating he gave you. He taxed you, didn't he? Well, here's your chance, Jānis, to show your bottle. We were planning to be at his house tomorrow with Kenny to get it rigged up. Me and Pat will be with you for 8 tomorrow. Text me your address.'

'Tomorrow?'

'Yep, tomorrow. Events of earlier today mean we can't delay it. 8 o'clock OK?'

'8 it is, Archie. See you tomorrow.'

Archie placed his phone on the table. 'See, you've just got to have the right contacts, Frank,' he said mockingly.

Frank smiled. 'Nice one, Son.'

Frank and Archie then discussed the plan at length. Phoebe rang Andrea to inform her she'd need to go round the back with her car as she did normally. She explained she'd have to get the two security men to her car by pretending there was a knocking sound or a flat tyre.

Andrea was glad to be back in the fold. She was annoyed when she was cast aside. She'd been banking on the money she was going to get for her role in whatever Jānis's contacts had been planning, and if she was honest, she'd even contemplated tipping Fletcher off, just out of spite. That little thought, however, soon disappeared from her mind once Jānis told her in no uncertain terms to not even consider doing anything like that, and explained fully who they were dealing with. She didn't like what she'd heard about Frank and Archie Pearson, so she sucked it up and just accepted that her rather uneventful life was to continue as such. Now, though, she had a chance of some excitement again and she was well up for it.

Even though she enjoyed bouncing up and down on Fletcher's cock once a week most weeks, she'd never really liked him. She'd seen the way he'd treat Kat and she'd certainly heard the way he spoke to most people, so, in her mind, he could well and truly fuck off and she'd take her money and run. Her wedge was a lot less now, of course, but she'd take it and bank it along with her other savings. That's all she could do. Andrea wanted her own little business and this would be a way of earning a bit towards it for very little effort whatsoever.

chapter thirty-nine

Fletcher stood in his large hallway. He could hear some music playing in the kitchen. He knew Kat would be having a glass of wine. She'd been for a swim earlier and would have showered before she came back into the house. She would do as she always did and would be sat at the island in the kitchen reading some gossip magazine. That's all Kat ever read. It allowed her to keep up with what was happening in the celebrity world. She wasn't really that interested, but it's what her and her few friends did. She would then finish her wine and put the children to bed. They were both playing in their playrooms upstairs, well out of earshot.

Fletcher walked through and, as he expected, there she was flicking the pages of the glossy. Fletcher could never see that that's all she would do – just flick through the pages. He genuinely thought she was interested in that world, but that just showed how little he knew his wife.

'Interesting, is it?

Kat looked up and smiled. 'Nah, not really. It never is, but I look anyway. Here, come here and look at this,' she said, as she flicked her hair. 'Have you ever seen anything like it? Bloody ridiculous, look.'

Fletcher walked over slowly. Kat had her eyes fixed back on the pages.

'Do you know what I've been up to today?' Fletcher asked, stopping a few feet away. His stance was subconsciously masculine. It didn't need to be.

Kat answered without taking her eyes off the page. 'No idea,' she replied.

'Do you know where Leeds is?' he asked, without any feeling in his voice at all.

Kat sensed it. She felt a pang of apprehension. Her breathing pattern changed. She didn't notice. Fletcher did. He looked out for things like that.

'Leeds? No idea. Down south, isn't it, somewhere?' Kat kept her eyes on the magazine. She didn't want to look Fletcher in the eye. She didn't want to give anything away. She could see in her top vision that he'd moved closer. He was now standing next to her. He could hear her breathing was quick. He grabbed her hair and pulled her head back. She squealed. 'Fletcher, you're hurting me!'

'You knew, didn't you? Don't lie to me, you fucking bitch! You heard me. Where you been today, eh? Why did you go to that fucking spa you go to today, eh? You never go on Sundays. Ever. I should've known, you fucking whore!' He dragged her off the stool by her hair, letting go when she was on the floor. She tried to get up. He slapped her with the back of his hand. She fell back.

'Who did you tell? Tell me, you bitch!' he shouted.

Kat didn't answer. Her mind was racing, trying to think what to do. Her next move or her next reply would make a huge difference to how this all played out. As she got up with her hand held out in front of her to protect herself from any further attack, she decided to play the only trump card she had.

'Fletch, baby, I have no idea what you're talking about. I never listen to any of your conversations. I have no interest in them. My only interest is you. I'm here just to make you happy, baby. Your business interests are nothing to me. I love you, babe.'

Kat was now stood right in front of him. She knew her only chance to defuse this situation was to get his cock hard. Fletcher could never resist any female who made the dick in his pants grow. That was his Achilles heel and Kat was about to expose it.

'Someone knew about Leeds today. *You* knew. You must have,' he said, his voice far less threatening than it had been a moment ago.

'Not me, babe,' she said whilst stroking his growing member. She could see he was struggling to remain angry. Kat could sense his desire to rip her clothes off and fuck her hard. She knew the children would be far too busy upstairs in the other side of the house to think about coming down.

Fletcher was enjoying the moment, but he just could not shake the feeling that Kat had betrayed him. The trip to the spa was the defining factor. Without that, he could accept what she was saying but Kat never went to the spa on a Sunday, and for her to go on the very same day he seriously suspected he'd been betrayed just did not add up. Kat lowered her head and then got on her knees. She took his cock out and sucked it hard. She was sure by the time she'd swallowed his load he'd have fully calmed down. She was wrong. Just as he'd finished coming and Kat was still swallowing it down, he slapped her across the face with the back of his right hand. He then zipped himself up and dragged her round the kitchen floor by her hair. She didn't want to scream too loudly for fear of the children hearing her.

'Fletcher, stop, please! It wasn't me, I swear!' she cried out, tears rolling down her cheeks. He let go. Her head was hurting so much. She felt her hair to see if any had come out. A few strands in the palm of her hand was all she saw.

Fletcher put his face right into hers. 'I think ya lying, bitch. If I find out you are, I'll kill ya and if you are, I'll find out.' He stood up. 'BITCH!' he roared, as he left the room. She heard him get his keys. A minute or so later the front door slammed.

Kat lay there sobbing. She knew she'd just dodged a bullet. She knew she only had to survive a couple of more days, but with Fletcher being so suspicious, survival was not guaranteed. She got up and saw a figure at the window. It was Duffy, one of Fletcher's guards. She could see the despair in his face. He remained expressionless, but she knew he'd probably witnessed what had just happened. Kat smiled. Duffy turned and walked away. She headed to the spa and pool building. She'd put the burner phone in a drawer in the changing room. Fletcher had never set foot in that room in all the time they'd had it. It was still there. She switched it on and texted the number under the letter P. *Still on for tomorrow?* Kat waited a full three minutes before the reply came back: *Absolutely. Can you talk?* Kat said she could.

Phoebe told her about the slight change of plan with Jānis. Andrea was to still do her bit. Phoebe confirmed they would be there before 9am. Kat had mixed emotions. On the one hand, she could not wait to be free of the monster she lived with, but on the other, she knew she was making her children fatherless. Mixed emotions she could cope with; the need to be free of Fletcher was greater than being a single mother. That was the easy bit. Surviving for two more days was going to be the hard part.

Fletcher was on autopilot. He had no idea where he was going, but he needed to think, he needed some air, and to gather his thoughts. He'd certainly not expected today to have happened. He could not believe that none of the men he'd sent over to Leeds had been heard of since. That scenario had never crossed his mind. He'd expected some grief maybe and some sort of aggravation, but this unnerved him. And he'd still not had any communication from either of them. Fletcher was not used to feeling nervous. He made other people nervous. The men he'd sent over were no amateurs. Benny, in particular, was a proven asset. Fletcher trusted him. Harry and Stuart were the same: seasoned criminals who he'd put up against anyone in that sort of situation. Fletcher had resigned himself to the fact that he might not see Benny again, or any of the others for that matter.

As he drove around Manchester's ring road, he tried to get his head around things. Maybe he should have gone himself. Maybe he should have made sure that the men Benny chose to take with him were of a certain calibre. He was annoyed at himself that he didn't even know who Benny had taken other than Harry and Stuart. Fletcher recalled the conversation in his head. He'd just told Benny to "take a few of the lads from one of the estates". He now realised that he'd been far too cocky, far too flippant. How the fuck could he have been so stupid? He thought Frank and Archie's lack of response was a sign of weakness. He now realised it was their strength. It took a lot of self-control to remain silent when under attack. But that was not Fletcher. That was not how he operated. He was not the silent type. Fletcher was loud and arrogant, and he was not about to change now. He dialled Archie's number. He reasoned he'd get more of a reaction from Archie. He wanted a reaction. He wanted Archie to get angry, to be upset and to let something slip.

Archie answered. 'Yeah?'

'*Yeah?* Fucking *yeah*. Is that all you've got to say?!' Fletcher barked down the phone. His face was taut with anger.

'What else do you want me to say?' Archie was staring straight at Frank. Frank was telling him with his hand to remain calm. He mouthed at him silently, 'Stay in control.'

'If you've done anything to my lads, Archie, I will personally make you pay. You might think you're in control, but I'm comin' for ya and I'm gonna take everything you've got, including that lovely wife of yours. She'll be something special. Picture it, Archie lad. Picture me all over your lovely wife. I'll lick her dry.'

Archie was struggling. His breath was heavy. 'You touch a hair on her head, Fletcher, and you will suffer pain like you've never suffered before. You hear me, you wanker!' he shouted.

Frank had heard Fletcher's remark. He couldn't intervene now. Fletcher had made it personal.

Fletcher laughed. '*Wanker*? I was calling people that in the playground, Archie! This is the BIG league. Put your toys away and climb back in your buggy. You're out of your depth, lad, and that grandad of yours is too fucking old. You can't take me on, Archie. And let me remind you, if you've hurt my lads, I'll be gunning for ya, so let them go and send them back unharmed. That way, I'll take everything you have, but I'll leave your wife alone. It's your call.'

Fletcher hung up. He laughed again. He then stopped as he remembered Kat. He was sure she'd tipped someone off. It had to be her, he told himself again. There is no way Benny or any of the others would have betrayed him. No one had ever betrayed him. He always commanded loyalty, always had. He decided he would visit Kat's spa after his Monday meeting with his men. That was a priority. They needed a plan. Archie and Frank needed sorting once and for all – Fletcher was sick of biding his time. If they were not going to bring the fight to him, he was going to them. How and when would be decided tomorrow morning. He'd find out for himself who, if anyone, Kat had been seen with earlier that day. He knew she went there; his men would confirm it whenever they got back. He just didn't know with whom.

'I'm doin' 'im tomorrow, Frank. He ain't gettin' away with that. I'll fuckin' kill him. Tomorrow, I'm doing 'im,' Archie seethed.

'You ain't doin' nothing of the sort, Archie. We stick to the plan. Jānis does his thing tomorrow. We then go over, get in the house and we make it look like an accident. A house fire. That's the plan. We ain't movin' from it, so fuckin' take it like a man and play the game.'

'Did you hear what he fuckin' said, did ya?'

'Of course I did. I'm not fuckin' deaf, but we stick to the plan. If you can't, then you ain't goin'. I'll send Jez here and Pat – two men who can handle it.'

'What, you saying I can't take it?' Archie shouted. He was livid at being expected to take shit like that about his wife, Sarah.

'I am, yes. It's just words, Archie. Look, 48 hours and it'll be over. I know it's hard to take and the easy thing to do is to react, but you have to take the words and let them go over your head. How many times have I fuckin' told ya that I've been there, done it a million times? I'm telling ya, listen to me and let it go. You can tell him what you think when we have him in his own house.' Frank walked over to him. 'Look, we'll put Steven and Pēteris at your house 24/7, OK? They can make sure that Sarah, and Alice, are protected until this is over. I get it, Son, I really do and this *is* hard for me. I've never held back so much in my life. Tell him, Jez, this ain't me, is it? You know me better than anyone.'

Jez raised his eyebrows and nodded. He remained in his seat but looked at Archie. 'This ain't quite the Frank of old – that I do know, mate. I'll agree with that. Frank has always been calmer than the rest of us in situations like this, we all know that, and that's what sets him apart. Without his calmness, we'd all be pushing up the daisies by now, Frank included. The Frank of up to even five years ago would've been over the Pennines by now, and someone'd be in a coffin – probably Fletcher. As I'm sure Frank has said to you many times, Archie, there's a void in our hierarchy and that void is a generation. And that makes us slightly vulnerable. That's what this is all about: negating that vulnerability. You are still as old as most people at university. Frank is as old as most people who've retired, so that leaves a gap, so we have to act differently. This is alien to us all, this degree of cautiousness, but unless your mum here wants to fill Daniel's shoes, we have that gap. Don't let Fletcher fill it with dead bodies by reeling you in. Listen to your grandad. That's the best advice I can give you.'

Everyone was blown away. Jez had just said more in a minute than he ever had at any top table meeting. Jez was a listener, a man of few words. He preferred to watch from the wings than to tread the boards. No one said a thing. Jez looked around the room and realised the reason for the silence. 'Someone speak then, for fuck's sake,' he said.

'That was beautiful, Jez. Really beautiful,' Phoebe said. She got up and kissed him on the forehead. She then turned to her son. 'I'm not filling that void, Son, so do as Jez said, and take the advice.'

Archie felt humbled. Everyone was just looking out for him, and he knew the strategy was right. He felt very lucky to have people around him who cared for him. 'I want Steven and Pēteris or someone over there at the house, though.'

Frank nodded. 'Make it Ryan and Steven. Pēteris can go with you tomorrow. Jānis will like him being around I think.'

Jez was sat wondering where all that came from. He'd liked giving that little speech. He'd liked it very much.

Everyone knew the plan. The next two or three days were going to be some of the most testing in Frank's career. Everyone had left and he was sat on his own in the boardroom, reflecting on his life. He thought about Renee and what life may have been like for him had she survived childbirth. It had been a while since he'd thought about her. He used to think about her daily many years ago, but as time had passed and as Gloria had become more of a life-long partner to him, the memories had faded. Every time he remembered her, he would be sad at how long it had been since he'd last given her a thought; however, he was aware that it was a natural part of the grieving process. He thought about Daniel and Richie as young men, about how Richie had been into football violence as a late teenager and twenty-something; how he used to swagger about in that world. He smiled. Even though at the time he had despised Richie, they brought back memories all the same. Memories of the old days. He then remembered the way Daniel came into his own, when he shot Gary Wallace, Steven's brother. That was the day Frank knew he was the right man to take over the business. Frank thought about the subsequent years and how he'd made peace with Richie, but also how it had all gone wrong. His eyes filled as he remembered the moment he'd found out about Daniel's death, the aftermath and how Richie had played a big part in it all. He then thought about Richie, wasting away in the care home. 'What a life you've had, Frank,' he told himself out loud. 'What a fucking life,' he said, raising an imaginary glass.

As he continued to reflect in this rare moment of peace, he thought again about the next few days. For such a young man, Archie had huge responsibility on his shoulders. These were the moments when Frank realised the vulnerability around him. Archie was a main player in the making, of that he had no doubt, but he also saw glimpses of a boy in a man's world. Glimpses that no one else saw. People didn't catch the regular glances at Frank for recognition and assurance. Frank saw them, of course; in fact, he looked out for them. Archie needed time and he needed support, but he couldn't publicly show that too often. Frank did wonder whether Archie would cope quite so well without him. People needed to see Archie as a strong, decisive leader, not a young man that had been thrust into his position far too early. Frank tried to ensure he appeared a leader as much as possible.

He picked up his phone and rang George Burbanks. It rang four times before George answered.

'Evening, Frank.'

'Evening, George.'

'You sound sombre. You OK?' George asked.

'Yeah, fine. You asked me to tell you when we planned to make a move.'

'I did. I assume this is that call.'

'Archie and some of my men will be around Fletcher's place tomorrow. You don't need to know the details, but we will be back Tuesday to sort this out once and for all. By Tuesday, Fletcher O'Brien should be out of my hair and yours.'

'OK, Frank, thank you for the heads-up. My men will be nowhere near the vicinity. I'd appreciate a call when it's done.'

'No problem, George. Take care.'

Frank put down his phone. For the first time in his life, he was apprehensive. If it went wrong, he could be well and truly finished. For the first time in his life, he felt vulnerable. And he didn't like it one bit.

chapter forty

It was Monday morning. Archie was on his way over to Jānis's house. He had Pat and Phoebe with him, along with Brian, Del and Pēteris in the car behind. Archie had wanted a good solid team with him. He knew that even though it had all been planned meticulously, he still wanted to feel he could put up a show of strength and if it came on top, he wanted Del with him. He'd promised him. That was planned for tomorrow, but even the best-laid plans went wrong. They were going into the home of one of Manchester's main criminals after all.

The mood in the car was tense. No one had really said much, other than a few pleasantries. Pat was driving, Archie was in the passenger seat and Phoebe was in the back. They drove over the Derbyshire Dales towards Sparrowpit and on towards Disley. They picked up Jānis from his house just outside Stockport and then headed out towards Altrincham.

They reached the outskirts of Altrincham around half an hour later. Pat pulled into a side street. Pēteris pulled in behind. Archie turned to Jānis, in the back.

'Still up for this, Jānis?' he asked, knowing what the answer would be.

'No problem, Archie. As I said, once I get in the house, I can do this – how do you say – standing on my head.'

Archie smiled. 'Well, don't do, that pal, will ya. Make sure you're stood upright. Right then.' Archie checked his watch. It was 8:32am. 'Kat said Fletcher always leaves at 8:30, didn't she?' he said to his mum.

Phoebe nodded. 'That's what she said, but she said she'd text me once he had.'

'Any message?'

'Not yet.'

'Well, let's just wait here until she does,' Archie said. He looked at the sat nav. It said they were seven minutes away. He got out to tell Brian in the car behind what was happening. Brian rang Frank to keep him updated.

Jānis wound his window down and popped his head out. 'She's just messaged, Archie!' he shouted.

Archie got back in the car and asked Phoebe to read it out. *He left 5 mins ago. Andrea is here. Her car is round the back.*

'Text her to see if she can talk,' Archie said.

Thirty seconds later, Phoebe's phone rang.

'We'll be seven minutes or so, Kat. So, in six minutes, get Andrea to get those two men you'll have there with you to look at her car. We will let ourselves in and come straight into the house. It will just be me and Jānis. I assume the key code is the same?'

'It is. Same number as I told you. Six minutes and I'll make sure both of them are round the back with Andrea. Hurry up, Phoebe. I'm bricking it here.'

Pat was already turning the car round. The two cars made their way to Fletcher's house, arriving in a little under seven minutes. There was no time to spare. Phoebe and Jānis got out and walked briskly over the road. The house was on a private road, which no one had given a thought to, with maybe seven or eight very large houses on it. They were all set back, so it was difficult to see any of them properly from the road, but it was clear this was millionaire country.

Phoebe entered the key code. The gates slowly started to open. Thankfully, they made little noise. Archie watched as his mum and Jānis disappeared behind the gates.

'Where we gonna park, Archie?' Pat asked. Archie looked up and down the road. Any cars here would stand out like a sore thumb. There were no cars parked anywhere. It wasn't that kind of street.

'We'll have to park on the main road at the bottom. We can't park here. Someone is bound to come out and ask what the fuck we are doing. At least on the main road we can see if anyone comes onto or off the street.'

'Are you sure? We just seem a long way away on the main road.'

'Got no choice, Pat, have we?'

Phoebe and Jānis ran towards the house. Kat was stood at the kitchen window pointing towards the front door. They ran that way. The door was slightly ajar. As they entered, Kat came out into the hallway. 'Quick,' she said, as she turned to run upstairs. 'The control panel and everything is up here, but you'll need to erase the CCTV first as it will show you coming into the house.' Phoebe and Jānis followed her without question. They were taken into a room at the back. Jānis looked at the CCTV monitors and quickly scanned the system. It all looked pretty simple to him.

'I'll leave you two here. I'll have to go downstairs. I need to try and act normal. How long will you be?' Kat asked.

Phoebe looked at Jānis for an answer. 'An hour, maybe less, but certainly no more.'

Kat looked anxious. 'OK, but please do not come downstairs until I come and get you. Stay here. I'll come up in half an hour. I just need to get the children from the playrooms and take them to school. It's only a three-minute drive, so I'll be back in no time.'

'You never said anything about that,' Phoebe said, trying hard not to raise her voice.

'Well, I do have to get them to school. I can't not take them. I'll be back within ten minutes. Just stay here. No one knows you are here. No one will come up. They have no need to.'

'OK, but hurry,' Phoebe ordered her.

Jānis began to work on the CCTV system. He wanted to erase them coming in before he rigged it up so that it was no longer recording. No one would know unless they tried to look back at any recordings. It would appear just as it always did to the naked eye.

Phoebe texted Archie. *Kat is taking the kids to school. No drama. She'll be back in 10. We're both OK.* She then put her phone on silent. She didn't want a text or anything giving them away.

Archie saw Kat's car pull out of the road. They were parked twenty yards or so along the main drag. Kat didn't even notice them. He rang Frank just to keep him updated.

chapter forty-one

Fletcher left as usual that morning. Same time every Monday morning to drive to his club for his weekly meeting with his men. It was something he'd done for many years and had found it very beneficial to keep abreast of things. This morning, he was to have his meeting as usual, but just a little later than normal. He'd had a change of plan from last night. He had planned to call into the spa after his meeting, but when he woke up and saw Kat parading around in her skimpy nightie, he decided to go there first. He rang Newbie and told him that the meeting was to be later than normal, but didn't tell him why. Newbie knew better than to ask if nothing was forthcoming. He'd just been told to get everyone there for midday. Fletcher knew if he found out anything incriminating at the spa, he'd need time to deal with Kat. He was waiting in reception for the manager, a very effeminate young man called Tony.

Tony came out and invited him into the office. Tony knew who he was and this made him anxious. He was anxious at the best of times. He lived on his nerves.

Everything was a drama and everything was done at a hundred miles an hour.

'What can I do for you, Mr O'Brien?' he asked, with a definite nervousness in his voice.

Fletcher could see he was shitting himself. 'Look, pal, I don't want any resistance from you. I just want to know who my wife was with yesterday when she was here. You do know who my wife is, don't you?'

'Er, yes, Mr O'Brien, I do. We love Kat. Everyone loves her.'

'I couldn't give a flying fuck who loves her and who doesn't, I just want to see the CCTV of her visit yesterday, that's all.'

'Er, well, I'm not sure I can do that.'

'Are you not? Well, I am, and believe me you can, so let's stop fucking about and just show me the CCTV.'

'Well, er, there's only CCTV in the reception. There's no CCTV in the actual spa areas or the changing rooms.'

Fletcher stood up. 'Well, let's see what you have then.'

Tony's breathing was heavy. His heart was pounding. 'Yes ... well, yes ... er ... OK, Mr O'Brien, er, please, please, follow me. This way, sir.'

Fletcher was struggling to contain his composure, but followed Tony out into the reception area. He watched as Tony navigated the screen monitor with the mouse. He could see the receptionist looking at him. He could sense she was in awe of him. She studied him like she was looking at a famous celebrity. He liked that. Even in this situation, he couldn't help but wonder what kind of a shag she'd be. He thought he might come back later and see if she was up for it. Her eyes told him she would be.

'Here we are, Mr O'Brien,' Tony said, turning the screen to face Fletcher. 'Here is Kat arriving on her own. Look, she goes straight through into the spa areas. There's no one with her, Mr O'Brien.'

'Leave it playing!' Fletcher ordered. 'Leave it playing. I want to see who comes in after her.'

'Well, we could just fast forward until people come in?' Tony suggested. Fletcher nodded.

They saw five people come in after Kat. None of them were anyone that Fletcher recognised. It was now seventeen minutes since Kat had arrived. 'Keep going,' he told Tony, who continued to fast forward the recordings. He then stopped as two ladies came into the reception through the front door. He stopped and paused it, as he had with the others. Fletcher looked closely.

'Are these the ladies you are looking for, Mr O'Brien?'

Fletcher said nothing. He studied the images and saw a face he recognised. 'It may well be, Tony. Play it at normal speed.'

Tony did as instructed. They all watched as the two women talked to the receptionist, the same receptionist who had now stopped looking at Fletcher. They then watched, as Phoebe signed the day pass forms.

'Where are those forms?' Fletcher asked.

The receptionist turned to open a cabinet door behind her and took out a black file. 'Here,' she said, placing it on the front desk. She opened it and gave it to Fletcher. He looked at the name on the top form – Tracy Wright. The next was a Rebecca Dawson. He turned to the third piece of paper – Phoebe Pearson.

Fletcher bolted out the door. No thank you, nothing.

Tony looked at Wendy. She shrugged her shoulders and closed the file. Tony got up and walked into his office. Wendy answered the phone as it rang for the third time. By the time she'd finished the call, Fletcher was at his car. He screeched out of the car park.

chapter forty-two

Archie watched as Kat returned. She indicated to turn into the private road and disappeared out of sight. He sent a text to Phoebe: *She's back.*

'I wonder how long it'll take,' Pat asked, with a sigh. 'Could be a long morning,' he said yawning.

'No idea. I don't think Jānis did until he saw what system it was. It can't be that long, though. I mean, he knows what he's doing. I'm not expecting to be here all morning, that's for sure,' Archie replied. He then relaxed back in his seat and closed his eyes. 'Anyway, just relax. Phoebe will keep us up to speed.'

Pat turned round in his seat to look at the car behind. He could see the others chatting away. He couldn't make out what they were saying, but they seemed in good spirits considering. With Pat looking at Brian waving his hands about, obviously telling a story, and Archie resting his eyes, no one saw Fletcher turn into his road. By the time Pat had turned back round and glanced over to the junction, he'd already disappeared out of view.

Kat walked back into the house. There was no sign of either of the two men that were supposed to be guarding. Kat had no idea who was on duty today. She never did until she saw one of them. She knew there was a pattern to their shifts, but never really took any interest. The only one she liked was Duffy and he was on last night, so she doubted he'd be on today. She assumed Andrea must still be with them looking at her car.

Kat was nervous as hell today. She'd been unsure whether to take the kids to school, but then reasoned that things had to appear normal. That way at least, she may be able to keep her nerves in check. She knew if Fletcher got wind of anything, she was done for and his behaviour last night had done nothing to calm her nerves. When he'd returned from his drive, he'd hardly said a word to her and had just gone straight to bed.

She decided she'd make a drink. She put the kettle on, thinking she'd make Phoebe and the man she was with a drink too. They were bound to want a cuppa. Kat had been told the man's name, but she couldn't remember it. As she got the mugs out of the cupboard, she thought she'd pop up to see what they wanted but before she got half way across the kitchen, the front door flew open. Fletcher came storming in and slapped her in the face. She was knocked back into the island. Before she had a chance to react or even speak, Fletcher had her by the throat.

'I fuckin' knew it was you! You've betrayed me,

haven't you? What have you been telling that bitch Phoebe?' He stepped back and slapped her again. Kat screamed for Fletcher to stop. He grabbed her by the shoulders and headbutted her. Her nose cracked and blood began spurting out. He threw her to one side. 'I'll fuckin' kill ya, you fuckin' bitch!'

Fletcher was frothing at the mouth. He started to throw things around the room. He picked up one of the stools that was in a row of four at the island and smashed it onto the worktop. Kat cowered on the floor, screaming at him to stop.

Phoebe and Jānis heard the commotion. Jānis stopped what he was doing and looked straight at her. Phoebe's eyes were transfixed on him. She then opened the door of the room and walked onto the landing. She could hear a man shouting, and Kat screaming, 'Fletcher! Stop! Please!' She got her phone out of her pocket and saw Archie's text: *She's back.* She'd forgotten her phone was on silent. Phoebe replied, *Fletcher's here. Get here now*, then watched it go from *Delivered* to *Read.* Archie was typing. *1 minute.*

Jānis had now joined her on the landing. They both heard Fletcher say, 'I'll fuckin' kill ya, you fuckin' bitch!'

'Come on, we have to go down and help her. He'll kill her, Jānis,' Phoebe said. She knew they may not have a minute. Phoebe felt they owed Kat. She had to help her. Jānis took the lead and ran downstairs. Phoebe followed a step or two behind.

Andrea was still with Marcus and Dec, the two guys who were helping her fix her car. She'd let the tyre down slightly and had knocked a screw into the tyre wall a few hundred yards from the house. She was handy with things like that. Her dad had shown her from a very young age how to change a wheel, change the oil and other bits of basic car maintenance. He'd always told her that it could save her life one day. They could hear shouting coming from the house. Andrea's heart was in her mouth. She had to concentrate on not shaking with fear. Marcus shook his head.

'Duffy said he was in a foul mood last night. I suggest we keep our heads down and leave them to it. They do nowt but fuckin' argue these days.'

Andrea quickly supported his theory. 'Yeah, I think we are best staying here.'

Dec shrugged his shoulders and continued to watch Marcus sort the tyre.

Dec's phone rang. It was Fletcher.

Jānis ran into the kitchen, but instinctively stopped as soon as he saw Fletcher stood with a knife in one hand and his other holding Kat by her hair. Phoebe was a pace behind him. She nearly ran into him. Fletcher saw them both. He immediately stopped what he was doing and slowly nodded his head as he looked them both up and down.

'And what the fuck do we have here? What's your name again? I know you,' he said to Jānis. He still had the knife in his right hand and Kat's hair in his other. Her head was pulled back.

'Well, Phoebe, so nice to see you. Good to see someone from your lot has some balls!' He laughed at his attempt at a joke. 'This is gonna be very interesting.' He took a couple of steps towards them, still holding Kat in his left hand. He laughed as the penny dropped. 'Jānis, isn't it? That's it, Jānis. Well, come on then, what the fuck are you two gonna do?'

Jānis looked at Phoebe. 'One step forward and she dies, Jānis,' Fletcher said. Phoebe looked behind her and saw two men pushing Andrea in front of them. One had a gun. Marcus pointed to Phoebe and Jānis to move into the kitchen. They did as instructed.

Fletcher heard the screech of car tyres. He looked out of the window but recognised none of them. He then saw Archie get out of the driver's side of the front car. 'You betrayed me, bitch!'

Kat groaned as Fletcher plunged the kitchen knife into her stomach. He twisted it and pulled it out. As he let go of her hair, she fell back into the island, cracking the back of her skull. Kat was dead before she hit the floor.

'Come on!' Fletcher roared, as he swung the knife at Jānis. Jānis put his arm out to defend his face. The knife cut through his coat sleeve, slicing his left arm. He staggered back. Phoebe lunged forward to push Fletcher out of the way. He swung his arm. It cut through Phoebe's coat. Jānis punched Fletcher hard with his right hand. Phoebe looked down. She saw blood seeping through her coat. Archie came in first through the front door. Marcus pushed Andrea to one side and turned to shoot. Pat hit him before he could line his shot up. He staggered back. Pat hit him again with his right hand. Archie went straight to the kitchen. Pat and Marcus continued trading blows. Del, by this time, had followed Archie.

Brian fought with Dec. He was struggling a little. Dec was young, strong and fit. Brian was a man in his late sixties, and it showed. Dec had the better of him. Brian took punches to the head. Pēteris jumped on Dec's back to pull him away and bit into his ear. Dec screamed and tried to wrestle him off, but Pēteris held firm. Brian then composed himself and punched Dec hard three times on the head. Dec pushed firm with his legs and backed hard into the wall. That made Pēteris loosen his grip. It winded Pēteris as the force of the wall hit him hard into his back. The gun went off. Andrea had picked it up. She didn't mean to fire it. It hit Brian in the left thigh. He went down on one knee clutching his leg. Andrea dropped the gun. Dec had by now wrestled free of Pēteris. He picked it up and aimed to shoot him. Brian then thrust the knife he'd taken from inside of his right boot into Dec's side. He winced and arched his side as he fired. The bullet hit Pēteris in the shoulder. It knocked him back, but the wound was superficial. Andrea pushed Dec. It was all she could think to do. It knocked him enough off balance that he dropped the gun. Brian managed to pick it up and shot Dec through the back. He fell forward to the floor. The gunshots made Pat and

Marcus momentarily stop. Marcus reacted first and knocked Pat into the staircase. Brian wanted to fire but was afraid the bullet would go straight through Marcus and hit Pat too. He had the gun aimed on Marcus as he managed to get to his feet. Pēteris hit Marcus in the lower back. He couldn't put his full force into it due to his shoulder, but it was enough to make him wince with pain. That gave Pat his chance, who kicked him hard between the legs. Marcus bent over, doubled up. Pēteris took Brian's knife out of Dec's side and thrust it into Marcus's back. He fell to his knees. Pat punched him in the face as he looked him straight in the eye. The blow knocked him to the floor.

Fletcher had been swinging wildly with the kitchen knife. He'd not only cut Jānis and Phoebe, but Archie too, on his left bicep. Fletcher was backed into a corner, still swinging the blade. It was hard to get near him. No one could get round the back. To get close to him would mean risking being stabbed. He was still raging, 'Come on! I'll take you all on!'

When Archie and Del realised that Brian and the others were now in the kitchen, they realised Fletcher was on his own. They backed off, giving him room. Fletcher continued to swing, but slowed down to a stop as soon as the realisation dawned on him too. He saw that he was now one against six men and two women. He was panting hard, as were the rest. The adrenaline had started to subside a little and there was a lot of huffing and puffing going on.

'You may as well put that knife down Fletcher, don't you think?' Archie said, as he manged to catch his breath.

'Six of ya! Fuckin' amateurs, the lot of ya!' he shouted, as he waved the knife again.

'I think you'll find there's two of your fellas through there!' Pat shouted as he nodded towards the hallway. 'So, let's not debate who the amateurs are, shall we?'

'So, what now, Archie lad?' Fletcher said, as he finally put the knife down.

Archie took a deep breath. He stepped to the side and surveyed the room. He was cut, not badly, but he'd have a pretty scar. Brian had been shot in the thigh by the looks of it, Pēteris had been shot in the shoulder, Jānis was cut, as was Phoebe. In the melee he'd not noticed she'd been cut. He walked over to where she was stood, leant against the kitchen wall.

'You OK, Mum?'

'Oh yeah, I forgot she was your mum. I'd have done her serious damage if I'd remembered!' Fletcher shouted. Archie ignored him. He had no need to react now.

'Yeah, I'll live,' she replied. She opened her coat to reveal her top had been cut too, but allowed Archie to inspect the damage through the opening where she'd undone two of her buttons. It was quite a cut, but not too deep. A flesh wound, Frank would have said. 'Yeah, you'll live, Mum. Made of strong stuff you are.'

'Did you have to kill Kat?' Archie asked of Fletcher, as he walked the few steps back over.

'The bitch fuckin' betrayed me. She was dead the minute I found out. You can blame your pretty mum, though. She signed the forms at the spa in her own name.'

Phoebe closed her eyes, cursing herself. She looked at Kat's body. *I'm sorry*, she said in her head, hoping that Kat could hear her. Wherever she was, she hoped she didn't blame her.

Archie turned to look at Del. The look was enough. Del knew Archie was asking him if he wanted to do the honours, and Del's face said that he most certainly did. He walked the few paces towards Fletcher without averting his gaze. Fletcher knew what was coming and stiffened his stance. He then took up his fighting pose and stood slightly side on with his fists out in front of him, as a boxer would facing his opponent.

Del looked at Archie. There was no way Archie was going to allow Fletcher the opportunity to inflict any pain on Del. He shook his head. 'No way, Fletcher. You ain't earned that.' He looked to Pat, who threw him a gun. Archie aimed it at Fletcher's head. 'You have two choices, Fletcher. We can either torture you to death or you can go quickly, but either way, you're dying in this kitchen. Now step forward.'

Fletcher felt fear for the first time in a long time. He didn't want to die. He was too young to die. Kat's body looked so lifeless, but then it was. He took a step forward. He then saw the one other person left alive who had betrayed him – Andrea. He pictured Marcus and Dec coming in with her a yard or so in front. He knew she must have distracted them, the bitch. He then picked up the knife from the worktop in front of him and threw it expertly towards her. It hit her straight in the chest. She grabbed the handle with both of her hands, as she groaned. She dropped to her knees. Phoebe, although in pain herself, ran to Andrea's aid. She was dead before she reached her.

Phoebe ran towards Fletcher, screaming 'You bastard!' Pat grabbed her and held her firm as she wailed again; this time because her actions had aggravated her wound.

Del calmly walked over to where Andrea lay and took the knife from her chest. Fletcher had been swinging the very same knife only moments before, but was now stood legs apart, in defiance. Del said nothing as he approached him with a cold, hard stare. Archie still had the gun aimed at Fletcher's head.

Fletcher didn't flinch as Del came up behind him. And just like that, Del slit his throat – just like Shaney, one of Fletcher's men, had done to his son Paul. Fletcher gasped for breath. He held his throat and staggered as the life drained out of him. He dropped to his knees and Del then plunged the knife into his stomach. That was for John. Fletcher fell forward onto the blade and the knife exited through his back. Fletcher O'Brien was dead.

The room fell silent as they took in Fletcher's lifeless body. This was not how it had planned to be. Archie's phone rang. He picked it from his pocket. Three missed calls from Frank. He'd not even heard his phone ring in all the chaos.

'Archie! For fuck's sake. Thank fuck you've answered. What the fuck's happening?'

'Well, things have moved on a little,' he said.

'How? Come on, what's happened? Is everyone OK? I've tried you numerous times. I've rung Brian and Pat too. Is there no fucking signal over there?'

'Fletcher's dead, Frank.'

'Eh? Dead? How come? I fuckin' told ya not to go over there all guns blazing, for fuck's sake!' he bellowed.

Archie held the phone away from his ear and shook his head. He then told Frank what had happened in as much detail as he could remember. It was all a blur if he was honest, but Frank got the picture. He calmed down and told Archie what a good job he'd done, but that they now needed to act fast. There were bodies that needed disposing of in a way that wouldn't come back to them. Frank told Archie what to do. Archie listened intently. He was aware of the gravity of what could happen if he got this wrong. Frank reminded Archie of their deal with the Burbankses. He now had to ring them and put them in the picture. They needed to know quickly.

Frank had told Archie to still torch the place. It needed to look like an accident. Brian, Pat, Del and Phoebe made their way out of there. The private road seemed totally unaware of what had gone off. There was no sign of anyone. The residents were either too busy with their own lives or they were all out at work, but in all the time they were there, no one saw a soul from that road. All the houses were in large grounds and appeared to be well set back. No one, it seemed, had heard a shot. For that, everyone was thankful.

Archie and Pēteris stayed with Jānis. He made sure the CCTV was wiped and that it was no longer recording. Jānis then rigged up an electrical short circuit that, once he'd switched on the lights remotely, would start a fire. The fire would ignite in several rooms. Frank had told him to find some fuel of some sort if he could and to dowse the bodies. They were both aware this would lead to suspicion, but Frank had told Archie that he was sure the Burbankses would see to it that there was little investigation into the finer details. They had a payroll as big as Frank's, if not bigger. Frank was counting on everyone in Manchester to be glad Fletcher was out of the picture. It was a risk worth taking. The bodies had to be unrecognisable. By the time Archie had hit Manchester's ring road, Fletcher's house was ablaze. The fire service did their best later that day but it more or less burned to the ground.

Frank's conversation with the Burbanks brothers went well. They seemed non plussed by Archie leaving a few bodies and were happy for them to be burned. They assured Frank they could put on enough pressure if needed to ensure it wasn't investigated too well, but in return Frank had to forgo any retribution on the men who killed Paul and John. George told Frank there were enough bodies already and any more would make their job at silencing any investigation a stretch too far. Frank argued his corner, telling George that they needed to pay. They'd killed two of his men and others had smashed up his club. But George and Ivan didn't budge, and Frank did not want another war on his hands. He reckoned they'd done well to avert this one, so he accepted the terms. He knew he had no choice and that sometimes, even at the top table, you had to swallow things and move on.

The person he was most nervous about telling was Del, but that was only because he'd given him his word. And if there was one thing Frank was, it was a man of his word. This did not sit well with him, but sometimes the bigger picture was the best thing to look at. He told Del personally; he felt he owed him that much. Del took the news badly, as Frank had expected. He threatened to go over there himself with Michael and his boys, but Frank managed to persuade him that that would be a disaster all round. He wanted the men who did this, Shaney in particular, to suffer real pain, but he eventually accepted that he was never going to be able to avenge his son's death how he wanted. Frank Pearson did not go back on his word lightly, so Del knew Frank would've had no choice. Frank would be feeling just as bad as he did.

George and Ivan Burbanks had their men over at Fletcher's main club that afternoon. They took over his operations without too much aggravation. Newbie and Tiny tried to assert some authority but by tea time, they too were in the Burbankses' employ. The next day, George and Ivan, along with three of their men, visited Alderley Edge. They sent Frank a photo of Shaney with a bullet in his forehead, slumped over the bar. Frank showed it to Del. It pacified him.

Alfie and Courtney, Fletcher's children, were taken in by Kat's parents. They doted on them. Always had. They had never approved of Kat's choice of husband and for that, they had not seen as much of their grandchildren as they would have liked. And that had been painful for them. It had taken something like Kat's death to finally give them the time they deserved with them. Alfie and Courtney were, from that day forward, well-loved and well-nurtured children. It was just a shame that unconditional love and safety had come at such a high price.

chapter forty-three

Three days later

It was early morning, at the crematorium. Del got out of his car and straightened his tie. He'd not been to this crematorium before. Ted had decided on one well outside of Frank's patch to keep it further under the radar. He hugged tight his two sons, Ryan and Des, before following Frank and Archie. Michael, Jez and Pat followed, with the rest of the mourners behind them. The numbers were limited for obvious reasons – this was a funeral that was not officially taking place.

Frank and Archie had broken the news to Del two days before, the day after they'd torched Fletcher's house. Initially, Del had been angry at not being told that his son's body had been in a cold store for the past week and a half, but he soon calmed down to appreciate what was being offered to him. Today was important to him and even though he knew it was under the radar, he was so grateful that his son could have a send-off.

Del, Ryan, Des and Michael acted as the bearers and carried Paul's coffin in. Frank, Archie, Pat and Brian carried in John's. A local celebrant had been paid to deliver the service. He'd spoken to Del at length only the day before and had quickly put together a brief outline of Paul's life. There was only ten minutes allowed for each service, but although they were brief, they were delivered with affection and passion. Del was thankful for small mercies, but all too quickly it was over and they were being led out of the chapel by Ted, who was acting as a funeral director.

Once they were outside, the flowers were brought through and were laid out, although they had to be removed straight away and taken to the garden of remembrance, where they would stay for one day only. Frank paid extra for that.

Everyone went to Frank's house for a drink and a sausage on a stick afterwards, where the solemn atmosphere soon evaporated. Once a few alcoholic beverages had been poured, everyone, including Del, toasted Paul's and John's lives. Stories of the past few days were told more than once; Archie holding court for most of it. He was proud of the way he had handled things at Fletcher's and was revelling in the plaudits. Frank was full of admiration for his young heir. He'd met with unexpected circumstance and had dealt with it like the criminal Frank wanted him to be. Laughter flowed, with Brian taking a ribbing due to his walking stick, a result of his bullet wound in his thigh, and Pēteris too, with his arm in a sling.

Frank had heard from the Burbankses of how they'd taken over Fletcher's operations. It didn't appear that there would be retribution from any circle. Fletcher would not be missed. At times like this, Frank would get quite philosophical and remember Daniel's funeral. He was in the kitchen with Gloria thinking about Richie. The past couple of weeks since seeing him had been quite a time. Even though Frank only usually went once a month, he decided he'd go and see him the following week. He had a lot to tell him. Richie wouldn't want to hear, but Frank would tell him anyway. He always told him what was happening, never realising, of course, that hearing stories of the outside world, stories of which Richie could and would have been a part of, only served to fuel his anger and resentment. Frank never gave that a thought, though.

'Another cup of tea, Frank?' Gloria asked.

'Yeah, go on then, luv. Why not?'

chapter forty-four

One week later – The Shetland Isles

Kenny opened a tin of dog meat for Bertie. He bent down and scraped half of the tin into Bertie's bowl to go with the dry biscuits he'd already put in there. He then put the tin in the fridge. As he closed the fridge door, Bertie barked. He never barked, mainly because there was never anyone to bark at. He only ever barked if a bird came into the garden, and that was once a flood.

'What's up lad?' Kenny asked, taking his very creased face into his hands. 'What you barking at, eh? There's no one here.' Kenny kissed him on the top of his head.

His brother, Alan, had gone to Lerwick in the car around twenty minutes before and wouldn't be back for a good hour or so. Bertie barked again. Kenny was intrigued. He couldn't hear anything, but went to the window and looked out into the garden. Nothing but acres upon acres of fields, and the sea in the distance. He loved it up here and since coming back, he'd often wondered why he left Scotland in the first place. He wasn't from the Shetland Isles. Kenny had been brought up in Peebles in the Scottish Borders. Moving to Glasgow for work in his late teens was the start of his delinquency. He'd always liked the Scottish countryside, but had forgotten how much until now.

Bertie barked again. Kenny went outside, shutting the door behind him. As he did so, he felt a blow to the head, which knocked him back into the door. He was dazed but could make out two men in front of him. One of the men grabbed him and dragged him out into the garden.

'Frank sends his regards,' Trainer said.

They'd found him. He knew they would. Even when he was on the ferry from Aberdeen and felt a million miles away from Nottinghamshire, a voice kept telling him that they'd find him. He assured himself that he'd be ready for them but, of course, when it happened, he'd not been. In fact, it dawned on him that Frank Pearson hadn't even entered his head when he'd looked out of the window just now.

Kenny put his hands out in front of him in an act of compliance. He wasn't going to struggle. There was no point. There was no one for miles around and Alan was an hour away, plus Kenny knew full well these guys would be well prepared – one thing that he was not.

'Look, fellas, I know the score. I know you have a job to do, so let's just get on with it, eh,' he said, hoping that would appease them slightly. It didn't.

Frank had sent Trainer and Ryan, one of Del's lads, up to do Kenny. Frank had high hopes for Trainer.

He could see, even early on, that Trainer was the real deal and Frank wanted him to get as much experience under his belt as possible, as quickly as he could. He wanted Trainer to be one of Archie's main men moving forward.

'You fucked off, Kenny, and that cannot be tolerated. A bit like your brother. We watched him fuck off in the car, but don't worry, he's OK. We haven't harmed him too much. We'll release him once we've finished with you.'

Kenny's heart sank. The one thing he'd wanted to try and ensure was that Alan was kept out of it. Alan wasn't up for any bother; he was quite a handy fella in his own right, but he was no criminal. Kenny was never sure that Alan ever really understood the kinds of people he talked about. Alan knew the stuff Kenny had been involved in, and Kenny was straight with him when he arrived unannounced, but, in truth, Alan thought it was more a case of dealing with a few heavies who just liked a fight. He'd soon got the message, though, when Trainer and Ryan ran him off the road. They'd beaten him up badly and he was now tied up in the boot of his own car with the threat of death, should he breathe a word.

'Do you know how much grief you caused Mr Pearson, not to mention Archie too?' Trainer asked. Kenny said nothing. 'Now, Frank has been quite specific in his instructions as to what punishment you are to receive, Kenny. I can either tell you what we are going to do to you or we can keep that to ourselves and let it all be a surprise. What would you prefer?'

Kenny lowered his head. 'Just get the fuck on with it.'

Trainer and Ryan punched the hell out of him before pulling out his finger nails one by one. Kenny screamed, but, of course, there was no one to hear him, other than Bertie, who barked and cried for his master. They then chopped off his big toe and little toe from his right foot so that if he ever wanted to "fuck off" from anyone again, it would be a damn sight harder.

Trainer was a dog lover, so while Ryan stayed with Kenny, Trainer went inside and fussed over Bertie, who, in all the hugs and kisses, had completely forgotten about Kenny. Trainer wanted to take Bertie with him, but even he wasn't that cruel. He could see how much Kenny adored him. They then set off to catch the ferry back to Aberdeen, leaving one brother in agony and stopping to untie the other. They told Alan what they'd done to Kenny, making it clear that if he said anything, there would be more men sent to deal with them both once and for all. Alan now fully understood the kind of world Kenny had been mixed up in. He couldn't help but wish his brother had stayed the fuck in England.

chapter forty-five

Frank was at the care home, sat in Richie's room. He'd taken a call from Trainer to tell him the job in Shetland had been done. Frank was pleased. That was the final piece of the whole Fletcher saga put to bed. There were no more loose ends. Frank didn't like loose ends. He always said loose ends hanging about would only trip you up at some point. He'd learnt that early on in his criminal career, to always tie up loose ends.

Frank had only been there a couple of minutes. He'd only just arrived when Trainer had called. He had meant to come a couple of days ago but whilst ever there were loose ends to tie up, his mind had been occupied. Now he could relax a little and enjoy his time with his son.

'I've got loads to tell you, Son,' he said as he switched his phone onto silent. 'Loads. You won't believe what's happened since we last came to see you. It's not been three weeks yet, but bloody hell, what a time we've had. It all started once we'd left here really. Archie took a call in Clumber Park. We went there straight from here, you know, to have a walk and an ice cream and that, as you do. Well, that kicked off a chain of events that got us into a bit of a war with Fletcher O'Brien from Manchester. You'll remember him maybe. You'll remember his dad anyway, Arnie. Nice fella was Arnie; old style, a man of his word. A bit like me, really, I suppose. Well, anyway...'

Frank sat there for about forty minutes retelling Richie the story of the past three weeks. He went into some detail telling his son, who couldn't really give a flying fuck, all about Paul and John being murdered, the club getting smashed, how they sorted out the guys who came to Leeds and finally about Archie and the rest of them and how they put an end to it in Manchester. 'So that only really left that twat Kenny Walters to sort out. That was Trainer, the new guy running Leeds, on the phone earlier when I came in, telling me he'd sorted it and he was on his way back. He said the Shetland Isles are really nice. Maybe I'll go there one day. Maybe I'll take Gloria. She'll like that. She likes it nice and quiet, which Trainer said it is by the way. He says you can drive for miles and not see a soul.'

Frank had been telling his tale whilst staring out of the window most of the time. He did that so that he didn't have to look at Richie's face. He knew if he did he'd see how he didn't give a shit and that would just remind Frank that he wasn't really welcome there. If Richie could talk, he'd tell him to fuck off. Frank had thought about getting him one of those machines where he could talk through movement in his eyes, but he'd never done anything about it, only because he didn't want to hear what Richie had to say. Frank was in denial, you see. He regretted his actions and if he could turn back time, he would. He would forgive Richie for his part in Daniel's murder, realising that it was him who'd made Richie the way he was. Frank knew only too well that all behaviour is learnt and that the way he'd treated Richie for most of his life meant he was only ever going to turn out one way. It was his biggest regret, except for losing Renee, but bigger even than Daniel being taken so soon. No one knew that, though, only Frank, and it was a secret he would take to his grave. Even now at his time of life, Frank could not handle any perception that he was weak. To admit now that he'd been wrong all his life in how he'd treated Richie was something he just could not deal with. Frank was a stubborn man and that stubbornness would override any regrets he had about Richie. He did accept it, though. Frank was able to own it and to look in the mirror, and know only too well that he was the loser in all of this. But he also accepted that it was just how he was and he was never going to change now. He was prepared to take second best and to have his time alone with Richie once a month.

He changed his gaze to look at his son. Richie stared right back. They stared at each other for a whole minute before Frank spoke. He looked back out of the window first, though.

'I do love you, Son. You know that. I've told you often enough, but I'll tell you again. Do I have regrets about us? Of course I do. If I could turn the clock back, I would. I know you did what you did because I made you into that person. I take responsibility for that, Son, and I suppose growing up in the world in which you did and having me treat you like I did, just meant you never really knew how to act any differently.' Frank paused a moment before continuing. 'I still often think about your mum, you know. Not as much as I used to, but when I do, I get angry with myself because the gap seems to get longer and longer. I've never loved anyone like I loved your mum, Son. She was my soulmate. Even at a young age, I knew she was the one for me. I would've been different with your mum at my side. Don't get me wrong, I'd never have been a 9 to 5 man, I'd have always strayed over the line, but your mum would have kept me in check. Plus I'd never have risked a lifetime in prison if I'd been with your mum. All my life I've done things that, in different circumstances, would have resulted in a lifetime behind bars, and even though I had you and Daniel, I was prepared to risk it. I wouldn't have done that with your mum. I loved her too much. It's funny 'cos without her, all I had was you two, and you two were the only thing I had left of her, but once she'd gone, there was only one way I was going, and that was down the path I ended up walking.'

He paused again. 'I do love Gloria. She's been my rock for so long, my wingman and the one person I have in my life who has never been a part of my criminal activities. But the love I have for Gloria, as strong as it is, is not like the love I had for my Renee.' He then turned to Richie, who was still sat looking straight at him. Frank wished he could sense what Richie was thinking. Maybe Richie was thinking *It's OK, Dad. I forgive you.* 'I hope you can forgive me, Son. They say you are in good health, so I have to live with the fact you will be like this for a long time yet, but then I know you do too.' He got up and walked over to him. He kissed the top of his head and then bent down to Richie's eye level. 'It is my biggest regret, Son. Other than losing your mum, it's my biggest regret, bigger than losing Daniel so young. I've never told you that before, but it lays heavy on my shoulders. I love you, Richie Pearson.'

Frank then stepped out of the French doors and into the garden. Today's visit was over. He wiped a tear from his eye as he quietly closed the doors behind him and sniffled. He took a moment to compose himself and then walked to his car, texting Faye, the nursing home manager, on his way.

Faye was in her office as usual. She heard her mobile ping and knew what the text would say. She was right. *All OK as usual. I'll be in my car.* She grabbed her handbag and headed out the back door into the rear car park. Frank saw her coming. He took a brown envelope out of his inside jacket pocket and held it out of the window. Faye took it and quickly placed it into her handbag. Frank winked at her and said, 'See you in a month. I'll confirm the day nearer the time.' Faye nodded and watched Frank drive off. She smiled, as she usually did. Frank always said the same one line. Nothing more, nothing less. She returned to the back entrance of the home, over the pebbled car park, thinking about what she'd buy with her wedge.

Richie thought about what his dad had said to him. *Blah, blah, blah. What a load of fucking shit that was.*

chapter forty-six

Two weeks later

Everyone was at Frank's house: all of the family, his top table, plus a few of the other more senior members of his businesses and one or two acquaintances. It had been three weeks since the incident at Fletcher's place and two weeks since Trainer had made his visit to Shetland.

Frank and Archie had thought to let the dust settle before throwing a celebration party to mark the occasion – that Archie had finally made the crucial step into the big time. Frank had been impressed with his grandson, not only how he had dealt with Fletcher on the day when faced with unexpected danger, but the whole thing. From taking the call from Paul at Clumber Park at the end of May, after the family had visited Richie, to torching Fletcher's gaff, Archie had shown his true colours. He was now the main man and today was about Frank officially handing over the reins to the young gun. Frank had decided to take a step back. He'd tried a couple of years before to let Archie come through, but he'd always been there a quarter step behind as a safety net. If truth be known,

Frank was still the one steering the ship. That was now to change, though. From this day onwards, Archie would carry the weight of the Pearson empire on his shoulders. Frank would still be in the background, to assist and advise where necessary, but he'd made it crystal clear to Archie that he now had to stand and fall by his own decisions. Frank would now only be there when absolutely necessary.

Everyone present knew what they were going to be told that day. It was no secret, but officially, until Frank made the announcement, things were as they always had been. Everyone was pleased; everyone except Jez. Jez liked and respected Archie as much as everyone else, but he'd seen more in his life of crime than most – and recently, he'd seen things that caused him concern. Jez was a wingman, a second, someone who was always there to serve and protect, and that meant he saw things others didn't. It's amazing what you can see and hear in this world by being in the shadows. Jez had seen Archie look at Frank for support. He'd seen Frank waiting for that assuring look from Archie, and it had made Jez nervous. It seemed he was the only one with any reservations about Archie's pedigree for being Frank's successor at his young age. He said nothing, though, not even to Frank. He just hoped he was wrong.

One man who was very pleased with how things appeared to be unfolding was Steven Wallace. Steven had been in Frank's employ ever since he and his brother, Gary, had tried to muscle in on the Pearson criminal empire back in 1990. They'd banked on a guy from Leeds called Gerry Clarke to assist them, but he, like them, had come unstuck. Frank killed Gerry at point blank range. Gary was shot dead by Daniel, and Steven, it appeared, had got off lightly, with superficial injuries in comparison. He'd lost an eye and some fingers, but he'd been allowed to live, although he'd been made to work for Frank. For nearly thirty years Steven had worked for the very man who had been instrumental in not only his brother's death, though it was Daniel who had pulled the trigger, but also, in the early days, of humiliating him in his home town. Frank had reckoned all those years ago that making Steven his lackey was a great punishment for him.

Steven and Gary had been the top dogs of Leicestershire for a while and had commanded respect. All of that disappeared overnight and it took a long time for the humiliation Steven felt to go away. He couldn't look people on the street in the eye and had to suffer the whispers of how he could only look people in the eye with one eye anyway. He'd worn a glass eye for years, and the jibes did die down eventually, but it was still, after all this time, something that raged within him. He'd learnt to live with it and had, for twenty years or so, accepted the hand that he'd been dealt, and any desires to make amends or to get revenge had long since subsided. That was until around four years ago, when his sister-in-law had reared her ugly head again.

Gary had been married to Lorraine. When Gary was murdered, she went off the rails. She couldn't handle his murder and had taken to sniffing the very drugs she used to help distribute. In her day she'd been a shrewd young lady, but the drugs had soon taken their toll. She ended up pregnant after a one-night stand and had fucked off when the baby was a toddler, leaving her son to be brought up by her parents.

Four years ago, after having no contact with any of the family for over sixteen years, she came back. At first, it had been hard, both for Lorraine and her son. Steven had initially wanted nothing to do with her, but one day, around three months after her return, she told Steven something that knocked him for six. The father of her son – then 19 – was none other than Richie Pearson. She'd met him in a bar one night in Loughborough and, well, she'd had sex with him over the bonnet of her car and Johnny was the result of that night. That was why she'd not been able to cope and had fucked off. She'd knowingly slept with the brother of the very man who was suspected of killing her husband, and had had a baby boy with him.

Lorraine couldn't take to Johnny, but the whole scenario just showed how screwed up she was at the time. Steven didn't believe her at first, but she assured him that he couldn't possibly be anyone else's. Richie Pearson was the father of Steven's sister-in-law's illegitimate child. Steven could well call Johnny his nephew; not technically, of course, but close enough for Steven to forget the technicalities and use it to his advantage. He had seen young Johnny a couple of times over the years, at family get-togethers, when his own parents had made a fuss of their grandchild, but other than that, up until a few years ago, he'd never bothered with him.

At first, Steven had not known what to do with the information. It had taken him a few days to really process it, before deciding to get a DNA test done. He needed to know for certain. He couldn't risk going to Richie's care home. It was only a fairly small place, so getting in and out undetected would be hard. So, instead, he took hair from Frank's head and used that. He faked a trip and a stumble, falling into Frank, to get the hair, but it had been easy enough. He had a contact who could get DNA tests done under the counter and who assured him that a grandad and grandchild match was no problem, and that a hair from the grandad would be good enough. The contact knew nothing of their identities, and it had to stay that way: the Pearsons had used the same guy before themselves.

Steven couldn't trust his sister-in-law to keep it to herself, so he'd paid her a large stash to fuck off again, on the promise never to return. Lorraine was only interested in money. That's why she'd returned when she did; that was obvious quite early on. With this information, Steven could not have her staying put. Lorraine was happy with her pay-off and disappeared with not so much as a goodbye or fuck all, knowing that her brother-in-law would kill her if she ever breathed a word.

Lorraine's bombshell had been the catalyst to bring all of those feelings back to the fore. They'd long been buried, waiting to erupt, and Johnny, his nephew of sorts, was going to be the vehicle for that opportunity. After getting Johnny on board, which, to be fair, had been quite easy, Steven set up a meet between him and Alice. Johnny saw him as his uncle. They both knew it was stretching it a little, but neither of them cared a fuck. He was a nasty fucker, was Johnny, with an explosive temper. On the outside, he looked so sweet and pleasant, but rub him up the wrong way and he could wrestle with the best of them. Johnny was, at this point, training to be a physiotherapist, which Steven, even with one glass eye, could see the benefit of that in his little plan. He just needed to get Johnny in with the family. He needed him on the inside and Johnny, being the young short-tempered wannabe that he was, was only too keen to get involved. To get him on side, Steven plied him with tales about how the Pearsons had murdered his mum's husband and how badly they'd treated Steven himself. He left a few details out, of course, to blur the facts, but it had worked, and after listening to a few of Steven's tales, Johnny was as vengeful as Steven. He was always amazed at how young lads like Johnny, who had a bit of rawness about them, could so easily be swept up by the gangster life. Lads like Johnny were in awe of blokes like Steven. Fellas like Steven were heroes to them. It had been so easy to get Johnny fired up, especially given the fact he'd never even known Steven's brother, Gary. To listen to him talk now, though, you'd think Gary had been his favourite uncle.

Steven then paid a local guy to make advances towards Alice one afternoon at The Burnt Stump pub, just off the A60, and for Johnny, of course, to sort him out. That had all led to Alice swooning over him and, well, the rest just fell into place. Steven was in it for the long haul and planning to topple the Pearsons from the inside was not going to be easy. Frank was Johnny's grandad after all, but after listening to Steven's version of events, any concerns he had of Johnny pining after his long-lost grandad were well and truly unfounded. No one could suspect a thing, and that took time and patience, but here Steven was, sat in Frank's pile, enjoying the hospitality, waiting to hear how young gun Archie was taking over and Frank was moving well into the background. That move could just well be what Steven had been waiting for. It all depended on whether Johnny could get his bit sorted soon. Time would well and truly tell, but Steven Wallace was becoming impatient. He had waited long enough to avenge his brother's death. He was sick of waiting.

Frank clinked his glass and cleared his throat. 'Now then, ladies and gents, I think you all know why I have called this little get-together. Trying to keep things a secret with you lot is nigh on impossible, so I'll not string it out.' He turned to Archie, who knew that was his cue to get up and join his grandad on the floor. He stood next to Frank, who put his arm around him.

'Today is a momentous day in the Pearson family business. I've been around a long time. Me, Brian and

Jez started out together running the doors of Mansfield, back in the day when we were no more than teenagers really, and, well, together, and I mean together, we built up an unrivalled business – unrivalled in the sense that at the heart of who we are is loyalty. There is no one in this room I would not trust with my life, and that is unheard of in our world. But, listen, I'm digressing and if I don't get back on track, I'll end up filling up.'

The room chuckled as everyone sat in awe of the man they would, indeed, all take a bullet for. Everyone except Steven Wallace. Steven sat there stony-faced as Frank continued.

'So, today is the day that I officially retire from being head of operations. Archie here, my grandson and heir, is now officially head of the family business. He is the one you will all now report to and he will be making all of the decisions. I am having a well-earned rest.'

Frank then looked over to Gloria. She too got up and joined Frank on stage. Archie took a step to the side, as Frank put his arm around her. 'A well-earned rest with my wife-to-be. Gloria and I are getting married.' Frank then hugged Gloria as the room stood to applaud their news. Steven Wallace got up and clapped with the rest of them.

Archie raised his glass. 'Hip hip hooray!' he shouted. The room did the same and Archie repeated this two more times as Frank and Gloria happily received congratulations from their nearest and dearest.

Frank had asked Gloria two days ago. It had been a lifetime in coming, but, at 69 years of age, Frank was finally ready for marriage. He always said that if he couldn't marry Renee, then he'd marry no one and Gloria had always respected that. But in retirement, Frank wanted to be man and wife. It was time to tie the knot. All that was left was to fix the date.

Frank clinked his glass again and waited for the noise to lower. 'I nearly forgot ... there's one more announcement.' Frank looked at Jez, who walked on over to him. Frank stuck out his hand in readiness for a handshake. Jez shook his head and smiled and then hugged Frank like a long-lost brother. Frank returned the compliment. Everyone stayed silent in admiration of two men who had seen it all. Frank Pearson and Jez Carrington were of the old style. They were men of a different time and men like that might never be seen again. Frank finally pulled away. He wiped away his tears with the back of his hand. 'This man,' he said, 'this man has been at my side for fifty years. He has been my wingman for so long I just cannot put into words what he means to me. Jez, it's been an absolute pleasure, my friend.' Jez nodded, tears rolling down his cheeks. He was never comfortable with the limelight. 'Jez is retiring too. It's time for him to hang up his holster and, like me, enjoy a quieter time.'

The group stayed silent, only because what everyone was witnessing was so powerful, to break the silence would be criminal.

It was Jez's turn to say a few words. He took a deep breath and faced his audience.

'Thanks.'

Everyone burst out laughing. Jez had broken the silence. Frank looked at the floor and shook his head as he laughed. 'You're a funny fucker at times, Jez Carrington, but I love ya to bits, my friend.' They shook hands and embraced once more.

The only dry eye in the room was Steven Wallace's false one.

Frank was in his element. He loved jovial occasions like this. Everyone seemed to be having a good time. The drinks were flowing, the food was good, courtesy of outside catering, and there were pats on the back aplenty. He'd even had a whisky to toast the occasion. He was back on builder's tea soon enough, though.

'So, come on, Gloria. When's the big day?' Alice asked. 'Can I be a bridesmaid?'

'Of course you can, sweetheart. I want all of you ladies to be my bridesmaids,' Gloria replied, looking at Alice, Phoebe, Raquel, Sarah and Marie. 'There's no limit on bridesmaids, is there, so I can have you all! How the hell I'm going to choose my maid of honour God only knows. Just promise me you'll all be supportive of who I choose. I don't want anyone upset.'

'Of course we will, won't we, girls?' Phoebe said, raising her glass. They all clinked glasses together and reiterated Phoebe's words.

Archie was stood in a circle talking with Pat, Steven and Brian. 'When did you know about Jez?' Pat asked.

'Last week, mate. Couldn't say owt but Frank told me of his own plans, and mine of course. He just told me I was taking over. You know how he is. He doesn't ask, does he, but then he dropped it in about Jez, which to be fair I'm not surprised about. He's earned it, ain't he?'

'Too fuckin' right he has. The man's a legend, only one step behind Frank,' Pat agreed. 'What about you, Brian? I thought you might take it easy too?'

'Nah, not me, mate. I've always said I'll die on the job – and not that job either,' he said with a wink. 'I've got nowt else to do. Without this lot, I'm nobody. I'd just be a miserable fucker. I'm here till he says otherwise,' Brian said, pointing his glass to Archie.

Frank and Gloria had chosen August Bank Holiday weekend for their big day, around six weeks away. They were banking on the sun shining to help make it a day to remember. It had taken Frank nearly fifty years to marry. Now he was retiring, he wanted to spend the rest of his years married to the lady he loved more than life itself. Gloria had been his rock for so long, and Frank would often ponder as to where he would be without her. She had kept him grounded on so many occasions, it was hard to recognise the enormity of her influence over the years. Everyone was happy for them, which only went to further cement Frank's standing in not only the criminal fraternity but the local community too. Frank knew he had hanger-ons and people in supposed positions of authority and influence in his circle, but he also knew that they needed him, as much as he needed them. It had always made Frank laugh how alleged pillars of the community were often as bent as he was, just in different ways. Everyone seemed to be out for what they could get and knowing Frank Pearson well enough to shake his hand at any public gathering, was as lucrative for them as it often was for Frank. Everyone scratched one another's backs. Frank just scratched a little harder. The difference was, Frank knew why they courted his favour and always made sure he had leverage. They, on the other hand, seemed to genuinely think Frank liked them, even that Frank was in awe of them. That would always make Frank laugh. Leverage was one thing Archie understood well. Frank had drilled it into him early on and, as a result, Archie had things on people that he could present to them at any time. Frank played the game, though, and took the pats on the back from all the well-wishers and would ensure they all had their opportunity to be seen at the wedding. He would do it for Archie to keep the relationships well placed for him.

One person that gave Frank cause for concern, though, was Richie. No one knew of his visits to his son. They assumed his hatred was as intense as ever. Frank could deal with the regret at putting him in a wheelchair – he had to, he couldn't turn back time – but he now had a chance to show Richie that the things he said to him were sincere. On nearly every occasion, Frank would tell him he was sorry for the past, and he prayed that Richie had accepted his apology, but if he then went and excluded him from his wedding, he would not be able to look him in the eye. Frank wanted him there. What he was struggling with was how people would react to that. Gloria would be fine, he knew that, but Frank found it hard to show any sign of weakness to the outside world, especially when he'd carried on the pretence for so long. Frank was resolute on Richie being at his wedding. He just didn't yet know how he was going to announce it.

chapter forty-seven

Archie was enjoying a stroll with Sarah and Mary around Rufford Park, a beautiful area of North Nottinghamshire, off the A614 near to Edwinstowe. He'd just bought them both an ice cream. Mary was fast asleep in her pushchair. The park was busy with families picnicking on the open grassed areas and walking around the lake. It had been three weeks since the announcements of the wedding and Archie being the official new head of the Pearson empire. He'd received lots of support from criminals around the country all saying that he was a chip off the old block and that he'd be welcomed to the top table. No one ever said whether the old block was Frank or Daniel, and Archie never clarified it. He was only too happy to be receiving the plaudits.

Even though they were both still young and only really just starting out in adult life, Sarah knew her husband better than he knew himself. Like a lot of the women in the Pearson family, Sarah was happy to sit in the wings. She was placid and caring and whilst she understood how things were, and how the future was likely to be for her, she would do anything to change the life Archie had been given. Was he the man he pretended to be? She saw the anxiety in his face, the nervousness in his mannerisms and when he lay in bed at night, unable to sleep, she knew he was worrying about the life he led. She never said anything, of course. She knew better than to suggest Archie was struggling. She was well aware of things he'd done, things he'd had to deal with and the end of Fletcher O'Brien. If anyone had ever harboured doubts about Archie, that had put them to bed. He'd shown his mettle there, yet that had been done with Grandad Frank never being more than half a step behind him. Sarah wasn't sure if her husband was the man to take on the legacy of Frank Pearson. Without Frank in the shadows, even two steps behind, did Archie have what it took to be head of a firm like the Pearsons'. One thing she did know was that there was nothing she could do about it, and that, more than anything, scared her to death.

'Great here, innit?' Archie said, licking his ice cream. 'Great to just get away from it all for a bit and well, you know, just be a normal family having a stroll around the lake with an ice cream and not having any shit to deal with.'

Sarah smiled an ironic smile. Yes, it was nice and something that she would love to do more often. She lay her head on his upper arm as they watched the ducks. They almost looked like any other family of three. She thought of the other husbands there who worked in factories, husbands who worked in offices and husbands who did things on computers. Then she thought of her husband: the head of one of the UK's biggest and most feared criminal families.

'Yes, it's great,' she replied. 'Lovely to just, as you say, get away from it all. We should do this more often. I'm sure we could.'

'We will. I promise.'

It was an empty promise. He meant it, in that moment, but it wouldn't happen. She watched a young boy feeding the ducks out of the white paper bag he was holding close to his chest, and said a silent prayer to keep Archie safe. It wasn't the first time she'd prayed for him to find the strength to leave and hand the baton to someone else, but she'd long given up on that hope. Archie would never do that. He'd always be keeping up with being the next Frank Pearson. But he wasn't Frank. Sarah now just prayed for him to remain safe. That was all she could do.

chapter forty-eight

'Come on, Frank! For fuck's sake, spit it out!' Jez barked, his hands clasped with his elbows on his knees. 'I know you want to tell me something. Fuck me, I've known you long enough to know when you need to get something off your chest.'

Jez continued to sit forward as he studied his old boss. He'd taken a well-deserved holiday after Frank announced his retirement. He'd been to Croatia and then Montenegro before stopping off in London for a few nights on his return. He'd only been back three days when that morning, Frank rang to say he was popping round. Jez was pleased. He was quite missing the day-to-day craic with Frank. Jez was ready to call it a day, of that he was still sure, but the buzz of the life was missing, so Frank calling had him itching to find out what had been happening. He knew Frank, even from the back seat, would know everything that was going off. Jez was dying to know, but all Frank had done was ask him about his holiday. This wasn't Frank, not even in retirement. He never gave two fucks about your holiday, so either he'd changed beyond all recognition or it was just small talk for what he really wanted to discuss.

'What you on about? I'm just interested in your holiday,' he replied defensively.

'Fuck off, Frank. I know you have something on your mind and I'm sure you popped round here today to tell me all about it. Like you, I'm officially retired, so we can sit here all day if you want, but we both know at some point it'll all come out. Always does. So, I'll put the kettle on and we can have another brew.'

Jez walked into the kitchen. He lived in a nice stone cottage with sash windows just off the A617 towards Newark. It was double fronted with a small garden to the front and had a very neat rear garden that Jez loved to potter in. It was semi-rural, secluded and just enough off the beaten track for no one to really know it was there. He'd been there for just over ten years and loved it. Everyone thought he was mad, being cut off on his own, and it was well rumoured that he'd have it back up for sale within a few months of buying it, but he liked everything about it and had no plans to move. He could never understand why people couldn't see why, after his years of protecting Frank, he loved to retreat to his cottage and be on his own. Jez enjoyed his own company, although he did miss the action during the day.

Frank followed him and stood in the doorway whilst he made the tea. Jez knew he was there, but didn't look up.

'I want Richie at the wedding,' Frank blurted out like

a schoolboy admitting he was the one who'd smashed the window with his football.

Jez said nothing as he poured the boiling water into the two mugs. He poured in a drop of milk, stirred them both and walked silently to his sofa, brushing past Frank in the doorway. Frank went and sat opposite, just as he had been a moment or two before.

'Wow, wasn't expecting that, Boss,' Jez said, stroking his chin. 'Why?'

This was the reason Frank had been so hesitant to tell anyone, Jez included. He knew he didn't have to explain his reasons, but deep down he wanted to get it all off his chest and Jez was the one man he knew he could confide in before he told the world. He took a deep breath.

'If I could turn back the clock, I'd not have done what I did. I regret doing that to him, Jez. He's my son. No father should do that to their offspring.'

Jez stuck his bottom lip out as he nodded slowly, taking it in. 'How long you had regrets?'

'More or less from the moment I saw him after Bonnie had finished with him. I was angry, Jez, you can understand that. He was responsible for Daniel's murder and, well, I had to do it, didn't I?'

Jez didn't answer. He was a big believer in that we all have a choice. No matter what the situation, we always have a choice. But Frank didn't need to hear that.

'Have you told him?' Jez asked.

Frank nodded. 'Yeah, many times. I go and see him. No one knows and I mean no one. Well, except Faye at the nursing home, the manager there, but she has to. She makes sure no one sees me and I pay her in return. Been going for a long time. It was good for me. I needed to do it. I needed to tell him I was sorry.'

Jez shook his head in amazement. 'Well, I can honestly say, Frank, I had no idea and for that matter, to my knowledge, neither does anyone else. Everyone thinks you still despise him and that seeing him like that is what you wanted. What you still want for that matter. Fuck me, Frank, this will be a shock to everyone.'

'I know. That's why I need to ask a favour of you.'

'What?'

'I want you to be seen as the one to plant that thought in my head. I'd like you, in front of everyone, to tell me that I should have him there. I will say no way and all that shit, but you then tell me that life's too short and all that bollocks. We'll think of something, but that way, I can sit on it for a day or two and then, you know, just say that I've mulled it over and he is my son and that kind of stuff. I'll be able to keep face and Richie can be there. It would mean a lot to me, Jez. I wouldn't ask otherwise. But I can't face everyone knowing I've been lying to them all this time.'

Jez held Frank's gaze. 'But you can face telling me?'

'Yeah, strange, innit? But yeah, with you, I've got no hang-ups about it. Don't ask me to explain it 'cos

I can't, but I love you more than life itself, Jez, and I know ... well, I'm pretty sure ... you'll not judge me.'

'You're a strange man at times, Frank, but of course I will. I'd do owt for you, you know that. And when I think of what I've done for you over the years, this'll be a piece of cake. When am I to do it anyway?'

'Tomorrow. Be at mine 6ish. Just having a few drinks and a bit of food. Gloria is sorting stuff out with the bridesmaids and all that, so everyone who I need to witness this will be there.'

chapter forty-nine

Frank splashed a bit of aftershave on his face and then looked in the mirror. He was nervous. He could count on one hand the number of times in his life that he'd been nervous. Tonight, he had to play a blinder. He had run through things with Jez and was quietly confident that if they both stuck to the script, he'd be OK.

The house was busy. Archie was there with Sarah and Mary; Phoebe too, with Alice and Johnny. Pat, Brian and Jez were reminiscing about old times, as were Steven, Del and Michael. Del's sons, Ryan and Des, were chatting with Trainer. Raquel was talking in equal measure to the fellas about torture and beatings and to the women about flowers and dresses. There were a few others who had also been invited but the main people who needed to hear tonight's events had come and were either supping expensive fizz or the usual beers.

Frank went down to mingle. He couldn't help but hold court, even though he tried hard to leave it to Archie – he was used to being the centre of attention. His very presence had meant people looked to him to take the lead. Even Archie would still look to Frank to take over if he felt the spotlight too much. Tonight was one of those nights. No one really noticed how Archie instinctively took a sidewards step as Frank found his feet. No one except for Sarah. She always noticed when Archie searched for back-up.

'I bet you're so excited, Gloria. I know I would be,' Alice said, looking round for Johnny as she spoke. Johnny was with Steven, so had no chance of hearing her. Alice dreamt of getting married. Everyone knew except Johnny. Either that or he just didn't want to see it.

'Ooh I am, luv. Been a long time coming, as I've already said, but I'm so chuffed. I never thought he'd ever ask me, you know, with how he felt about Renee and all that. I'd have been happy as I was – I always told him that – but every girl loves to get married, don't they?'

'Yeah, I wish my Johnny would take the hint,' Alice said, rolling her eyes. 'Fat chance there, though. You ever wanted to be walked down the aisle, Raquel?'

Raquel smiled and laughed a little. 'No chance. Not the marrying kind, me. When I was little, I always did, but once I left home and, well, got into the "trade" so to speak, there was little chance of that. And, I don't know, over the years, I've never given it much thought.'

'You've had your fair share though, lady,' Phoebe quipped with a smirk.

'Hey, you're not wrong,' Raquel said, keen to end

the conversation there and then considering she'd shagged Phoebe's husband, for years. Her encounters with Daniel, and Richie for that matter, had, as far as she was aware, remained a secret and she was keen to keep it that way. Raquel took the opportunity to catch Pat's eye and make out that he wanted a word. She made her excuses and left the little posse of women talking about marriage and sex to go and chat with Pat, who was careful not to appear too surprised when Raquel stood next to him and joined in their conversation.

The evening was going well. Everyone was in good spirits. The finer details of the wedding had been discussed, but Frank was keen to get the real reason why he'd arranged the evening over with. He caught Jez's eye and as discreetly as he could, gave him the nod. Jez was in a small group with Frank, Gloria, Sarah, Archie and Phoebe.

'Anyway Frank, is everyone you wanted to be at the wedding coming? No no-shows I presume?'

'What! Give over, Jez, this is the society wedding of the year! In fact, have we sold the rights to it yet, Gloria?' Frank joked. 'Everyone who's been invited is coming. They wouldn't dare not turn up, would they, let's be honest,' Frank continued, making the group laugh. 'Everyone that I care about will be there.' He raised his mug of tea and the others their glasses.

'No chance of Richie coming then?' Jez said with a smile.

'There's no fucking chance of that! I'd rather call it off!' Frank said angrily.

'Shame, though – you know, when you put everything aside – that he won't be there.'

'You what? A shame? Is it fuck a shame! Let's not forget what he did, eh!' Frank replied, his voice getting louder.

Jez put up his hands in mock surrender. 'Just a thought, Frank, that's all. Just a thought. Time goes on, you know. Time's supposed to heal, that's all I'm saying.'

There was silence, just as Frank had hoped. No one had yet supported Frank, which he'd banked on.

'Well, I take it the silence means you all think Jez is right, does it?' he snapped.

Again, silence.

'Look, let's forget it. I wish I'd not said owt,' Jez said, from the script.

'No, fuck that. This silence speaks louder than words. So, come on then, does anyone think that me not having Richie at the wedding is wrong somehow, eh? After what he did?'

Frank took a step back as he said it, as did Jez, so as to open their small group up to the wider room. Everyone could now hear what Frank was saying, just as he'd planned. He wanted the whole room to hear people's responses. Frank looked at Phoebe – nothing. He looked at Alice, then Archie and, finally, at the one person who he counted on more than anyone to give him the response he wanted: Gloria.

'Maybe Jez is right, Frank. It would be nice to use our wedding as the platform to new beginnings. He *is* your son at the end of the day. Just think about it.'

Frank glared at her. His outward glare was one of anger and frustration, but inwardly it was one of love and admiration. He knew she wouldn't let him down. Gloria could forgive anything. That was who she was. She didn't have a nasty bone in her body.

Frank scanned the room. He looked at Archie, who had idolised his uncle growing up. He and Richie had, for a while, been inseparable. And there was Phoebe, who deep down knew it was Richie who had saved her from being raped all those years back. Something she'd never forget.

Phoebe spoke first. 'Just think about it, Frank, eh? Like Gloria says, think about it. No one here would have an issue with it, I don't think,' she said, addressing the room to give them an opportunity to say their piece. But no one said a thing.

'I need a fucking drink,' Frank said, as he marched out of the room to his study. Gloria made a move to follow him. Jez put out his hand. 'Let *me* go,' he said, reciting the script. Gloria, as ever, accommodated.

For the next two days, Frank appeared to be in a mood. He was sharp with almost everyone, except Gloria. Gloria was a peacemaker; she avoided conflict wherever possible, but she was also not afraid to tackle difficult subjects with Frank when appropriate.

Frank knew Gloria better than anyone; at some point she would talk to him about it. He just had to bide his time.

He came in from the garden. He'd been pottering about, keeping himself busy – and keeping out of the way. Phoebe and Alice had been round with his granddaughter, Mary, and Frank knew that while Mary was asleep they'd have been discussing things. As he slipped off his shoes, Gloria spoke. 'You can't go on being off with everyone. It's not fair. We have a wedding to organise and I don't want you spoiling it with your funny moods, Frank.'

Frank put his boots in the cupboard, without acknowledgement.

'Are you listening to me?' Gloria continued. She was seldom sharp, but on this occasion, Frank felt it. He'd dragged it out long enough now.

'What do you want me to do – let him come? The person who ruined everything?'

Frank purposely played the injured party, rather than the aggressor. Gloria changed her body language. She stepped forward and stood him square on. She stroked his cheek and said the one thing Frank was hoping she would say above all else.

'Can you do it for *me*, Frank? Can you, for me, let the past stay in the past? You're too old now to be holding grudges and letting the past eat away at you. I know who you are, Frank Pearson. Lord knows I know who you are – and *what* you are for that matter. I love you and I never ask you for anything, but, for me, put it to bed. He's your son. Let the celebration of our wedding be the time you let it go. Don't have regrets, Frank, not at your age. You may never get another chance to put it right. No one will think any less of you; in fact, people will respect you doing this. And look, you can always say you did it for me.'

Frank tilted his head. That last comment hit a nerve. What did she mean? Gloria sensed he had picked up on that.

'I know you, Frank, better than you know yourself. You're an open book as far as I'm concerned. I know you have regrets. You don't need to tell me; I know you. Take this opportunity to lay it to rest – in front of everyone – and use me as your reason for doing it. Say you did it for me because it's what I wanted – Richie, your son, at our wedding.'

Gloria stared into his eyes, those piercing blue eyes she fell in love with many years ago. The eyes that told her she was right. Frank said nothing but hugged Gloria like he'd never hugged her before. They embraced for what seemed an age.

Frank was reminded of how lucky he'd been in so many aspects of his life. Gloria really was the best thing that had ever happened to him. He loved her more today than he'd ever loved anyone and that he now admitted to himself for the first time. Today had not only put to rest the ghost of Renee, but all that had happened with Richie. Today was a good day. Frank Pearson was a happy man.

He pulled away and smiled at Gloria as he said, 'Where have you put them little blue pills?'

Gloria laughed as she replied, 'In your sock drawer.'

chapter fifty

Faye was in her office looking at the rota for the following week. She had two members of staff on holiday, so needed to organise cover. As she was thinking about who to ask first, her phone pinged. She ignored it as she wanted to try Darren first. Darren was saving for a deposit for his first house with his girlfriend, so was never one to turn down overtime. She got up to go and find him. She needed to sort this quickly, in case he wasn't able to do it. The rest of the staff never really wanted the extra hours. They were all middle-aged or older, and more financially free than Darren, so the lure of a few hours' overtime never floated their boat. Her second choice was Delia, but only because Delia found it hard to say no to anyone. She left her phone on her desk. It pinged for the second time. She heard it, but thought she'd look at it after she'd spoken to Darren.

Johnny was with his father. He was coming more often of late, mainly because Richie's progress with his hands was coming along better than he had expected.

'That's great, Dad, really great. You are getting more movement every time I come. That grip was awesome, I tell you, really awesome. And you held that fork in your hand for a good three minutes before it dropped.'

Johnny was so pleased with how he was doing. He could see Richie was too. The glint in his eye told him so. He only wished his dad could communicate with him. It was the one thing he wanted more than anything else. Growing up, all he'd ever wanted was to know his father. It was only when Steven, the man he looked on as an uncle, told him that he had any clue of where he came from. His mother had known, of course, but being the bitch she was and the fact she'd fucked off when he was so young meant he'd always wondered where he came from. When she returned, she pretended to be interested in him, but Johnny saw through her and was glad when Steven paid her to fuck off. Johnny wanted nothing to do with her; he only wanted to help his father as much as he could and to be there for him. He harboured a lot of resentment. One day, someone would pay. Uncle Steven had promised him that, together, they would avenge not only Gary, Steven's brother, but Richie too.

Frank was getting annoyed. He'd sent two texts. Not a fucking dicky bird. He knew she was at work as she gave him her four-weekly rota in advance. Frank had insisted on it, mainly for eventualities like today. He wanted to tell Richie that he was coming to the wedding and he wanted to tell him today. Frank had laid it on thick, fooling everyone into thinking that he was very reluctantly allowing Richie to attend for Gloria's sake. Everyone bought it, knowing full well how much Frank despised his son. Gloria played her part, backing Frank up, saying how it'd taken all of her powers of persuasion. Frank continued to be like a bear with a sore head, but only to prolong the pretence. Only Jez knew the score and he would take it to the grave.

Frank rang Faye again. 'It's me again. Where the fuck are you? I'll be there in five minutes. Ring me straight back. I'll park round the back as usual.' He was angry and frustrated. This had never happened before. Faye wouldn't have been expecting him to turn up that day, but Frank didn't take being ignored too well.

Johnny was having a brew and talking to Richie about the wedding. He rolled his shirt sleeves halfway up his forearms as he spoke, having placed his gold cufflinks on the coffee table. He didn't know whether Richie knew yet, but by the look in his eyes, he suspected not, so he decided not to tell him he was invited. He told Richie about the wedding the first time he saw him after finding out and could tell then he was fuming, so he had expected him to know about his invite by now.

Faye burst through the door, causing Johnny to spill hot tea down his front. 'For fuck's sake!' he shouted.

'Frank's just pulled up!' she blurted out.

'What? For fuck's sake!' he repeated, putting his tea down on the table. 'When? Just now?' he asked frantically.

'Yes, just now. I didn't know he would be here today, honest. I had a text, and rang him just as he was pulling into the drive. He's as mad as hell!'

Faye was frantic too. Johnny could hear it in her voice.

'Quick, he'll be coming through them any second,' she said, pointing towards the patio doors.

Johnny was in a panic. He ran his hands through his hair as he turned 360 degrees.

'Look, I'll stall him. Just get out of here, Johnny. Quick, and take your tea with you. Bloody hell, I'm shaking.'

Faye opened the patio doors and ran out through the garden, stopping at the gate that led to the gravel path behind. She could hear footsteps. She took a deep breath and walked out.

Frank stopped when he saw her. 'I don't pay you every month to have this!' he growled.

'Frank, listen, I'm sorry. I didn't know you'd texted. I wasn't expecting you today,' she replied, struggling to contain her composure. Frank could hear the fear in her voice.

'I've also left you two messages, Faye. We agreed you'd keep your phone on you at all times at work, just in case I wanted to come unannounced. Remember?'

'Yes, I do. I can only apologise. It won't happen again.'

Frank nodded. 'Yeah, OK. Look, no harm done, but last time, Faye. Is that clear?'

'It is, yes. I'm sorry. I didn't know you'd rung as well. My fault entirely.'

Frank felt bad. He didn't like being aggressive with the likes of Faye. That wasn't him, but she had to know. That's just how it was.

'Come on. Take me to my son.'

Faye walked in front of Frank, hoping and praying Johnny had left it as it should be. Her heart was pounding. She'd recently managed to pay for a new kitchen, courtesy of the payments she received from Frank, but as she walked towards the patio doors, she remembered how much she'd actually liked the old one.

'Your dad's here, Richie!' she called. Faye always said it as though Richie was a child, like he would be excited to see him. Faye had no idea whether he was, but she always spoke to him in the high-pitched voice you'd use with a five year old.

'Hello, Son,' Frank said, walking in a step or two behind. He turned to lock the doors behind him.

Faye glanced around the room and saw the cufflinks on the coffee table. Her heart missed a beat. While Frank's back was turned, she picked them up and in one movement placed them on a shelf behind a photograph of Daniel and Richie when they were toddlers. Frank didn't notice.

'Right then, I'll leave you two to it.'

'An hour, Faye. I'll see you at my car in an hour.'

Faye smiled a warm smile and nodded as she left the room, closing the door quietly behind her. In the corridor, she took two deep breaths, before walking swiftly back to her office. Her heart was still beating fast and as she sat behind her desk, for the first time in a long time she wished she still smoked. She closed her eyes and imagined herself having a long draw of a cigarette. She could really do with a fag.

Johnny was by now on the main road towards Ollerton, on the phone to Steven.

'Fuck me, Unc, that was a close fucking call. I've never shit myself so much in my life. I really thought he was gonna walk in as I was there. Thank fuck I parked my car in the front car park.'

'I dread to think what would've happened. Fucking hell, I can't believe it. Weird coincidence that,' Steven replied.

'I know. The thing is, now I think of it, Faye seemed surprised he was there, but she said she didn't know he was coming *today*, which makes me think he's visited before.'

'Hmm, yeah, strange thing to say. You think he's been going then?'

'No idea, but I'll find out next time. She definitely was not surprised he was turning up, only that he was turning up today. If she's known and never told me, I'll fucking do her, the bitch. Every time I've been there, paying her to keep her fucking gob shut, she's probably known all along that there was always a chance Frank could turn up. I tell ya, Unc, if that's the score, I'll make sure she fucking regrets the day she thought she could play me.'

chapter fifty-one

'Look, Son, I'll not beat about the bush. That's not my style, you know that. Mind you, the way I've gone about orchestrating all of this is a major fucking embarrassment .... so make sure you don't tell anyone!' Frank laughed.

'But listen. You know I have regrets about everything. I've told you often enough, haven't I?' Frank looked at his son as he spoke. He paused a second and stared as Richie looked blankly at him. Shame came over Frank once more. It often did whenever he visited as he would go over the same old thing. It was the only way Frank could cope with it. He'd maimed and killed in the past, he'd been responsible for inflicting more pain than he could remember, some of it directly, most of it indirectly, but the one thing he wished he could change more than anything was what he'd done to his son. It had eaten away at him for seven years now, although he was surprised at how much better he felt, having told Jez. Frank was a big believer in talking things through, getting things off your chest and on the table, but with how he'd really felt about Richie was something he just could not put out there. Jez was the only one he could confide in, not even Gloria. He'd have been too ashamed and would have felt as though he'd been living a lie for the past seven years. Jez was the only one who he knew would understand, though Gloria had as much as confessed the other day that she'd known all along. However, since she'd not actually said the words, Frank could convince himself that was not the case.

'Me and Gloria are getting wed, Son. Yep, I finally got round to asking her. I don't know what your thoughts on that are ... I only wish you could tell me ... but I hope you're pleased. She's a good'un is my Gloria. Always been there for me she has. She's been my rock on so many occasions, you know. As gentle as she is, and she's a peacemaker is Gloria ... you know that too, don't you ... she's still shown strength that beggars belief.'

Frank paused again. He wasn't sure why, but he seemed to be stalling telling Richie the biggest news of all. Maybe it was because he was unsure whether Richie would be pleased.

'I want you to be there, Son. I want you to be at our wedding, in front of everyone, to be front and centre. This is a chance for me to show the world that the past is the past and well, you know, that we're OK again.' He looked for some sort of reaction. There was none.

Richie stared at him blankly as he always did. It was a control thing. He knew Frank searched for emotion in his eyes, to try and get an angle on what he was thinking, but there was no way Richie was going to give him any insight into what he was feeling. Richie was laughing inside. In fact, he was struggling to remain emotionless.

"That 'we're OK again'? What fuckin' planet are you on, you stupid old twat?! You do this to me, leave me in here, come once a month or so and tell me how sorry you are and then once a year you parade me round in front of the family, telling me you fuckin' despise me. Then you come here to tell me you want to parade me at your wedding to show the whole fuckin' world we are OK again. Well, you can fuck right off, Dad. Go fuck yaself ten times over, you absolute wanker!"

'I wish you could show me how you feel, Son. I know you'll be made up. After the wedding's over, I promise I will not keep my visits a secret. Things will be different, I promise. I'll make it up to you, whatever it takes, and I'll even get you one of those things that will mean you can communicate. You can talk then. It'll be great, Son. I can see you're excited.'

Richie squeezed his fists under his blanket. He was seething. The only thing he could think of was Johnny's next visit. He was sure that the anger raging within him right now meant he had more strength in his hands than ever before.

Frank continued to talk about the future, about how things were going to be and how thrilled he was about the wedding. Richie remained disconnected and harnessed his anger through his hands. He knew he hated his dad, he just never realised how much until now.

chapter fifty-two

Archie was in the main club in Nottingham with Pat, Raquel, Steven and Del. He took Pat with him everywhere now. Pat was not only his number two but his bodyguard. He needed to be the kind of man Jez had been to Frank over the years, always in touching distance whenever they were out and about on business. Frank would often tell Archie that he needed to do that, but it was only now that he was the top man, that Archie felt the need to have Pat with him at all times. Archie no longer relied on Frank, but Pat Steadman.

He was having a catch-up meeting with Raquel about things on her patch. Raquel was, as ever, on top of everything. The only time she'd ever looked as though she'd taken her eye off the ball was when Fletcher's gear had ended up on her patch, twice.

Raquel told Archie about a fella who was causing her a bit of aggro. 'The only issue I have is with Mokker in Ripley. He just never comes up with the money on time. I'm always chasing him. Well, Steven is via Dickie's lot. He's a nightmare, ain't he, Steven?'

'Yeah, we always get it but it's as though he's trying to push back, you know. Fuck knows why. He's had a few slaps about it, but just never seems to take the hint,' Steven replied.

'Well, fuckin' break the fucker's fingers. In fact, Steven, that should be right up your street. You know what it's like to lose a finger. Break every finger in his best hand. That's what you should've fuckin' done.'

Archie then looked at Del. 'Find out if he's right- or left-handed, Del, and break the fuckin' lot of 'em.'

'I can do it, Archie, I'll sort it,' Steven insisted.

'You should've done that already. We need to hit 'em hard. They'll only take the fuckin' piss otherwise.'

Steven was mad. He'd just been made to look weak in front of everyone. He was Raquel's number two, but it would appear Del was far better equipped than he was to deal with this little problem. He glanced at Raquel. She gave him a look that told him to keep quiet. Del felt a little uncomfortable but knew he had to do as he was asked.

'OK,' he said. He looked at Steven and then Raquel. She shook her head, meaning that Del was not to suggest taking Steven with him.

'Right. That it then, Raquel? We done?' Archie asked.

'Yeah, nothing else to report. Everything's sweet.'

'It will be once that Mokker fella has had what's coming to him. Report back to me, Del,' he said as he looked at Pat, as if to say it was time to go.

Archie walked out across the main floor towards

the front entrance. 'I fuckin' hate people taking the piss. What are we Pat, eh? Does my fuckin' head in.'

Pat kept quiet. He thought Archie was out of order, not in this Mokker fella needing to be taught a serious lesson, but in the way he'd dealt with it. Archie needed to learn a bit of class, but he was young. Pat hoped it would come in time.

'Calm down, Steven. Look, it is what it is. It's just Archie's way of doing things, that's all,' Raquel said, as Steven paced up and down the office.

'I tell you something, though. He's changed since he took over. He wouldn't have spoken with such disrespect a few weeks ago. He needs taking down a peg or two. Am I right, Del?' Steven asked.

'I know what you mean, mate. He's got a real edge to him and not a nice edge, but look, let's me and you go together and sort this fella out, eh?' Del looked at Raquel as he spoke, hoping it would be OK.

'Yeah, go on, but for fuck's sake, make sure he gets the message.'

'He'll get the fucking message all right.'

'Steven,' Raquel said, as they walked towards the door. 'Don't go overboard. That can have consequences. Just do what Archie said. Break his fingers, no more. Don't bring any shit down on yourself unnecessarily. You hear me?'

'Yeah, I gotcha. Don't worry, I'll have calmed the fuck down by the time we get there.'

Raquel thought about what had just happened.

Archie *had* changed. He was far less approachable and seemed to have forgotten a lot of what Frank had taught him in such a short space of time.

'Who's driving?' Del asked.

'You can, mate. I still need to calm down,' Steven replied, chucking Del the keys. 'I tell you something, Del, someone needs to have a fuckin' word with Archie. I'm fuckin' sick of the lot of 'em, I am. I don't know about you but if anyone took them out, I certainly wouldn't lose any sleep over it.'

Del looked at Steven and frowned. 'Fuck me, mate. Talk like that will get you killed. I'll pretend I didn't hear that. Fuckin' hell, chill out. He'll have forgotten about it by tomorrow. If the Pearsons ever got taken out, it'd be carnage. And who's gonna fuckin' do it? Not me that's for sure. Look, they have everything sewn up. Things run smooth, so for fuck's sake, don't let anyone else hear you talk like that.'

They went to Ripley and found out Mokker was right-handed. He now uses his left hand, not very well, but he's learning fast. He now always pays on time.

Del couldn't shake from his mind what Steven had said. He'd never heard anyone speak like that before, ever. It didn't sit right with him. He parked it in his memory bank and decided to watch from the wings whenever he was around Steven. Del knew all about things back in the day with him and Gary and was well aware of what it was like to lose a close family member to the life they led. He also knew blood was thicker than water.

chapter fifty-three

Faye was getting ready for her shift. It had been three days since the close call with Johnny and Frank – long enough for her to have largely forgotten about it. There had been no harm done as far as she knew. Johnny had been a bit agitated but had left without being seen and Frank, after his initial annoyance, had left in good spirits. When she met him in the car park at the end of his visit, he had been quite jovial, like he normally was, so, other than realising how close she'd been to disaster and being more aware of the potential pitfalls of her little arrangements, she'd hardly given it another thought.

The doorbell rang. She was just finishing the final touches to her make-up in the hallway mirror. After putting her lipstick back in her handbag and placing it on the bottom stair, she opened the door.

With one hand on the wall, Johnny asked, 'Can I come in?'

'Well, er, I'm just about to leave for work. Why are you here?'

Johnny pushed his way in. Faye closed the door.

She was afraid. Johnny didn't look in a good mood. 'Wh-wh-why are you here?' she stuttered.

'How long's Frank been visiting Richie?' His voice was assured; not so much aggressive as assured.

Faye's mind raced. She couldn't think. She felt under pressure. 'What? Eh? What do you mean?' she replied, as she tried to think about his question. How did he know? She was the only one who knew. Frank had always told her such.

'Don't fuck me around, Faye.' He suddenly put his hands around her throat and pushed her against the wall. 'Don't take me for a prick! How long has Frank been visiting Richie?'

She was thinking so fast it was hard for her to process her thoughts clearly. One thing she did know, which had been clear to her all along, was that under no circumstances could she grass on Frank Pearson. She didn't like Johnny, never had really. He had his hands around her neck and she feared him, but not how she feared the wrath of Frank.

'He doesn't. Only you visit him.'

Johnny squeezed her neck harder. 'You fuckin' knew he was coming the other day. "I didn't know he was coming today" was what you said. Don't lie to me, bitch. You might be afraid of Frank, but let me tell you, getting on the wrong side of me is not advisable.'

He then placed his left hand over her mouth and took his right hand off her throat. He looked into her eyes as he slid his hand down her body, over her breasts and down between her legs. She had her work trousers on but he pressed hard as he rubbed her. She wanted to scream. She wanted to knee him between the legs, but she was paralysed with fear. After a few seconds, he removed his hand and placed it back over her throat.

'A little warning, Faye, a little warning. Heed it,' he said, as he took both hands away.

Tears filled Faye's eyes. She tried hard not to let them run down her face.

Johnny smiled with the power he had. 'If you tell anyone I visit Richie, I'll be back – and I won't be on my own.'

He left and Faye slammed the door shut behind her. She moved her bag off the bottom stair and sat and cried. She had been frightened of this all along. As she wiped her tears and looked at her watch, she wondered whether to go into work, but recalled that she had two people off on holiday. She needed to go. She re-did her make-up and went to work as usual, trying her best to be strong, but deep down she was scared shitless.

chapter fifty-four

17th August 2019 – The weekend before the wedding

Frank and Gloria had decided to have a pre-wedding party. Frank thought he was too old for a stag do, and he didn't want a weekend of drink and drugs. He hardly ever drank and had never taken drugs. He'd seen far too many people in his line of work, on all rungs of the ladder, fall foul of the gear they peddled and made money from. Neither of his sons had ever taken drugs and neither, to his knowledge, had Archie. Frank would never have stood for it. No one at his top table or at any senior level within his organisation could be a user. Everyone knew it and everyone towed the line.

Gloria hadn't really wanted a hen party either, so a family get-together with their nearest and dearest, plus the chosen few within the family business, some close friends and associates was what they went for. It was their way of having their own night before the big day, when the crème de la crème of the criminal elite would be present. Frank had been very selective on who attended the service. Everyone else would just have to be happy with a ticket for the night bash. There had been a few moans and groans throughout certain factions, but Frank was too long in the tooth to be worrying about who he upset.

Today was a special day too in that it was the first time Richie had been seen at Frank's house since 2012. Frank had explained to everyone that it would be a great opportunity, before the actual wedding, for them all to get used to him being back in the fold. Frank didn't want to have to deal with everyone fussing around Richie, plus he genuinely wanted him to feel a normal part of the day's events. Gloria could see how pleased Frank was. She observed how he looked at Richie and could sense the relief he felt in finally having him around.

For the most part, Frank still played it down and acted as though he was doing it through gritted teeth and "for his Gloria". No one else noticed it was an act, except for Jez, of course, but even Gloria and Jez couldn't confide in each other as Frank hadn't told Gloria he'd breathed a word to him. It was their secret and that's the way it was to stay. Frank could enjoy Richie being back within the family, leaving the others thinking he was just doing it for his intended, for Gloria.

Everyone was in the garden. The sun was shining, people were chatting and mingling. The celebration had started at noon, with most people arriving by 1 o'clock. Frank had, as ever, been a superb host. He and Gloria had spent most of the afternoon joined at the hip as they entertained their guests, but by 4 o'clock, he'd had enough of talking about the impending nuptials. He whispered to Gloria that he was going to catch up with Brian and Jez, his two oldest friends. He managed to drift off largely unnoticed, leaving Gloria talking about her dress for the umpteenth time. He walked past Johnny, who was standing with Richie, and took the chance to have a word with his son.

'I hope you've not been manhandled today, Son. I've tried to keep an eye on you to make sure people aren't fussing over you. I know you wouldn't appreciate that.' Richie looked blankly at him as always. 'You warm enough?' Frank continued.

'I've made sure he's had that blanket over his legs all day, Frank. I've got another one here, look, to put over the top if it drops cold later on. I've enjoyed looking after him, so to speak. He'll be fine with me, honest. You go and do your thing, Frank.'

Frank smiled at Johnny. He'd always liked him. 'You're a good lad, Johnny. Our Alice has done well. When are you gonna get married anyway? I'm sure Alice will have dropped a hint or two. She's not backward in coming forward when she wants to be, is that one.' Frank glanced at Alice as he spoke. She was chatting with Sarah, who was rocking Mary's pushchair from side to side.

'Not anytime soon, Frank. We will one day, I'm sure, but there's plenty of time for that. Look how long it took you!'

Frank gave a hearty laugh. 'Well, don't leave it *that* long, lad!' Frank patted him on the back and wandered over to Jez and Brian.

'Fucking hell, Brian! Leave some for everyone else, will ya,' he joked.

'It's only my second plate, funny fucker,' he said in reply, as he munched away on a salmon and cream cheese sandwich.

Frank stood in the middle and put his arms around his two oldest friends' shoulders.

'Great idea this, Frank,' Brian said, taking another bite.

'Fuck me, you can't even stop munching to speak!' Frank teased, squeezing Brian close to him.

Johnny was pushing Richie their way and smiled at Frank.

'Yeah, can't beat time spent with family. They're my life, Brian, this lot here. You two included of course. I love each and every one of you dearly.'

Frank proudly looked around the garden at his loved ones: Gloria, Archie, Phoebe, Alice, Sarah, Mary – Richie. Johnny had stopped and was kneeling behind Richie's wheelchair.

Frank felt good inside. 'I'd die for any one of you; every single one of you.'

No one heard the shots. The garden was too noisy, with the music. Brian looked round to answer his boss, who he hadn't realised had fallen to the ground. Jez shouted 'Frank!' as he crouched down. Gloria shrieked and dropped her glass. Phoebe screamed. Jez looked up; he had blood on his hands. Brian froze;

his mouth wide open, plate still in one hand and a sandwich in the other. His world stood still. People ran in slow motion. Brian snapped out of it as Archie charged past him, knocking him sideways. Alice shouted for Johnny, who was wheeling Richie away and putting the second blanket over his legs. Steven was now with them. She ran over. She wanted Johnny to do something.

Jez pushed everyone away – everyone except Gloria and Archie. Gloria was hysterical. Archie was numb. Frank was dead.

chapter fifty-five

It had been less than a minute since Frank had been shot. He'd been shot twice: once in the stomach and once in the chest. The garden was now full of crying women, speechless men and everyone looking for some sort of leadership. Archie stared at his grandad, unable to comprehend what had happened. Phoebe tried her best to comfort Gloria but she was inconsolable. Alice was crying into Johnny's chest. Johnny was explaining how his first thought was to get Richie away as he had been so close to Frank.

Two people who knew this had to be contained were Raquel and Steven.

'Archie's not moved. He's numb,' Raquel said.

Steven immediately saw his chance. 'I know. Come on,' he replied, as he walked the few steps to Jez.

'Jez, what happened?'

'No idea. Me and Brian were talking to Frank. Next minute, he's on the ground. Fuck me, Steven, I can't believe it.'

'Someone needs to take a look outside. It must've come from over the fences or one of the hedges.'

'I'm no leader, Steven. Never have been. Archie, for fuck's sake, look at me!' Jez shouted, as he spun him round. Archie looked straight through him. 'What do we do? For fuck's sake, Archie, what do you want us to fuckin' do?!'

Jez slapped him, but Archie's eyes remained glazed. He slowly brought his hand up to stroke his sore cheek.

Jez turned to Steven. 'What shall we do?'

Steven sensed a chance to take charge. Maybe, he thought, it should be Pat, Archie's number two, but Jez had turned to him. The fact Steven had taken the lead ahead of Raquel meant people were looking to him.

'Del, Ryan, Des: you three search the outside. Quickly. Search for anything, anything at all.'

He then shouted at the top of his voice. 'RIGHT EVERYONE, LISTEN UP! EVERYONE.'

The garden fell silent. Everyone fixed their attention towards Steven, the man with a glass eye and missing fingers. The man who Frank had humiliated all those years ago and the very man who had lost a brother to the man who now lay dead a few feet in front of him.

'NO ONE LEAVES HERE WITHOUT BEING CHECKED. ANYONE WITH ANY FIREARMS ON THEM LEAVES THEM WITH US AND NO ONE, AND I MEAN NO ONE, IS TO POST ANYTHING ONLINE. IF I FIND OUT ANYONE HAS POSTED ANYTHING – PHOTOS, MESSAGES OR ANYTHING – WE WILL COME AFTER YOU. DO I MAKE MYSELF CLEAR?!'

A young lady who Steven didn't know raised her hand. 'I posted some photos earlier,' she confessed, shaking as she did so. Steven sighed. 'THEN I SUGGEST ANYTHING, AND I MEAN ANYTHING, THAT HAS BEEN POSTED GETS DELETED, RIGHT NOW. DO NOT MAKE US COME AFTER YOU.'

Steven needed to give an order to Pat. He needed to see if Archie's second in command would take the instruction.

'Pat, you and Trainer make sure no one leaves without being checked. If we find any guns, I want them all checked against the bullets. If anyone in this house is responsible, I want them found.'

Now to see if Raquel, the lady he'd reported to for so long, would also take an instruction from him. 'We've got to inform the Old Bill,' he said to her. He guessed she'd either ask him who the fuck he thought he was, or she'd be with him.

'I know,' she replied. 'You're right. There's no way we can keep this under wraps.'

'Jez, any ideas who to ring about this lot?' Steven asked.

'Hazlehurst is the most senior guy we have, so I guess let's start with him.'

Steven told him to get him on the phone. While Jez informed Hazlehurst of Frank's death, Steven, Brian and Michael carried Frank's body into the house. As the guests waited to be frisked, they could be seen on their phones, frantically deleting anything they'd posted about being at Frank Pearson's pre-wedding party.

Gloria was still crying. Phoebe, Alice and Marie were consoling her. Johnny had offered to take Richie back to the care home. He'd not had a drink as he'd somehow been left in charge of Richie all afternoon. Alice offered to go with him, but he insisted she stay and look after Gloria with her mum. Steven made sure everyone agreed that was a good idea. No one questioned it. Throughout all of the commotion, Steven had kept an eye on Archie. He saw a young man out of his depth. He laughed a very smug laugh inside. He could not believe what was happening in front of his very eyes.

Archie was at the bottom of the garden with Sarah and Mary. Sarah was leaning into him. He had his arm around her shoulder. He'd let everyone down. Frank had been killed. The wave of responsibility that he'd managed to keep at bay enveloped him like a huge dark cloud on a miserable wintry day. Being the top man in the family business brought expectation. He thought about Atlas bearing the Earth on his back. That's how Archie felt – having the world on his shoulders. He was ready to admit to himself that he was not the new Frank Pearson. Without Frank at his side, he was not who he needed to be. Archie wanted to run. He wanted to run so far and so fast he couldn't settle his breathing. His heart felt like it was ready to burst.

'What we gonna do?' Sarah asked.

Archie hadn't said a thing, but she knew. She always had done. He continued to stare at the hedge that ran along the bottom of Frank's garden while other people, people who reported to him, took his role and sorted things out. His silence was confirmation of what Sarah had known for a long time. In a way, she was glad. She wanted out too, but wherever Archie went or whatever he did, even if that was to stay and front it out, she would be with him. Of that, there was no doubt.

Pat and Trainer didn't find a single gun on anyone. No one had turned up tooled up but then again, they wouldn't have expected anyone to. This was a party at Frank Pearson's house. No one had needed to be in fear. No one had needed to feel as though they had to defend themselves. No one, including within the firm, had brought a gun. Every single person in that house had been checked – every person except one. But who in their right mind would check a guy in a wheelchair, supposedly unable to move any part of his body except his eyes?

chapter fifty-six

Hazlehurst arrived just over an hour later. He came on his own, which he felt very uncomfortable about, but Jez had insisted. Archie had by now involved himself a little in the proceedings, but Steven and Raquel were the ones taking the lead. For now, everyone seemed happy with that. No one else really wanted to step forward. Jez was the old hand they were both subconsciously relying on, though. Jez could feel it, even if Steven and Raquel couldn't.

Hazlehurst was taken through to the downstairs study. He'd already been shown Frank's body, which was now in the utility room. Gloria had wanted him to remain with them in the house, afraid he'd get cold, but they'd managed to persuade her that having him in the utility room was best.

Steven sat down and spoke first. 'Look, we know your lot have to be involved – we get that – but we don't want a big thing made of this. We will sort this. We will do our own investigations, so we are looking at you to keep your lot low key and to do the basics, just to show you're doing your job.'

Hazlehurst looked at Jez, then at Pat, before returning to Steven. 'This is a murder, you know. Fuck me, there's procedures in all of this. I can't stop the police doing their job.'

Jez sat forward. 'Look, all we're asking is that you do your bit. Earn your fucking dough – you know, that dough you've taken off us for years – and make sure that whoever is investigating just does enough to keep your superiors out of our faces. Do that and we'll be good. If you don't, well, you know the kind of information that can come out when things get messy...'

Hazlehurst knew what Jez was referring to. They had enough on him to put him away for the foreseeable.

'Look, luckily for you guys, I will probably be the SIO.'

Archie suddenly sat forward. 'What the fuck's that? Talk fuckin' English.'

'Senior investigating officer, Archie. It will more than likely be me, so look, don't worry. The fact you've moved the body makes the crime scene murky for a start. Plus it happened outside and loads of people, I presume, were there, which makes the crime scene even less like it was.'

'Correct,' Archie said, as he sat back.

'Look, we ain't keen on giving you too many names. That ain't what we do, you know that. So, don't be surprised when we tell you we don't know who was here,' Steven said, keen to get that in to make it very clear to Hazlehurst what he was likely to be up against.

'This will be in the press, you know. There's no way this'll be kept out of the papers. Probably go national,' Hazlehurst said, aware that wouldn't go down too well.

'Look, just make sure you keep it fucking low key on every score. That's what you're paid for – to do as we ask – so don't fuck it up now. This is what you earn ya fucking dosh for, Hazlehurst. We'll do what we need to do, and you do what you need to do to make it all go away. You just draw a blank your end and leave it up to us. That's it in a fucking nutshell. Got it?'

Jez was starting to get angry. This was when they needed Frank. Frank would have had Hazlehurst singing his tune without any fuss. Jez wanted to make sure he knew things were going to remain the same as they'd always been.

Hazlehurst nodded. 'Look, just let me do what I need to do. Don't interfere – just trust me and trust the process. You've made it loud and clear what you need from me, but the first thing we need to do is to make this official. This has to be made a crime scene. The forensic pathologist will have to be involved, as will the coroner, and there will have to be a post-mortem. These are things we cannot bypass – you know that – but look, I have friends, you have friends, so we can speed things up and get things done as you wish, but these processes need to take place. It'll be a few weeks at best, even with our friends, before the body is released for any funeral.'

'Just make it happen,' Steven said. He then sat back and looked around the room. 'We need to find out who did this.'

chapter fifty-seven

Johnny arrived at the care home and took Richie into his bedroom. He stayed with his dad for a while talking about the day's events, but was mindful not to stay too long as that wouldn't be expected. He'd not had a chance to speak to his Uncle Steven as yet, but they'd exchanged enough glances back at the house to know that the plan had seemingly gone smoothly.

He folded the blankets up and placed them in the drawer under his father's bed. He then picked up the gun and planted a big kiss onto the silencer. The gun had been placed in Richie's hand moments before he shot the man who had indeed put him into the very wheelchair that Johnny had wheeled towards Frank. Richie needed to be close enough to ensure the correct angle and to get a clear enough shot. It had been a gamble, especially as Frank was stood in the middle of his two closest friends, but because Frank had been with Gloria all afternoon, that was the first chance they'd had. Johnny had been bent down behind the wheelchair making sure, as best he could, that the angle of the gun was correct. He knew Richie had enough strength in his hand to pull the trigger. They'd agreed on two shots to make sure.

Richie had played a blinder.

'We fuckin' did it!' he said, careful to keep his voice low. 'We fuckin' did it. Well, you did really, I suppose, but he's gone. The man who put you in here, who despised you and belittled you for years is gone. The man who killed my mum's husband and my uncle's brother. The man who took Steven's eye and his fingers too. Gone forever. He can do that no more.'

He then sat down so that he was at the same height as his dad. 'And you will soon be the head of that family. Me, you and Steven will run that fucking firm. Steven's gonna hatch some sort of plan to take over, not sure what yet, but hey, no rush, is there. And then once he has the top seat, and the right people in place, we will reveal everything and you will inherit what's due to you. We will run it for you, but you will be at the top – where you should be, Dad.'

Richie looked at his son with such pride. He only wished he could tell him.

Johnny stood up. 'Look, I've got to go. Everyone will be wondering where I am. I need to be there for Alice. She'll no doubt be crying like a baby. Does my fuckin' head in, she does. Anyway, I'll see you soon, but I might have to keep away for a few days – you know, play the game, the grieving son-in-law to be and all that shite. I tell ya something, Dad, you better be in that fuckin' will. I want paying handsomely for all this.'

He then put the gun in the safe he'd installed at the back of the wardrobe. Only he knew the code. Not even Steven. He and Steven had agreed that's where it would go. They knew the family would search everywhere and everyone. They would leave no stone unturned, but no one would ever think of searching Richie's room.

Killing Frank had been planned for so long, but even they couldn't believe it when Frank announced he was bringing Richie back into the family fold. That had been a godsend and had solved the re-occurring problem of when and where. They had initially planned to do it at the actual wedding, once it had been announced, but the pre-wedding party seemed even better, because there was a chance, just a chance, that Frank still had Richie down as a beneficiary of his will. He was his last surviving direct blood relative. Had Gloria become Mrs Pearson, things may have changed. Neither Johnny nor Steven were sure about wills, but what they did know was that without a Mrs Pearson getting in the way, Richie just might be the one to inherit Frank's fortune. And that, as Johnny had told his uncle right at the beginning, would be a very nice little cherry on top of a very nice, very large, slice of cake.

Richie watched him go until he disappeared from the garden. He then heard footsteps coming towards his door, which he knew were Faye's. She came in and spent the next few minutes making sure he was OK.

She talked the whole time. Richie often wondered if it was her way of dealing with what she was doing. He had worked out early on that she was dealing with both Johnny and Frank, so he understood her need to calm her nerves. He didn't really ever listen to what she said, and tonight was no different. It was too early for bed, so after she left, he sat and replayed the day's events. He thought of his upbringing. His earliest memory was of his dad telling him he should never have survived his birth and how he was responsible for his mum's death. He smiled inside as he recalled the football away days and the tear-ups. He thought of Goldie and his death. He remembered how he and Frank had made it up. He thought about how he'd been playing his dad all along. He was just glad his Johnny was different. He thought about their relationship and how Johnny would never do that to him.

Richie remembered his time in Venice, chasing Andy Barnes out to Italy, and how he never did get his fifteen grand back. He wondered what Andy was doing now. He then thought about the guy at the hotel in Venice – about how he killed him, and the guy in the next room. He realised he never knew their names, but the guy he killed first – he heard his name in the hotel lobby. What was it?

He then thought about the day they came and killed Daniel, obviously thinking it was him. He felt sad. He regretted that. Daniel didn't deserve it. He put that out of his mind as he thought about the aftermath, his dad, Jez and what Bonnie did to him to put him in there. Then he came back to the present day and considered how revenge, even though he couldn't really enjoy it, was still sweet. *Fuck you, Frank Pearson. See you in hell.*

chapter fifty-eight

Three days later

The boys in blue did their job. People came in white suits and took photos, dusted things down and, to be fair, it looked as though they were doing what had been asked of them. In reality, they were just doing their job. Hazlehurst was in constant touch with Jez. He was the man he always rang. He'd dealt with Frank and Jez over the years more than anyone else. He kept reminding Jez to let the process play out and that he would take care of things his end.

The family had spent every waking hour trying to piece it all together, but they, like their friends in uniform, were drawing a blank. No weapon, no witnesses, no motive. Hazlehurst was amazed that Frank, being who he was, had no real enemies. There was no one, it seemed, who had any real motive to kill one of the most feared men in the UK. The police knew nothing of the recent events with Fletcher O'Brien, so were certainly not poking their nose in over the Pennines, something George and Ivan Burbanks were grateful for. That whole episode had been kept under the radar. Even Hazlehurst was unaware of the families' involvement in Fletcher's demise. Frank had always been good at keeping his activities from anyone who was not in the know. He'd never involved the Old Bill unless it was for his gain. The world he'd operated in sorted things out themselves. Coppers were never invited to those kinds of parties. That had, on numerous occasions, kept Frank from any spells at Her Majesty's pleasure.

Phoebe and Alice were in the kitchen with Gloria and Sarah. Gloria had been coping surprisingly well. She'd cried all of her tears the night it happened. She was a tough cookie on the inside when it mattered; one of the keep calm and carry on brigade. She'd dusted herself down and now wanted to put all of her efforts into making sure Frank had the send-off he deserved. However, nothing could be planned until the body was released.

Archie had received a lot of calls from those at the top offering their condolences and assuring him that no one would try and muscle in. They'd all asked to be kept informed about developments and, of course, with details of the funeral. Archie relayed that to Jez, who was now seemingly out of retirement, and the rest of the firm. Archie thanked Steven for taking the lead on the day and for his leadership since.

Phoebe had left a third message for Archie to ring her. He wasn't answering his calls and no one had heard from him all day. They were all worried, especially Sarah.

'He's not coping at all, you know,' she said, repeating herself.

'So you keep saying, Sarah. We all know that.' Phoebe was sharp in her delivery. Sarah said nothing and lowered her head.

It was 6 o'clock. Archie had left before breakfast and everyone had assumed he'd gone to sort some business.

'He'll come home when he's ready. He's got a lot to think about. It'll all be weighing on him,' Gloria said, forever trying to make things sound OK.

Sarah was not so sure. 'I think he's gone AWOL,' she said.

'What do you mean "AWOL"?' Alice asked.

'Well, I mean gone.'

'We know he's gone, but he'll just be getting his head straight. It's only to be expected. He's tough, you know. He'll be OK,' Phoebe said, trying to defend her son as best she could.

'I don't think so, Phoebe. You don't know him like I do—'

'What do you mean I don't know him like you do? He's my son! I raised him. I've known him all his life. I know him better than anyone, so don't tell me otherwise.'

The atmosphere was tense.

'You don't lie with him at night when he's awake for most of it, worrying about everything. He's not like Frank; he just isn't that man. Frank was different. He wanted this life. Archie was born into it and had no choice. Believe me, he ain't the man you all think he is. With Frank at his side, he maybe could've been, but without Frank he doesn't have it in him. He's lost without him. He's gone. I knew it would happen. He's gone, I tell ya!'

Sarah broke down and sobbed her heart out, which made Gloria cry, and Alice too. Phoebe remained resolute.

'Rubbish,' she said. 'Of course he's got it. He always has. His dad had it and he has it. He'll be back. You just watch.'

Phoebe stormed out. She was angry; angry that Archie had not been able to step up and angry because she feared Sarah was right. He was supposed to honour his father's name. Daniel was the true heir, but he'd had that snatched from him. *Why can you not step into your father's shoes?!* she shouted to herself. *'Why?!'* she cried. She then turned round, wiped a tear from her eye and walked back into the kitchen.

'I'm sorry, Sarah,' she said, standing with her arms out in front of her.

Sarah looked up. She sniffled, wiped her cheek, stood up and accepted Phoebe's embrace. They hugged tightly.

'I'm sorry,' she said again, as she stroked Sarah's head.

Gloria and Alice joined in. For two minutes, they all apologised and comforted one another in a group hug.

Phoebe knew what she had to do.

chapter fifty-nine

Archie arrived at Stansted Airport. He'd parked his car in a car park in Stamford, just off the A1, and had ordered a taxi to take him the seventy or so miles to the airport. He had no idea where he was going. He had nothing with him, except a small suitcase with a few clothes and a couple of bundles of cash. He also had his debit card for an account no one else knew about. Frank had told him three years before that in this game you always needed access to cash that no one, not even your wife, knew about. Frank had never needed his, but Archie knew where he'd kept the debit card for his account. He had that one too. Frank's had far more money in it than Archie's did and the fact no one knew about it meant no one was likely to notify the bank of Frank's death.

He headed in and looked at the departures board and thought for the hundredth time about Sarah and Mary, the two people in his life he loved more than anything and who he was leaving behind. It had all been too much. Archie needed to get away. He needed to own his shit and accept who he was. More importantly, he needed to accept who he wasn't. He told himself, again, that he would send for Sarah and Mary once he was settled. He knew Sarah understood. She'd understood things for a long time now.

There were flights going to all over Europe. He had a wide choice. He decided on Portugal. Archie walked up to the desk and booked a one-way ticket to Faro.

chapter sixty

Phoebe was sat in her kitchen diner at her house in Southwell. She had called a meeting with Jez and Brian and was waiting for them to arrive. They'd received word that Archie's BMW X6 had been found in a car park in Stamford. It had been there for over 24 hours.

As soon as the news had filtered through, Sarah texted him. *Please tell me you are OK. I love you. We both love you. I just want to know you are safe. Surely we deserve that at least xx*

Within ten minutes Archie had replied. *I'm sorry. I just can't be who everyone wants me to be. I need time on my own. I'm OK. I love you. I'll be in touch x*

Sarah showed it to Phoebe, who passed it on to Brian and Jez. They were the two men within the business who she felt she could trust with it at this stage and who would offer the advice she was looking for. When it first appeared Archie may have gone, Phoebe had realised that she needed to ensure that Daniel's legacy was intact. Without Frank, there was Archie. Without Archie, there was her. That was it.

With Richie as he was, she was the only one who could preserve the legacy of Daniel's name.

She was well aware of the calls Archie had received from the criminal top table, assuring him there would be no takeover attempts, but she was also acutely aware of events involving Fletcher O'Brien. So, whilst she took them at their word, she couldn't be convinced it would stay like that for long.

'It's only us!' came the shout from the front door. Jez and Brian came through and both hugged her, before taking a stool around the kitchen island.

'Tea?' she asked.

'Could murder one,' Brian replied. Jez nodded.

'How is everyone?' Jez asked, knowing Archie's disappearing act could well have had a mixed response.

'Well, we're all shocked to say the least. No one could see this coming, gents. He was always, from a young age, so entrenched in the family business. I remember Daniel, and Richie to be fair, having to put a rein on him. Sarah knew the truth. She never said anything, of course, but since the other day, when we first suspected all was not good with him, she's let things be known.'

'Like what?' Jez asked, intrigued.

'Like how he'd lie awake at night worrying, and how she could see it whenever he looked to Frank for assurance. We knew he did, and that was only to be expected given he was so young, but she saw it more than most. She knew he was not cut out to take over, but like the good wife she was, she never interfered.'

'I saw it too to be honest, Phoebe. I saw how he leaned on Frank. Probably too much, even taking into account his age. But you know what he was like. You could never have said owt. He would never have admitted it,' Jez said, hoping that wouldn't cause any friction.

'Did you see it too, Brian?' Phoebe asked.

'To be honest, no. I never did, but then again, I don't notice things, me. Never have.'

'True. You've always been the same, Brian. Anyway, here's ya teas. Drink them while they're hot.'

'What's gonna happen with Frank's will? Archie is executor, isn't he?' Jez asked.

'Yeah, he is, but only one of them. The solicitor's also an executor.'

'Sanderson?'

'Yep, Sanderson. He's a good bloke, as you all know. He's certainly earned his money over the years.'

'He's fuckin' had plenty, that's for sure,' Brian replied.

'It's what they do apparently, which makes sense, I suppose. He can't do anything until the body's released anyway, so if Archie doesn't resurface, then he will deal with it all. He will make sure Frank's wishes are carried out and that his estate is left to the right people. To be honest, no one knows when he last changed it,' Phoebe continued.

She sat down and took a moment. She then looked up as she spoke. 'Look, let's put the will business to one side. I need to talk to you both. Someone needs to take command. We need someone at the top. Frank always said that there has to be the captain of the ship, the one steering it through both calm and rough waters. If we don't agree on a new leader, despite what we've been told, we'll open ourselves up to all sorts. We need one voice.'

'I agree,' replied Jez. 'We were on about it on the way over. Archie's gone and, to be honest, I think he'd struggle to regain authority if he came back. I know it's not been too long, but – and I say this with all due respect, Phoebe – he's shown his true colours. And in this game, as you well know, any sign of weakness gets jumped on by all and sundry. So, no matter what transpires with Archie, for me, he's finished in this life.'

Phoebe remained silent. That was her son he was talking about, but she knew she had to be strong and she had to be ruthless, or else she would not survive. She gulped.

'I want to take over, gents. I want to be Frank's replacement – well, Archie's replacement, but you know what I mean. I want that mantle. I owe it to Daniel.'

'Can you do it?' Jez asked.

'Do you think I can?'

'Doesn't matter what I think right at this moment in time, Phoebe. I'll ask again. Can you do it?'

'Too right I can. I'm no match for Frank or Archie, or any one of you guys really, in terms of brute strength, but I'm measured and calculated and someone who can make the right calls. All I need is guys like you two around me, younger guys of course,' she said with a smile. 'But you understand what I mean. I can be ruthless when I want to be. I'm not afraid of taking the tough decisions and if I have guys like you two, guys who would die for me, as you two would have done for Frank, I'll be OK. The Pearson name is staying, gents. I'm gonna make sure of that. I just want you two's approval. With that, I can take on anyone.'

'Then you have mine, Phoebe. One hundred per cent. I'd die for you, just as I would Frank,' Jez said without a moment's hesitation.

'I'll second that Phoebe, luv. I'm in it till I die anyway, so I may as well die for you if anyone,' Brian said, as he raised his mug of tea.

'Whisky?' Phoebe asked.

'Lovely,' they both said in unison.

Phoebe walked through to get the bottle and three glasses. When she returned, Jez looked a little concerned.

'We'd both take a bullet for you, Phoebe, you know that and I'm happy to come out of retirement, but you will need a strong, younger team around you. We are too old for you to rely on totally. You understand what I'm saying?'

She smiled as she poured the whisky. 'You didn't think I was putting all my ambitions and plans on you two old farts, did you?'

They laughed, though they were still unsure what she wanted from them.

'Look, all I wanted was your backing. As I said, with that, I can do this. I want your experience, your advice, your muscle if I need it, and I certainly want your bottle. But I want you two to be my sounding board. I want you two at my side, as advisers or consultants, you know, helping me steer the ship. You know what I mean.'

'That sounds good to us, Phoebe. Brian here is still ready to mix it with anyone, but we will be at your side, every step of the way. Brian one side and me the other. No one will get to you and no one will fuck with you. That's a guarantee we can both make you. All we ask, Phoebe, is that when we give advice, you listen. With that, we can do this too.'

'I will. I promise.'

'So who's gonna be doing what?' Brian asked.

'Well, I must say I've been impressed with Steven recently. He really stepped up when Frank was shot. I've never really warmed to him, I'll be honest, but credit where credit's due,' Phoebe replied, waiting to see their first response.

'Fair play – he did. And he's a credible bloke, although he didn't really give anyone else a chance. I know Pat was a little annoyed at himself for not reacting quicker and letting Steven slip in like he did. You know Pat, he's not naturally a centre-stage kind of man, but I know he wishes he'd taken the lead. And he would have done, but he was just a split second too late,' Jez pointed out.

'Hmm, sometimes that split second can make all the difference in this line of work, though ... as we all know.'

'Yeah, we all know that, Phoebe, as you say too well, and maybe this is my first piece of advice...'

'What's that?' Phoebe asked.

'Steven Wallace has never forgotten what Frank and Daniel did to him and his brother. I know it was thirty years ago, but trust me, it's always there, so my advice would be to keep Wallace at arm's length. No matter how much time passes, your Daniel shot his brother and Frank took his eye and his fingers. That memory never fades. He'll be reminded of it every day.'

'Advice noted, gents, thank you. Any news from Hazlehurst?'

'Not yet, other than he's trying to hurry things up as much as he can. His team are drawing blanks, though. I know he's had a tough time over the lack of names we gave him, but he's had enough off us over the years, so fuck him.'

'Everyone kept to the script I presume?'

'Yep, to the letter. Hazlehurst said, at some point, they'll come to a dead end and then they'll wind it down unless something new comes to light. Ey up, speak of the devil.'

Jez answered his phone. 'What you got?'

Phoebe and Brian studied Jez's face as he listened

to Hazlehurst. He looked grave. 'And that's definite, is it?' he asked. 'This can't change your investigation. As far as you are concerned, this changes nothing. Understand?'

'You ain't gonna believe this,' Jez said to them.

'What?' Phoebe asked.

'Hazlehurst reckons the bullets that killed Frank were fired from fairly close range, certainly within the garden grounds. He's just told me the killer must have been at the party.'

A look of horror came over Phoebe's face. 'But everyone was checked. Everyone, even us. That can't be.'

'Well, that's what he said. Who checked everyone? Pat and Trainer, wasn't it?'

'Yeah, definitely. Pat checked me himself. Did they check each other?' Phoebe asked.

'No idea. I would assume so, but hey, come on, surely you're not suggesting what I think you are,' Jez said, with a certain annoyance in his voice.

'I checked them two,' Brian said.

'Eh?'

'I checked them. They both insisted on it, so you can both get that little theory out of your heads.'

'Thank fuck for that,' Jez said in relief.

Phoebe walked towards the window and looked out into the garden. Jez and Brian watched as she pondered. Looking out of the window was something

Frank always did. They both liked the fact she was reminding them of Frank.

'We keep that to ourselves, gents. No one else must know that at this stage, but we need to get the perimeter checked again, just in case they are wrong and it was fired, as we suspected, from the edge of the garden. I mean, how far were you two and Frank from the hedges?'

Jez turned to Brian. 'What you reckon? Thirty foot maybe? I mean, we were just to the left of the large Buddha, so, yeah, I reckon thirty foot or so at the nearest point.'

'Well, that's close range, wouldn't you say? I mean, who was nearer to you than that anyway?'

'No idea. Bloody hell, people were walking around all the time, chatting and that. I couldn't tell you.'

'OK, well, I'll arrange for the perimeter to be checked again. There must be something that will give us a lead. Someone must know something.'

'As we've said many times over the past few days, Phoebe, Frank had no known enemies. I mean, we've said more than once that the only possibility was from Manchester, but, as you know, I've been to see the Burbankses and they assure me one hundred per cent that this was nothing to do with them.'

'And you believe them?'

'Yeah, I do. Look, I've known George and Ivan for donkeys' years and they're like Frank was – if they had beef with us, they'd tell us. This was not the Burbankses, Phoebe, I'd bet my life on it.'

'Could have been one of Fletcher's men though, getting payback.'

'Yes, it could have been, but if that was the case, why stop at Frank? Look, with Frank gone, we are more vulnerable than ever, so if it was one of Fletcher's men, they'd have picked some of us off by now and the Burbankses would know about it. Fletcher's men all work for them now. That's just how it is. Trust me, Phoebe, I've been in this game long enough to know these things and if someone from Fletcher's old firm, or even the Burbankses, wanted Frank dead, they would not have done it at Frank's house, at a party with all of those potential witnesses. No way. Am I right, Brian?'

'He's right, Phoebe. If it was one of them, it would have been a quiet affair, with no fuss, when Frank was alone. Not like this, at a party.'

'Yeah, I suppose you're right. But who then? Who would want Frank dead and who would be silly enough to do it when they did?'

'We may never know, Phoebe. Again, that's just sometimes the way it is. In this life, you're always a split second away from being taken out. It's something we all have to live with, but it's part of the attraction. Well, for me it is anyway.'

Jez's phone rang again. It was Hazlehurst.

'Yeah? OK, brill, at least that's something.'

'What did he say?'

'The body can be released. He's had to call in a fuck

load of favours he said, but we can have the body for the funeral.'

'Well, at least we can sort that out. The funeral directors are fully versed on what we want, so I'll make the call. I bet they already know anyway,' Phoebe said, as she sat back down. 'Then I'll call Sanderson and tell him. At least we can get the will sorted too.'

'I'll call a full top table meeting for tomorrow to let everyone know the funeral details and also about me taking over.'

They raised a toast. This was a new dawn. Did the business need a woman's touch? The world was about to find out.

chapter sixty-one

Gloria pulled into the car park of Romsey nursing home. She had known about Frank's visits for a while. She'd told Frank as much when they spoke about telling everyone that he only wanted Richie at the wedding for her. She knew how much the visits had meant to Frank, so she'd come to see him, with a view to carrying them on, but that really depended on how today went. She was a little nervous. She knew Richie couldn't convey his emotions, but she was still anxious as to how he would receive her.

She met Faye at the front door, as agreed. Faye had explained to her that Frank had always gone round the back to avoid being seen, but Gloria wasn't bothered about that. She had no reason to keep it from anyone. She'd not told the family yet, but if today went well, she would do. Gloria didn't want any secrets.

'Do you want a cuppa first, Gloria, in my office? Or are you happy to just got through?'

'I'll just go straight through, luv. I'll have a cuppa, though, if there's one going.'

'Of course. I'll get one brought through to you. Milk and sugar?'

'Just a dash of milk, please.'

'Come on, I'll take you in and then I'll sort it.'

Gloria followed Faye down the corridor and into Richie's room. It was very spacious and more luxurious than she'd imagined. It was the first time she'd been in. Every year, when the family all came on the anniversary of Daniel's murder, they'd wait in reception for a carer to bring Richie through. She was surprised that he had a separate lounge and bedroom.

'Hello, Richie,' she said.

'I'll leave you to it. I'll get your tea brought down in a few minutes.'

'Thank you.'

Gloria sat down opposite Richie. He looked straight at her, but there was nothing in his eyes. She felt sad.

'Lovely room. A lot nicer than I thought it'd be. I love the patio doors and the garden. I bet you love to sit and watch the wildlife. Do you get much?' she asked.

Richie stared blankly at her. She realised it was silly asking him as he couldn't answer. She felt awkward. *Why did you ask that?* she said to herself.

'I know your dad used to come and see you. He didn't know I knew, but I did. To be honest, I can't remember how I knew but I just did. Funny that, isn't it, when you know something but can't remember how. Well, I just wanted to come and see you because, well, to be honest, I'd like to keep the visits up. You know, to keep them up as Frank would have done. Would you like that?'

Again, she wondered why she was asking, but it just felt the right thing to say. 'I'd like to come. Faye said your dad used to come monthly. She said he'd been a bit more recently, but I suppose that was to tell you about the wedding and that, so if it's OK with you, I'll come once a month and we can just sit and, well, I can tell you things. I can read to you if you like. I'd like that. I like reading.'

She looked at him, hoping for a sign that he was happy with that. 'I don't know what you think of me, Richie, but if there was ever a chance that you enjoyed your dad's visits, I want to carry them on. I know your dad liked them. He loved you. I know you might find that hard to believe, but he did. I'm sure he told you himself, but he did regret what he did. He would have changed it all if he could.'

The door opened and in came Louise, one of the carers. 'Here you go, Gloria. Nice cup of tea. I've put you a biscuit on there, too.'

Gloria stood up and took the cup and saucer from Louise, who then bent down in front of Richie and wiped a tear from his eye. When Gloria noticed the tear, she shed one too.

'Look at me,' she said. 'I told myself I wouldn't cry.'

'Here, give me that,' Louise said, taking the tea back from Gloria. She placed it on the shelf, just to the side of a photo of Daniel and Richie when they were younger. Gloria took a tissue from her bag and wiped her eyes.

'You OK?' Louise asked.

'Yes, thank you. We'll be fine. I'm just going to chat with him.'

Gloria took a sip of her tea. 'Ah, look at you two,' she said. 'Proper young tearaways, I bet.' She picked up the photo and showed it to Richie. 'It's almost impossible to tell who's who,' she said smiling, as she turned round to replace it. 'Ooh, some cufflinks here. They must be Frank's.' Gloria picked them up, studying them in her right palm. 'Yep, I've definitely seen these before. I'll take them back with me and put them with his others. I'd like to keep them. He loved his cufflinks, did Frank, especially gold ones. Always immaculately dressed your father, wasn't he?'

Gloria talked with Richie about nothing in particular for the next forty-five minutes before giving him a kiss goodbye and assuring him she'd be back in a month's time. Even though Richie had shown no emotion, Gloria convinced herself that he'd enjoyed her visit. He'd actually fucking hated it. Anything to do with his father got him fired up, and Gloria was no different. She went away happy, though, sure she was doing a good thing. Besides, visiting Richie had given her momentary relief from her grief.

chapter sixty-two

Phoebe thought long and hard about what Jez and Brian had said about Steven. She knew she had to get these first decisions right and above all else she had to be strong in her delivery of them. She just had a feeling that Steven would be expecting to be rewarded. She had a private word with Pat, telling him of her plans, of her conversation with Jez and Brian and that she wanted him to be her number two. Pat told her he'd be honoured and that she had his support.

Alice, as usual, took the tea and coffee orders as everyone took their places. For the first time, Phoebe felt the absence of their two formidable family figures. She took a deep breath.

'Well, good morning everyone. You'll all be wondering why I've called this meeting, I'm sure, so I'll get straight to the point. I am taking over as head of the family business.'

She paused and scanned the room. 'As you all know, Archie has decided it's best for him to get away. For how long we are unsure, but for now at least, I will be running things. Pat here will be my number two. Jez is coming out of retirement and will, along with Brian, act as my advisers, being only half a step behind Pat and me. Raquel, I want you to take a step up and oversee all areas of the day-to-day business. You will relinquish your daily running of Nottingham, Leicester and Derby. Steven, you will replace Raquel as head of operations in those areas. Del, you will move up to be Steven's official number two. Trainer, you will continue to run Leeds and Doncaster.'

Phoebe broke off to observe their reactions. Everyone seemed to be taking it all in and were OK with everything thus far. Phoebe continued. 'So, Raquel, yours is a newly created position. Steven and Trainer will report to you, and you will report to me. In my absence, you'll report to Pat, but Pat, in the main, will be at my side. Is that clear to everyone?'

They all at slightly different times said yes. All except Steven.

'Just a minute, Phoebe. Who voted you in as head doorman?'

'No one, just me. Why? Problem?'

'Yeah, if you like. It was me who took the fucking lead when Frank was shot. Me who stepped up. It was me who showed he had it, me who picked up the baton in a moment of crisis. Maybe I want to be head of the business. Maybe I want that seat.'

Phoebe had expected something like this, not so much a direct challenge for the leadership but discontent at the very least. She had instructed Jez, Brian and Pat not to intervene if she encountered any resistance. Phoebe knew she had to stand her ground and was aware this was her first test. She stood up and stepped to the side, leaving her chair empty.

'Well, here it is, Steven. Now's your chance to see if you have what it takes to take it.' She held his gaze firm as she spoke, well aware that if he stood up to make his move, she could fail at the first attempt. Her reign would be short-lived.

You could feel the tension. No one spoke for what seemed an age. Steven continued to stare at her. Phoebe returned his hard stare. He got up and as he did, Del, who was immediately to his right, placed himself in front of him to block his path to Phoebe. Michael did the same. Steven now had two hardened criminals between him and the empty chair he could just about see over their shoulders. Rooted to the spot, he realised everyone else had now stood up, he assumed, in support of Del and Michael, and, more importantly, of Phoebe as head of the family. He shook his head as he sat down, knowing his act of leadership on the day of Frank's murder had not had the effect he'd hoped.

'Well, I think it's clear which way the votes would fall, Steven. Thank you for your interest in the top job, but, as you can see, there is no longer a vacancy.'

She sat back to address the room. 'I think we all know we have a big job on our hands, but the first thing we need to do is get the message out there that it's business as usual. There's been a change at the top, but that message has to be felt loud and clear. So, I want a firm hand given to anyone who steps the slightest bit out of line. No second chances. There will be people who will try it on – don't allow it. I want you all to be extra vigilant. We cannot afford to show any sign of weakness. That clear to everyone?'

Everyone nodded, including Steven. He was fuming, but told himself his plan had only been temporarily thwarted. It would take a little longer, but he was now surer than ever that he would, somehow, take that seat from Phoebe Pearson.

Phoebe closed the meeting around two hours later, having discussed specific issues on specific areas she needed to be aware of. She had chaired the meeting well and not encountered any further problems. Steven had been quiet throughout, deep in thought about how he was going to further execute his takeover plan. Phoebe had noted his quietness, but put it down to the outburst at the start of the meeting. As people started to make their way out, she asked him to stay behind. She remained seated. Pat closed the door behind Jez, the last one to leave the boardroom, before returning to his seat next to her.

'So Steven, are we good?' she asked.

'Yeah, no issues. I was just pissed off, I suppose. I thought I had a chance to be at the helm. I didn't for one minute expect you to be taking over. You have to remember, me and my brother, many moons ago, had what you have – even if on a smaller scale. We were the top dogs in Leicester at the time, so I suppose that fire was still burning a little. No issue, though. I'm clear as to where I stand.'

Steven surprised himself at how genuine he sounded. He suspected Phoebe would have a word and he wanted any tension laid to rest, so he'd prepared this speech during the meeting. He needed Phoebe to trust him if he was ever going to have any chance of carrying on with his plan.

'Good. Glad to hear it. We'll just pretend that little episode never happened. Any repeat and you'll be out for good. Clear?'

'Crystal,' he replied, promising himself he'd keep any anger in check.

Steven left the house and rang Johnny immediately. 'The fuckin' bitch has taken over!'

'Who has?'

'Phoebe. She's now running things. Fuckin' Phoebe! A woman! How the fuck can we have a woman running the firm? Fuck me, we'll be a laughing stock. We need a plan, Johnny boy, and we need one quick. Any news on the will?'

'Not heard owt yet,' Johnny replied, a little stunned.

'Well, keep ya ears close to things. If we're lucky, that will may just be the leg-up we need.'

chapter sixty-three

Gloria was getting ready for what was going to be a very emotional day. She'd hardly slept a wink. She and Phoebe had spoken at length about what kind of funeral to give Frank. Neither of them wanted it to be a showcase. Every criminal the length and breadth of the UK wanted to be there; most of them had never actually met Frank, but wanted to be seen mixing with the elite. After much family deliberation, they opted for as low a key affair as possible. Hazlehurst had also told them that given the circumstances, a low-key affair would be best too.

Jez had been responsible for contacting those who had been invited from the fraternity, which mainly consisted of the main players and their own top tables. These mourners along with the family and their own firm members would make up the majority of the people in attendance. Brian had organised some heavy security for the day to ensure no hangers-on caused any trouble. No one wanted Frank Pearson's funeral to turn into a spectacle. The family had booked a double slot at the crematorium, to guarantee enough time for people who wanted to, to get up and have their say.

Everyone wondered if Archie would turn up.

Gloria looked at herself in the mirror. She was determined to remain steadfast, just as Frank would have wanted. As she walked out onto the landing, she heard Johnny shout downstairs to Alice.

'Have you seen my gold cufflinks, Alice?'

Gloria stopped and took a step back into her bedroom. She couldn't make out what Alice was saying.

'What do you mean "which ones"? I've only got one gold pair. I can't remember when I last wore them, but I'm sure I left them here. They're not at my house. I checked this morning,' Johnny shouted. He then walked back along the landing to Alice's bedroom muttering about how he wanted to wear them.

A feeling of immense doom washed over Gloria. She took a deep breath as she stepped into her and Frank's dressing room and opened Frank's top drawer. She opened the box where he kept all of his cufflinks and took out the ones she'd found in Richie's room, before walking onto the landing. Her heart was beating fast.

'Are these them, Johnny?' she asked, praying he'd say no.

'Yeah, that's 'em. Cheers, Gloria. Where were they?'

'I found them in the bathroom last week. I meant to tell you but, you know, with everything that's happened...'

Johnny planted a big kiss on Gloria's forehead before walking away, fastening his left cufflink as he did so.

Gloria walked back into her bedroom. What the hell were those cufflinks doing in Richie's room? She did not like the feeling she had in the pit of her stomach. Nor did she like the thought that was running through her head.

The horse-drawn carriage drew lots of attention as it held up traffic along the A60. It was surprising how long it took to get from Papplewick to Mansfield. The line of traffic was so long, you couldn't see the end, but no one tried to overtake. Phoebe was unsure whether it was because everyone knew whose funeral it was or whether it was etiquette, but either way the respect shown was admirable.

The driveway of the crematorium was lined with mourners. This had been expected. Phoebe hoped there would be no problems. As the horses pulled up outside the chapel doors, the line of cars behind were visible all the way back down towards the entrance. Phoebe, Gloria, Alice, Sarah and Mary were in the front car. They waited for the funeral director staff to open the doors after the music had all been checked. As they got out, Phoebe and Gloria took a moment to speak to those at the front. Phoebe immediately scanned for Archie. Deep down, she knew he wouldn't come. She'd not heard from him, but a little part of her had hoped he'd show up. She was angry at him for not being there, but she held back. He had his reasons, but to miss his grandad's funeral, the man who had been like a father to him in recent years, was something she would find hard to forgive. She would never understand, she knew that, but would she ever be able to forgive him for his no-show?

She saw Richie being wheeled up to the front. The funeral director had organised a car for him and two of his carers. She smiled at him. He gave nothing back. Phoebe noticed people staring.

'Here! Bring Richie up here!' she beckoned to his carers.

As they were instructed to the front of the queue, Alice looked for Johnny. He'd been in the car behind with Jez, Brian, Pat, Raquel and Steven. She couldn't see him. She wanted him with her.

'Where's Johnny?' she asked Jez.

'He was here,' he replied, as he pointed to his side. 'Maybe he's nipped to the toilet. Don't worry, I'll bring him in to you. Save him a seat.' Jez moved to the side and then walked to the toilets next to the chapel entrance door. Raquel could see Alice was anxious. She stepped out of the queue and looked down the line. She could see Johnny remonstrating with a woman in the car park.

'What the fuck are you doing here?!' he asked.

'It's a free country. Why wouldn't I want to see that bastard dead? You can't stop me being here. No one can. It's a funeral and I can be here if I want,' Lorraine replied. Johnny could see she'd taken something. This was the last thing he needed.

'Mum, look, you can't be here. For fuck's sake, just go. Just fuck off!'

'Charming. That's no way to speak to your mother. That bastard lying in there was responsible for everything. Him and that fuckin' son of his, not the slavering one that I shagged, the other one who died – fuckin' Daniel. They ruined it all. Bastards. I want to make sure he's dead!'

Johnny was starting to panic and he was getting more and more angry. His mum being here was not good; in fact it could spell fucking disaster. He pulled his wallet out of his pocket.

'Here, take this.' He gave her a hundred quid in twenty-pound notes. 'Just take this and leave. Go and get some more of that shit you take.'

Lorraine looked at him as if to say not likely with a hundred quid. Johnny took some more twenties out of his wallet. Here, that's two hundred. Now just fuck off!'

Lorraine smiled a sarcastic smile, blew him a kiss and snatched the money from his hand. 'I hate funerals anyway,' she said, as she marched off.

Johnny straightened his jacket, turned and walked towards the entrance door. He saw Raquel with Jez. They both looked curious.

'Who the fuck was she?' Jez asked.

'Oh, just one of my clients from the hospital. Just one of them people who are intrigued by gangsters and all that. She said she was gonna turn up. I didn't think she would, but she's a bit erratic, you know. A bit loopy at times, so I've told her to go. Can't trust her to not cause a scene if she's not allowed in,' he said convincingly.

'Oh right, good call. Alice is waiting for you, come on,' Jez said, as he put his arm around his shoulders.

Raquel stood fixed to the spot. Where did she know that woman from?

Jez turned and noticed Raquel was deep in thought. 'Raquel!' he shouted. She turned and followed, but was racking her brain as to where she knew her from.

The chapel at the crematorium was full despite the family restricting attendance, with some having to listen to the celebrant on the outside speakers. Johnny couldn't help but think of his mother and prayed she'd taken the money and fucked off.

The funeral went well. Jez said a few words, something he found really hard to do. He spoke of their early days and how Frank had always been the one man he had looked up to. Johnny spoke too, concentrating on how Frank had welcomed him into the family and how there was only one Frank Pearson. Then George Burbanks spoke, saying how they don't make 'em like Frank any more.

Outside afterwards everyone gave their condolences to Gloria. People were catching up, talking about the old days and how Frank was someone who could always be relied upon. Raquel, however, was watching Johnny. He scanned the area as soon as he came out and though he did his best to be part of the family and be at Alice's side, he was constantly searching the grounds. He was looking for someone.

The family held the wake at Phoebe's house in Southwell, opting to have it there rather than at Frank's house, where the murder took place. The mood was fairly jovial, as Frank would have wanted it to be. The sun came out from behind the clouds on a couple of occasions and the rain that was forecast managed to keep away. This meant people were in the garden most of the time.

Jez was talking to Bonnie, asking what he'd been doing since he retired.

'Not torturing people, that's for sure, Jez. I miss it sometimes, though. I suppose what I did for a living is not something most people can comprehend, but I fuckin' loved it. I do sometimes think I might get a call from someone one day and get my old tools out. I've still got them all, you know.'

'I bet you have. You were the best, Bonnie. I can vouch for that. The only one Frank ever rang.'

'He was the best was Frank. One of a kind, you know,' Bonnie said, raising his glass.

Jez spotted Raquel. He needed to speak to her. 'I'll see you in a bit, Bonnie. Just need a word with Raquel.'

'Don't mind me, Jez. I know you'll have business to attend to.'

Raquel saw him, sensing he wanted a word.

'You recognised her too then?' he said.

'The woman at the crem?'

'Yeah, Johnny's "client",' Jez said.

'Yeah, who was she?'

'I was hoping you'd know. I can't place her, but like you, Raquel, she looked familiar. I know her from somewhere and it's not from round here.'

'Yeah, me too. That sarcastic smile and the way she blew that kiss was a déjà vu moment. I've seen that before, but I can't think where from.'

'He was looking for her when we came out, you know.'

'I saw him. He was looking for her all the time. It'll come to me, Jez. Leave it with me. It'll come to me. He gave her a wad of cash, you know.'

'I saw it. Don't worry, I saw it.'

The afternoon went well. All the talk was of who could have done it. Everyone had their theories, but, interestingly, no one theorised that it could have been the guy in the wheelchair, who was being pushed around by Johnny all afternoon. No one really noticed that Johnny never left Richie's side. No one except Gloria. Gloria couldn't take her eyes off them, but then no one noticed that either.

chapter sixty-four

The day after the funeral was the reading of Frank's will. The family solicitor, Arthur Sanderson, had invited some of the family to his offices. Gloria, Phoebe and Alice were present. Archie was the only one who should have been there that wasn't.

Arthur Sanderson was in his mid-sixties. He had known Frank for as long as he cared to remember and had dealt with many of his affairs over the years. His firm was well respected within the area, although his association with Frank over the years had been frowned upon from some quarters. Arthur was a shrewd fella, someone who a man like Frank would want in his corner. Arthur knew where the line was and nudged it daily, but he was skilful in sticking to the right side of it. Frank had paid him well, and Arthur had kept Frank out of prison. That was the agreement they had, with both parties keeping their side of the deal. Arthur was old school like Frank. His handshake meant something. The two men had seldom had a cross word. They were very similar, the only real difference being Arthur stayed on the right side of the law.

'So, how are you all?' Arthur asked.

Phoebe spoke on behalf of the three of them. 'We're all fine, thank you. You?'

'Oh, I'm always fine, Phoebe. Always fine, me. Well, let's get down to business, shall we. As you all know, Frank liked things simple. He was not a complicated man in life and in death he is no different. He's left just about his entire estate to four people, and that's you three here and Archie. There are a few others he's looked after, of course, but the majority of it all goes to you and Archie. We are only talking about the tangible assets and Frank's legitimate businesses here, of course. Many of his, how shall we say, "other" business interests, as you all know, are not something that he would leave in a will. That part of his life I will have to leave to you to sort out amongst yourselves, but in terms of property, money and other material assets in his legitimate activities, he basically left it all to the four of you.'

'What about Richie?'

'Nothing. He left Richie nothing. I'm sorry to say that Richie gets nothing.'

'When did he last change his will?' Phoebe asked.

'After Daniel passed away. It was one of the first things he did, but since then, he never contacted me to change it. It is as it was seven or so years ago.'

Phoebe looked at Gloria, who looked at her in return. Alice looked to the floor.

Sanderson proceeded to read the contents of Frank's will. He left Jez, Brian and Pat some money, as he did

Del and Raquel. He left nothing for Steven. He also left a few quid for Marie, as a thank you for her involvement in helping to solve the mystery surrounding Daniel's death. Everything else went to the three people in the room, and Archie. Arthur explained who got what. It was as expected really. The three of them had spoken about it beforehand. Gloria got the house and a share in the main club in Nottingham. Phoebe, on behalf of Daniel, got a share in the same club, plus in other properties with Archie and Alice. The money was shared out in a similar vein. Frank had looked after everyone well. Everyone except Richie. There wasn't even a provision for the cost of his care. That was something they were all keen to sort. No one wanted to see Richie removed from his care home. Phoebe promised she'd sort it out. She still owed Richie from saving her all those years ago. She would pay the fees personally. It was something she both wanted and needed to do. It would make her feel good inside.

Alice had arranged to meet Johnny afterwards. She still needed him to hold her and to tell her things were going to be all right. Alice relied on Johnny such a lot, more than she probably ever realised. She was so grateful that Johnny had nothing to do with the life everyone else around her seemed to be involved in. He was her saviour in so many ways. Alice enjoyed being on the fringe of it all. She secretly liked the adulation it gave her, but she never wanted to be a bigger part of it. She made the tea, kept notes of meetings and did some office work here and there for the family business, but that was it. Johnny was no part of it and that was one of his best qualities.

She had arranged to meet him back at his house in Blidworth. It was an ex-pit house, but it was his. He'd bought it just before they met. He was now earning good money, so could easily move to something bigger, but for some reason he wanted to stay where he was. That was another quality she liked about him – he wasn't materialistic. Alice parked in front of his house on Dale Lane. His car was on his drive.

She sat a moment and looked around her. Blidworth was an old mining village where everyone knew everyone. It was a community that looked after their own. She watched two young mums walk past her, both pushing a buggy, both no older than 18, but happy in their own little world. Alice suspected they'd only ever lived in Blidworth and wondered if they'd ever leave. It was one of those villages people seldom left. Everyone was happy with what life had afforded them. Alice smiled a wry smile as she thought how different the lives of those two young girls were from her own. They may well have heard about, or read of, Frank Pearson's death, but neither of them would have known his granddaughter was sat in the very car they'd just walked past. Maybe, she thought, they couldn't give a shit.

Alice got out and walked towards Johnny's front door. He opened it as she was halfway up the path. 'You looked deep in thought there,' he said. 'I was watching you through the window. Penny for them?'

'Those two young lasses just made me think, that's all. Just about how different our lives are.' She kissed him. He kissed her back.

'Cuppa?'

'Yeah, please.'

'So, how did it all go?' Johnny asked, as he picked up the kettle.

Alice sighed and puffed her cheeks as she exhaled.

'That bad?' he said, now really curious to know.

'Well, yes and no really. Most of it was as we'd expected. Me, Archie, my mum and Gloria have been left the majority of money, property and shares in the businesses. Jez and some of the others got left a few quid, enough to see them all right, but nothing for Richie.'

Johnny, immediately, without realising it, folded his arms. His face changed. He looked stern. 'What, nothing at all?'

'Not a bean, not even any money to pay his home fees, although my mum is gonna sort that, so he'll be fine. He won't know any different really, but it was still a shock. I mean, we all know he despised him, but we all still thought he'd leave him money to see him right. I mean he's paid his home fees all of these years, so to leave him with nothing was a surprise. We were all as shocked as each other. I mean my grandad was always about family.'

Johnny was struggling to contain his anger. He needed to ring his uncle. He turned his back to make the tea.

'You OK?' Alice asked.

'Yeah, course. I suppose I'm just as shocked as you lot. As you say, Frank was always big on family. I'd not thought anything about it – nowt to do with me – but now you've said, I'm really shocked. I thought Frank would have looked after his only surviving son, especially as it was him who put him where he is.'

'Well, we can't change it, Johnny. It is what it is, but we'll all make sure he's OK. My mum will anyway.'

'So, you said Jez and the others got some money. Who else other than Jez?'

'Er, well, Brian, Raquel, Pat and I think Del did too.'

'That's nice. Good old Frank. I suppose Steven got some too eh?'

'No, funnily enough he didn't. I did think that when we were there. The solicitor never mentioned Steven for some reason. Probably 'cos of some shit that happened years ago. I don't know the full details, but him and Grandad had some beef before I was born. Grandad would never forget things like that.'

Johnny was having to try really hard to mask his frustration.

'Right, well, after this cuppa, I've got to go into work.'

'Eh? You never said!'

'Sorry, luv, but I have to go. I'll make sure I come round later, though, I promise. We're short-staffed in the department. I have to do my bit to cover.'

Johnny wanted to ring Steven and ring him quickly.

chapter sixty-five

Steven Wallace was parked in the car park in the reservoir opposite King's Mill Hospital. He was waiting for Johnny, who was meeting him prior to starting work. Johnny had rung and texted him saying they needed to talk before he started his shift. He knew from the voicemail it was not going to be good news.

Steven had kept a pretty low profile since the top table meeting, but had made sure he knew what was happening with regards to the investigation into Frank's death. He could not believe how they had pulled it off. It had been so easy. No one suspected a thing, and no one suspected Richie. He couldn't believe how, after thirty years, he had managed to finally avenge his brother's death and what had happened to him. Frank had mellowed towards him, but it had taken a long time. For years, he had ridiculed him in front of others, which Steven had had to just take. When Frank had taken him and his brother, Gary, out, he'd shown that he was the undisputed king of the East Midlands. Steven had, as the years rolled on, accepted his place in the criminal hierarchy and had slowly gained the family's trust, if not Frank's

432

entirely. Through hard work, he had gained Archie's and Raquel's trust. He had always vowed to one day take Frank out, but if he was honest, he never thought he'd ever really have a chance. Johnny had given it to him. It had been a small chance but, with planning, he knew he could pull it off, and he had. It had been a long time coming, but as his mother had always said to him, good things come to those who wait.

Johnny opened the door. 'All right, Unc?'

'Get in quick. You never know who's watching.'

'You're fucking paranoid. No one's watching.'

'So, what happened?'

'Richie's got fuck all. That fucking wanker dad of his left him fuck all. Not a bean. Nothing.'

'Not a penny?'

'Not one penny, Uncle, not one fucking penny.'

'For fuck's sake. I fuckin' knew it, though. I knew deep down that bastard wouldn't leave him anything. Well, that's your inheritance gone then.'

'I know that. I'm not fuckin' stupid. That was my fucking way out of here. I was only in this for the dosh. I know he's my dad and all that but come on, he's never gonna take me for a pint, is he? I'd resigned myself through all of this that once we had the money we'd be doing away with him 'cos then I'd inherit his share. Legally.'

Johnny ran his hands through his hair before continuing. 'You don't realise how nice I've acted towards him all of this time. If anyone had heard me or seen me with him, they'd really think I loved him. In fact, I think I've told him so a few times. If only he knew it was all just to make sure he pulled that bastard trigger. For fuck's sake!' he shouted.

'Calm down, Johnny. Look, this wasn't what we planned. Neither of us knew Frank would leave Richie fuck all. I never thought he'd leave him the whole lot, I mean how could he, but I thought he'd leave him a tidy sum. A tidy sum that, as you pointed out, would see us both all right.'

'So, what's the plan now then, 'cos I ain't going back to that room. Never.'

'Well, there's nothing coming to light about Frank's killer. They know fuck all, so unless Richie blabs, we're in the fucking clear on that score.'

They both laughed at the thought of Richie spilling the beans.

'The gun still in the safe?' Steven asked.

'Yeah, still there. No one knows anything about it, not even about the safe, so there's no drama there. Fuck, I'll have to go back to get that, won't I?'

'Yeah, at some point we need that gun, but look, it's safe there. We don't want it out in the open. Leave it there a while.'

Steven stroked his chin – with the hand that was missing some fingers. As ever, that reminded him of Frank.

'I still can't believe we pulled it off, Johnny. When I think back to that day, I'm amazed how calm I was through it all. Even when I saw you wheeling Richie towards Frank and I knew what was gonna happen, I was still as calm as fuck. I tell ya, Gary would have fuckin' loved it. I hope he's giving Frank a good kickin' up there.'

'Or down there, wherever they are,' Johnny replied. They smiled.

'So, Richie lives then, is that what you're telling me?' Steven asked.

'Well, he ain't gonna blab, is he? And look, as much as I hate having a slavering fuck for a dad, I ain't gonna kill him for no reason. If he had a boat load of cash from the will, then yeah, it would have been OK to carry on with plan A no drama, but even he doesn't deserve that for no reason.'

'You got time for a cuppa in the café round the corner?'

Johnny looked at his watch. 'Yeah, go on then, a quick one.'

They both got out and walked towards the water.

'So, what's the plan now? Surely that can't be it?'

'Be patient, nephew. Things come to those who wait. It took me thirty years to get rid of Frank, so hang fire. We need to let things settle a bit more, but I'm on it. I'll have a plan, don't fret. I haven't taken out one of the biggest villains in the UK to stop now. Frank was the hard bit. Phoebe won't last, Johnny. She's no fucking criminal, not one for running Frank's empire anyway. Unless Archie boy returns, we'll just have to wait for the dominos to fall. They will, 'cos Phoebe is out of her depth. She's a fuckin' joke. It won't be long, trust me.'

'Can't we just pay someone to take her out? After her, there's no one. You'd be able to slip in unchallenged and take over.'

'I said, I'm on it. Just let me think. Anyway, get that table over there and I'll get the teas in.'

chapter sixty-six

Emma Black was driving to Papplewick to see Gloria before going on to a couple of nursing homes. She had a session booked with her to give her some Reiki. Gloria needed it. In the past two days she'd had the funeral to get through and then the shock of Frank's will. No one expected Frank to leave Richie with nothing. Gloria felt partly responsible, mainly because she'd suspected how Frank felt about Richie, but only discussed it with him a couple of weeks before his death. She felt guilty. If she had spoken to him before, she would maybe have thought about getting Frank to change his will. Phoebe and Alice both told her not to be silly. Frank was the only one responsible for his will. No one else and certainly not Gloria.

She was looking forward to her Reiki today, but was apprehensive also. She had something she needed to talk to Emma about, something she was not looking forward to. It had been a last-minute booking after Gloria ringing Emma late the night before to see if she could squeeze her in. Emma, the ever-accommodating lady that she was, said she'd come before her pedicure appointments at the homes later in the afternoon.

Emma was on her way, singing her heart out to her favourite eighties tunes as she drove along Blidworth Waye. Emma loved the eighties. It was her era and she would tell anyone that there was never any better music than the eighties. Some agreed, many didn't, but for Emma, it would always be the decade that defined her.

She pulled into the driveway. As she got out of the car, humming a tune to herself, she saw Phoebe come to the front door. 'Hiya!' she shouted. Phoebe waved and smiled, but seemed rather preoccupied. Emma then remembered. Shit. Bloody funeral two days ago. She changed to her best sombre expression and approached Phoebe, who had now opened the door fully to allow her in.

'How is everyone?' Emma asked, her voice quiet and solemn.

'Bearing up, Emma. You know how it is. Takes it out of ya.'

Emma hugged Phoebe, who returned the gesture. 'I'll go and see Gloria and then I'll come and get my couch out of the boot. Is she in?'

'Yeah, kitchen as always. She'll have the kettle on.'

Emma walked through and hugged Gloria. Gloria squeezed her tight. 'I'll make a cuppa and we'll go through, eh,' Gloria said, as she turned to take three mugs from the cupboard. 'You want one, Phoebe?'

'No, it's OK. I'm off out. I won't be long.'

'Ah, well, just the two then.' Gloria replaced one of the mugs.

'I'll nip and get my couch then and I'll set up, eh. Once we've had a natter and a cuppa, you can lie back and relax.'

Emma smiled before heading out to her car. She watched Phoebe drive off, then closed her boot lid as she walked back to the house, struggling to carry the massage couch.

'Just drop it there, Emma. Come in here. We can chat in the kitchen first. I've got something I need to ask you.'

'Is everything OK?' she asked, taking a sip of her tea, knowing full well that given Gloria had only buried her husband-to-be two days ago, it was probably a silly question.

'Have you ever seen Johnny at Richie's nursing home?'

Emma burnt her lip on her mug. She felt herself colouring up. Emma couldn't lie; it just wasn't in her. She struggled to keep a secret, never mind tell a lie. Gloria could see straight away the answer was going to be yes. She could sense Emma felt uncomfortable all of a sudden.

'Just be straight with me, Emma. I need to know.'

'Yes, I have. Only once, though, but yes, I have seen him there.'

'Did he see you?'

'Yes, we spoke. I bumped into him not so long ago. I'd left my diary in the car and gone back for it. That's when I saw him and when he saw me too.'

'What did he say about why he was there?'

'Just that he visited Richie sometimes. He said that he felt sorry for him and was doing some physio or something with him. He did ask me to keep it a secret, though. I'm sorry, Gloria. I didn't like having to keep it from you, but he just said that Frank wouldn't have liked it and, well, that it was to be our secret. I just pushed it to the back of my mind. You know I don't handle things like that well.'

'It's OK. Honestly, it's fine. Anyone would have done the same. Frank can't be angry at you now, can he?' she said, cupping her hands over Emma's. Emma smiled a nervous smile wondering why she was being asked.

'How did you know?' she asked.

'No matter. Now this may seem ironic, but the fact I know Johnny has been going is our secret. Understand?'

Emma put her head in her hands. 'Bloody hell, Gloria! That ain't fair!'

'Maybe not, but trust me, just forget we ever had this little chat. Anyway, drink up, I'm looking forward to my Reiki.'

Phoebe arrived at the main club in Nottingham. She had no real reason to go there, but wanted to keep her mind busy. She didn't even know who was going to be there, but knew someone would be. She was pleased when she pulled into the car park to see Raquel's car. She could have a good old chinwag with her, a proper girls' chat. She was ready for one of those given what she'd had to deal with lately. She'd spent most of the time at the wake talking about her new role at the helm. The London main faces were all happy with her. She'd not met any of them prior, but Greg West, in particular, was pleased to hear of a seemingly easy transition of power. He was old school was Greg and liked the fact it was staying within the family.

None of them was pleased with Archie, of course, but were very respectful in their choice of words when talking about his disappearing act. Phoebe had been ready to defend him, but, save for Tariq Mali, who was close to the knuckle in his feelings, she had been OK with what had been said. She knew Tariq had some beef from years ago, so had put it down to that. Tariq had been supplying the women to two men who Frank had taken out in Leicester twenty-five years ago and he'd never forgotten Frank cutting off his supply chain. That was ancient history, but Phoebe was aware it still rankled Tariq. She'd heard Frank mention it a time or two.

'Drink?' Raquel asked, as Phoebe walked into the office.

'Just a small one. A glass of Chardonnay, please.'

'Pat not with you?'

'No. I just wanted to get out, you know. Just to keep my mind from wandering. It's only a social call. Just needed someone to talk to, that's all. Pat's sorting out an issue for Pēteris anyway. Nothing major, but Pēteris needs his help.'

Raquel walked to the office door and shouted an instruction into the bar area.

'You were a bit preoccupied the other day. Every time I looked over, you seemed miles away. Reminiscing?' Phoebe asked.

Raquel sighed. 'No, not really. Not reminiscing exactly, just thinking.'

'Bout what?'

'Something that happened at the funeral. Something I think you need to know. Not to act upon, but just to have stored away. I've sat on it over the last couple of days, so I'm glad you've popped in.'

'Come on then, spit it out.'

'Johnny.'

'What about him?'

'He's from Loughborough, isn't he?'

'Yeah. He has a place in Blidworth now, but yeah, from there originally. Why?'

'How well do we know his history?'

Phoebe was intrigued. She sat forward just as a member of staff brought her wine.

'Thank you.' She took a sip. 'Well, come on. Bloody hell, spit it out!'

'Well, when we got there, as you were all shaking hands and exchanging pleasantries, Johnny went missing. Alice was looking for him. Anyway, I saw him thirty yards away talking to a woman. It was obvious by the way he was acting that he wasn't happy to see her. He gave her a wad of cash – a fair few quid by the look of it – and I managed to hear him tell her to fuck off. She gave him a sarcastic smile and tilted her head – you know what I mean – then blew him a kiss, and off she went.'

'Right. Go on.'

'Well, by this time Jez was stood next to me. He'd been looking for Johnny in the toilets for Alice. Jez asked Johnny who this woman was. He gave us a load of shit about it being a client who was a bit loopy. He said she could cause trouble so had told her to go. Neither of us believed him, but the thing is, I had a bit of a déjà vu with that smile and her blowing that kiss. I've seen that before. I've seen her before. I can't think where, but I have. The other thing is, Jez recognised her too, but again can't remember where from. She was no client, Phoebe, but why would Johnny lie? And give her a load of cash too?'

Phoebe didn't like what she was hearing. Why would he lie? Why would he be so keen to get rid of a woman at Frank's funeral? Her gut instinct told her there was something in this, something she needed to get to the bottom of.

'You need to find out who she is. Do some digging. Someone from your past must know her. That smile or that kiss you spoke about – it must have been something she did, something she was known for. It might be nothing, Raquel, but whilst we still have no idea who killed Frank or who was behind it, everyone is under suspicion – even Johnny, a physiotherapist from Loughborough.'

That last part stuck out to Raquel. "A physiotherapist from Loughborough." That was where she needed to look, she was sure of it. Loughborough, she thought to herself. Yes, he was from Loughborough.

The chat with Raquel did not turn out to be the girlie chat Phoebe was hoping for. All the talk was about the day Frank was shot – who was where, who said what, who acted strange – but still nothing came to light. They talked about how the police had drawn a blank, as they'd suspected they would. The people who were there that day were all very wary of the police and had been told by Steven, Pat and Jez in the aftermath to keep their mouths shut. As much as everyone wanted to find Frank's killer, no one wanted the police to do it for them. This was how things were in their world. Frank had spent all his life staying clear of the filth, having coppers in his pocket, keeping under the radar. He was always sure to have legitimate businesses to explain his wealth, meaning he'd be left alone, so there was no way the family wanted heavy police involvement in their affairs now. Frank would not rest if he thought they had relied on the Old Bill to find his killer. They did things their own way, and that was not going to change now.

Once Phoebe had gone, Raquel racked her brains to try and picture where she knew her from. She then had a thought that made her sit up. The only other person she knew of any importance from Loughborough was Steven Wallace. He and his brother, Gary, who ran Leicester in the early nineties, were from Loughborough. Her immediate thought was to ring Steven to get him in, to see if he could place this woman. She picked up her mobile, but slowly placed it back on the desk. Something was telling her to keep that information from him. Her gut feeling, that sixth sense, was talking to her. Raquel listened to it. She didn't like what it was saying. She didn't know why, but she did know she was off to Leicester. She needed to see Tracey, who used to work for her many years ago in the Leicester clubs within the business. Maybe Tracey knew her, or if not, someone else on her payroll down there might do. She picked up her keys and shouted to Del she was off out.

chapter sixty-seven

Phoebe was driving to meet Pat and Pēteris at the club in Mapperley. Pat had rung her about a local main dealer who he'd gone to have a word with. Pēteris had alerted them to the fact he'd been late with his payments recently. It had seemed nothing, but quickly transpired that not only was he late but he was a fair bit short too. Phoebe had made it clear to everyone, Pat included, that if anyone appeared to be trying it on, she was to be informed. This guy appeared to be. Phoebe needed to nip it in the bud, ensuring word would spread.

During the drive, she'd not stopped thinking about Johnny and why he would lie like he did. She liked Johnny. She always had. He had been good for Alice and the thing she liked most about him was that he wasn't interested in being part of the family business. That was the best thing about him. Maybe, she thought, he was telling the truth. Maybe this lady *was* a client who was a bit loopy, and just maybe Raquel and Jez had got it wrong. She would keep it to herself for now, though, and see what developed over the next day or two. Raquel was on her way to Leicester, so if this mysterious woman was from her past, she'd get to know about it pretty quickly.

Phoebe pulled into the car park, and found Pat's car next to Pēteris's. There were two others parked up, both of which she assumed were to do with the guy she was about to deal with. One was a soft top that she liked the look of. The guy she'd come to deal with was called Steffan, a Welsh guy who had lived in Nottingham most of his life. He was a respected dealer, who had bought off the Pearsons for years and who had, up until now, never missed a payment. He was a bit of a loose cannon, though, who was well known to need a firm hand every now and again.

Phoebe walked upstairs to see Steffan sat on a chair, looking rather chilled and certainly not someone who looked concerned in any way. Pat and Pēteris were stood in front of him with a rather nasty-looking guy stood behind him. Phoebe did not know him. She hoped he was one of Pēteris's men. Phoebe had not yet managed to get to know everyone on the firm's books.

'Pat,' she said in acknowledgement, before looking and nodding to Pēteris. 'Hello Pēteris.'

'Hello Phoebe,' he said in return. 'This is Jase,' he said as he turned his head to the big fella stood behind Steffan. 'He's my new head doorman.'

'Hello Jase. I'm Phoebe. Nice to meet you.'

'You too, Mrs Pearson.'

Phoebe smiled. She liked the fact he called her Mrs Pearson. 'Please call me Phoebe.'

Jase smiled.

'Pat, can I have a word please?'

Pat followed her into the main office. 'So what's the crack here with Steffan? He's never missed before, has he?'

'Never. Classic case of someone getting above his station and testing the new broom if you ask me. I would've just beat the fuck out of him, but you did say to let you know of anything like this before handing out any retribution.'

'I did, thank you. I need to show my presence, Pat. Word needs to spread. Do we have a broom of any sort?'

'What, a brush?'

'Yes, a long-handled broom. We must have one somewhere.'

'Two minutes,' Pat said and left the room.

Phoebe walked back out. 'So, Jase, how long have you been working for Pēteris?'

Steffan shuffled from one arse cheek to the other. Phoebe knew it was a sign of nerves but deliberately didn't acknowledge him.

'Three weeks. I've known him for a few years, though. I did a bit of work for him importing foreign labour initially, but I had a spell inside. Came out a couple of months ago.'

'How long were you inside?'

'Two and a half years.'

'Working for us could well land you back at some point, Jase. Bear that in mind, won't you?'

'Occupational hazard, ain't it? It won't stop me working hard for you, though. I'm loyal. Pēteris will vouch for me.'

'That your car outside?' she asked, wanting to account for every vehicle that was there.

'Yeah, mine's the convertible.'

'Here you go.' Pat came back into the room holding a stiff yard brush in his hand.

'Thank you,' Phoebe said, as she took it off him. Jase looked at Pēteris, who looked as perplexed as anyone, including Steffan.

'Steffan, I understand you're late for, what, the second time recently?' Phoebe looked to Pēteris for confirmation. Pēteris nodded.

'Mrs Pearson, I can only apologise. It won't happen again.'

'And short too, I understand. Creaming off the top, I think the technical term is.'

'Nah, not me. I'm only short 'cos a couple haven't paid me.'

'Not my problem, Steffan. As you well know, any shortfalls your end are made up by you. As with my father-in-law, God rest his soul, and as with my son, I am not to be short-changed.'

Steffan smiled. 'How is Archie. Heard from him?'

Phoebe ignored the comment. She held out the broom. 'This,' she said, 'is a broom. It's an old broom. I would have preferred a new broom but, well, we can't have everything, can we, and I suspect you are testing the new broom.'

Phoebe then took two steps forward towards Steffan and whacked him hard to the side of his head with the brush end. He brought his hands up to protect himself as she repeated it twice more. Steffan tried to get up but Jase held him down by the shoulders, making sure he arched his back to keep out of line of the swinging brush head.

'All right, all right!' Steffan shouted, as he wiped blood from his nose and mouth. His head was pounding.

'*All right?* I ain't started yet. You think you can fuck with me?'

Phoebe looked at Jase. 'Hold his head back!' she ordered, as she straddled him.

She cupped her hands around his jawline. 'Poor little Steffan. Thought he was the hard man. Thought you could be the one to show me what was what, did you? Aw, poor little Steffan.'

She smiled as she stroked his cheek, running her nail through his smeared blood. Phoebe stood up.

'Hold him down, Jase. Pēteris, Pat, take it in turns. How much was he light?'

'Just over 300.'

'OK, three punches each. That's six punches, so fifty quid a punch, give or take.'

Phoebe sat down as Pat, then Pēteris, took it in turns to punch Steffan to the face. By the fourth punch, he was out cold. By the sixth, he looked like he'd been in the ring with a heavyweight boxer. His eyes were closed, his nose and mouth were bleeding and he'd lost five teeth. They waited for him to come round. When he did, she walked over and grabbed his head by his hair.

'Don't ever be late with your payments again, Steffan, will you? And please, whatever you do, never cream off the top. This new broom will sweep you up next time and leave you in a skip. Understand?'

Steffan nodded as best he could. It hurt like hell, but he nodded.

'Right, gents, I'm off back home. Do with him what you like. Any repeat, I want to know. I'll be at home if you need me, Pat.'

Pat winked at her. They both knew the new broom had just swept clean. Pat liked what he'd seen. He liked it very much.

Phoebe was nearly home, pleased with how she'd handled that little episode. It had felt good; in fact, she'd loved every minute of it. The power was immense. She now knew why Frank had loved it so much, and, if she was honest, couldn't understand why Archie had not been able to seize his opportunity.

She drove down the drive and saw Gloria's car. She wasn't expecting to see Gloria here. She'd left her earlier with Emma and wasn't anticipating seeing her again. She was intrigued, but in equal measure, thought maybe she just wanted some company. Gloria had her own key, so would be inside, having a cuppa no doubt, even if she was on her own.

'Gloria?' she shouted as she opened the door.

'I'm in here, luv. Kettle's on. Hope you don't mind me coming in.'

'Course not. That's what your key's for.'

'I know but I still feel strange using it.'

'Fancied some company, did you?'

'Well, yes, but I need to talk to you.'

'What about?'

'Johnny.'

'Johnny?' Phoebe said, aware she'd not masked her surprise. Twice in one day was surely no coincidence. She was now expecting Gloria to tell her about the mystery woman.

'Yeah. Listen, I keep myself away from all of your business dealings as much as I can, you know that, but I went to see Richie a few days ago, before the funeral.'

'Right. Why did you go to see Richie?'

'Look, Phoebe, you need to know something. Frank used to go. All that stuff about him despising Richie was all a front. He regretted what he did to him and, well, he used to go and see him. Did for a few years. I knew. Frank didn't know I knew, but I did. I know a lot, Phoebe, you know that, but anyway, it sort of all came out recently with the wedding and everything. Frank wanted Richie there, but couldn't find a way of doing it without looking silly. You know what he was like, so I sort of let him know I knew, and well, before we knew it, we'd agreed that he could do it by saying he was doing it for me – you know to save face. After Jez brought it up that day, it just kind of spiralled from there.'

'The old bugger. He had us all convinced. Every year we would go and see him and every year Frank would make out he hated him.' Phoebe shook her head in amazement. 'And all the time he was visiting him. He played a bloody blinder, Gloria, I'll give him that.'

'You're not mad with him, are you?' Gloria asked.

'No, of course not. I'm just amazed he had us all believing him, that's all. You old devil, Frank,' she said, looking up to the ceiling still shaking her head. 'You know what, I really hope Richie knew how he felt. He must have told him, eh?'

'He will have done. Not sure how Richie would have felt, though. When I went to see him, there was no emotion there.'

'So, what's this about Johnny?'

'Oh yeah, sorry. Well, when I was there, I found some gold cufflinks behind a photograph of Daniel and Richie as boys. I thought they must have been Frank's, so I brought them home. I knew I'd seen them before, but if I'm honest, I couldn't remember Frank ever wearing them. I just assumed they must've been his, so I put them in his drawer upstairs with his others. Then, on the day of the funeral, I hear Johnny shouting downstairs to Alice asking her if she'd seen his gold cufflinks—'

'And they were Johnny's.'

'Yes. I showed them to him, saying I'd found them in the bathroom a few days earlier. But yes, they were his. So, this morning I asked Emma if she'd ever seen him at the home.'

'Had she?'

'Yes, only once, but she did confess that he visited regularly to do some physio on him or something and that he'd asked her to keep it a secret. You know Emma, she wouldn't say boo to a goose, so, of course, she just put it to the back of her mind.'

'So Johnny has been visiting Richie all of this time too?'

'Appears so.'

'Do you think Frank knew?'

'No. Emma said that was why she was to keep it a secret. Johnny was petrified that Frank would find out. He's mentioned it to her a couple of times since – you know, to make sure she wasn't gonna say anything.'

'OK, Gloria, thanks for that. Listen, this has to remain between us. I need to think about this. Do not breathe a word to anyone.'

'I won't. Trust me. You're the only one I've told. What are your initial thoughts?'

Phoebe's mind was racing. With this and the mysterious woman, Johnny was becoming a very interesting piece of information. Why, she did not know, but Gloria had no need to.

'Not sure, Gloria. Just leave this information with me. Make me that cuppa as I need to go somewhere. I'm parched.'

Gloria went to make the tea, leaving Phoebe to think about the two bits of information she'd received today. Raquel was on with finding out more about the woman at the funeral. Phoebe needed to find out more about Johnny's visits. There was one woman who would know about that. The same woman who would have known about Frank's visits too. Phoebe, after her cup of tea, was going to see Faye Johnson. She'd ring Raquel on the way.

chapter sixty-eight

Raquel pulled up outside Tracey's house. She was thinking about what she'd just heard from Phoebe, about the cufflinks. That had really cemented her thoughts. Johnny seemed to have a lot to hide. He wasn't the placid, kind and thoughtful man he portrayed himself to be. She opened her car door and walked through the little gate at the end of the path that led up to Tracey's front door. It had been at least a year since she'd last seen her.

Back in the mid-nineties, Tracey and her friend and neighbour Brenda had worked for a couple of local gangsters. When Frank took over, they then worked for Raquel, who ran Frank's operations for him. Brenda retired a few years after the takeover, but Tracey stayed on until around five years ago. She'd saved hard, had Tracey, and was now mortgage-free, with a part-time job in the local supermarket. Life in the underworld had taken its toll on her and she'd had enough. She'd stayed in touch, and every now and again Raquel would call in on her.

Tracey flung her arms around her as soon as she opened her front door.

'Bloody hell, girl, let me breathe!'

'Sorry, come on. I'll put the kettle on, unless you'd prefer something stronger?'

'No, coffee will do for me, please.'

Raquel was pleased with how Tracey had turned out. She had a lovely three-bed semi-detached, which was very neat and well presented. Her eldest daughter had gone to university and was now an accountant working for herself and, from what Raquel heard, was doing well. Her second, a son, was at some university in the North East doing economics.

'So, with what do I owe the pleasure?' Tracey asked, as she shouted from the kitchen. Raquel walked through.

'Can't I just call and see my old mate for a catch-up?'

Tracey laughed. 'I could hear it in your voice, Raquel. I've known you long enough to recognise that tone. You've come for a reason.'

Raquel held her hands up. 'Guilty,' she replied. She took the coffee mug from the worktop once Tracey finished stirring it.

'Can you recall anyone, a woman, from the past who always had a habit of tilting her head to the side, blowing a kiss in a sarcastic manner, with her hand on her hip?'

'Yeah, Lorraine her name was. It was something she always did.'

'Lorraine who?

'Never knew her surname, but she was friends with Annabelle. That's how I sort of knew her. I think Annabelle went to school with her.'

'Annabelle who ran reception for us for a few months?'

'Yeah, that's her. This Lorraine used to come in the club. She was always after a job, but she was always on the gear. The bouncers used to chuck her out when she got lairy, which she often did – always spouting off about her husband or something. That was when she would blow them a kiss – you know, when they chucked her out – and she'd tilt her head like she did.' Tracey did her impression of her, with her hands on her hips.

'That's it! That's exactly what she did!'

'Did what? When?'

'No matter, but I need to get in touch with Annabelle. Have you got her number?'

'Yeah. I'll ring her now.'

As Tracey put her mobile to her ear, Raquel thought back to the days when Lorraine would be at the club.

'Annabelle, hiya, it's me. Guess who I have here with me?' Tracey put it on loudspeaker and nodded to Raquel as if to say go on, say hello.

'Hiya Annabelle, Raquel here.'

'Bloody hell! Raquel, how are you? I didn't expect it to be you. What you doing there?'

'On a fact-finding mission. Look, I haven't got time

to chat, sorry, but you remember Lorraine who used to come in the club?'

'Yeah, Lorraine. I used to go to school with her. Lost touch with her for years, but then caught up with her again when she used to come in looking for a job.'

'What do you know about her?' Raquel asked.

'Er, well, not a lot really, other than she was as bright as they come at school, but once we left, I hardly saw her. She did get married, though. Gary, I think her husband was. Got killed apparently. He was in a similar line of work to you guys I think back in the day, so you may have known him.'

'What was her surname?'

'Well, when she was young, it was Connell, but when she married I'm sure it was Wallace.'

Raquel's blood ran cold. Tracey could see that last bit of information had hit a nerve. The atmosphere suddenly turned tense.

'Lorraine Wallace, you say, Annabelle, and her husband was Gary Wallace?'

'Yeah, for sure. That's her. I ain't seen her for ages, though. I have seen her knocking about since I stopped working for you, but not often.'

'Thanks, Annabelle. Sorry I can't chat, but we'll catch up another time.'

Tracey said goodbye and, placing her phone on the coffee table, looked at Raquel. She could see her mind was racing.

'Anything I can do?' she asked.

'Yeah, there is actually. Ring Annabelle back for me.'

'Annabelle, it's me again, Raquel. Did Lorraine ever have any children?'

'Er, yeah, I believe she did. One of my neighbours who used to live two doors down knew her and she told me she had a kid. A son, I think, but she buggered off when he was only a toddler. She never set eyes on him again, as far as my neighbour knew. No idea who he is or where he is.'

'Do you remember her parents?'

'Yeah, I do. Mr and Mrs Connell. Not sure if they're still alive, though.'

'Do you remember where they lived?'

'Yeah. If they're still in the same house, yes.'

'Text Tracey the address please, Annabelle, and thanks. Speak soon.'

Raquel nodded to Tracey to take it off loudspeaker. She said her goodbyes again and waited for the text message. She showed it to Raquel.

'Fancy a trip to Loughborough?' she asked.

'Yeah, can do. Is this gonna involve me doing anything dodgy?'

'Not really. I'll tell you on the way. Come on, get your stuff.'

As Tracey put on her shoes and grabbed her keys, Raquel realised she'd not even told her about Frank. She told her as they drove out of Braunstone. She then told her what she needed her to do.

chapter sixty-nine

Phoebe stood in the doorway of Faye Johnson's office. She watched Faye working away with her head down, when she happened to look up and jump in her seat on realising who was stood before her.

'Mrs Pearson, hello. Sorry, I was busy, er, well, just working.'

'I know. I could see. Can I have a word?' Phoebe asked.

'Er, yes. Please, come in and take a seat. Are you wanting to see Richie?'

'Maybe, but first I'd like a word.' Phoebe took the seat in front of Faye's desk. Faye walked back round to her side and made herself comfortable.

'How long have you kept it a secret from us about Johnny coming to visit Richie?'

Faye bowed her head. She'd been expecting this, but not from Phoebe.

'How do you know?' Faye asked.

'That's irrelevant. How long?'

'I'm not sure exactly, but a couple of years. Maybe longer.'

'And Frank?'

'You know that too?'

'How long?'

'Frank started coming about a year after Richie arrived here. Mrs Pearson, I had no choice. I had to keep it a secret. This is Frank Pearson, we're talking about.'

'I'm aware of that. I get it with Frank – I'd have done the same. But Johnny? Why did you keep that a secret?'

Faye again bowed her head.

'Let me guess. Money. I assume both were paying you. I know Frank would've done. He would not have expected that kind of favour for nothing. With Johnny, I can only assume there was financial reward for your silence. He must have made it worth your while to keep that from Frank and the family. You must have been shitting yourself every May when we came for the charade that it all appears to have been.'

Faye tried to look Phoebe in the eye. 'Yes, it was for the money. This job doesn't pay well, Mrs Pearson. The money allowed me to get nice things and, well, do up my house. I'm not going to lie, it was for the money. Plain and simple.'

Phoebe appreciated her honesty. There was no flannel or shifting of responsibility. Faye was able to own her stuff. Phoebe liked that.

'Johnny is not who he appears to be, Mrs Pearson,' Faye continued.

'What do you mean?'

'Well, Frank nearly caught him here a few weeks ago. Frank always let me know in advance if he was coming at any time other than his monthly visits. That way, I could keep them apart, but a few weeks ago, he came unannounced. Well, he did pre-warn me but I didn't get the message. Johnny was here as Frank pulled up. He managed to get away quickly. He left his cufflinks behind, though, which I had to hide. He came to see me at my house afterwards. He said that I'd let on that Frank had been visiting all along, and that all this time I've been putting him in danger. He was very threatening.'

She lowered her head and wiped a tear before continuing.

'He sexually assaulted me and told me he'd be back if I breathed a word of it. Oh shit, what am I doing! He said he wouldn't be alone next time.' She got up and put her hand to her mouth. 'He'll kill me. I know he will.'

'Faye, calm down. Sit down. Let me tell you how things are going to be. Johnny will not hurt you. You have my assurance of that. Now take me to Richie's room, but get him out of the way first. I want to be in there alone. This conversation stays in this room. No one will hear it from me. But Faye, you need to understand something.'

She wiped her tears. 'What?'

'You kept a secret from the family, that may, and I say may, have dire consequences. You owe the family.

One day we will collect that debt. Me or someone else will one day ask you for a favour to repay it. Do you understand?'

'To do what?'

'I cannot say. But all actions have consequences, Faye, yours included. I will protect you and look after you, but that is on the proviso you repay the debt. Do that and we are good. Understand?'

'I think so, but you will keep Johnny from me?'

'I promise Johnny will not hurt you. Now get Richie out of his room.'

Tracey was at the house which she believed Mr and Mrs Connell lived in. It was well looked after, but was obvious it was occupied by an old couple. There was nothing modern about its exterior. There wasn't a weed to be seen at the front. The windows were clean, as were the fascias and soffits – a clear indication of a couple brought up to take pride in their house.

'This it?' Raquel asked.

'This is the house Annabelle said.'

'You ready?'

'As I'll ever be.'

Tracey got out of the car. Raquel pulled away, turned it round and parked a few doors down on the opposite side. Tracey rang the doorbell. She could hear a woman's voice. A few moments later she was greeted by a lady in a pinny. She had neatly swept-back grey hair and wore glasses, with a complexion that defied her years. She definitely looked after herself; a lady who complemented the house.

'Hello, can I help you?' she said, as Tracey tried to recall her opening line.

'Oh hello. Is Johnny in?' she asked, knowing full well if the lady in the pinny replied *"Johnny who?"*, then Raquel was barking up the wrong tree.

'Johnny? Ooh no. He's not lived here for a few years now. Do you know him?'

'Er, yes, I used to. I studied with him a few years ago. I said I'd look him up one day. He gave me this address, you see.'

'Oh, come in, dear. I've just put the kettle on.'

'Oh no, it's fine, honestly. Please don't go to that trouble,' Tracey replied, keen to keep the conversation brief. Her knowledge of physiotherapy was limited to say the least, but they'd guessed Johnny's grandma would know no more.

'It's no trouble, dear. We don't get to see many people. No one ever comes to visit. The kettle's on.'

Tracey looked behind her at Raquel's car as she took a step inside. The hallway was as she'd expected. Clean and neat, but dated.

'Take a seat in the front room. What did you say your name was?'

'Maureen,' Tracey replied. Her mum's name was the first that came into her head.

'So, where does Johnny live now?'

'A place near Mansfield. I can never remember the

name of it, dear. It begins with B, but it's just outside of Mansfield. He's doing really well, you know. We are so proud of him. He works in the hospital up there. He has a girlfriend. A lovely girl. But we don't see him as often as we'd like.'

'I suppose he'll go and see his mum when he's down here, won't he?'

Johnny's grandma's demeanour changed. 'No, he won't see her. Certainly not.'

'Oh, sorry,' Tracey said, knowing that it would have been a touchy subject.

'No, our Lorraine is a real disappointment to us, but that's another story. Biscuit?'

'Er, yes, OK, thank you. What's your name?' Tracey asked.

'Iris. And that grumpy old man there is John. Johnny was called after his grandad,' she said, pointing to her husband, who was dozing in his chair. 'We could have a party in here, Maureen, and he'd never know,' she sighed, shaking her head.

Tracey and Iris spoke for twenty minutes about Johnny. Tracey kept her replies brief. Iris told her that Johnny was a bit of a bugger as a youngster, how Lorraine had had nothing to do with him and how he was now happy in Nottinghamshire. She told her about Lorraine's husband, Gary, and his brother, Steven. It had surprised Tracey how, after just a few minutes, Iris was happy to talk about Lorraine and the past. She never mentioned Johnny having anything to do with Steven now, though. Tracey guessed Johnny had kept his involvement with his uncle away from his grandparents so as not to risk them ever mentioning Steven in front of Alice, who they'd only ever met twice.

'He said he never knew his dad. So sad, isn't it? I suppose Lorraine never knew him either?' Tracey asked.

'Oh, she knew him all right, did our Lorraine. Never said, though. Well, never told me or her dad anyway. Johnny never needed his father. Me and his grandad brought him up. We did our best for him. We never had much, but we gave him all we could.'

'Do you not see Lorraine now then?'

'We didn't see her for years, then she turned up like a bad penny. She was only after money. Thing is she now lives three streets away, but we don't want to see her. She only bothers with us when she wants something.'

'Wow, so close. Three streets away, you say?'

'Yes, three streets down,' Iris said, pointing her finger through the living room wall. 'The one with the different coloured gate to the rest of the fence. You can't miss it. She wasn't brought up like that, you know. She changed once her Gary died. Mind you, he was a bugger too. Up to all sorts he was. I rue the day she ever met him.'

Tracey thanked Iris for the tea and hugged her as she left. Iris was a sweet old lady. She'd give you her last penny. John stirred once, had a sip of his tea, and dozed off again.

Tracey walked back to Raquel's car.

'So, what's the verdict?' Raquel asked.

Tracey pulled down the sun visor and checked her hair in the mirror as she replied. 'Yep, that's them all right. They are definitely Johnny's grandparents and Lorraine is one hundred per cent his mum. Lorraine was married to Gary Wallace, who had a brother called Steven. Poor old Iris spilled the whole lot. That fella Alice is in love with is related to Steven Wallace.'

Raquel sat back. She had a lot to tell Phoebe.

'And the best bit is, Lorraine now lives three streets away, down there,' Tracey said, indicating down the road.

'Lorraine does?'

'Yep, that's what she says. Moved in about six weeks ago. It's the one with the different coloured gate to the rest of the fence. So, what are you gonna do with that information?' Tracey asked.

'Take it back to the boss. That's all I can do. People will lose their lives over this, Tracey. This ain't gonna end well, girl. Fuck!'

'Do you need me to do anything else?'

'No. I'll take you back, but thanks for that.'

Raquel took a last look at Iris and John's neat little house before peering down the street where Lorraine now lived. She thought of going to see her, but decided she better talk to Phoebe first. Raquel was starting to piece together a jigsaw. The picture on the box was not looking good.

chapter seventy

Phoebe waited while Faye arranged for Richie to be taken to the day room. Her phone pinged. She read the text from Raquel.

Ring me when you can speak.

OK, won't be long. Are you on your way back?

Yes.

OK, see you at mine.

'You can go down now, Mrs Pearson.'

Phoebe walked the short walk down the corridor towards Richie's room. Like Gloria, this was the first time she'd seen it. And, like Gloria, she was surprised at how plush it was. She took in the surroundings and stepped into the bedroom, marvelling at the décor. She didn't know what she was looking for, but began looking behind things, opening drawers and doors, going through whatever was inside. There was nothing to suggest Johnny had been here. She stood hands on hips as she looked around again. She went back into the bedroom and surveyed the furniture. It was then she noticed the drawers underneath his bed. She opened them and saw two blankets neatly folded. She raised her head in disbelief. These were the blankets he had over his legs on the day Frank was murdered. She recognised the pattern. She got them out and opened them up to smell them. She put one down as she sniffed the other. She then swapped them over. It was on both – the distinct smell of gunshot residue. Phoebe smelled both blankets again and again. It was unmistakeable, that smell of sulphur. In Phoebe's world, that smell was all too familiar. Yes, there was gunshot residue on these blankets.

What the fuck, she thought to herself before folding them up and putting them on the bed. She then searched the rooms again – the bedroom, living room and bathroom. She opened the cupboard door in his bedroom. She knelt down and felt about the floor with her hand, not sure what she was hoping to find. She touched something cold, something hard, something stuck to the wall. She crouched down further and poked her head in. It was a safe. She tried turning the knob but was not surprised to see it was locked. She fell back and sat on her bum as she pondered. What was a safe doing in Richie's bedroom?

She went to find Faye, who was by now back in her office. 'Did you know there was a safe in Richie's bedroom, Faye?'

'What, a safe?'

'Yes, a safe, fixed to the wall inside his bedroom cupboard.'

'No. There should not be a safe there. Any valuables

are locked away for safekeeping,' Faye replied, genuinely puzzled.

'Keep that to yourself, Faye. Don't breathe a word and bring Richie back to his room, please. And can you bring me two plastic bin bags. Large ones.'

Faye rose from her chair and as quick as she could went to find him and to get the bags. Phoebe walked calmly back to his room. She waited for Faye to return with him.

'Leave us, please,' Phoebe instructed. Faye placed the bags on the sofa and did as Phoebe asked. Richie stared straight ahead.

'Richie, I know you can't respond to me, but I'm gonna put you in the picture. Mainly because if what I'm starting to think is right, I want you to know, because it will eat away at you and you won't be able to do fuck all about it.'

'I know Johnny has been coming here and I know Frank used to as well. Johnny coming is of real interest to me. The one thing I don't know is why the two blankets you had covering your legs when your father was shot have gun residue on them. That is a question I need to find the answer to.'

Phoebe saw Richie's eyes widen. She stood up and took a step back, when she saw something that sent a shiver down her spine. Richie Pearson had made a fist; well, two. He was squeezing his hands shut. She looked at his eyes. She could see the hatred and venom. She took a step further back.

'Your hands – you can make a fist.'

Richie relaxed, slowly opening his palms. She said nothing as she walked through into his bedroom and picked up the blankets. As she came back through, she placed the blankets in the black bin bags.

'I'll be opening that safe, too,' she whispered in his ear, 'but don't tell anyone, will you?'

Phoebe walked out, stopping at Faye's office door on the way.

'No one knows I was here, Faye. Understand?'

'Yes.'

Phoebe then threw Faye her phone. 'Put your number in there. I'll be in touch.'

She rang Raquel from the car. 'Make it Frank's house, Raquel. Don't go to mine.'

'Why?'

'I'll explain when I see you. Go straight to Frank's.'

Phoebe then rang Gordon Bilson, a well-known guy who could unpick any lock in the world and, more importantly, any safe.

'Gordon, it's Phoebe.'

'Phoebe, how the devil are you? How's things? Everyone OK?'

'Yes. I have a job for you. Interested?'

'Always, Phoebe. Where and when?'

Phoebe looked at her watch. It was just coming up to 6:25. It had been a long day, but she needed to know what was in that safe.

'Can you do tonight?'

'Where?'

'A village called Walesby, about a half hour outside Mansfield.'

'I'll be an hour and a half, but yeah, could do. It'll cost ya, though. Frank and Archie always paid extra for last-minute jobs.'

'I thought as much. Look, I get it. How much?'

'What is it I'm gonna be doing?'

'Need you to get into a small, domestic safe. Should be a walk in the park for you, Gordon.'

'A grand, all in. Satisfaction guaranteed.'

'Eight hundred and it's a deal,' Phoebe replied, knowing he was trying it on a little.

'Send me the details. The address etc. Will I see you there?'

'No, it'll be Del probably.'

'Brill. I ain't seen Del for ages. Could've got it for seven hundred, Phoebe, if I'd have known Del was gonna be there,' he said with a certain joviality in his voice.

'I'll make a note of that for the future. I'll text you the details, but Del will wait for you in the car park. He'll be there for 8.'

Phoebe rang Del with the instructions. She explained she needed to know what was in the safe, if anything at all. She rang Pat, Jez and Brian and told them to meet her at Frank's. She rang Faye to tell her two men would ask for her around 8 o'clock and she was to let them into Richie's room. Richie was to be out of sight. Faye explained to Phoebe that her shift finished at 8. Phoebe explained to Faye that tonight she was working overtime. Faye rang her friend to say she couldn't meet her for a drink as planned. Phoebe also explained tonight's overtime was unpaid.

As she pulled into Frank's driveway, she saw Raquel was already there, along with Jez and Pat. Only Brian was yet to arrive. Phoebe sent him a text asking him how long he was going to be. He replied saying he'd be five minutes. She walked into the house carrying the two blankets, to be met by Gloria.

'They're all in the boardroom, Phoebe, luv. I'll make you a cuppa. You go on through.'

Phoebe smiled at Gloria and mouthed thank you as she walked towards the other part of the house. She turned and shouted. 'Gloria!'

'Yes, luv.'

'I want you to be part of this meeting. Frank was your soul mate. You need to hear this lot, I think.'

Gloria thought a moment. She'd never before been privy to anything that happened in the boardroom. She'd never wanted to be, but with Frank gone and Phoebe suggesting what she had to say was something to do with Frank's death, she decided to take her up on the offer.

'OK, I'll just make a cuppa and I'll be through,' she replied.

'Brian will be here in a couple of minutes, so may as well make his too,' Phoebe called.

Brian arrived right on cue, taking his seat next to Jez. Phoebe looked serious. Brian looked at Jez and raised his eyebrows.

'OK everyone. I have some news that I want to share with you all and then Raquel has some too – news that even I've not heard yet. My news is that Johnny has been visiting Richie for a good couple of years now.'

'Johnny?' Pat interjected.

'Yep, Johnny. It came to light when Gloria found his cufflinks in Richie's room a few days ago when she went to visit him. Anyway, the short version is the manageress there was being paid by Johnny to keep it quiet. We have no idea why he was visiting him, but since he obviously felt he could risk going behind the family's back, we can assume it wasn't to drink tea. I went there today to see what I could find and, well, I found two blankets.'

Phoebe bent down and picked them up. 'And a safe drilled into the wall of the inside of his wardrobe. A safe that Del, and Gordon Bilson, are going to get open later.' She glanced at her watch. 'In about thirty minutes, actually ... but the really interesting – alarming – thing right now, before we know the contents of the safe, is that both of these blankets have gun residue on them.' She then threw one blanket to Jez and one to Pat. 'Smell 'em.'

'Unmistakable,' Jez replied.

'Same,' Pat said, as he swapped blankets with Jez and sniffed at the other one they were now holding.

'Those were the blankets Richie had over his legs the day Frank was shot,' Phoebe told them.

'What are you saying?' Pat asked.

'Just a moment, Pat. That's not all. When Richie saw I had the blankets, his eyes changed. They were full of hatred and ... he clenched his fists in anger!'

'What, he can't do that!' Pat said, shaking his head.

'Well, he did, Pat, I saw him. Richie Pearson can make a fist. He has strength in his hands. I could see him tensing them. I'm telling you all, Richie can move his hands.'

Everyone was in shock. Brian then spoke. 'There was only one person who wasn't checked for firearms that day.'

'Richie,' Jez said. 'Fuckin' Richie.' He then looked at Brian. 'He was right in front of us when Frank was shot. Johnny was coming towards the three of us, pushing Richie. Remember?'

Brian thought for a moment. 'You're right, he was. And then Johnny wheeled him off. We all thought he was just getting him away.'

'Well, before we put two and two together and make five, let's hear what Raquel has to say, and remember, I haven't heard this before. Raquel, over to you,' Phoebe instructed.

'Well, if you think that's created conspiracies,

wait until you hear this. You ain't gonna like it. Jez, remember the woman at the funeral who we both recognised?'

'Yeah, go on.'

'Well, her name is Lorraine—'

'Lorraine Wallace, that's who she fuckin' is! Fuck me, Lorraine Wallace. It's her, ain't it?'

'It is. For those of you who don't know, Lorraine Wallace was the wife of a gangster from the early nineties called Gary Wallace. Gary was shot by Daniel and his brother was maimed by Frank. His brother, Steven.'

Raquel paused as she heard the pennies drop.

'So, what's this got to do with what we are on about?' Pat asked.

'Lorraine Wallace turned up at Frank's funeral. We only knew that because Johnny was arguing with her, getting her to leave. He lied about who she was. Me and Jez both recognised her, but neither of us could remember where from. Anyway, turns out I remembered her from when she used to frequent Goldie's club down there. She was always looking for a job. And Jez, I assume you, from your dealings with the Wallaces back in the day.'

Jez nodded his head.

'So, what's it got to do with Johnny?' Pat asked, annoyed.

'Lorraine, ladies and gents, is Johnny's mum.'

'Fuck off!' Pat shouted. 'No way!'

Phoebe interjected. 'So, Raquel, let me get this straight, 'cos I'm struggling a bit here, but Johnny is related to Steven Wallace? Is that what you're saying?'

'That's what I'm saying, Phoebe, but not directly.'

'What do you mean not directly?'

Raquel looked at Jez. 'When did Daniel shoot Gary Wallace?'

Jez tilted his head back as he thought. 'It's gotta be 1990 or maybe '91, certainly no later. '91 latest, I'd say. Why?'

'Johnny was born in '96, so there's no way Gary, Lorraine's husband, could be Johnny's father. Steven is an uncle of sorts, but not really if you get my drift – only through Lorraine, Johnny's mum, being Steven's sister-in-law.'

'Johnny doesn't know his father,' Phoebe said.

'Maybe he does, Phoebe. Maybe he does,' Raquel replied.

Phoebe sat back. 'Fuck me,' she said loudly. 'So, Steven can't be trusted – neither can Johnny – they're working together – and Frank gets shot by, as it would appear, a man in a wheelchair. Do we know where this Lorraine is now?'

'Yes, sorry, we do. She lives three streets away from Johnny's grandparents,' Raquel replied.

'Me and you are paying her a visit tomorrow morning, first thing, Raquel. Pat, I want you to keep tabs on

Steven. Not too obvious – he can't suspect anything, but I want you to know where he is at all times.'

She then looked at Gloria. 'Gloria, I need your help. I need you to keep close to Johnny. I have no idea how you do that, but you out of anyone can make a nuisance of yourself around Alice and Johnny without raising suspicion. Alice cannot know of course.'

Gloria nodded in reply. 'Leave that to me, Phoebe. I won't let you down.' Phoebe smiled a reassuring smile Gloria's way.

'This stays in this room, folks,' Phoebe ordered.

Her phone rang.

'Hi Del. Just a minute, I'll put you on loudspeaker. Can you hear me OK?'

'Yeah, clear as a bell. Well, we've got the safe open and you ain't gonna believe what's in there.'

'What?'

'A gun.'

'A gun?'

'Yep, a fucking gun,' Del confirmed.

'Get it to me, Del. I need to get it checked out.'

'On my way.'

Pat said what everyone was thinking. 'That will be the gun that shot Frank.'

'And the residue will be all over those blankets,' Jez added.

chapter seventy-one

Steven Wallace was in a car park in Bingham, a small town just off the A46 in between Nottingham and Leicester. It was 9:45pm. He was waiting for a guy called Simon Kelly, from a small village just off the A1 near Scotch Corner. Simon was from the underworld of the underworld. No one knew about him. He went about his business so far under the radar, he was almost undetectable.

A car pulled in. The car looked so ordinary it stood out – probably not to anyone else, but certainly to Steven. Simon got out, straightened his jacket and walked over towards him. He looked ordinary too; the sort of person who should be tapping away on a computer in a call centre, not someone about to have a dark conversation with Steven. Simon opened the passenger door and got in. He nodded to Steven before holding out his hand. Steven nodded in return.

'Good trip?' Steven asked.

'Steady, you know. A bit of traffic but nothing major, not at this time of night anyway. So, who do you want me to take out?'

'Phoebe Pearson.'

Simon didn't flinch.

'You know who she is, don't you?'

'Of course I do. When, where?'

'I'll be in touch with those details. I just wanted to make sure you could do it.'

'What's special about Phoebe Pearson?' Simon asked.

'Nothing.'

'Then why would I not be able to do it? That's what I do. I take people out. It's my hobby. I can't call it a job – I enjoy it too much. I always say it's my hobby.'

Steven laughed. 'Ten grand, as agreed?'

'Ten grand, Steven. That's what we said. Not a penny more, but not a penny less either. Five grand up front. Five on completion, as agreed.'

Steven held out his hand. Simon shook it.

'Right, I'll be off. Long way to come for a two-minute chat, but that's hobbies for ya. And I never do business with anyone I ain't met.'

'Can't fault you, Simon. It's the only way to do things in this life. How much notice will you need?'

Simon laughed. 'I can generally be available immediately. In this game, I don't work eight hours a day, ya know. Not that many people need bumping off.'

Steven grinned. 'I'll be in touch, but it'll be soon.'

'I don't start my car without the five grand up front. Just remember that. And I only accept cash.' Simon opened the passenger door and walked the few steps to his car.

Steven was in awe of how ordinary this bloke looked.

Just then, his phone rang.

'Steven, how's tricks?'

'OK Pat, why?'

'Nothing, just wondered. Not seen you for a bit. What you up to?'

'Nowt really. Just popped out for a sly one and a bite to eat. You?'

'Nothing. Just chilling, pal. Anything happening out there that we need to know about?' Pat asked, coolly.

'Nothing, but hey, I heard Phoebe sorted old Steffan out. Well, you guys did, but I heard she was as cool as fuck.' Steven was keen to massage both Pat's ego and Phoebe's.

'She was, mate. The real deal. She sent a message all right. There'll be a few others try it on, I'm sure, but with us lot behind her, she'll be fine. They'll get the message just like Steffan did.'

'Anyway, gotta go, Pat. I'm just getting my snap.'

'What you having?'

Steven looked at the chippy across the square. 'Fish and chips, pal. Can't beat it.'

Pat laughed. 'I could just do with some of that. Anyway, enjoy 'em, me old mucker.'

Pat rang off and watched Steven drive off, past the chippy and onto the main road out of Bingham.

He called a copper on the payroll, a rookie called Sheryl, who was the granddaughter of one of Pat's old schoolfriends. From the moment she'd completed her training, she was onto Pat for a bit of extra pay. At first, he'd been a bit hesitant, mainly because of her association with his old mate, but also because coppers tend not to hunt down the extra pay and certainly not so early on in their careers. But his old friend had vouched for her, so Pat had put a bit her way. She'd not let him down yet.

'Hi, it's me. You on duty?'

'Yeah, night shift worse luck.'

'Can you talk?'

'Just a second.' Sheryl walked out into the street before continuing. 'OK, Pat, I'm good.'

'I'm gonna send you a photo of a reg plate. Need to know whose it is ASAP.'

OK. I can do that now if you send it straight through,' Sheryl replied, careful to keep her voice low.

'Just sent it. You got it?'

'Hold on.' She took her phone from her ear and looked at the image. 'Got it. I'll ring you back.'

Phoebe was in her bedroom wiping off her make-up. She was thinking of Archie and how he'd not been in touch with Sarah. She was pining for him. Even Mary, as young as she was, seemed to be missing him. It pained Phoebe to think he'd not been in touch with his wife. That wasn't him. It wasn't the way this family did things, but there was nothing she could do at this moment in time. It was down to Archie to make contact. Phoebe just wished he would do it soon. Sarah needed to know he was OK. She was lost without him and was hurting. She couldn't understand why he was treating her like this.

Oh Archie, Phoebe said to herself. She missed him too. It was a hard life they led she thought, as she squeezed some night cream into her hand and applied it to her face.

Del had brought the gun to her earlier. He'd made sure he'd worn gloves the whole time, as did Gordon, so the only prints on it, if any, would be of the person who pulled the trigger. Hazlehurst was collecting it first thing.

Her phone rang. 'No rest for the wicked,' she said, before answering it.

'Hi Pat, you OK?'

'Yeah, but you might not be when I tell you this.'

'Go on.'

'I followed Steven to a car park in Bingham tonight. Straight after I left Frank's earlier, I went to the main club, just to show my face. Anyway, as I got there, Wallace was just leaving, so after what you said, I thought I'd follow him. He met a fella in this car park in Bingham. It was no longer than a five-minute meet. When this guy left, I rang him, Steven that is, and casually chatted, asking him what he was up to.

He lied. Said he was out for a sly drink and a bit of snap. No mention of this fella, so I rang Sheryl, you know the young copper on the payroll. She checked the registration and it belongs to a guy called Simon Kelly.'

'Who's Simon Kelly?' Phoebe asked.

'Simon Kelly is arguably the best hitman in the UK, possibly Europe. I've never met him, but I think Jez has. Frank never used him. I often heard him say he never needed to. He lives up near Scotch Corner, a little village called Bowes. We need to pay him a visit, Phoebe. We need to find out what Wallace is up to and quick.'

'Agreed, Pat. Take Jez and Brian with you and pick Trainer up on the way. Steven won't notice any of them missing. I'll make Raquel aware so she can make sure she knows where he is. Why do you think he was meeting this guy?'

'Can only be one thing. He's looking to take someone out.'

'Me?'

'That's where I'd place my money, Phoebe.'

chapter seventy-two

Raquel pulled up outside the house with the different coloured gate. It was scruffy, as were most of the houses in the street, but this was the one house as a kid you never wanted to be yours.

'She must be in. All the curtains are closed. Whoever lives here hasn't surfaced yet,' she said to Phoebe.

'It's 11 o'clock. Some people amaze me. Come on,' she said, opening the passenger door.

Phoebe knocked twice and then took a step back. Raquel looked around, noticing the rubbish that lay nestled up to the kerb and the beer cans resting in the hedges that ran along the top of the fences. Phoebe knocked again, louder this time.

'OK, OK, hang on!' she heard a voice shout.

'She's up,' she said to Raquel.

They were welcomed by a woman in her nightie and dressing gown. 'Yes? What d'you want?'

Phoebe looked her up and down, noticing the cigarette stains on her hands. She still had last night's make-up on. She looked rough as fuck.

'Lorraine, can we come in?' Phoebe asked.

'No, who are you?'

Phoebe pushed her way in, knocking Lorraine into the hallway wall.

'Hey, get out!' she shouted. Raquel closed the door behind her.

'Who the fuck are you?!' Lorraine screamed.

Phoebe ignored her and walked through into the kitchen. Last night's pots were still in the sink; the remnants of a chip pan splattered the wall above the cooker; and an ashtray sat on the kitchen table, full of half-smoked fags.

'Nice place you have here,' Phoebe remarked.

The sarcasm was lost on Lorraine, who said, 'Thanks. I try to keep it nice. But who the fuck are ya?'

'No matter who we are, Lorraine. You don't need to know who we are, but we want to talk to you about your son.'

'Johnny, why what's he done? He ain't got one of you two pregnant, has he, 'cos if he has, he's fuck all to do with me. I don't see him. In fact, I've disowned him. If you want to see anyone about Johnny, then see those two old biddies round the corner. They're responsible for him, not me.'

Phoebe sighed. 'We also want to talk to you about Johnny's father.'

'His father? What the fuck?'

'Yes, his father. You must remember who his father is, surely. One-night stand, was he?'

'Look, I don't know who you two are, but you best get out of here before I call the police!' Lorraine spit-screamed. She grabbed her fags, lighting one as quickly as she could.

'You ain't calling no one, Lorraine.' Phoebe gave Raquel the nod. She grabbed Lorraine from behind, wrapping one arm around her neck as she forced her right arm up her back. Lorraine shrieked with the pain, dropping her fag. Phoebe picked it up and went to place it back in her mouth, but as Lorraine parted her lips, Phoebe stuck the end into her cheek. Lorraine hollered as her skin burned.

'Now then, who was Johnny's father?' she asked.

Tears trickled from Lorraine's eyes, but she still kept quiet. Phoebe pushed the cigarette into her neck. 'Richie! His father's name's Richie. He was one of the Pearsons from Nottingham. I don't know where he is, though, I swear.'

Phoebe dropped the cigarette and looked at Raquel, who looked as horrified as she did.

'Richie Pearson, Frank Pearson's son, is Johnny's father?'

Phoebe indicated to Raquel to let Lorraine go.

'Yes,' she cried, holding her face and neck. 'It was as you said – a one-night stand. I met him in a bar one night and, yes, Johnny is his son.'

'Does Richie know?'

'Well, if he does, he ain't heard it from me. He's in a fucking wheelchair, ain't he?'

'You turned up at Frank's funeral. Why?' Raquel asked.

'To make sure he was fuckin' dead. Him and that son of his, Daniel, ruined things for me. Killed my Gary, they did. That's why I fucked off when I did. I couldn't bear the fact I'd not only slept with Richie, Frank's son and Daniel's fucking brother, but I'd produced Johnny. Too much for me, that was. I had it all. Me and Gary had it all, but they had to kill him, didn't they?'

Phoebe sat down and passed Lorraine a fag from the packet on the table. Lorraine leant in as Phoebe lit it for her.

'Him and that brother-in-law of mine are up to something. I just know it. Don't know what, but they are up to something, so if you know any of this Pearson lot, you better warn 'em to watch out. He's a nasty fucker is Steven and Johnny's no angel. I blame myself for that. I should have been a mother to him.'

Raquel dabbed Lorraine's wounds with the cleanest cloth she could find.

'Is that it then?' she asked. 'Is that all you wanted to know?'

'That's it. Sorry about the fag burns, but we needed to get it out of you. They'll heal.'

Phoebe dropped five twenty-pound notes on the table. She then picked up the fag that she'd left burning on the worktop, which Lorraine hadn't noticed, before pulling her head back by her hair. She put the burning end of the fag millimetres from Lorraine's right eye.

'No one knows we are here, Lorraine. If we find out anyone has been furnished with that information, I'll take that eye of yours, just as Frank did to Steven all those years ago. Understood?'

Lorraine gave a careful nod, the fag end so close to her eye.

'Good. We're all friends again, then,' Phoebe said, as she stubbed the fag out.

They got back in the car and looked at each other, both knowing what the other was thinking.

Trainer was sat in the back with Brian, looking out of the window as they passed yet another sign stating how far it was to Scotch Corner.

'I never got why Scotch Corner was so well signposted. I mean, it's just a roundabout. One way goes to Cumbria and one way goes to Middlesbrough and if you carry on, you get to Geordieland. What's the big deal?'

'I always thought that at some point it was the border between England and Scotland, but I could be wrong. Fuck knows, but the main thing is, it's only four miles away now,' Pat said, pleased they were nearly there.

'How far is this Bowes place then once we get to the old border?' Trainer asked.

Pat looked at the sat nav. 'Fifteen miles or so.'

'We'll be there in about twenty minutes then?'

'Yeah, bout that.'

'Good, 'cos my arse is numb.'

'Think yaself lucky, Trainer. We had over an hour before we picked you up,' Jez shouted from the front.

Trainer closed his eyes for a power nap. Jez and Brian followed suit, and Pat kept his eye on the road ahead.

They approached Bowes eighteen minutes later. The sat nav told Pat he was just under a mile away from the address. They didn't know what they were going into, but had to assume Simon would be alone. Pat just hoped he was in. The last thing he wanted was a waiting game for him to return. As they came to a row of four cottages, he saw another detached cottage a hundred yards up ahead and noticed the same car he'd seen at Bingham.

'That's it, up there, lads. Brian, you and Trainer get out here and walk the rest of the way. I don't want him seeing four burly-looking blokes get out. It could spook him. He's bound to have shooters in there. I'll park a quarter of a mile up the road, and me and Jez'll walk back. You two wait here until I'm at the front door.'

'Why you going a quarter of a mile up the road?' Trainer asked.

'So this motor ain't seen outside his house, that's why. You lot wait here just in case he's spotted me and Jez. You can see things from a different angle down here.'

'Four burly-looking blokes? Where?' Brian quipped. 'I can only see two here.'

'Get fucked,' Jez said, as Trainer and Brian got out. Brian and Jez laughed.

They waited until they saw Pat and Jez come into view and watched as Pat walked towards the front door and rang the bell. He saw a figure through the frosted glass coming towards him. Pat readied himself. As the door opened, he recognised the man standing in front of him. Pat swung and caught him square on the nose. Simon reeled back. Pat followed straight up with another punch that knocked Simon to the floor. He was now inside the house. He put his size tens hard onto his face, squashing it sideways into the tiled floor. Simon lay on his back, with his hands facing upwards at the side of his head, in surrender. Jez and Brian were now in the hallway. Trainer was stuck in the doorway. He was looking for signs of any neighbours, but given the nearest one was a hundred yards away, he had no need to worry.

'Simon Kelly, I presume?' Pat said.

Simon muffled a reply. 'Yes. Now get off my face.'

Pat removed his boot and took a step back to allow Simon to stand. Jez had a gun pointing towards him.

'Jez, you should've rung,' he said, wiping his nose. He looked at the blood on his hand and shook his head. 'I take it you aren't lost and just wanted a cuppa then?'

'Sit down Simon. We need to talk.'

'I think I know what this is about.'

'Oh yeah, what's that then?'

'Well, given who your new employer is and given my meeting last night, I don't think we need to insult each other with mind games, do we?'

'What did he want?' Pat asked.

'Who?'

'Don't fuck me about, Simon. Steven – what did he want?'

'I can't tell you that, mate. I'm a stickler for that, me. What I discuss with a client remains confidential.'

Pat whacked him with his gun. Simon spat out a tooth.

'Jez, you know me. Tell him I ain't gonna grass. It's not what I do.'

'And me telling Pat here what to do ain't what I do, Simon. Just tell us what it was about. Who does he want taking out?'

Simon stood square on. 'Look, fellas, I ain't gonna tell ya. You can do to me whatever you like, but I ain't telling ya. But let me tell you one thing, Pat, or whatever your name is, you will spend the rest of your life watching over your shoulder, 'cos I'll take you out. No one comes into my house and whacks me over the head with a gun, you fuck!'

Pat shot Simon straight through the forehead. He dropped to the floor like a stone.

'Sorry, lads, but I ain't takin' a threat like that from no one,' Pat said, stepping forward and allowing Trainer in.

'I think we'd have all done the same, Pat. We need to move this, though,' Jez said, as he kicked Simon's leg.

'Best bet for me, gents, is to take the road to Reeth. I know this area well. It's over the hills, and the middle of nowhere. We can dump it there. It'll not be found for days, maybe weeks.'

Pat walked to get the car. They swiftly cleaned the place, before putting Simon Kelly in the boot. Trainer then showed Pat the way over the remote road to Reeth. He was right. It *was* the arse end of nowhere. They dumped the body in a stream, away from the road, careful that no one saw.

Pat then rang Phoebe, apologising for reacting like he did. Phoebe didn't seem bothered. She knew Steven Wallace was a dead man. Phoebe told Pat to drop Trainer off and get back to Frank's house as quickly as possible with Jez and Brian. She had some news of her own to spill.

Raquel and Phoebe were approaching the M1 at junction 24. Phoebe needed a coffee. They were headed towards the services near to East Midlands Airport. She had just spoken to Pat. Another body was all she needed.

'I tell you something. I've certainly jumped in at the deep end here,' she laughed. Laugh was all she could do. 'We'll have more bodies piled up than old Ted at this rate.'

'He had to do it, though. If Simon wasn't going to

spill the beans, Pat had to take him out. He must have known that. But fair play to him sticking to his principles. We could have done with him on the firm,' Raquel replied.

'Was thinking that myself. We have a good team, though. I'm happy with our lot, except Wallace of course. I never really trusted him. Mind you, I did promote him, didn't I, so that last sentence must be a load of rubbish.' Phoebe laughed at herself.

Raquel pulled into the services, parking as close to the entrance as she could, to get their two coffees.

'Who did it then?' Raquel asked.

'Well, it can only be Johnny or Richie. I can't believe I'm saying this, but after what I saw with Richie's hands and the fact Johnny's his son, maybe it was Richie. He could pull a trigger, I'm sure of it. And he's had plenty of practice down the years. I tell you what, Raquel, if Richie killed Frank right under our noses with the help of Johnny and Steven, then as much as they will all pay, I've got to take my hat off to them. I mean, what a bloody plan. I can't believe Johnny fooled us all like he did. I liked him, treated him like a son and all the time, he was playing us. Alice will be distraught. She loves him more than life itself. I'm not looking forward to that conversation. Unless Hazlehurst tells us otherwise, I reckon Steven got Johnny involved after realising who he was, saw it as a way to bring down Frank probably. Johnny then painstakingly used his physio to get Richie's hands working. I mean how the bloody hell can that be after what the doctors said?' She took a sip of her coffee. 'And then, they decide to do it at Frank and Gloria's party. That's why Steven was so keen to take the lead. It must have been. He must've seen that as a way to take over – you know, with Frank gone. What do you think?'

'I think from what we know so far, that's about right.'

'As soon as we know for sure that the gun Del found was the weapon, then we act swiftly. There may not be any prints, but the fact it was in a safe in Richie's room has to be enough. Well, it will be. That's what I'm waiting for from Hazlehurst.'

They drank their coffee, continuing to talk about ifs, buts and maybes, but Phoebe was sure she knew roughly what happened. She only needed to receive one more call.

They made their way to Frank's house. As they approached the Badger Box at Annesley, Phoebe rang Hazlehurst.

'Any news?

'Phoebe, give me a chance for fuck's sake. This ain't a two-minute job, you know, and I have to get this done under the counter if you know what I mean. You did tell me you didn't want the fact you'd found the gun made public, remember? I'm on it. I'll be back to you as quick as I can.'

'I need to know and I need to know quickly,' Phoebe said, hanging up.

'It's just gonna confirm what we think. It can't be anything else. I can't tell Alice until we know for sure.'

There were three cars parked up in Frank's drive: Gloria's, Johnny's and Alice's.

'I was hoping he wasn't going to be here. Just smile and wave, Raquel. We can't give him any indication.'

'Don't worry about me. I've had my share of smiling and waving at fellas whilst I've been secretly fucking them over. I'm a dab hand at this,' she winked.

Gloria was in the hallway. 'He's here.'

Phoebe put her hands on her shoulders. 'Don't worry, just keep calm. We have it under control, but, for now, act as if everything's normal.'

Gloria nodded. 'I'll put the kettle on,' she said.

'There you go, see. Just act normal.'

Phoebe walked through into the living room. Alice was sat with her legs up on the sofa. Johnny was flicking through the TV.

'Hi you two. You both OK?'

'Yeah. I think Gloria's struggling a bit, though. She can't settle. Just keeps walking around,' Alice replied.

'She's had a lot to deal with, sweetheart. It's probably hitting her hard now. We all deal with grief in different ways, remember. Just give her space and a bit of time. She'll be OK. You working today, Johnny?'

Johnny shot up like a coiled spring.

'Yep. In fact, I gotta go now really. I'm on till 8 tonight.' He stood tall, stretched his arms above his head and yawned. 'I bloody hate this shift.' He leant into Alice and gave her a kiss. 'I'll see you at mine around 8:30. If I'm gonna be late, I'll ring or text, but make sure my tea's ready.'

'Have a good day,' Alice replied, with a real smacker of a kiss. 'And yes, sir, I'll have something nice waiting for you.'

Raquel had texted Jez to see how long they were going to be. He said about an hour. Raquel showed the text to Phoebe, who nodded. Gloria brought the teas through, passing Johnny in the doorway. 'See ya, Gloria,' he said, kissing her cheek. She'd normally kiss him back, but didn't. Johnny noticed, but said nothing. He put it down to what Phoebe had just said.

For the next forty-five minutes, the three of them mainly talked about Frank and the things he used to do. They laughed, they cried and they sat in silence, reflecting on whatever they'd just discussed.

Phoebe's phone rang. It was Hazlehurst.

'Can you talk?'

'Just a mo,' Phoebe replied. She wandered out through the house into the boardroom. She needed privacy. 'OK. I'm OK now.'

'The gun is definitely the gun that killed Frank. One hundred per cent.' He waited for a response. 'Phoebe, did you hear me?'

'Yes, sorry. You're sure?'

'As I said, one hundred per cent. But that's not all.'

'Go on.'

'There are two sets of prints on the gun and you ain't gonna believe this...' Phoebe knew what was coming, but she still readied herself. 'Just spit it out.'

'One set belongs to Richie. The other set belongs to a "Johnny Wallace". You know him?'

'Yes, I do.'

'It's not Alice's fella, is it? I thought his surname began with a C?'

'It does. Connell, like his grandparents. Well, we thought it was Connell, but he must've legally taken his mum's surname at birth if you had him as Johnny Wallace. How do you know they're his prints?'

'He's on file from around eight years ago. He got pinched a couple of times for shoplifting and once for assault when he was sixteen. He could have done time by the looks of it, but got off with community service and a fine. The most interesting thing, though, Phoebe – and this is something I wasn't looking forward to telling you – but the prints on the trigger belong to Richie. His were the only prints we found on that part of the gun. Richie must've pulled the trigger. But how the fuck can someone like him, in a fuckin' wheelchair, paralysed from the neck down, pull the trigger?'

'You've done your bit. Leave all that with me. Return the gun to Frank's house straight away and your large envelope will be here for you, with a nice bonus on top. This ends here. From now on, you leave it all to us. Is that clear?'

Hazlehurst cleared his throat. 'I knew you'd say that. Don't worry, I've been in this game long enough to make sure there's no trail back to me. As far as we're concerned, Frank's death will remain a mystery. Whatever you do from here, just make sure my name is kept out of it all. One last thing, though. With a surname like that, don't tell me he's related to Steven?'

'As I said, you've done your bit. Now leave this to us. That's what we pay you for – and pay you well for. So, no more questions.'

'Fair enough, I've got the gist. I'll be at Frank's in half an hour or so with this piece.'

'Just before you go … what about the residue on the blankets?'

'Bloody hell, sorry, yes – the residue is from that gun. No doubt.'

Phoebe sat down, taking in what she had just been told. Richie had murdered his father, and Johnny and Steven had helped him do it, just as she thought. She looked to the ceiling. 'I didn't think I was signing up for this, Frank,' she whispered. 'But I'll get them all. I won't let you down.'

Hazlehust arrived at Frank's just before Pat and the rest returned from Bowes. Phoebe had briefed Raquel about the gun, but not yet broken the news to Gloria. She put on some gloves as she studied Frank's murder weapon.

'With all the talking, the music and the general atmosphere, it was no wonder no one heard anything with this on the end,' she remarked, making reference to the silencer.

'Glad you mentioned that. There is DNA on the end of that bit. Someone kissed it.'

'Who?'

'Johnny. It's his DNA.'

Phoebe shook her head in despair.

Hazlehurst continued. 'I tell you something, Phoebe. I was flabbergasted to find Richie's prints on the trigger. I did not expect that at all.'

'Surprising what you can achieve when you are fuelled by hatred,' she replied.

Pat walked through the door, flanked by Jez and Brian. They had been surprised to see Hazlehurst's car in the driveway.

'Do we know for sure then about the gun?' he asked.

Phoebe looked at Hazlehurst, indicating it was time for him to leave.

'Right, well, I'll be off,' he said. He stood a moment or two unsure what to say. Phoebe twigged and walked to the safe.

'Here you go. There's some extra in there, but it's a one-off. You did good turning this round so quickly.'

'Cheers. I'll leave you all to it, but for fuck's sake, whatever you do, make it clean. Don't leave any trail.'

'I can assure you, Hazlehurst, there will be no

comeback. Not on you or anyone else. Nothing's changed on that score.'

Hazlehurst peered into the large brown envelope on his way out. He loved it when he got his hands on some cash – untraceable cash that he could have a fuckin' good time on.

'Sit down. You all need to listen. Me and Raquel have some news that is going to change things round here forever.' Phoebe looked at Raquel. 'Just pop out there and see if Alice is with Gloria, please.'

Thirty seconds or so later, Raquel came back through. 'Alice is having a shower. Gloria is, well, you'll all know what Gloria is doing.'

'Making tea?' Jez guessed. They all laughed.

'Yep, good as gold, making tea.'

'Give her a shout, will ya. I want to brief you all before Alice comes back down.'

Gloria took her seat next to Raquel. She looked worried. Everyone else looked intrigued.

'We went to see Lorraine today, that lady you saw at the funeral, Jez. The father of her son, Johnny, is Richie.'

'Richie?' Brian asked in amazement.

'Yes, Richie. One-night stand apparently. That's why she left Johnny when she did. She couldn't cope with knowing she'd had a son with a man whose father and brother had killed her husband. But, yes, Richie is Johnny's dad. We can only assume that Steven got to know and the two of them have been hatching a plot to kill Frank ever since.'

'So, it must've been Johnny who shot Frank? It must've been. He was the one coming towards us when it happened,' Jez replied.

'Wrong, Jez. This...' she said, picking up the gun, 'is definitely the gun that killed Frank. And there are two sets of prints on it.' Phoebe paused. 'One is Johnny's – they know that because he was known to the police as a teenager –and the other set belongs to Richie. Remember, I've seen him clench his fists. But, and this is the big one, the only set of prints on the *trigger* were Richie's. Richie killed his father. He murdered him, with the help of Johnny and, we assume, Steven.'

Gloria burst into tears. 'I can't believe what I'm hearing. Frank was a good man. He didn't deserve that. He was sorry. He really was. I know it.' Raquel comforted her. Gloria rested her head in Raquel's chest.

'It's the truth, Gloria, and now we have to sort it,' Phoebe said with authority and determination.

Alice walked in, her hair still damp. 'Shall I make the tea for everyone, or has Gloria beat me to it?' she said in a slightly sarcastic but jovial manner.

'Sit down, Alice. I need to talk to you,' Phoebe instructed, knowing what her daughter was about to hear would bring her world crashing down.

Alice sat dumbstruck. She refused to believe what

she was hearing. Her mum had told her everything, from the cufflinks to the secret visits, right through to Johnny's fingerprints being on the gun.

'This can't be true, Mum. It can't be. Johnny wouldn't do that. You must have it wrong. There must be a mistake. I love him!'

Gloria moved over, put her arm around Alice and pulled her close. 'This has come like a bolt out of the blue to us all, sweetheart. I didn't want to believe it myself, but your mum would not tell you unless she was one hundred per cent sure.'

Alice sobbed. 'But I love him. I love him, Mum!'

Phoebe knelt down in front of her. 'I know you do, but Alice, darling, you must understand I have to deal with this. I have to deal with it all. Johnny included.'

Jez, Pat and Brian felt awkward. They wanted to go. They didn't want to see Alice like this. 'Shall we leave you to it?' Jez asked.

'No. We need to discuss what we're going to do. Gloria, will you take Alice through, please.'

Alice walked out through the house, wiping her tears. Gloria kept her arm around her. She looked to the heavens for some guidance. *Help us, Frank*, she begged. *Get us through this.* Alice went up to her room. She flung herself on the bed and sobbed into her pillow. 'You bastard!' she screamed at the photograph of Johnny on her bedside table, before picking it up, spitting at his image and then throwing it at the wall. Alice knew she would never see Johnny again. There was no way her mum would allow her to go to his house tonight, as planned. She knew Phoebe would have to act quickly. She knew her mum had the length of Johnny's shift at the hospital to put whatever plan she devised in place. Alice went into her en suite and stared at herself in the mirror. She dried her tears, knowing what she had to do. Alice put on her jacket, walked downstairs, put on her shoes and slipped out of the door, ringing Johnny from her car.

Phoebe finished talking to Jez, Pat, Brian and Raquel, before making a phone call.

'Phoebe. How are you? Didn't expect to receive a call from you.'

'You up for a job at the lock-up in Arnold?'

chapter seventy-three

Steven Wallace was on his way back from seeing a dealer in Derby. The guy he'd just had a meeting with was one of their main faces, who looked after Derby city centre. He made sure they ran all of the doors in the city and that they retained control of the supply and who was allowed to deal in the city's pubs and clubs. Steven was putting time and effort into getting the main players on the second rung of the Pearson empire on side. He reckoned having these well-respected fellas in his pocket would stand him in good stead for his plan to take over once Phoebe was out of the equation. He rang Simon Kelly for a second time, but again it went straight to voicemail.

'Fuckin' useless!' Steven shouted into the phone.

A minute or two later, as he was driving along the A52 towards Nottingham, his phone rang. He instantly thought it was Simon ringing him back, but no such luck.

'Hiya,' he said.

'Where are ya?' Raquel asked.

'Just on the A52 on my way back from Derby. Been chatting with Chris.'

'Ah, brill. Come straight to the lock-up in Arnold. We've had some beef with Steffan again. He needs sorting once and for all. Phoebe's ordered it.'

'Fuckin' hell, must be serious if he's being taken to Arnold. OK. See ya there. Won't be long.'

Steven thought about the lock-up. That was where Frank had traditionally taken anyone who needed sorting out. It always brought back memories of his own experience there, on the receiving end. It was where Gary was shot by Daniel and where he'd lost his eye and fingers. He hated that place, but he'd been in it many times since, dishing out punishment. These days, it sort of held a feeling of nostalgia to people in the firm. It had always been referred to as "Frank's Place". He couldn't help but wonder what Steffan had done. He failed to recognise that Raquel never actually said what.

'He's just rung this,' Jez said, showing Raquel Simon's phone. 'Twice today, that is. Let's listen to the message.'

Pat, Del and Pēteris were waiting a hundred yards or so from Johnny's house. They were expecting him home very soon.

'I still can't believe all this, ya know,' Del said, having been briefed by Pat on the way there. 'I mean, fuckin' Johnny. Nice as they come. He should've been an actor, mate, 'cos he had me fooled. Had us all fooled by the sounds of it.'

'He did, but he'll fuckin' regret it in a bit. He has no idea what's gonna happen to him,' Pat replied, thinking of what was to come.

'Well, as they say, if you can't stand the heat and all that...' Del said, mimicking the drums.

'Ey up, he's here. That's his motor.' Pat started the engine and waited to see Johnny lock his car. He then drove towards Johnny's house and watched him enter through the front door.

Johnny walked in, wondering what time Alice would turn up. She'd rung earlier to say she'd be late, and had asked him to make supper. He'd taken the easy route and got a takeaway on the way home. He switched on the light, walked through into the kitchen and turned on the oven to keep the chicken tikka warm.

'Forgot your key?' he shouted, hearing the doorbell ring.

As he opened the door, Pat burst in, sending him flying into the stairs. He fell, as he stumbled on the bottom step. Pat grabbed him and pushed him through the doorway into the lounge. 'What the fuck, Pat?!' Johnny shouted.

Pat decked him, knocking him onto the settee. He grabbed him, pulled him up and held him as Del punched him twice. He then threw him towards

Pēteris, who grabbed hold of him, spun him round and held him tight around his throat from behind.

Pat straightened his jacket before saying very calmly. 'You, boy, are in deep shit. You, my friend, will never see this house again, so say your goodbyes.'

Before Johnny could answer, Pat nodded to Pēteris, who stepped aside to make way for Pat to knock him clean out.

'Me and you will get him in the car, Del. Pēteris, clean up, make sure there's no trace of us being here and then drive his car to the lock-up.'

Pat checked Johnny for his keys, finding them in his front pocket.

'There's a house key on here, so lock up. But bring that takeaway with you. I'll have that later. I love cold curry. And switch that oven off. We don't want any accidents here tonight.'

Twenty minutes later they arrived at the lock-up. Phoebe, Jez, Brian and Raquel were already there. Johnny was in the boot, but had by now come round. The reality of the situation was clear to him. It had all happened so quickly back at the house. Pat opened the boot. He and Del marched Johnny into the lock-up. Johnny put on a show of bravado, trying to wrestle himself free of the grip he was under. Pat had seen it all before.

Johnny was placed on a chair in the middle of the room. His face was bloodied, his right eye was swollen, but he could clearly see Phoebe walking towards him.

'You know, Johnny – I have to take my hat off to you. It took some balls some real balls to play us like you did all that time. And to get Richie to be able to move his hands is, well, a miracle really. You'd have gone far, you know. They all said he'd never move any part of his body again. That's a real talent you have. Under different circumstances I'd offer you a seat on the board, but, you know, doing what you did cannot go unpunished. Just so you know, you will die tonight. I think it's only right to put my cards on the table, face up, but we're just waiting for someone else to arrive. A family member, I think he is. He'll be here soon.'

'Look, Phoebe. It wasn't me. I swear. It was Steven all along. He made me do it. I'm no killer. I'm no gangster. I'm just a physio. You know me, Phoebe. Come on, you know I am not capable of this!'

'Of what? No one said anything about anyone killing anyone, but now you've mentioned it, yes, I do think you're a killer. Richie pulled the trigger, we know that. Maybe you helped him – who knows? Maybe you had your finger around Richie's to make sure he had the strength to do it. We do not know, Johnny, but it matters not. You may as well have pulled the trigger yourself and shot Frank. And for that, you will die a painful death tonight.'

Johnny's head flung back as the bullet hit him smack in the face. He was dead before his head rocked back forwards, resting on the chest of his limp body. Everyone looked behind them, startled. Jez and Pat had drawn their guns simultaneously, both aiming them at the figure who stood motionless with their gun still pointing towards Johnny. Alice was transfixed. Tears streamed down her face as she lowered her hand, dropping the gun on the floor.

'I hope you rot in hell, you fuckin' bastard!' she wailed, as she walked towards Johnny and spat on his lifeless body.

Phoebe took her daughter in her arms and held her tight. 'I had to do it, Mum. I wanted to be the one who killed him.'

'It's OK, sweetheart. It's OK.'

'I suppose I've crossed the line now, have I?' she asked.

No one said anything. Del picked up the gun and placed it on the bench, which doubled as some sort of kitchen worktop.

Phoebe looked at Pat as they heard a car door slam. 'Wallace,' she said.

Brian stood at the door entrance. 'Steven! About time, pal. Where ya been?' he asked, sounding as normal as ever.

Steven was about to answer, when Brian grabbed him and pulled him inside. He threw him by the scruff of his jacket into the room. Pat grabbed him, as did Del. They held him tight as Jez pummelled him.

'You're getting old, Jez. I bet Phoebe could hit harder.'

Jez thumped him again, catching him sweet on the jaw.

'That's better, old man. Much better! I see my nephew has had a good evening,' he said, pissing everyone off with his brave-man act, Phoebe included.

She looked at her phone. *Two minutes away.*

'You may come across as not being bothered, Steven, but we both know deep down your arse will be twitching. Fair play to you, though. You'll be remembered as taking it all like a man. Sit him down, please, gentlemen.'

Phoebe stood a foot or so away from him. 'You thought you'd gotten away with it, didn't you? To be fair, had it not been for these, you probably would have done.'

Phoebe showed him Johnny's cufflinks. 'Oh and a certain lady called Lorraine too. She was most helpful when we went to see her.'

Steven smiled. 'I'd do it all again, you fuckin' slag. You can do whatever you want to me, but I'll die a happy man knowing I took out the man who killed my brother.'

'But you didn't, did you? Daniel killed your fucking brother and you never got to avenge that, did you? You had the opportunity for years. For twenty years, you worked for the very man who shot your brother and did fuck all about it. You took orders off him, you fetched and carried for him. You made money for the man who killed your brother and you did fuck all. So, don't sit there and tell me you took out the man who shot Gary Wallace. You were not man enough to take my Daniel out. Instead, you licked his arse for years and took out a man nearing his seventieth birthday, using a guy in a wheelchair to do it for you. You are fuck all, Steven Wallace. Never were. So, you will die a painful death, knowing you were never the man you always wanted to be. You were never the man who could avenge his brother's death.'

Steven stared at Phoebe, not saying a word. She had cut through him with ease, and had hurt him more than any tool they would use on him tonight.

'A car's just pulled up, Phoebe,' Del said, as he popped his head outside the door.

'Ah, an old friend, Steven. Someone you will recognise, I'm sure.' Phoebe watched the door.

'Evening, gentlemen,' Bonnie said, nodding to Jez. 'And ladies, of course.'

Steven's heart sank. A pang of fear came over him. He was instantly transported back to 1990, the last time he was sat in this room on a chair. The day he was last tortured by Bonnie, the best in the business.

'Steven! How nice to see you again. You know it feels just like yesterday when I took that eye from you. I'll be sure to take the other one tonight. How I've missed this.'

'Just the one then, is it?' he said, making reference to Johnny.

'Yes, just the one, Bonnie.'

'It's good to be back, Phoebe, my dear. I'm gonna

enjoy this. Shall I still chop that fella up too?' he asked, pointing to Johnny.

'Yes, please, Bonnie – if that's not too much trouble.'

Bonnie tortured Steven Wallace all night. He savoured every moment. Bonnie didn't always chop up dead bodies. Sometimes he preferred ones that were still alive.

Within 24 hours, Steven Wallace was taken to a farm and fed to the pigs bit by bit. Johnny's body was dumped along the A617 towards Newark. His death was never solved. It was assumed he was targeted by association with the Pearsons, a theory that was supported by the family. His car was torched; the gun that killed him never traced. The coppers investigating filed it away unsolved.

The day after Steven and Johnny were murdered, Phoebe visited Faye Johnson at her home. Faye had not been expecting her, so was shocked to see her at the door.

'Mrs Pearson. Er, hello,' she said, feeling fearful all of a sudden.

'Can I come in?'

'Er, yes, please do. Would you like a coffee or something?'

'No, it's OK. This won't take long. It's payment time, Faye.'

'Payment time?'

'Yes. As I explained when we had our little chat, you are in debt to me and the family. And today is the day I call in that debt. The day you pay me back.'

Faye's legs buckled. 'What do I have to do?'

'You have to kill Richie.'

'What?! I can't kill anyone. No way. I'll go to the police.'

'No you won't. If you do, I'll kill you. Well, maybe not me, but I'll order it.' Phoebe fixed her eyes firmly on her. Faye didn't know where to look.

'It's simple, Faye. You kill him. How you do it is up to you, but that is how you repay the debt to us. You made a decision to keep things from us. That has consequences. The consequence is you now have to do this. Otherwise, you will die a painful death. The police will not be able to protect you from us.'

'But I don't know how to kill anyone. I can't. Ask me anything else! Please! Anything but this!'

'You have 72 hours.'

Phoebe let herself out.

Faye didn't sleep a wink that night. She couldn't believe the situation she found herself in. She was up at 5:30 the next morning, feeling as though she'd been run over by a bus – which seemed an attractive proposition given the ultimatum she'd been given.

She went to work as usual that day, had her morning meeting with her staff, did her rounds and then drove the specially adapted vehicle round to the back of the home. It was a people carrier for staff to take some of the service users out in on occasion. The staff looked forward to it, as did the residents. Richie, however, hated it. He detested people, even those who didn't know him, seeing him like he was. Faye drove him into Mansfield town centre. She walked for nearly three hours around the streets, with no real idea where she was going. She wanted to have some space to think about how she was going to deal with the mess she was in. She stopped at the roadside, looked left, then right, remembering her thought that morning. She then stepped out, still pushing Richie, straight into the path of an HGV lorry. It wasn't a bus, but it may as well have been. Faye Johnson died instantly, regretting the day she ever met Johnny Connell. Richie Pearson died thinking of nothing at all.

chapter seventy-four

Two months later – December 2019

Archie was sat in a bar on Spain's Costa del Sol. He'd come here a few weeks after arriving in Portugal. Portugal wasn't for him. He made contact with a couple of associates who'd been there escaping the attentions of the British police for the best part of the year. He was listening to the news about some virus causing concern across the globe.

He was waiting for someone to arrive. That someone didn't know he was there. He ordered another beer, making sure he drank it slow. He was unsure how long he'd have to wait. He'd grown both a beard and his hair. He looked quite different to how he did when he left Stansted, especially with his sunglasses on.

He picked up his beer, on hearing the news he'd been waiting for. Two men behind him, two tables away, had arrived ten minutes after Archie. He'd been keen to keep as inconspicuous as possible.

'Here he is, Julian – my old pal Benny. Benny, this is Julian. Julian, this is my old mate Benny Lancashire.'

Archie listened intently as this Julian fella, his mate and Benny talked about life in the sun. Benny mentioned contacts he'd made since arriving on the Spanish shores and how he could orchestrate things his end to make money. He also told Julian and the other fella about the very nice hotel he was staying in, which Archie knew well. He finished his beer, left a twenty-euro note on the table, picked up his book and left.

He walked five hundred yards, put on his sun hat and walked into a hotel bar. He ordered a glass of water. He read his book and waited. He ordered another water, read some more and waited. He then saw Benny waltz in and say something sexual to the waitress, before waiting for the lift. Archie watched as the lift indicated the twelfth floor. He put down his book, walked to the stairs, before running up them as fast as he could. Breathless, Archie watched Benny vacate the lift and walk to his room. He smiled to himself. Benny hadn't even noticed he was there, even though he'd been sat a couple of tables away just earlier.

He waited a few minutes while he regained his composure and got his breath back. He adjusted his sunglasses and walked towards Benny's room, knocking twice. Benny opened the door.

'Yeah,' he said, looking Archie up and down.

Archie took off his sunglasses, put them in his shorts pocket and barged his way in. Benny swung a punch, which caught Archie on the temple. He took a step back to steady himself. Benny flung towards him, but Archie side-stepped him, sending Benny hurtling towards the wall. Archie grabbed him, turned him round and kneed him in the bollocks. Benny doubled over. Archie punched him twice hard on the head. Benny was coughing. Archie continued to punch him. Benny fell to his knees, holding his left hand out, as his right held his crown jewels. 'Who the fuck are ya?!' he spluttered.

Archie kicked Benny in the head with his right trainer. Benny sprawled forward as he struggled to keep himself on his knees.

'Archie Pearson, that's who, you bastard. Remember me, do you?' he said, sitting on top of Benny, raining blows to his head.

Archie stood up and looked over to the balcony. He walked over and using the bottom of his T-shirt, opened the patio doors. He looked outside at the hotel grounds below. A few people were round the pool further down the steps towards more gardens. He turned round, pulled Benny up and threw him over his shoulders. With Benny's weight on him, he walked slowly out of the doors and threw Benny over the balcony wall.

Archie heard the thud. He walked calmly out of the room, collecting his hat and sunglasses, before picking up a brisk pace down the stairs. Archie heard screams and commotion as he walked into the main foyer. Hotel staff rushed past him towards the pool area. People turned 360 degrees on the spot, wondering what the hell had happened.

Archie walked back to where he was sitting, picked up his book he'd purposely left behind and slowly walked out of the hotel door, making sure he had his hat and sunglasses on all the time. He turned right, took a stroll and then stopped at a café. As he waited for his coffee, he made two phone calls.

'I won't be long, luv. Just having a coffee. I'll be back within the hour.' He could hear Mary laughing in the background.

He then made the second call. 'Hi, it's me. It's done.'

Phoebe sat back in her chair in the boardroom. The last loose end was tied up. She smiled at Alice. 'Here's to the new dawn, sweetheart. Or, as Jez said, the new blood.'

Acknowledgements

Writing this sequel was just as exciting as writing the first; in fact, maybe even more so because the story had already developed. I just needed to keep the action going. As always, I needed people who would give me honest feedback before I handed it over to the professionals to *"tighten it up and make it look like a book"*.

Therefore, I would like to thank the following people for helping me, once again, to get this novel to print and, most importantly, into your hands.

My wife, Debbie, who inspires me and has been my rock, best friend and soulmate over the past thirty years. Without her, I would not be the man I am today. Debbie helped me put the characters and plot together for both *New Blood* and its predecessor, *The Wrong Man*. Every time I'd written a few chapters, I would read them to her and await her candid and, at times, critical comments. I love you, Debbie, more than you'll ever know. Thank you for always being at my side.

Our very good friend Heather Brown, who has been a constant reader for me and who always amazes me with how quickly she gets back to me. Thank you, Heather.

Bob Hart, who I have known for nearly 25 years and who is unique. Your pointers were superb, Bob: very descriptive and very constructive. You will be over the moon to see the page numbers in this, the finished product! Thank you, Bob.

Our next-door neighbours, Nick and Mandy, who are so encouraging and supportive. They are great people to know and do a great G&T and a glass of fizz.

Andy Shaw, who has also read all three of my novels to date and who, like the others, always gives me frank feedback. Thank you, Andy.

And, finally, the two professionals who have taken my manuscript and turned it into this fantastic product. Yasmin Yarwood, from Meticulous Proofreading, has improved the wording, taken out those filler words I tend to use and who, along with me, has thought of alternative phrases to enhance the reading experience. She also makes sure those little commas are all in the correct place.

I had already worked with Alexa Whitten, from The Book Refinery, on *The Wrong Man* and *A Bitter Pill* to convert them both into Kindle formats. Alexa not only put me in touch with Yasmin for *New Blood* but managed the process from start to finish once I'd sent her the manuscript. She formatted the content, designed the cover and, ultimately, she made it look like a polished and finished novel. To both of you, thank you.

Without Alexa and Yasmin, *New Blood* would not be the novel you are holding in your hands right now, or reading on your Kindle. It really is amazing the work that goes into the making of a novel.

About the Author

For many years, Michael Elliott worked in 9 to 5 jobs, leaving the house early in the morning and not getting home until ten or eleven hours later. He'd seen, from a very young age, his father working hard in a factory to provide for his family. Like many people, Michael just thought that was life, though his wife would often tell him that it didn't have to be that way.

In 2019, Michael decided to do something different with his life and left a well-paid position in a company that he had shares in to do what he wanted to do. Initially, he had planned to go into buying and selling property or to become a landlord, but, of course, the pandemic hit and lockdown came, so he put the property dream on hold.

He then decided to become a funeral celebrant, providing services for non-religious funerals. He does this on a part-time basis and meets some wonderfully interesting people. He finds it very rewarding, and the families are so appreciative of what he does to help them during such an emotional time.

But Michael still had one other dream: to write a novel. He had always been a fan of crime fiction and psychological thrillers.

His debut novel was the prequel to New Blood: The Wrong Man. After publishing The Wrong Man, he set about publishing his second novel, A Bitter Pill. His wife, Debbie, has always believed in him and knew if he put his mind to it, he could do it.

Michael wishes he'd done it years ago. He remembers sitting in his garden, with the sun shining, listening to the trickle of the water feature, writing away and thinking, this is how life should be. This isn't work! So, between delivering funeral services and writing, he feels very fulfilled and content.

Michael and Debbie have been married for twenty-seven years. They have two daughters, Heather and Georgina, and three grandchildren. Michael is fifty-one years old and lives in Mansfield, in the heart of Nottinghamshire, a short drive from Sherwood Forest. He hopes that he can make a career from writing novels to sit alongside the funeral services he does.

Contact Michael

Email: michael@mjelliottauthor.co.uk
Facebook: mjelliottauthor
Instagram: @mjelliottauthor

Other titles by M J Elliott

The Wrong Man — The prequel to New Blood

Frank is at the top of his game. He has grown through the ranks of the criminal underworld and is now at the top table. Born into violence, for Frank's twins, Daniel and Richie, there are certain expectations. Yet, there can only be one heir to the kingdom.

Frank doesn't see any of it coming. He has to face his demons and look at himself for once. Just maybe, Frank is the one who is ultimately responsible – responsible for it being the wrong man.

A Bitter Pill

Anna Fox has been in an abusive marriage for far too long. Desperate to find a way out, a chance to change her life presents itself in the most unexpected way. Is Anna willing to do anything to escape? She must dig deep if she is going to succeed, but she soon realises that her husband has other ideas.

Anna used to be a bubbly person. Then she met Jonathan. She wants to be that person again. She wants to be free. She sees a chance, and takes it. She's scared, but excited. Jonathan is smart, cute and plays the long game. Can Anna outwit him and play the long game too? Can she finally get her freedom and meet her Simon? It will take courage and it will take help. Has Anna got enough of both?

Available on Amazon as a paperback and Kindle and of course on his website www.mjelliottauthor.co.uk

Printed in Great Britain
by Amazon

41719257R00300